F   HU    W9-BRD-382

Without Fear

Without Fear

COLONEL DAVID HUNT
AND R. J. PINEIRO

A TOM DOHERTY ASSOCIATES BOOK

NEW YORK

WITHOUT FEAR

Copyright © 2018 by David Hunt and R. J. Pineiro

A Forge Book
Published by Tom Doherty Associates
175 Fifth Avenue
New York, NY 10010

www.tor-forge.com

Forge® is a registered trademark of Macmillan Publishing Group, LLC.

The Library of Congress Cataloging-in-Publication Data is available upon request.

ISBN 978-0-7653-9400-2 (hardcover)
ISBN 978-0-7653-9401-9 (ebook)

Our books may be purchased in bulk for promotional, educational, or business use. Please contact your local bookseller or the Macmillan Corporate and Premium Sales Department at 1-800-221-7945, extension 5442, or by email at MacmillanSpecialMarkets@macmillan.com.

First Edition: August 2018

Printed in the United States of America

0 9 8 7 6 5 4 3 2 1

To our wives,
Angela Hunt and Lory Pineiro

ACKNOWLEDGMENTS

Hats off to Robert Gleason for his continued support, as well as the rest of the staff at Tor/Forge, in particular Tom Doherty, Linda Quinton, Elayne Becker, and Karen Lovell.

Thanks to Matthew Bialer from Greenburger Associates, for a lifetime of guidance and friendship.

Our gratitude goes to Judge Jeanine Firro of Fox News, Peter Kostis of CBS, and Howie Carr of Boston's WRKO *The Howie Carr Show* for their continued support and unflagging friendship.

A special thanks to Lt. Col. Steve "Coach" Fournier, USAF pilot, and Col. Delbert "Hound dog" Bassett, U.S. Marine Corps aviator, for their technical assistance.

A very special thanks to Lynda Tocci, Mary Anne Marsh, and Maria Hardiman of the Dewey Square Group for their very generous assistance in marketing efforts.

Hillarie Olson also has our sincere appreciation.

We are grateful to Alice Frenk for her terrific proofreading help.

And last but not least, we wish to thank our families.

Courage is fear holding on a minute longer.

—GENERAL GEORGE S. PATTON

Without
Fear

PROLOGUE

I hate this fucking country.

Mikhail Tupolev glared at the starry night beyond the armor-glass canopy of his Su-25TM jet cruising at twenty thousand feet, feeling anxious to exit the airspace of this godforsaken land. The Red Air Force colonel hated its people, its customs, its food, its climate, and its infernal terrain.

From scorching deserts and wind-whipped plateaus to icy mountains and treacherous caves, everything about Afghanistan was harsh, bitter, unforgiving, and particularly cruel. It was hell on earth; truly the land that God forgot.

And Mikhail cursed the day his country chose to invade it.

But above all, the Soviet pilot hated the *mujahideen.*

Down to my fucking bone marrow.

Mikhail tightened his grip on the control column of the Sukhoi close air support jet. Visions of maimed bodies were superimposed on the star-filled sky surrounding the wide-angle heads-up display painting the center of his canopy with flight telemetry.

Those ruthless insurgents, bearded sons of the devil, weren't content with simply killing Mikhail's comrades. The zealous bastards took pleasure in brutalizing young Soviet men in ways that had forever scarred his soul. And sometimes the mujahideen would even lack the decency of finishing them off, leaving them alive for rescue crews to face the horror of their wounds.

Images of the scourged and writhing bodies of his friends crying in agony as they arrived at Kandahar pierced Mikhail's mind like burning splinters, disturbing memories stabbing what semblance of sanity he had left. They dominated his days and especially his nights, when demons armed with long and curved *pesh-kabz* knives crawled out of the darkest corners of his mind.

But it was his survivor's guilt that ate him from the inside like a ravenous cancer. Mikhail had lasted six years in Afghanistan while everyone in his flight unit had succumbed to the dreaded Stinger missiles. Or worse, they had managed to eject into the mad world rushing beneath the Sukhoi while holding four hundred knots in a westerly heading of 280 degrees.

But the madness ends tonight.

By dawn, he would land at Astrakhan, North Caucasus Military District.

Home to the Soviet Air Force 116th Combat Training Center, Astrakhan marked the place where the battle-hardened pilot would make a much-welcomed transition to flight instructor.

The reality, however, was that Mikhail would have welcomed *any* redeployment.

Anywhere.

Anywhere but here.

Though he had to admit that getting the opportunity to pass on everything he had learned to a new generation of pilots, including his experience of years at the Gagarin Air Force Academy, certainly felt like a second lease on life.

Mikhail glanced at the class ring adorning his right hand holding the control column and slowly filled his lungs with the hope of a new beginning—a new dawn—away from this place. He also looked forward to the opportunity to see Irina, his wife, and also his daughter, Kira, who had just been accepted to the KGB academy in Minsk when he'd kissed them good-bye on the eve of his deployment.

The forty-year-old pilot sighed. That was yet another reason to hate this country.

The Afghan campaign had kept Mikhail from his family, especially from watching Kira graduate and become a promising KGB officer, currently on her first assignment in East Berlin.

But all of that was about to change. Irina waited for him at

Astrakhan, and as chief instructor he would have certain freedoms, including flying anywhere in the Soviet republics over weekends and state holidays, and the list included East Germany.

The future did seem bright for the veteran pilot, but as he lifted his gaze, he noticed the darkening horizon under a moon in its third quarter.

Like a pulsating curtain, the weather front swirled by the foot of the Sulaiman Mountains, north of his flight path, and extended south, veiling the desert plains as far as he could see.

Sandstorm.

His eyes shifted skyward. The incoming gale crested well above his service ceiling of 22,965 feet, swallowing the stars. The Su-25TM was a close air support platform created to help ground troops. It was Moscow's answer to the venerable American A-10 Warthog. Its designers built it to take abuse while assisting infantry and engaging tanks. But like the Warthog, it lacked the high ceilings and supersonic speed of an interceptor.

Inside his oxygen mask, Mikhail frowned at a storm that had most definitely not been in the forecast during his briefing three hours ago.

He shook his head. Even *leaving* this country was difficult.

Sighing, he considered his options: return to base or go around the storm. The latter meant flying over the Sulaimans, the southern extension of the Hindu Kush mountain range controlled by the mujahideen. Mikhail had flown countless sorties over those rugged and forested slopes traversing this nation, but always accompanied by his flight squadron plus swarms of Mi-24 Hind-D gunships in coordination with infantry divisions.

Strength in numbers.

That had been Moscow's answer to the exponential increase in Stinger attacks by the mujahideen: overwhelming and coordinated firepower. And even *that* had failed to strip the determination from the obstinate insurgents.

But tonight Mikhail flew alone—alone with his precious cargo: a single RN-40 thirty-kiloton tactical nuclear bomb secured to its port inboard pylon.

Moscow had secretly ordered the RN-40s to the Afghan theater as a desperate measure to root out the rebels from their mountain hideouts. However, for a number of reasons—including the Kremlin's growing fear of America's President Ronald Reagan—it never used them. Now the time had come to ferry them home as part of his country's massive troop and equipment withdrawal from the region. But it had to be done as covertly as when they were first delivered here: via solo night flights.

The logical decision would have been to turn back and wait for the weather to clear, especially given the high sensitivity of his cargo. But after a decade of the most brutal fighting imaginable, logic had long given way to emotion among the tens of thousands of Soviet troops living in this worldly version of Dante's *Inferno*. And this sentiment burned even brighter in Mikhail, whose mind replaced the images of his lost comrades with that of the green fields of the Soviet Republic of Turkmenistan, on the other side of the Afghan border.

And beyond it, the Caspian Sea at dawn and—

His right hand tilted the control column to a northerly heading while his left hand worked the throttles to their highest setting short of afterburners to conserve fuel while minimizing the time spent over the mountains. He still had a long flight ahead of him, and his hands were a bit sore, probably from handling the controls harder than normal. He eased the pressure, returning to fingertip touch as the Sukhoi accelerated to just under its top speed of 526 knots, or Mach 0.82.

Mikhail gave his safety corridor a backwards glance over his shoulder as he placed the storm off his left wingtip and pointed the nose straight toward the distant snowcapped peaks. The desert rushed beneath him for another five minutes as he shot over the town of Lashkar Gah before reddish-brown sand dunes glistening in the moonlight gave way to the rugged terrain rising sharply to become the Sulaimans.

Skirting the northern edge of the squall, Mikhail slowly banked the Su-25TM back to a westerly heading. But he kept the deadly sandstorm at least five kilometers off his left wingtip, well aware that the dual Soyuz/Gavrilov R-195 turbojets would not react well to the high concentration of sand inside that boiling cloud.

As he exited the turn and leveled his wings, Mikhail realized the depth of the storm. The northern edge of the front resembled a torrid vertical wall extending at least fifty miles to the west. And that meant he would have to fly over the mountains for several minutes before he could return to his safety corridor.

With a little luck—and considering his speed, altitude, and the late hour—he hoped to be back on track without incident.

However, for reasons he could not explain, Mikhail Tupolev did something he had not done since he was a boy dragged into church by his Russian Orthodox mother: he briefly closed his eyes in prayer.

Wide awake, CIA officer Glenn Harwich bolted up in his cot. Sleep was a luxury. Those deployed in every war or dangerous assignment yearned for it but never got it, until they were back home—and sometimes only with pills.

He turned his head slightly to the source of the noise and stopped breathing, trying to discern its source.

A jet . . . A Sukhoi!

Even on less than four hours of sleep a day for weeks, Harwich recognized that sound.

Leaping to his feet, he grabbed a pair of field binoculars and his .45-caliber SIG Sauer P220, tucking the latter into the holster designed for the small of his back.

Wearing desert sandals, faded jeans, a cashmere tunic, and a *pakol*, an Afghan round cap made of fine wool, Harwich rushed out of his tent, which was nestled beneath a rocky outcrop at the edge of a plateau halfway up the mountain.

The air was dry and cold, and the young CIA officer filled his lungs while blinking rapidly, trying to clear his sight as well as his mind. Walking briskly, he reached the edge of the narrow plateau where they had made camp for the night.

To the south, a sandstorm swept across the desert, its leading edge swirling like a vertical cyclone, kicking up sand and debris in an impressive display of nature's unbridled power.

Harwich had been alarmed by the South Asia storms in the beginning, when he had first arrived in this country after graduating from the Farm, the CIA training facility in Williamsburg, Virginia. No one liked to talk about it, but environmental adjustments to time zones, climate, altitude, food, and clothes—all tied together with anticipation and fear—took some getting used to, and not all could handle it. Harwich's adjustment had meant being tired for the first few weeks in-country, where he learned that physical training, diet, and hydration were not just buzzwords but really helped his transition.

He was part of Operation Cyclone, the code name for the CIA program to arm the mujahideen in their fight against the Soviet invaders. But after two years rotating through countless rebel groups operating in the region, Harwich viewed the storms as a royal pain in his ass, and he was glad that his missions kept him mostly high up the mountains. Here, the much colder air sweeping down the sides of steep slopes resulted in an outward flow near the base that countered that of the desert storms, keeping them a good distance away.

A tall and bearded man in his early thirties, in charge of this rebel group, ran up to Harwich from another tent. He had a long and wide nose, dark eyes, and full lips under a white turban. Harwich only knew him by his nickname, "Al-Amir"—meaning "the Prince," because rumor had it he came from some billionaire Saudi family. If that was true, then Harwich had to truly tip his pakol at the man, because he sure as hell wouldn't be in this lovely corner of the world if his parents were billionaires.

Al-Amir had his ever-present SVD Dragunov sniper rifle with its wooden thumbhole stock and matching two-piece wooden hand guard slung behind his back. The SVD's long barrel, thinly profiled to save weight and ending with a slotted flash suppressor, projected above his right shoulder like an antenna. A thick Russian Army belt crowned the top of his *partug* pants, from which hung a Tokarev 7.62×25mm pistol in a desert camouflage holster. According to yet another rumor, the mujahideen fighter had allegedly pried both weapons from the dead fingers of some elite Russian sniper.

His young nephews followed him. Akhtar was the oldest, at around ten or eleven years old. Pasha looked around seven or eight. The kids yawned while rubbing the sleep from their eyes. The boys referred to Al-Amir as *Akaa*, "Uncle." The rest of the dozen men in the mujahideen enclave, whom Harwich had trained for the past two weeks in the use of the FIM-92 Stinger missile system, also emerged from their tents. Everyone gathered by the brink of the gorge, overlooking the desert and the edge of the storm.

Scanning the western skies while fingering the binoculars' focusing ring, Harwich quickly located the jet just above the horizon.

"It's a TM," he whispered, referring to the improved version of the original Su-25, which had engines positioned so close together that missile damage to one caused collateral damage to the other. The TM model sported 5mm armor plates between the two engines, and it also increased the flare capacity from 128 to 256, making it quite difficult to shoot down with a single Stinger.

Harwich frowned while tracking the jet, wondering what in the world it was doing out here alone in the middle of the night. The latest Soviet tactics always called for multiple attack jets and Hind-D gunships in support of ground troops. But there were no other planes in sight, and Red Army soldiers had not ventured up these mountains for months.

Is this guy lost?

"Can it be done, Ba'i?" asked Al-Amir in his thick accent, which sounded a bit British, calling Harwich by the nickname that translated loosely to "merchant" or "provider of goods." The man seemed well educated—far more than anyone Harwich had trained in this country—speaking good enough English to lessen the need for Harwich to use his bastardized Pashto.

The CIA man lowered the binoculars and considered the question while gazing into the determined dark eyes of this enigmatic warrior. Over the past two years, he had shown mujahideen enclaves like this one how to use Stingers to shoot down Hind-D gunships, transport helicopters, and also the original Su-25. But never a TM.

"Only one way to find out," Harwich replied, deciding that, lost or not, the lone Sukhoi presented them with a unique opportunity to see if the new and improved Soviet jet could be brought down with a coordinated attack. "But we'll need *two*," he added, stretching the index and middle fingers of his right hand like a peace sign before pointing them at the containers of missiles stacked by the side of his tent. The Stinger had a range of twenty-six thousand feet on paper. But on a cold night, the denser air worked in his favor. Plus their plateau stood at almost nine thousand feet, increasing the weapon's actual ceiling to thirty-three thousand feet.

Al-Amir gave the command and his men retrieved two Stingers from their round containers and rushed them over to him.

Akhtar and Pasha snagged a pair of wooden launcher mock-ups Harwich had carved out of tree branches to minimize handling the real thing during basic training. The Afghan men nodded approvingly and patted the boys on the back as they took their positions next to Akaa.

Harwich ignored them while verifying that the battery coolant unit was in place inside the handle before shouldering the thirty-three-pound weapon and grasping the pistol grip with his right hand. Al-Amir copied his movements, just like in training—and to Harwich's growing annoyance, so did his nephews, whose seriousness matched those of the craggy and unshaven warriors observing the live demonstration.

Using his left hand, Harwich unfolded the antenna, removed the front-end cap, raised the sight assembly into position, and inserted the IFF interconnecting cable into the grip stock.

The identification, friend or foe circuitry was designed to avoid shooting down friendly aircraft, though in these mountains every aircraft was a "foe." Still, Harwich wanted to instill some level of discipline in these characters so they didn't accidentally take down a commercial jetliner if they ever operated near the borders with Pakistan or Iran. But it wasn't just the moral dilemma of killing hundreds of innocent passengers that made Harwich fastidious about his training. He was also trying to cover the Agency's ass. Traditionally, the CIA provided insurgents with Soviet or Chinese-made weapons in order to plausibly deny its involvement. The Stinger had been a gross deviation from that policy. He'd even heard a congressional staffer say once that with the Stinger, Congress had finally popped the Agency's cherry.

Using his right thumb, he released the weapon's safety and the actuator, pushing the lever forward, outward, and down until he heard a click, activating the BCU. Within a few seconds, the gyro spin-up noise signaled the weapon becoming operational. He then moved his left hand forward and grasped the missile's Uncaging switch but did not throw it. The switch worked in conjunction with the trigger to unlock or "uncage" the missile from the launcher the instant Harwich pulled the trigger mechanism to ignite the two-stage solid-fuel propellant.

Aiming the launcher at the distant target. Harwich looked through the peephole of the sight assembly, positioning the jet in the center of the range ring. The IFF system responded immediately with multiple beeps, confirming a "foe" target.

He continued following the Soviet jet, keeping his left foot directly toward the incoming threat and his body leaned slightly forward. In his peripheral vision, he noticed the mujahideen chief mimicking his movements.

The coolant in the BCU chilled the detector cell in the Stinger missile seeker, making it ultrasensitive to any radiation in the infra-red frequency spectrum. Given the lack of any other heat source on this cold night, the system responded with a steady, high-pitched sound, the acquisition signal tone that the missile's infrared seeker had located the Sukhoi's superhot exhaust plume.

Slowly, Harwich pressed the Uncaging switch with his left thumb and held it while continuing to track the jet. The IR tone became louder, signaling that the seeker had achieved a full lock on the Su-25TM.

Keeping the silvery target in the center of the range ring, and while continuing to press the Uncaging switch, Harwich held his breath and squeezed the trigger.

The missile shot out of the launching tube in a blaze that momentarily bathed the plateau in pulsating yellow light. And an instant later, Al-Amir fired his missile.

Harwich counted to three before simultaneously releasing the trigger and the Uncaging switch, lowering the launcher. He took several steps to his left, still holding his breath to avoid inhaling the toxic fumes.

Al-Amir, however, remained in place, undisturbed by the smoke swirling about him, launcher still pointed at the night sky, where twin bright contrails rocketed toward the target.

Mikhail spotted the dual flashes off the side of the mountain just as missile warning lights and alarms came alive inside the cockpit.

Stingers!

His reaction followed his training. He notified his base at Kandahar of the attack while cutting hard left, forcing the Sukhoi into an evasive turn toward the northern edge of the storm and dispensing flares.

Cringing as the g's piled up on him from the sudden 180-degree maneuver at high speed, the Soviet colonel momentarily lost sight of the missiles while getting dangerously close to the edge of the cloud.

The g-suit immediately inflated the bladders lining his pants, compressing his legs to force blood to his upper body, keeping him from passing out as the g-meter peaked at 8.4. His instincts screamed at him to cut back throttles to ease the pressure and also to shorten the turning radius to avoid the haze about to swallow him. But he needed the speed to distance his dual exhausts from the decoys blazing behind him.

Caught in between the storm and the damn missiles, Mikhail chose the lesser of the evils while broadcasting his position to Kandahar and ignoring the darkness suddenly enveloping him.

Sand hammered the canopy with an ear-piercing crescendo while he dropped the nose and shoved the throttles to the afterburners setting the moment he exited the turn.

The turbojets kicked him in the back as they roared, as the sandblasting intensified—as the sky ignited behind him when the closest missile lost its IR lock and scrambled after the white-hot countermeasures.

One down. One to go.

The control column trembled in his right hand as the Su-25TM shot past Mach 0.88, beyond its maximum rated speed. Debris struck all leading edges, peeling off paint and ripping into the jet's aluminum and titanium alloy skin.

Hoping that the sturdy TM, capable of withstanding sustained ground fire and flak, would endure the abuse—and also praying that the RN-40 remained locked in its mounts—Mikhail continued in the cloud for several seconds.

To his relief, the aircraft's self-defense suite—plus his engine's reduced heat signature from being immersed in the swirling debris—fooled the second Stinger.

But engine alarms suddenly replaced the missile warning lights. Although the fuselage appeared to be enduring the punishment and the RN-40 remained attached to the Su-25TM's underside, the turbojets were sucking in too much sand and starting to overheat.

Get out.

Quickly, he swung the control column to the left while pushing full left rudder, banking the Sukhoi hard toward the mountain and out of the northern end of the storm.

But it was too late.

A sudden reduction in thrust signaled the loss of his port engine. He immediately shut off the fuel and ignition to it while using the cross-bleed air from the starboard engine to spin the stalled compressor back up.

But as the Sukhoi burst out of the cloud and the mountains reappeared in his windscreen, the starboard engine also flamed out.

Mikhail quickly cut off its ignition and fuel to avoid flooding it.

"Red Eagle has lost both engines during evasive," he reported in a voice far calmer than he felt. "Attempting restart."

"Red Eagle, Kandahar. Copy."

The side of the mountain now filled his canopy as the Sukhoi decelerated to Mach 0.6 and the radar altimeter, which measured the true distance to the ground, told him he had two thousand feet left.

It all boiled down to the next few seconds. Mikhail engaged the onboard auxiliary power unit to windmill the turbojets' compressors, listening to the turbines spinning, gathering rotational speed while hopefully expelling enough rubble to clear them up.

But the moment he switched on the ignition and the gas, instead of firing up, the turbojets simply coughed up smoke.

Mach 0.5 and 1,300 feet.

Mikhail went through the emergency restart again, whirling up the compressors before throwing the ignition and injecting fuel into the turbines. But the result was the same.

Mach 0.4 and four hundred feet.

Out of options, he shoved the jet back toward the desert valley to give himself a bit more altitude margin before bailing out. Although the Sukhoi's Zvezda K-36 ejection seat was rated for zero-zero operation, meaning it could be engaged at ground level while standing still, Mikhail wanted to increase the distance from the bastards who had fired on him. With luck, the rescue helicopter would extract him before the insurgents got anywhere near his location.

"Can't restart. Getting ready to eject. Repeat. Getting ready to eject," he reported, as his eyes shifted between the terrain sloping down to the desert floor and the altitude radar. Although the Su-25TM was dropping fast, by forcing the jet in the direction of the very steep slope he momentarily gained significant separation relative to the sand dunes projecting south between the foot of the mountain range and the northern edge of the storm.

"Red Eagle, Kandahar. We have a fix on your position. Rescue is on the way. ETA two hours."

The response filled Mikhail with hope as he read two thousand feet and reached for the dual ejection handles by his thighs, pulling them as hard as he had ever pulled anything in his life.

The canopy swung open as the pyrotechnic charges of the solid rocket firing mechanism boosted his seat up the guide rails mounted on the rear wall of the cockpit.

The windblast struck Mikhail as the emergency escape system shot him away from the wounded jet at dizzying speed before the second stage hurled him skyward and back, toward the Sulaimans.

His vision tunneled from the extreme g-forces as steep slopes, the stars, and the storm swapped places.

Just before he passed out from the pressure, Mikhail watched the Sukhoi spin out of control and disappear inside the angered clouds.

The full force of the sandstorm broadsided the Soviet jet as it whirled along its main axis, severing the mounts securing the RN-40 to the titanium underside. The centrifugal force shot the weapon away from the fuselage before gale force winds carried it farther south.

Tossed about in the storm, the weapon finally stabbed the sandy dunes just south of the town of Lashkar Gah, where the storm buried it under several feet of sand.

Two miles away, the Sukhoi and its hundreds of gallons of fuel crashed in a fiery explosion that briefly lit up the skies before the passing storm smothered it.

The mujahideen began to chant and dance in the moonlight, but Harwich kept the binoculars fixed on the Sukhoi, watching it disappear in the storm after the pilot bailed out.

His training and intuition were both blaring in his head. Something hadn't been right with this whole picture from the start: a Sukhoi flying solo in the middle of the night over mujahideen country. And now Harwich had just noticed a very large and long weapon—at least ten feet long—secured to the jet's underside.

Su-25TMs typically carried a variety of missiles, like the AS-14 or SA-9 air-to-surface missiles, or B8M1 80mm rocket pods—all in support of ground troops. But he had never—*ever*—seen it carrying just one large bomb.

And a bomb which size suggested it to be . . .

He lowered the binoculars and looked over at Al-Amir. "We need to locate that wreckage."

The mujahideen chief tilted his head at him before unsheathing his pesh-kabz knife and using it to point at the storm. "Of course . . . but not until *that* passes."

Before Harwich could respond, Al-Amir added, "But first we need to go after *that*." He shifted the tip of the curved blade to the parachute blossoming over the mountains. The winds were carrying it in their direction.

Harwich brought the Soviet's red canopy into focus with his binoculars as it drifted in the wind, following the pilot's moon shadow rushing over the rugged mountainside. He estimated it to be at least four or five miles from their position.

"Is that necessary?" Harwich asked. "We've already shot it down, proving it can be done. And besides, the wreck is really more important."

Al-Amir placed a hand on Harwich's shoulder, smiled without humor, and said, "Then you do not understand, Ba'i."

"Understand what?"

Turning to face the distant parachute, he replied, "The kind of war we are waging."

The voice on the R-855UM transceiver secured to his survival vest pulled him back into consciousness.

Mikhail quickly came about, realizing he had landed in a small clearing, a ledge really, overlooking the desert under a sea of stars and a yellowish moon.

Where is the sandstorm?

Sitting up, he verified that the emergency locator transmitter, designed to self-activate upon ejection, was operational and broadcasting his position at 243.0 MHz. Reaching for the transceiver, he said, "Red Eagle, Kandahar. On the ground. Do you have my beacon?"

"Copy that, Red Eagle. Twenty minutes out."

Mikhail frowned. Upon ejection, Kandahar had reported that the rescue chopper was two hours away, which meant he had been unconscious for well over one and a half hours. The storm had already passed, its trailing edge barely visible in the eastern horizon. The fact that he had not yet been captured in these mountains amounted to a minor miracle.

And let's keep it that way.

Standing, he pulled up his helmet and gathered his parachute, quickly hiding it in the surrounding shrubs, before reaching for his old .380 ACP Makarov IZh-70, his country's version of the venerable Walther PPK/S. The semiautomatic had belonged to his father, Makar Tupolev, also a colonel in the Red Army, who had fought the Nazis at Stalingrad. He briefly stared at the inscription on the side of the stainless steel muzzle: COL. M. TUPOLEV.

Running a finger over his father's name for luck, Mikhail removed an RSP-30 signal rocket flare from his vest.

Inhaling deeply, he knelt in the bushes next to his chute and looked around him, listening to the wind whistling over the mountains under a majestic star-filled sky. The moon had risen higher behind the mountain range, casting the ragged shadows of trees across the narrow clearing.

Everything looked serene, peaceful, in sharp contrast with the violence of the Stinger attack.

But that was precisely what worried him. It was *too* damn peaceful, and there was no such thing in Afghanistan.

He shifted his gaze between the eastern horizon, where any moment now he should spot the incoming helicopter, and his immediate surroundings, looking and listening for anything that didn't belong.

His right hand held the Makarov and his left the flare while he remained in a deep crouch, measuring his breathing while constantly checking his watch. He just needed to survive for another ten minutes, and while he certainly didn't look forward to his debriefing back at Kandahar, anything was better than—

It happened very fast.

One moment he caught two shadows shifting from the trees off to his right before more silhouettes holding AK-47 rifles materialized across the clearing, their loose clothing swirling in the breeze. A few seconds later, he also recognized more shadows off to his left, and more behind him.

The bastards had already located and surrounded him and were tightening the noose, and that's when he spotted the curved knives extending from their fists.

His heartbeat rocketing, his choices suddenly as clear as the night sky, Mikhail stared at the Makarov in his right hand as images of his disfigured comrades flooded his altered state of mind. Rather than aiming the slim pistol and its seven full metal jacket rounds at the incoming shadows, he pressed the muzzle tight against his temple as his finger caressed the trigger.

Tightening his jaw and breathing deeply, he thought of Irina and Kira while building up the courage to—

A single shot cracked in the night, its report echoing off the mountainside as his right hand went numb.

Turning his head, Mikhail felt bile reach his throat when he saw the bloody stump where a bullet had severed his hand at the wrist. Dropping his gaze, he stared in horror at his hand on the rocks by his boots, still clutching the Makarov, his Gagarin class ring reflecting the moonlight.

Leaning forward, he vomited just as the distant sound of a heli-copter echoed up the mountain range. Operating on pure adrena-line, Mikhail mustered enough strength to rush to his feet, his left hand still holding the flare as he tried to make a run for the side of the mountain. Perhaps if the helicopter's gunners spotted him and gave him some cover, he could escape.

But he didn't get far.

The mujahideen converged on him like a swift and dark plague, grabbing him by the shoulders, arms, and legs before he could reach the clearing, dragging him back into the cold forest, away from his hope of being rescued.

Still, Mikhail tried to resist, to fight back, to wrestle himself free. He kicked and screamed, but the men, whose faces were hidden in the shadows, didn't utter a single word. They simply carried him in the direction opposite from the incoming helicopter, into a darkness that felt like hell itself.

Someone pulled off his survivor's vest and threw it toward the knee-high bushes by the tree line where he had hidden, while others tore at his flight suit and undergarments, shredding them.

"*Mehrabai wakrey*," Mikhail hissed in the limited Pashto he'd learned from local guides. "*Mehrabai wakrey yawazi mee pregda.*" Please. *Please leave me alone.*

But they ignored him as the exposure of his skin caused him to begin shivering in the cold air—as they slammed his bare back against the ground, where many hands held him down, immobilizing him.

Groaning in anger, in frustration, his eyes stared at the canopy overhead, at the narrow beams of moonlight filtering through branches swaying in the breeze.

And that's when he spotted two smaller figures crawling toward him, like faceless demons, dark and silent creatures, their hands clutching those curved knives, their movements slow, deliberate.

Mikhail gasped, his breathing short and raspy as raw fear dis-placed his anger, seizing him, arresting his soul, paralyzing him. He began to tremble, quivering uncontrollably.

The ghouls reached his legs, his waist, hovering over him like dark spirits, like the sons of the devil.

And just as these goblin-like creatures began to cut him, as

Mikhail's back bent like a bow while he bawled in agonizing pain, a slim ray of moonlight danced across one of their faces.

It was the face of a boy.

And it would be the last thing he'd ever see.

Harwich remained in the back, by the edge of the clearing, keeping an eye on the incoming helicopter while the mujahideen did what it did best: inflict terror into the heart of the enemy.

He wanted to turn away from the calculating mess that Akhtar and Pasha made of the screaming pilot, but he knew better. The eyes of the mujahideen were on him, looking for any sign of weakness.

Fortunately, it didn't take long to inflict the desired wounds before the men carried the maimed Soviet back to the clearing.

Then Al-Amir did the strangest thing. He picked up the Soviet's severed hand, pulled the bloody Makarov from its curled fingers, and gave the pistol to Pasha. He then removed the pilot's gold ring and, looping a string of black leather through it, he tied it around Akhtar's neck.

"So you remember," he whispered to the boys, touching their faces.

"Thank you, Akaa," they replied in unison.

Al-Amir then knelt by the Soviet and placed the bloody hand on the man's chest. "Take your trash back with you, Shuravi," he said, using the nickname given to the Soviet soldiers, derived from the similarly sounding Russian equivalent of *šouravī*, meaning "Soviet." "I want no part of you in my country."

Standing by the edge of the woods, the mujahideen leader fired the rocket flare as the rescue helicopter loomed off the eastern rim rock. The pyrotechnic arced across the night sky, bathing the rugged land in brilliant white light that momentarily hovered while cascading around the incoming craft.

Harwich recognized it as a Mil Mi-17 medium-lift transport with the NATO code name "Hip." Painted in the traditional Soviet desert camouflage pattern, it approached the narrow clearing with apparent caution, kicking up a cloud of dust while helmeted gunners hung out of both open side doors, manning 7.63mm machine guns.

And that's how they left the man whose name tags identified him as Colonel Mikhail Tupolev: with the helicopter's searchlights panning over the naked figure lying on his side in a fetal position in the middle of the clearing, writhing in pain.

The group became shadows, retreating to their mountain hideout as the Mi-17's lights pierced the woods in shafts of yellow light. The pilots paused their approach some fifty feet from the victim, who raised a trembling left hand—which clutched his severed right hand—in the direction of his rescuers.

Harwich gave the poor bastard a final look from the edge of the woods. And as he followed the mujahideen up the steep terrain, he prayed with all his heart that one day America didn't find itself at the receiving end of this war of terror.

1

Bastards

No bastard ever won a war by dying for his country. He won it by making the other poor dumb bastard die for his country.

—*General George S. Patton*

OCTOBER 2005.
COMPOUND 45. NORTH OF
LASHKAR GAH. SOUTHERN AFGHANISTAN.

Colonel Hunter Stark used an ATN DNVM-4 digital night vision monocular to follow the movements of his sniper, Sergeant Major Ryan Hunt, who advanced methodically, almost imperceptibly, under a quarter moon.

Like a predator, Ryan crept through the thicket in search of the perfect vantage point on the hill overlooking the compound designated by their CIA employer as a Taliban IED factory.

A ghillie suit, a net garment covered in loose strips of burlap designed to blend its user with the environment, broke up Ryan's slim physique.

Stark frowned. The same camouflage suit that helped keep Ryan hidden made it difficult for him to track the sniper's movements, even with the night vision gadget.

"Where the hell's Pretty Boy, Colonel?" whispered Master Sergeant Evan Larson, his large frame kneeling next to Stark on a wide ledge protruding beyond the rocky hill, roughly a hundred feet above their target. The windowless one-story structure surrounded by a six-foot-tall mud wall had a single access point wide enough for a truck. But it lacked a gate or outside guards. About a hundred feet separated the compound from the perimeter wall, forming an inner courtyard that Stark viewed more as a buffer zone, a place for those inside the compound to fire on anyone approaching the premises unannounced.

"It's okay to be jealous, Chief," replied Ryan over the secure channel.

Prior to the start of the raid, Stark had made sure his team switched off all sat phones and muted the sounds on all electronic equipment, including the black Casio G-Shock watches everyone wore. Only the AN/PRC-148 Multiband Inter/Intra Team Radios, the MBITRs, remained enabled, though connected to earpieces and voice-activated throat mikes designed to pick up the slightest of whispers.

"Not my fault you look like Steroids-R-Us and can't get dates," Ryan added. *"At least from two-legged species."*

Stark glanced over at his second-in-command and watched him grin. Even on his knees Larson's bulk rose above him ominously, his head wrapped in a desert camouflage bandanna, his eyes hidden behind a pair of PS15 night vision goggles. He held a massive M2 Browning .50-caliber air-cooled machine gun that made Stark's Heckler & Koch MP5A1 suppressed submachine gun look like something from aisle three at Toys-R-Us.

"He's almost in place," the colonel said, stretching a gloved finger toward an outcrop roughly five hundred feet to their right. "I'm more worried about those damn dogs by the entrance."

"Yeah," Larson whispered in his baritone voice, before pointing to their left. "And the goats."

"These hags aren't stupid when it comes to simple security," said Stark, shifting the DNVM-4 to the large clearing separating the compound from the foot of the hill.

The goats and dogs roaming around by the gateless entrance to the courtyard and inside the grounds served two purposes: to sustain those who cared for them with food, and also with money, once they were sold, and as an early warning system. Dogs and goats possessed great senses, barking and bleating when something bothered them.

Excellent proximity alarms on four legs, Stark thought, which also explained the lack of outside guards. As long as the animals remained quiet, there was no reason for anyone to venture out. But the presence of the animals meant there were no IEDs buried in the area.

The colonel fingered the adjusting wheel on the DNVM-4, scanning the edge of the trees until he spotted two more ghillie suits, worn by his last two operators, both former Navy SEALs, Michael Hagen and Danny Martin, the latter also a heck of a pilot. But on this pitch-black night they did not hold MP5A1s. Their suppressed weapons were slung behind their backs, freeing their hands for the bags they carried. Martin was after the Afghan shepherds, locally called *Kuchis*, and was armed with bags filled with chunks of raw beef laced with etorphine, a semisynthetic opioid one thousand times more powerful than morphine. Hagen had goat detail, carrying two bags of Manna Pro treats made with real anise, delivering a licorice flavor goats found irresistible—and also spiked with the powerful tranquilizer.

Stark watched the green images of his men, which the DNVM-4 amplified from the available starlight, toss their goods into the clearing before retreating into the forest.

"You guys missed your calling," said Chief Larson over the secure channel. "Petting zoo specialists."

Stark shook his head.

"*Hey, Ryan,*" said Martin. "*Didn't you tell me that using steroids shrinks the Big Dipper?*"

"*Yep. Turns it into the Little Dipper,*" replied Ryan. "*I keep telling the chief that.*"

"*Ahh,*" said Martin. "*That explains the Browning.*"

"*Think a mustache will help?*" asked Ryan. Martin had recently grown one that made him look like a 1980s porn star.

"*Nah,*" Martin replied. "*You need the rest of the package to go along with it.*"

"Screw you both," said Larson. "I'll have you know I'm proportionate *everywhere*."

"Knock it off," said Stark, focusing the DNVM-4 on the animals sleeping along the perimeter wall surrounding the dark compound.

Slowly, like ghosts materializing out of thin air, four Kuchis stood by the entrance and took a few tentative steps toward the lure. They were large, white dogs, measuring almost three feet at the withers and sporting massive jaws. Intrigued, they moved gradually—and most importantly, quietly—alerted by their olfactory receptors and possessing almost three hundred million of them, compared to the six million in humans. Primal carnivore instincts overpowered their normal reflexes to protect the grounds. Ignoring the goat treats, they went straight for the beef.

It took the strong narcotic less than a minute to drop the dogs as they walked back to the perimeter wall.

The goats came into view a moment later from inside the patio, dark green shapes appearing by the entrance and venturing beyond the wall, grazing about, pausing to test the air. Their sense of smell, although quite keen, was more optimized to detect predators than treats, so it took just a bit longer for the herd to pick up the licorice scent. Stepping around the sleeping lumps of their shepherd friends, they foraged the clearing quickly, and also quietly, and within a minute all movement ceased on the grounds.

"*Hey, look, Chief,*" Martin said. "*Sleeping goats. Maybe you'll get lucky.*"

"*Nope,*" Ryan chimed in. "*There will be absolutely no patronizing with sedated goats.*"

"That's okay, boys," Larson replied. "Sooner or later you *will* have to sleep."

Stark looked at his large second-in-command and sighed, focusing his energy on the task at hand by asking, "How's the range, Ryan?"

"*Comfortable, Colonel. Five hundred yards. In position.*"

The instant the sniper signaled that he had set up his McMillan TAC-50 rifle fitted with a sound suppressor on a rocky ledge, Stark put away the monocular and lowered his set of PS15 goggles.

"We're live," he said, starting the digital stopwatch on his Casio while giving the order to start this CIA-financed raid. According to satellite and UAV images, plus an earlier recon of the target in daylight, a dozen men occupied the compound, some as guards and the rest as explosives technicians. Improvised explosive devices were the number one cause of injury reaching the Role 3 Multinational Medical Unit at Kandahar Airfield, or KAF, and the U.S.

government had launched a covert campaign to eliminate them at their origin.

The team advanced in almost total darkness, reaching the edge of the clearing and pausing in the waist-high brush. Stark had considered a diversion, perhaps a car crash on the compound's north wall, but he feared telegraphing his position and having the rebels inside blow themselves up—and his team along with them. And besides, it was so damn dark that unless the residents had night vision equipment, all they'd see would be the muzzle flashes of his team's suppressed weapons before their brains were ejected from their skulls.

So stealth was the name of the game, and Colonel Stark left that in the capable hands of Martin and Hagen, who advanced first. The former SEALs covered the couple hundred feet of dark expanse in under thirty seconds, stepping around the still figures of dogs and goats with the grace of NFL running backs, finally reaching the perimeter wall just to the right of the entrance.

"*Still clear, Romeo?*" asked Larson.

"*Crystal,*" replied Ryan.

Stark checked his watch. Fifteen seconds.

Larson took off next while Stark brought up the rear, using his MP5A1's sights to scan the top of the compound's wall, the entrance, and the tree line behind them.

He pressed his back against the mud wall next to Larson, across the entrance from Hagen and Martin, whose camouflaged faces stared at him, MP5A1s held tight against their chests, bulky sound suppressors pointed at the ground.

Stark looked up the hill in Ryan's general direction.

"*'Twas the night before Ramadan,*" the sniper began, "*when all thro' the IED house, not a creature was stirring, not even a bag.*"

Stark pointed the index and middle fingers of his left hand at Martin and Hagen, before stretching his thumb toward the interior patio.

The two SEALs moved at once, covering each other while zigzagging across the courtyard, before settling on a spot to the right of the compound's metal door.

"Behind me, Chief," Stark said, also going through the entrance, taking fifteen seconds to cross the patio and reach the other side of the door, back pressed against the stone wall. Larson joined him a moment later.

There were a number of options available to Stark at that moment, including setting off a shaped charge to take off the door, getting Chief Larson to blast its hinges with the Browning, or even having Martin pick the latch, which appeared simple enough. But all of those options carried the risk of his team rushing into the business end of a half dozen AK-47s if the interior force was somehow aware of their advance.

Or worse, setting off a chain reaction of IEDs.

So the colonel chose another way, nodding to Martin, who produced a smartphone.

"Play it," Stark said, checking the Casio and reading forty-eight seconds.

"Play what?" asked Larson, obviously confused.

"Your girlfriend, Chief," whispered Martin. His thick blond mustache shifted as he added, "Taped her while you were tapping her."

Before Larson could reply, the audio clip of a couple of goats bleating broke the silence in the patio.

Even Hagen, who never smiled, could not hold back a grin while Larson gave Martin the bird. Stark kept his eyes on the door, MP5A1 ready.

The trick worked. Within thirty seconds the door swung open and three men hauling AK-47s rushed out.

But they didn't get very far.

Stark shot two in the back of the head, the suppressed mechanism absorbing the reports while exit wounds vaporized their foreheads. Martin took care of the third one as the hag realized the ruse and tried to pull back, putting a 9mm round through his left temple, dropping him right over his fallen comrades.

"No other hags in sight," reported Ryan, who had line of sight into the compound's open door. *"Must be nestled, all snug in their beds."*

The group went inside, Stark now leading, the MP5A1 up by his face, shooting eye scanning the foyer with Larson, Martin, and Hagen in tow.

Stark surprised two more guards drinking from cans of Coca-Cola in the hallway, and another one just beyond them, sitting by a pair of double doors with his head back against the wall, eyes closed, his AK-47 resting by his feet.

Two shots to the head each and the front of the factory was secured.

Ninety seconds.

Stark pushed the dead guards aside and kicked the doors open, surprising six technicians, each huddled behind a worktable under bright fluorescent lights, surrounded by what had to be at least several thousand pounds of Semtex. Shelves and tables were jam-packed with aluminum pipes, detonators, timers, coils of wire, assorted tools, and other hardware—all the necessary ingredients to separate NATO soldiers from their limbs.

The air was thick with grease, solder, and body odor. The techs glared at Stark and his men in disbelief, their wide-eyed stares telegraphing the horror they felt when facing four armed men in full tactical gear, including body armor and goggles.

One of the techs tried to reach for something under his table. Stark shot him twice in the face and he collapsed right over his work.

The remaining five quickly raised their hands when their colleague's brains splattered across the mud floor.

"Looks like the spooks were right for once," Stark mumbled, checking the Casio. Two minutes, to the second. They had found an IED mecca as well as several computers, tablets, and a dozen smartphones. "Call them, Chief."

Larson took off to contact the CIA contingent standing by a mile away.

Once the compound was secured and all technicians were flex-cuffed and hauled to the front of the building, Stark and team were to pull back to perimeter duty the moment the CIA showed up. Their goal this evening was to neutralize the site so that Langley officers could collect laptops, phones, and other gadgets that could be used to help locate other such facilities.

"Looks like we get full bonuses tonight, boys," said Ryan.

Their contract included a clause for cash—and therefore tax-free—bonuses for every live tech they could deliver to their CIA employers. And since they had caught five techs, it meant each member of the team would get a full share on top of their regular pay.

Stark had Martin use his smartphone to snap photos of their captives to include in his report.

"Vegas, here I come," said Martin, popping one of his watermelon-
flavored lollipops into his mouth before snapping images of each
tech. The man had managed to quit smoking a year ago and now
sucked on the damn things constantly. He rejoined Stark and Larson, who stood just beyond the entrance, by the comatose goats
and dogs.

Hagen, the quiet one of the group, caught up to Martin while producing a pack of Sobranie Classics, a heavy-tar brand of the legendary Russian cigarettes, and a lighter. Always a heavy smoker, Hagen
had gotten hooked on the strong brand during a short mission in
Moscow back in 2002. He lit one up and blew the smoke in Martin's
face as they walked side by side.

"You know, Mickey," Martin said, as they reached Stark and
Larson, pointing at him with the lollipop before shoving it back in
his mouth, "for being a damn mute you can certainly be an asshole."

Hagen grinned.

"Cover the perimeter," Stark told them, while Larson stepped
aside, the bulky satellite phone pressed against his right ear, the
Browning slung over his left shoulder.

Hagen and Martin walked away, their MP5A1s at the ready as they
disappeared beyond the outer wall's entrance.

Stark kept his weapon pointed straight at their line of cash cows
secured next to the building's entrance. Their hands were flex-cuffed
behind their backs, with the same large black zip-ties securing their
ankles. And just for added security, Hagen and Martin had zip-tied
the left ankle of one tech to the right ankle of the guy next to him.

They were all quite young, probably in their late teens, barely able
to sport some semblance of the Sharia law mandatory beards. Three
had already pissed their baggy pants from the same raw fear that
glared in their wide-eyed stares, and based on the pungent smell, at
least one of them had taken a shit.

Like most Taliban recruits, these kids were probably plucked
straight out of farming villages or the back alleys of Kandahar or
Lashkar Gah and forced to work at gunpoint or out of fear of retali-
ation against their families back home.

But to Stark, young or not, forced or not, afraid or not, the hags at his feet were directly responsible for the dismembering or deaths of American fighting personnel.

And today was judgment day.

Chief Larson kept the sat phone pressed against the side of his face, listening for about a minute. Nodding twice before saying, "Roger that," he hung up and clipped the phone to his utility belt before walking back to Stark. "Colonel, the spooks are on their—"

"Chief! Behind you!"

Two figures had jumped over the east wall, rolled when hitting the ground, and already had their AK-47s aimed at them. Larson was facing the wrong way, and worse, his broad figure prevented Stark from swinging his MP5A1 at the threat. And Martin and Hagen were out of sight on the other side of the wall.

The first rounds of the AK-47s hit high, over their heads, peppering the compound's wall, bathing them in reddish dust and debris.

Just as Stark and Larson dropped to the ground, Ryan's .50-caliber round parted the air like a whip from a distance of five hundred yards, tearing up the lead insurgent's chest. The bullet's momentum, the product of its 1,500-grain mass traveling at nearly 2,600 feet per second, flipped the man upside down, the AK-47 whirling in the air. The follow-up shot came precisely three seconds later, one second for Ryan to manually eject the spent round and chamber another one from the five-round magazine feeding the TAC-50, and two seconds to aim and fire. The full metal jacket round slammed the second rebel in the head, nearly decapitating him.

Stark stood slowly, looked in the direction of his guardian angel, and touched the tip of his shooting finger against his right temple.

Larson said, "Oswald and Whitman were pussies, Romeo. Drinks are on me."

"Anytime, Chief."

Martin and Hagen ran back to the courtyard but Stark waved them down while Larson knelt by the dead Tallies, noticing another of their captives soiling his trousers and crying.

It took the CIA almost fifteen minutes to arrive in three black Jeep Wranglers. Six men and a woman got out, all wearing jeans and T-shirts and hauling bags. The team lead, who looked like he still sucked on his mama's tit and who went by "Jones," nodded at Stark.

The colonel just pointed at the captives and showed the CIA man five fingers before rubbing the thumb of his right hand against his middle and index fingers.

As his team disappeared inside the building, Jones looked at the zip-tied techs, then back at Stark, and said, "They smell like piss and shit."

"Shit happens," Stark replied, walking away.

"Dammit," said the CIA man, before turning to one of his guys. "Find me some water, would ya? No way I'm smelling that crap all the way to KAF."

"Let's go, Chief," the colonel said, letting the spooks do what spooks do while his team fulfilled the last part of the contract by providing security for the site until Agency personnel left the area. Then Jones would call in an airstrike to blow the place off the map.

But just as Stark reached the edge of the clearing, by the waist-high brush, Larson's sat phone began to vibrate. The chief picked it up, listened for thirty seconds, and turned to Stark, his face suddenly gone ashen, as if he had just seen a ghost.

"Chief?"

"Sir, that was my guy at KAF Central Command. Apparently the Royal Canadian Air Force has launched a retaliatory strike on this place."

"That was the plan all along, Chief."

"No, sir, as in *right now*. Fighters are five minutes out."

"What the hell?"

"That's what he just heard, sir, and his intel is always right. A couple of IEDs killed some Canadian soldiers during an ambush an hour ago, wounded ten, and the hags even took three of the poor bastards alive—one of them a woman. Since Kandahar is under the command of Major General Thomas Lévesque, who happens to be French Canadian, well . . . there it is."

Stark had been around the block enough times to know that when it comes to a place like KAF, controlled by NATO but swarming with personnel from a half dozen nationalities, plus their intelligence services, the left hand sometimes didn't talk to the right hand. So, as a precaution, he always tried like hell to have someone on the inside at Central Command to warn him when hell was about to break loose anywhere near his team.

"Midnight!" Stark shouted into his mike. "Fucking *midnight!*"

Martin and Hagen scrambled up the hill, SEAL style, with ridiculous nimbleness. Larson, almost ten years their senior, tried to race after them but lost them in the dark forest, while Stark, the oldest of the group, did his best to keep up while changing frequencies. "Jones! Get the hell out of there!"

"Colonel?"

"Fighter strike . . . in five!" he screamed, as he nearly lost his footing, rushing through the slanted woods behind Larson while getting swatted by the branches as the chief's large bulk swept through the brush, crushing and parting vegetation like a mad gorilla. "Get your people out of there! Now!"

Without waiting for a response, as his lungs and legs burned from the uphill sprint, Stark switched back to the team's secure channel.

"Ryan! Where . . . the . . . hell . . . are . . . you?"

"Almost at the ledge, Colonel! Danny and Mickey are up here too."

Damn you, young guys.

He pressed on, feeling the strain of his forty-five years—plus his old wounds, which had a way of surfacing at the worst possible moments. As he pushed himself up the uneven incline, his body protested the effort, reminding him of the shrapnel fragments still lodged in his lower back from some Colombian asshole ten years ago, plus the stab wound in his thigh from a mission in Bosnia back in the day, plus the ACLs on both knees from jumping from too many damn planes too many damn times. And there were those titanium rods and screws holding his left leg together from that misguided missile strike in the waters outside Kuwait City during a mission with the U.S. Special Forces in support of Operation Desert Shield. But his mind worked through the pain, ignoring everything, even the branches whipping him as he tailed Larson while checking his watch and seeing one minute gone by.

Switching frequencies, he shouted, "Jones . . . you guys . . . out yet?"

"Almost, Colonel. Hauling everything out now."

Hauling everything? What the—

Taking a deep breath, Stark tried a final time to talk some sense into the stupid and inexperienced CIA operative before he got everyone killed. "Drop everything, Jones! Get out! *Now!*"

And once more, he returned to his team's frequency without waiting for a reply. In this type of asymmetric retreat, where the enemy—and any bomb, even those made in America—could be literally everywhere, you had to have a *stop what you're doing and leave right now* attitude. Such a moment had arrived yet again. In his mind, Stark had already done the math on the explosive charges of your typical NATO missile, plus the ridiculous amount of Semtex he'd just seen—enough to level a few city blocks.

But the colonel would later learn that, due to a mix-up with NATO commanders, a pair of Royal Canadian Air Force UAVs loaded with Hellfires would get there well ahead of the fighter squadron, with orders to fire as soon as they were in range.

"Damn Canucks!" Larson cursed, as they reached their emergency rendezvous, a wide ledge some seven hundred feet above the compound, where Martin, Hagen, and Ryan were huddled by the entrance of a cave-like rock formation lining the back of this plateau.

The master chief dropped the Browning and placed his hands on his knees as he tried to catch his breath. "You know, Colonel," he said, panting, "we all expect to die in this kind of war . . . probably *any* war . . . but you don't expect it . . . to be at the hand . . . of your friend."

Stark didn't reply, taking in lungfuls of air through his nose and exhaling through his mouth while checking his Casio. It had taken them exactly ninety seconds to get the hell out of Dodge, meaning he still had over three minutes left to seek even better shelter, and he could only hope that the CIA contingent had also—

The blinding flash made everyone hit the ground as a vertical column of flames and smoke licked the night sky, visible for miles. The ear-piercing blast gripped the entire mountainside, shaking it like an earthquake, so hard that Stark thought his teeth would come loose.

The shock wave propagated radially, tossing the operators across the rocky ledge, as the world seemed to catch fire around them. The energy bounced from the face of the hillside and joined the rest of the blast spreading in the opposite direction, toward the desert, colliding against the massive sand dunes east of Lashkar Gah.

And unearthing the tip of an old Soviet bomb.

2

Divine Sign

SULAIMAN MOUNTAINS. FIVE MILES NORTHEAST OF LASHKAR GAH. SOUTHERN AFGHANISTAN.

Mullah Akhtar Baqer traveled by night, avoiding all roads suspected to be under the surveillance of Predators or the even deadlier Reapers.

The forty-year-old Taliban commander gave the starry sky a contemptuous stare. Most of the three thousand men under his authority thought of Allah, or the Prophet Muhammad, or simply of paradise and virgins when contemplating the heavens on such a beautiful and calm night. A waxing gibbous moon hung high and proud over South Asia, adorned by countless stars blanketing the firmament from horizon to horizon.

But the magic or even romance of this moonlight-bathed arid wilderness, as seen from his side window, was completely lost on Akhtar, evoking only images of the unmanned aerial vehicles responsible for the deaths of so many of his brothers.

And almost of my own, he thought, shifting uncomfortably in the rear of an old UAZ-469, the Soviet version of the American Jeep, appropriately nicknamed *Kozlik*, or "Goat," a leftover relic from the war of his youth.

He grimaced while touching the extensive scar tissue beneath his *kameez*, the long shirt unbuttoned to the middle of his chest. Like clockwork, the muscle aches on his trunk and limbs had begun, along with mild stomach cramps. Soon the contractions would have him bent over in seizures as the pain squeezed his organs, ripping into his bones while perspiration oozed out of every pore.

A glance at his watch confirmed what his body already knew: it had been twelve hours since he last opiated. For a moment he considered reaching for the ever-present canvas knapsack by his feet, but the rough ride through this switchback trail would not be conducive to using the Chinese pipe. He would have to wait until they reached their destination, which should be within the hour, hopefully before his symptoms worsened to the point of alarming his men.

Sighing in anger for forgetting to medicate before leaving his compound, Akhtar took solace in toying with the gold ring hanging from his neck by a leather strap. But the breaking news that had pulled him from his nightly routine had distracted him.

Faiz, his driver and nephew, negotiated the hairpin turns of the steep trail with expert ease, winding down the southern face of the mountain under the protective canopy of a variety of conifers.

The mullah closed his eyes and tried to relax, taking a moment to enjoy the pine resin fragrance filling his lungs. Like the ring and the Goat, it reminded him of those glorious years when his people had defeated the Soviets.

The Americans had been their allies back then, supporters of their cause. But five years ago those same Americans had almost incinerated him and his beloved Akaa with a Hellfire while he was riding in a convoy just like this one. Akhtar had reacted quickly, pushing Akaa out of the burning vehicle, sparing the man who had founded al Qaeda—the man who taught him everything he knew—from the flames that disfigured him.

Akhtar shook the thought away as the distant lights of Lashkar Gah loomed over the western edge of the narrow trail, backdropped by snowcapped ridges lining the horizon's rim as the range curved south toward Iran. Nestled between the foot of the mountains and the confluence of the Helmand and Arghandab Rivers, the city was home to over two hundred thousand Afghans.

But Akhtar's destination on this starry night steered his three-Kozlik convoy away from the city and toward the vast desert dunes a mile east of the fertile strips of land flanking the shores of the rivers. It was there, by the edge of Afghanistan's largest desert, that Hamid, the young goatherd sitting next to him, had been leading his flock to the edge of a water reservoir. If Akhtar were the religious man his jihadists believed him to be, the mullah would have called it a miracle that the boy had noticed the tip of a strange metal object protruding from the sand.

But he didn't believe any more than did the infidels—though no one would ever know it from the brutality with which he enforced Sharia law among his people. Unlike Akaa, and even his own brother, Pasha, true disciples of the Prophet Muhammad, Akhtar's reasons for fighting this so-called holy war were quite selfish: under Sharia law, he was king. And for several glorious years, when the Taliban ruled this land, he had lived like a monarch, getting anything his heart desired—women, girls, land, and creature comforts. And total power over others.

Until the Americans took it away.

But it could all change tonight, he thought. The boy's sighting had been reason enough for Akhtar to abandon his secret headquarters high above Lashkar Gah in the middle of the night. The mullah was responsible for all Taliban engagements with NATO forces in the Kandahar region, plus he was directly accountable to Osama bin Laden, his Akaa.

It is the same location, he thought, ignoring another stomach cramp as Faiz turned the wheel, working the clutch and manual gearbox, downshifting as their descent grew steeper. The engine groaned, slowing them down while the oversize tires bit into the sharper grade.

Akhtar grabbed the window frame for support as the Goat tilted forward, its headlights washing the rocky incline in yellow light. Half the thread of the 4×4's left tires projected beyond the edge of the trail, over the gorge, while Faiz forced the right tires tight against the side of the mountain.

Hamid looked out his side window and into the void, but if the boy was afraid, Akhtar never noticed it. Rather, the goatherd showed far more interest in devouring the naan and figs in the basket between them.

In spite of his cramps, Akhtar couldn't suppress a grin. Hamid reminded the mullah of himself at that age, full of grit, eyes flat and impassive, hardened by their way of life, his young skin already dark and leathery from the desert sun.

And like Akhtar, Hamid was also growing up while his people fought off an invasion.

The path flattened after a while, as rocks turned to sand, as they reached the foot of the mountain and steered the Goats across the desert, past dozens of sand dunes glittering in the moonlight. This also meant leaving the protection of the conifers, but according to Hamid, they were almost there, just beyond the impressive blast radius of the latest American drone strike.

Akhtar frowned while staring at the distant fires to the east, still burning after twenty-four hours, where one of his largest IED factories had stood nestled against the side of the mountain. According to his scouts, however, the blast had also killed a number of CIA men after a team of Special Forces—probably SEALs—had secured the compound during a night raid. He had yet to understand why NATO had ordered a strike on its own people. But whatever the reason, and as much as it pained him to have lost good men plus thousands of pounds of explosives, hundreds of IEDs, and other raw materials, the resulting shock wave would be called by men of faith a gift from Allah.

A divine sign.

But for Akhtar it was simply a much-needed break in this war.

Since the beginning of this damn invasion, the Americans had had the upper hand. Using their technology, the infidels continued to find and kill his people, forcing them into tunnels.

Like rats.

And on top of that, they were now arming warring Shia tribes, compounding his problems. This discovery could turn the tide of the—

"That way!" Hamid shouted, pointing to their right at the steep and narrow valley formed by two immense sand dunes just west of them. A mile past the V-shaped rift, moonlight danced over the surface of one of many irrigation reservoirs fed by the slow-flowing Arghandab.

The almost magical sight of the towering mounds and the glittering water beyond them, however, was lost on Akhtar, who felt his heartbeat rocketing at the thought of—

Faiz swung the Goat sharply in that direction, forcing Akhtar and the boy to hold on tight as all four tires kicked up walls of sand and the vehicle slid into the turn, going around a shallow dune, steering them toward the edge of the mounds.

Akhtar looked behind them, making sure that the two Goats continued following them. It was quite easy to get lost driving in the desert, especially while navigating between sand dunes, and at night. But the trailing Kozliks remained glued to him, per his instructions, the drivers ignoring the spray of sand on their windshields. Before leaving his headquarters three hours ago, Akhtar had all seats, except the driver's, removed from the trailing 4×4, to use as a truck to haul whatever it was that Hamid claimed to have—

"There, Mullah!" the boy shouted with excitement. "Right there! Over . . . *there!*"

Jumping out of the Goat the moment Faiz stopped the vehicle, Hamid scrambled across the two hundred feet of sand separating the convoy from the rift between the dunes.

Akhtar understood why Faiz had not gotten any closer. This was the desert, and sand dunes could shift unpredictably, especially these crescent-shaped dunes called barchans. At a glance, the angle of repose of the pair of dunes seemed steeper than normal, so any foreign disturbance, such as low-frequency vibrations from approaching vehicles—even loud voices—could trigger a crushing avalanche. And if Hamid was right and the blast did indeed shift the sands enough to unearth this metallic object, then that meant that the dunes could be unstable.

But the fear of being buried alive was quickly overwhelmed by an enthusiasm Akhtar could not control—a boost of adrenaline that somehow even subdued his muscle spasms.

He too leaped out of the 4×4, and went after the boy, who seemed to float over the sand, reaching the closest barchan.

Akhtar filled his lungs with cold desert air, catching up to Hamid as he knelt by a handful of rocks stacked about a foot high near the point of inflection of the dune.

The men from the other two Goats pulled up behind the lead 4×4 and got out armed with shovels.

"Here, Mullah," he said, tossing the rocks out of the way. "This is where I found it."

Akhtar sank his knees in the sand next to Hamid, as the parting stones revealed something resembling a metallic fin painted in a light gray color, like those in the rear of large bombs. Flashlights converged on them as the group made a circle around Akhtar, who demanded complete silence. Any sound wave could trigger a deadly slump.

Using only their hands, Akhtar and the boy shifted some of the sand out of the way, unearthing a second fin at a right angle to the first one. The two were linked along their backs by a sturdy metal ring.

Definitely a bomb.

He ran his hand over the Cyrillic script adjacent to a red star on the adjoining ring, which was almost three inches wide and a quarter inch thick.

And definitely Russian.

Given the position of the fins relative to the desert floor, the bomb seemed to have stabbed the sand at a fairly steep angle, disappearing into the foot of the barchan.

Akhtar stood, ignoring a cramp twisting in his gut while the scar tissue on his chest and neck began to ache and itch. He needed to opiate soon.

But not yet, he thought, inspecting the wall of sand projecting up at a dangerous angle. An excavation could alter its delicate balance, the tension between the sand at the base and the sand rising up to the crest.

Kneeling down again, he inspected the solid fin section, fingers following the welding marks integrating the fins and ring into the steel body of the weapon.

"Put the shovels away and bring me the ropes," he whispered, continuing using his hands only to dig around the tail of the weapon and expose the other fins.

As his men headed back to the Goats, Faiz joined him, and the boy and mumbled, "What do you have in mind?"

"We can't excavate it out. Too dangerous," he whispered, eyes on the dune soaring over them, as he felt a shiver bouncing up and down his body from the growing chemical imbalance.

"Then?" Faiz asked.

But Akhtar didn't answer, inhaling deeply and mustering the strength to spend another fifteen minutes scooping sand out of the way while demanding silence as his men stood by with climbing ropes coiled over their shoulders.

He needed everyone to be absolutely quiet so he could listen to the crescent-shaped dune for any booming or burping sounds.

The desert, like everything else in nature, had a language, a set of sounds that foretold upcoming changes, and one of those was the whistling or barking that preceded sand avalanches. The pitch or frequency of the sound was controlled by the shear rate between layers of sand. As friction between grains and the compression of air between them increased, the sound would change from a light whistle to the low-pitch rumble of a major displacement.

The moment they exposed the tail section, Akhtar looped three sets of 11mm workhorse single ropes, standard for mountain climbing, around the base of the weapon. Akhtar and many of his men had received training years ago from Swiss contractors—training that had come in handy during this long war, to drop on an unsuspecting enemy as well as vanish down precipices following surprise attacks. Each rope was rated for seventeen UIAA falls, meaning they could withstand the impact of a 174-pound climber falling for the length of the rope, which was 120 feet, for at least seventeen falls, according to the Union Internationale des Associations d'Alpinisme.

Ignoring the slight trembling in his hands, he threaded each rope through the rings and secured them with figure-eight knots, the strongest for a loop at the end of a rope. Then he had his men back each Goat side by side, close enough to run each standing end to the rear bumpers, fastening them with a second set of figure-eight knots while applying an even tension to each rope.

Akhtar ordered Faiz and the other two drivers into position while getting everyone else a couple hundred feet in front of the trio of

Goats. He then walked back and forth between the bomb and the rear bumpers to make sure all was indeed in order.

Now for the tricky part.

Satisfied, he approached each driver and provided very clear instructions about when to shift into first gear and how to release the clutch, not too fast but not too slow. Too quickly and they risked snapping the ropes. Too slow and the probable avalanche triggered by the shifting mass seeking a new angle of repose would come down on the bomb—and even the Goats—before they could get the weapon and themselves out of the way. And on top of that, the drivers had to do it in perfect synchronization to even out the stress on the three ropes.

Standing in front of the Goats, in a way reminiscent of those American drag races he had seen on television as a boy, Akhtar did his best to ignore his nausea and spasms and held up his right hand, making a fist.

The men started the Goats and put them in gear.

In a single fluid motion, he lowered his hand.

Tires spun and engines groaned, spraying sand as the ropes whistled and vibrated, whipping into full tension. Their sound blended with the grumble emerging out of the barchan as the weapon shifted in the sand, shaking the dune's foundation.

The 4×4s spun in place, shifting sideways for a few seconds before suddenly leaping forward, plucking the bomb out tail first and dragging it away from the base.

But just as Akhtar caught a glimpse of the long weapon sliding out of the ground, the wall caved in with a thundering roar as a large mass sheared off the dune and slid to the base.

The Goats accelerated in a roar, tires whirling, towing the device for fifty-some feet. For an instant, the weapon, at least eight feet long, reflected the moonlight as it raced ahead of the avalanche. But the tip of the shifting sand caught up to it just before the dune reached a new angle of repose, burying it along with a dozen feet of rope.

Already broken into a sweat from opium withdrawal symptoms, Akhtar took a deep breath, working through the cramps and his aching skin while signaling the drivers to stop. Using a sleeve to wipe the perspiration off his brow, he breathed deeply again and again, swallowing a lump in his throat.

The Kozliks idled their engines as the mullah staggered behind them, inspecting each rope still secured to each bumper, before reaching the edge of the barchan, where the ropes disappeared into the sand.

His trembling hand gripped each rope and gave it a firm tug, verifying that they were still attached to the bomb, before finding the strength to walk back to the front and instruct the drivers to move forward, slowly, in first gear.

The Goats once more groaned with effort as the drivers released the clutches and all tires spun, spewing sand behind them but slowly inching forward. The ropes vibrated from the stress, resonating across the desert floor like a rumbling bass, but they held as the tail of the bomb reemerged.

Running four fingers across his neck, Akhtar signaled the drivers to cut off their engines.

And it was then, as he inspected the device and ran his quivering fingers over the severed mounting brackets that had once secured it to the belly of a Soviet jet, that Akhtar began to believe it could be the one from that night.

He remembered the American who had trained Akaa. He recalled the concern and the frustration painted on the infidel's face when they had left empty-handed after several nights digging through the wreckage. The Soviets had also failed to find it, using entire *divisions* of men and heavy equipment. And he especially remembered the American pointing to the broken mounts on the bottom of the Sukhoi jet, meaning the bomb and the jet had separated midflight.

The bomb had to be very important to get all of that attention.

And the bomb is ours, Akaa—ours!

As his men dragged the heavy weapon toward the utility 4×4s, Akhtar managed to drag himself into the rear of his Goat.

His fingers momentarily fumbled with the knapsack's zipper before grabbing the old Chinese-style wooden pipe and a butane torch lighter. The pipe was already stuffed with smoking opium. Also called *chandu*, it was processed from raw opium and enhanced with unadulterated opium ash, which contained the traces of morphine that had made those months following the UAV strike tolerable.

Akhtar glanced out the Goat's rear windshield to verify that his men were all still busy with the bomb. Satisfied, he held the end of the pipe over the lighter's bluish flame for thirty seconds, monitoring the drug as it vaporized.

Drawing deeply, he swirled the smoke inside his mouth for a moment before inhaling. The effect was almost instantaneous as his body reacted to the good-quality chandu, processed especially for him, feeling its power as it propagated to his fingertips.

He exhaled out the side window as the pure chemical energized him physically and mentally, unlike the low-quality opium sold by drug cartels. The latter, contaminated with cocaine or heroin to boost profits, caused users to lie around in the traditional opium-induced stupor, whereas Akhtar felt revitalized.

As his men hoisted the weapon into the cargo area of a utility Goat and used the same climbing ropes to secure it, Akhtar decided that he needed someone with the right technical expertise to inspect the bomb and assess its functionality, especially after it had been buried in the sand for so many years.

And that meant he had to get word out to bin Laden.

But given the importance of this discovery, it could not be done via standard channels. The Americans were always listening, and although Akhtar's messages were encrypted, he could not risk any dispatch that could tip the enemy to this discovery.

Placing a hand on his chest and holding the Soviet class ring as he took a final draw with his eyes closed, Akhtar's mind reached a state of unparalleled sharpness, of immense clarity.

And he suddenly realized how he could get a message out safely.

A message only Akaa would understand.

3

Al-Amir

He let them get close.

Very close.

It was a benefit of monopolizing the very top of America's Most Wanted list: the Saudi-born Sunni Muslim and founder of al Qaeda didn't need to go looking for trouble.

Trouble always found him.

Always.

And this evening it came in the form of a half dozen shadows materializing in his Russian "red star" night vision binoculars, crisscrossing the poppy fields skirting Darband Road, near his temporary headquarters on the outskirts of town.

One of his informants, a downtown rug merchant, had spotted the group earlier that afternoon driving up from Islamabad in a pair of white Toyota RAV4 SUVs. He had spent the following hour tracking their textbook movements through an assortment of local assets, all loyal to his organization—and all willing to die in his service for a chance to reach paradise.

The last message arrived via a burner phone text from a roadside vendor selling bundles of grayish-green stems topped with hairless round poppy capsules, harvested from the far end of the same field used by the approaching termination team.

Osama bin Laden calmly shifted the binoculars to scan the front of his headquarters, where his decoy had stepped onto the street for a night stroll a moment ago, followed by two of his own bodyguards for maximum effect.

He grinned. The resemblance was indeed amazing, down to the turban and prominent nose. And the ruse seemed to have worked. The instant his look-alike walked out, the shadows emerged from the rear of the field, silently cruising through the waist-high foliage like ghosts.

Professionals.

But it would not matter.

Not tonight, and certainly not in Pakistan, where the Americans couldn't use their Predators like they did in Afghanistan.

He set the binoculars down on the stone ledge of his rooftop vantage point and reached for his old SVD Dragunov sniper rifle lying next to him—the same one he had taken from that dead Russian boy sniper a lifetime ago.

Fingers worked the familiar weapon automatically, inserting a curved box magazine containing ten double-stacked 7.62×54mm cartridges, 151-grain steel-jacketed projectiles powered by the new 7N14 load developed specifically for the SVD.

He pressed the butt of the skeletonized wooden stock against his right shoulder, resting the side of his face against the stock's comb. Inhaling deeply, he positioned his right eye six inches from the end of the PSO-1 scope, cleverly mounted on the side of the SVD so as to not interfere with the weapon's iron sight line.

Shifting his head slightly to the left, then the right, the picture materialized in the PSO-1's reticle, illuminated by a small battery-powered light.

The scope's bullet drop compensation elevation turret, sloping down from a marking of 2 at the top to 10 at the bottom, along the left side of the reticle, placed his target—the group's point man—under the 6 marking, meaning six hundred yards. Measuring his breathing, he adjusted the BDC knob according to the chevrons running down the middle of the range finder. The reticle enabled him to observe the target in low-light conditions as it continued zigzagging through the waist-high vegetation. But Osama didn't follow the man's snaky pattern. Rather, he positioned the center of the scope steadily in the middle of the target's back-and-forth motion, letting the silhouette come to him.

Reaching for the radio next to his binoculars, he clicked the mike twice without breaking eye contact. A light breeze swept across the poppy field, swaying the lavender flowers toward the west, enough for him to make a slight compensation using the stadiametric marks in the PSO-1 windage turret.

Three sets of double-clicks on the radio signaled that three of his four snipers, already perched on surrounding rooftops, had acquired their respective targets behind the point man. His fourth shooter, Pasha, lay ten feet away facing the same poppy field—though his nephew favored the Remington M24 bolt-action rifle with a Leupold scope.

"Good here too, Akaa," Pasha whispered, without taking his eyes off his mark.

Five snipers against six targets meant a follow-up shot on the trailing figure carrying a backpack—easily done with the semiautomatic SVD. Unlike Pasha's bolt-action Remington, the SDV used the combustion gas of the discharging cartridge to eject the spent casing while chambering a fresh round. Plus the PSO-1's reticle offered a wide enough angle to easily shift targets.

But there was no talking Pasha into an SVD. His nephew had used the damn Remington to represent Afghanistan at the 2000 Summer Olympic Games in Sydney, Australia, winning a bronze medal in the men's fifty-meter rifle three positions. It was his baby.

Osama sighed while observing the team, letting them get even closer, watching the lead figure grow to touch the 4 marking on the BDC elevation turret.

Four hundred yards.

Making a final check of the crosswind, he tapped the radio once.

Shoot in five seconds.

Focusing on the lead figure, Osama let his mark return to the center chevron in the reticle.

Three.

Two.

He exhaled and squeezed the trigger.

4

Tradecraft

Multiple reports broke the silence across the poppy field, like whips cracking in the darkness.

In a most surreal sight, the head of each member of his team running ahead of him snapped. Exit wounds sprayed dark clouds behind them in unison and almost in slow motion, before their limp silhouettes sank below the layer of flowers.

CIA officer Bill Gorman reacted swiftly, hitting the ground as a near-miss buzzed his left ear a couple of seconds after the well-orchestrated volley of sniper rounds had practically decapitated his team.

What the hell?

But his mind already had the answer.

Ambush.

They were waiting for us.

Gorman had had a bad feeling about this op—the termination of one of bin Laden's generals—from the moment his boss, Islamabad Station Chief Les Finkle, had brought it up. And Gorman had argued against it, insisting on cross-checking the intel with his own assets inside the ISI, Pakistan's Inter-Services Intelligence, as well as with Army Intelligence. He'd even requested UAV surveillance before and during the strike.

But Finkle, freshly resting in peace some fifty feet ahead of him, wasn't having any of that, reminding Gorman of the many ops that the military had excluded the Agency from in the past year alone.

And besides, Finkle had claimed, the intel from his asset was golden, plus this location had been on his radar for a month. In addition, rumor had it that this compound was even occasionally visited by "Elvis," the nickname given to Osama bin Laden because of all the field sightings that turned out to be nothing more than wishful thinking.

The real reason, however, as Gorman knew quite well, was that Finkle saw the elimination of a bin Laden general as his chance to get promoted out of the shithole that was Islamabad. He wanted full bragging rights—which meant declining to ask Bagram Air Base for any assistance—as his ticket to head back to Langley.

As the new member of the team out of the Islamabad station, Gorman's recommendations had gone unheard. He had been out-ranked, outnumbered, and also assigned to the rear of the assault team, with the added shit job of hauling forty pounds of explosives and detonators. It really had not mattered that Gorman had been with Army Intelligence for three years and had done three tours, two in Iraq and another in Afghanistan, before the CIA recruited him. It also didn't matter that he had spent the following two years working his way through the ranks at the Baghdad and New Delhi stations before his assignment here. And it sure as hell had not mattered that during his one year in Islamabad, Gorman alone was re-sponsible for recruiting and handling four agents. He'd even made initial contact with a promising asset inside the ISI, the one whom Gorman had not been allowed to contact to cross-check Finkle's intelligence.

In the eyes of his boss, Gorman was still the fucking new guy, an FNG.

And it certainly hadn't helped that Pete Shaw, Finkle's second-in-command—also RIP, behind his boss—had reported a visual sighting of Osama bin Laden himself a minute ago, seen through a high-power night vision scope.

"Elvis . . . holy crap, it's Elvis! He just . . . left the building!"

"Seriously, Pete?"

"He really just stepped out, Les! I'm staring at the bastard. I'm telling you, it's him!"

"All right, One through Six . . . single file . . . go, go, go!"

Gorman shook his head before whispering into his throat mike, "Six here. Anybody?"

But as feared, he got no response in his earpiece.

"Guys? One through Five? Anyone?"

Nothing.

Removing his backpack, Gorman rolled onto his back, controlling his breathing while trying to assess his situation—which his operative mind quickly boiled down to a single word.

Fucked.

He was alone in the middle of this damn poppy field, surrounded by a team of well-trained snipers just waiting to smoke him the moment he lifted his head above the layer of flowers fluttering in the breeze.

So, yes . . . *very* fucked.

And that was just the beginning of his problems. His team was CIA operating in Pakistan—as in they weren't supposed to be here. They didn't exist, and that meant no one would claim them or come looking for them. Unlike during his military years, there would not be a rescue. There would be no helos coming for him. There was nobody to call for help. The instant he'd chosen to transition from Army Intelligence and Combat Support to become an operator in the CIA's Counterterrorism Center, he knew the day would come when he would have to rescue himself, and that meant—

Gorman cringed as two more reports cracked from unseen shooters, the rounds slamming the ground to his right.

They're trying to flush me out.

He was about to back away but then realized that was *precisely* what the bastards would expect him to do: to retreat, go back the same way he'd come. And since they had a pretty damn good idea where he had gone down, they would very likely try to cut him off at—

Three more shots, all just behind his feet, and each originating from a different source. A fourth shot nicked the heel of his boot.

Gorman scrambled forward while trying very hard not to think of multiple snipers with night vision scopes scanning the surface of the field.

Crawling through a dozen feet of swinging plants and loose soil, he ran right into Ken Hollis, another one of Finkle's go-to guys. The bullet had pierced his right temple and pretty much blown out the back of his head.

Damn.

Dragging the backpack, Gorman crept away from him and found the next member of the team, and the next, while more reports resonated in the night, though aimed downfield, toward his expected retreat route. And that told him that they could not see him in the poppy crop as he moved about.

Probably because of the wind.

It took him another minute to locate Finkle and Shaw, and the brutal reality struck him as hard as those sniper bullets pounding the ground around him.

Everyone is dead.

Everyone but me.

As he lay there staring at the lifeless eyes of a boss who'd been nothing short of an asshole to him for the past year—and whose arrogance had gotten his team killed—Gorman's tradecraft training gave him an idea.

It was obvious by now that the shooters suspected he had survived, and they were trying to force him to the surface. So why not give them what they wanted?

He crawled around for another minute, pulling the bodies closer together while inspecting each one, finally settling on Finkle.

"Are you sure we didn't get him already?" Pasha asked. "I saw him go down after your follow-up shot."

"I didn't hit him. He's still in there," Osama replied, regretting missing that follow-up shot, scanning the surface of the field with the binoculars, wishing that Allah would kill the damn breeze for just a minute. The constant swaying masked the movements the lone survivor would make when attempting to get away from—

"There!" Pasha hissed.

Bin Laden brought the PSO-1 over to the right, spotting the top of a man's head, and he immediately shot thrice in the time it took Pasha and everyone else to shoot once.

Multiple rounds found their marks and the figure vanished, but not before his head exploded.

"Move in," bin Laden said, while continuing scanning the area.

Gorman let go of Finkle's body and jumped back when several rounds tore apart what remained of Finkle's skull. He had held him up by the shoulders for just five seconds before blood, bones, and tissue went everywhere, spraying Gorman's face and chest as the headless body slapped the ground.

He wiped his face with a sleeve, fighting the nausea rising in his throat, taking a few deep breaths.

Jesus, he thought, staring at the carnage while feeling compelled to mumble something apologetic.

Sorry, boss.

Slowly and with effort, he dragged Finkle's remains over to the other four souls before lying sideways and opening the backpack. He produced a dozen M112 demolition charges—military grade C-4 blocks each roughly 2 inches by 1.5 inches and 11 inches long, weighing 1.25 pounds. He also grabbed a gray roll of PETN, a type of detonation cord made of flexible plastic tubing filled with pentaerythritol tetranitrate.

Using the SOG knife strapped to his right leg, Gorman worked quickly, connecting the C-4 with foot-long lengths of PETN and shoving them beneath the bodies. He made his way around the bodies before connecting the standing end of the PETN cord to one of the dozen remote control detonators in the bag, all slaved to a classified app on his smartphone.

Pausing, he closed his eyes, hearing the distant rustling of approaching men. As expected, the snipers thought they had killed him and were sending a recon team to check. With luck, it would be the snipers themselves.

Grabbing the backpack, Gorman gave his team a brief but heavy sigh. Assholes or not, they were CIA officers killed in the line of duty. And as such, the best way to honor them was by not leaving a single shred of evidence of them ever being here—nothing for al Qaeda to parade around.

He crawled on all fours away from them and from the incoming sounds, checking the compass on the top of the SOG knife's handle to move southwest for one minute, before once more rummaging through the backpack.

He connected a foot of PETN to a single M112 block and a second remote control detonator, set to go off ninety seconds after the main explosion. He buried the block of C-4 in the tilled and moist soil, like a mine, leaving just the detonator exposed.

Using the compass to navigate in a horseshoe pattern around his dead team, Gorman moved in twenty-degree increments. It took all of three minutes to bury seven more of the delayed single charges while keeping a respectful distance from the sounds of men still advancing toward his last sighting.

As expected, the incoming threat proceeded with caution, slowly, methodically, but getting nowhere near the location of his team before he was through setting up the timed mines.

Gorman turned southwest once more, clambering through the field like a reptile, ignoring his burning shoulders and thighs while putting two thousand feet between him and the explosives, then once more pausing.

He wiped the perspiration off his face while catching his breath. Now came the tricky part. If he were to assume that the snipers were still scanning the field, they would be doing so with their scopes, which provided a fairly narrow field of view. And if he could also assume that they would be limiting their scan to the area immediately around the last sighting, to alert the team on the ground, then it was fairly reasonable to think that he could chance a quick look to check their location.

But to mitigate the risk, Gorman smeared dirt and fallen lavender-colored petals on his head and forehead, while also shoving the ends of fallen stems between his neck and the top of the Kevlar vest to break up the shape of his head.

Very slowly, he got on his knees and rose just enough for his eyes to break the fluttering layer of poppy flowers.

Slowly and quite methodically, he scanned the surface in a slow circular motion, pausing every twenty or so degrees, like a submarine skipper with a periscope.

There.

He spotted their shadows waist deep in the poppy, coming from the northern edge of the field. There were seven of them, dark and loose tunics swirling in the breeze, heads rounded off with pakols, hands clutching the unmistakable shapes of AK-47s and their forty-round curved magazines. And that meant they were probably not the snipers, which further meant the area ahead of the incoming rebels was being scanned quite carefully.

Feeling damn glad he had taken the precaution to camouflage his head and keep it attached to his neck, Gorman tracked the shadows as they approached the kill zone. But he decided not to keep his body still. Rather, he swayed his head back and forth to the rhythm of the flowers around him, hopefully making it more difficult for a sniper to pick him out.

The moment the shadows got close enough, Gorman lay face down in the field and opened the app on his phone. The image of a red button materialized on the screen. Starting the digital timer on the watch hugging his left wrist, while opening his mouth, he tapped the red button three times.

Osama had followed the team using the red star night vision binoculars, which amplified the available light and channeled it to the center of his field of view, turning darkness into palettes of green. Pasha and the other snipers did the same, but using their night vision scopes, ready to strike if a survivor tried to make a run for it.

The poppy field was quiet, peaceful, almost resembling a rippling ocean as the wind swept over it under a yellow moon surrounded by a blanket of stars. And in the middle of it, like green ghosts, his men cruised toward the last known location of the survivor he had shot a few minutes—

The sudden intense light blinded him as the Russian binoculars amplified the white-hot ball of flames erupting where his men had been a second ago, shooting it right into his retinas. An instant later a powerful blast smashed into the building, the shock wave shoving him off his sniper's perch, tossing him in the air, and sending him crashing somewhere in the middle of the rooftop.

His back slapped the metal surface hard, skinning his shoulder blades and elbows as the explosion reverberated in his eardrums.

Stunned, Osama took a deep breath while trying to get his bearings, while forcing his shocked mind to figure out what the hell had just happened—while bright spots pulsated in his field of view.

A Hellfire?

But . . . drones are not allowed in Pakistani skies.

Rolling to his side, he blinked, trying to clear his sight, but the flash had killed his night vision. Everything was dark, save for the massive column of orange and yellow flames licking the night sky, turning the middle of the poppy field into a conflagration. The fire cast a pulsating dimness across the rooftop, where he spotted Pasha, also on his back, hands on his face.

Osama sat up with effort, swallowing, before standing and staggering over to Pasha, who was also sitting up, his round face tight under his short beard, eyes wide in obvious surprise.

"What the hell was *that*?" Pasha mumbled.

Osama lifted his gaze at the stars while blinking, wiping the tears off his sore eyes. "Not sure," he replied. 'A drone, maybe . . . Or perhaps . . ."

Realizing the other possibility, Osama rushed to the edge of the roof again and glared at the field. Although his night vision was shot and white spots still peppered the center of his field of view, the fire washed most of the surrounding farmland in shades of orange.

And at its farther end, between the fire and Darband Road, which connected the agricultural region to the northwest section of Haripur, he spotted a figure running.

Bill Gorman dashed through the night like a gazelle that had just pissed in the lion's den.

He ran for his life, gulping lungfuls of cold air, his eyes fixed on the road and the assortment of villages extending beyond it, sprinkled among farms and ranches surrounded by pastures dotting the north end of Haripur.

He ran as fast as his legs would go, ignoring everything else—

the inferno behind him, the heartbeat pounding his temples, the sweat dripping into his eyes, his burning muscles, and his drying throat.

But he did allow a quick glance at his digital watch.

Thirty seconds left.

He pressed on, his back tingling in anticipation of a sniper's bullet. But he had to trust the optics of his counterattack, the logic of his tradecraft. Anyone using night vision equipment should be momentarily blinded, in shock and pain, probably rubbing their eyes while wondering what the hell had hit them.

The blast had been more powerful than he had expected, lobbing him across the poppy field like a rag doll even at a distance of almost two thousand feet. But the soft soil and the vegetation had cushioned him, allowing him to leap to his feet and take off like an Olympic sprinter.

Twenty seconds.

He charged ahead, believing in his training, in the countermeasures drilled into him, both at Army Intelligence and at the Agency.

Ten seconds.

He thought about hitting the ground again but decided that he had already gained enough distance from those buried charges to fear any significant shock wave.

Osama worked quickly, reaching for his SVD and resting it back on the ledge overlooking the field. He acquired the runaway figure easily through the PSO-1, thanks to the scope's night vision feature, which amplified the dim orange light reaching the opposite edge of the field.

The bullet drop compensation elevation turret in the POS-1 reticle showed his target slightly smaller than the 10 marking, meaning just beyond a thousand yards. But the SVD could still make the shot, thanks to the unusually powerful 7N14 charge inside each cartridge in his magazine.

While Pasha stood by his side, acting as his spotter with the red star binoculars, Osama settled his breathing, ignoring his throbbing back and a flaring headache. He made a slight adjustment to the BDC and positioned his mark directly on the center chevron while exhaling and—

Multiple blasts erupted in the night like cones of fire, the flashes shooting through the reticle's advanced optics, piercing his vision again just before another shock wave pushed him back, though not as hard as that first one.

He landed on his butt, stunned, the SVD still in his hands, while Pasha, who had been standing, took a harder hit and rolled past him, landing on his side a dozen feet from him.

Mustering strength, and while Pasha groaned behind him, Osama stood and staggered to the edge of the rooftop, his aching eyes staring at the multiple fires spreading across the field, becoming a single blaze kindled by the breeze. It created a wall of fire and smoke that shielded the runaway figure from him and his other snipers, who also stood by the edge of their rooftops staring at the inferno.

Closing his eyes, he breathed in and out, trying to quench his growing anger at the infidel who had managed to outsmart—

The cell phone in his pocket vibrated twice, signaling a new message.

He frowned. Only a handful on this earth knew the number, and they all knew to use it *only* in an emergency, as one of his generals had done that afternoon when getting word of the incoming termination team.

Reaching into his pocket, he stared at it a moment. The message was a photo of a Russian pilot's ring. And below it read:

FOUND WHAT WE LOOKED FOR THAT NIGHT.
NEED ASSISTANCE TO ASSESS ITS CONDITION.

Osama stared at it, then at Pasha, who was standing, dusting off his tunic and pants, then back at the message.
Could it be?

"I will find him, Akaa," his nephew hissed while walking up to him and glaring at the furnace below, the Remington in his right hand. "I will find him and peel off his skin on YouTube."

Osama continued staring at the message while his mind grasped its profound significance, the reality of having control of a weapon with the power to destroy hundreds of World Trade Centers—an entire city full of infidels.

He closed his eyes, recalling that night in the mountains north of Lashkar Gah. He had been fighting with the mujahideen after leaving his family in Riyadh, where he had been born to billionaire Mohammed bin Awad bin Laden, a construction magnate with close ties to the Saudi royal family. Osama had studied economics at King Abdulaziz University in Riyadh before joining the Afghan resistance in 1979 to fight against the Soviet occupation.

That night in 1988, as the decadelong war drew to an end, thanks in part to the military aid provided by the same Americans who had tried to kill him tonight, his team had spent many nights searching for the missing bomb. His old CIA trainer, the Ba'i, thought the weapon important enough to risk leaving the protection of the mountains to find it.

But we never did.

"Akaa? Is everything all right?"

Osama turned to his nephew, dropping his gaze to the muscular warrior's waistband, which holstered the same Makarov pistol from that night.

"I will find him, Akaa," Pasha hissed again. "And I will—"

"Not you," he replied. "You have a new mission."

"A new . . . Wait, what are you talking about? That bastard just—"

"And we *will* find him, Pasha," Osama said, placing a hand on his nephew's shoulder. "But *not* you."

Before Pasha could reply, Osama showed him the message from Akhtar.

5

Alternate Plan

Gorman reached the edge of the poppy field, covered in mud and perspiration. Panting, he took a knee, hiding in the foliage, peering up and down Darband Road while he caught his breath. The two-way paved street leading into town smelled of cow manure and was nearly deserted.

Not for long.

Villagers from surrounding farms raced toward the field, and he could hear the distant alarms of the Haripur's municipal fire brigades. Poppy was essential to the local economy, so much effort would be devoted to cleaning up the mess he had made. Soon this place would be jam-packed with villagers, and if he had learned one thing after operating in the region, it was that al Qaeda had eyes and ears everywhere. He would not last a minute in the open while wearing his black tactical gear, smeared in soil and blood.

Unfortunately, Finkle's exit strategy had not been ideal—to which Gorman had also objected, to no avail. The Toyota RAV4s they had used to drive up from Islamabad were parked a kilometer away, hidden behind a cluster of trees, fully fueled and ready for their getaway.

But he had to get to them first, and that meant a change of clothes.

Gorman's answer came a minute later, when a group of farmers ran up the road, hauling picks and shovels. He watched them go inside the field a couple hundred feet from where he knelt.

The basic technique for fighting wildfires was fairly similar around the world: dig a trench around the existing fire to let it burn itself out while keeping it from spreading.

Gorman went after them in a deep crouch, aiming for the rear of the group. An older man roughly his height and sporting a long white beard tried to keep up with the rest of the younger farmers marching toward the southern edge of the fire to start excavating an isolation canal.

Confirming his target, Gorman scrambled closer, running up to the old man from behind, speedily but quietly closing the gap in under a minute.

Predatory eyes narrowed as he prepared to strike, checking his surroundings, making sure there were no other villagers coming up behind him or on either flank.

Waiting another thirty seconds for the rest of the group to get farther ahead, Gorman remained within striking distance, using the old man's noisy steps to mask his own.

Eyes flicked up ahead again, verifying a final time that the old man had achieved the desired separation from the rest of the herd. Gorman's movements were now almost on autopilot, honed to near perfection by years of training, closing the final gap.

He struck with the edge of his right hand the base of the neck, where the vagus nerve system ran from the cerebellum to the rest of the body. The shock triggered a vasovagal episode, and the old man fainted immediately.

Gorman caught him in midair, setting him down gently—and quietly—on the soil.

He now worked quickly, kicking off his own boots and slipping the stranger's baggy pants and long tunic over his tactical gear. He wiped off his face before donning the man's black pakol and leather sandals.

The transformation complete, Gorman grabbed the shovel and left him there to wake up in an hour or so with the headache of a lifetime.

He reached Darband Road in another two minutes. This time he just walked out, blending perfectly with the locals approaching the field from all directions on foot, in cars and trucks, on bicycles and mopeds, and even in carts towed by cows. Three showed up in small tractors driven straight onto the field, lowering their front loaders as they approached the edge of the blaze to carve wide isolation channels.

Gorman surveyed the horde without staring at anyone, his practiced eyes brushing dozens of faces in the semidarkness, searching for any gaze not focused on the inferno. But he saw no one interested in anything but putting out the fire threatening the area's livelihood.

Finkle's plan called for the team to reach the RAV4s, where they would shed their tactical gear for civilian clothes before driving back to Islamabad and storing the vehicles in a private parking garage a dozen blocks from the embassy.

But something made Gorman pause and turn around, his eyes staring at the two- and three-story mud structures along the northern edge of the field. The pulsating flames washed their facades in orange light, along with the two white-paneled vans parked in front.

As people rushed past him shouting, screaming, and even crying, Gorman couldn't help but wonder . . . What if Finkle's intelligence had actually been correct, just poorly acted upon?

And what if Shaw had indeed caught a glimpse of the elusive bin Laden?

As Gorman stared at the figures on those distant rooftops, his operative mind began to consider an alternate plan.

6

Thumb Drive

KANDAHAR AIRFIELD. SOUTHERN AFGHANISTAN.

Hunter Stark stood guard while his team slept on cots scattered around the nose of their C-21A military transport parked in a hangar near the south end of the runway. Fully fueled, it was always ready to leave at a moment's notice should their civilian employer decide to deploy them to another exotic destination.

The military variant of the Learjet 35A was a light jet designed to carry up to six passengers, the pilot and copilot, plus a couple hundred pounds of luggage. Or, in Stark's case, five contractors plus several hundred pounds of violence, since one of the contractors—Danny Martin—doubled up as the resident pilot. A former naval aviator, the man could fly anything from jets and prop planes to helicopters.

The two armored Chevy Tahoes parked by the tail of the jet were supposed to be black, but like everything else in this damn country, a thick coat of fine clay soil covered the CIA-sourced SUVs.

The colonel paced the interior of the structure slowly, methodically, a Heckler & Koch MP5A1 submachine gun in his hands, safety off, shooting finger resting on the trigger casing. On paper, he and his team were supposed to be safe behind walls of concrete and the millions of miles of barbed wire surrounding KAF, which resembled a midsize city in a third world country. But the colonel had been in the business long enough to know that, in Afghanistan, any feeling of safety was an illusion. Everything around here was a potential threat. Everything was hostile. Beyond those static barriers projected a land populated by a society that had a medieval way of inflicting terror on anyone stupid enough to invade it. And the long list included legends from Alexander the Great, Genghis Khan, and

Tamerlane to the British Empire, the Sikh Empire, and the once mighty Soviet Union.

And now us, he thought.

Of course, none of those ancient conquerors had to worry about IEDs or the three million mines left behind by the retreating Soviet Army in 1989.

Sighing, he checked his black Casio G-Shock watch before realizing the time and murmuring, "Damn."

He turned the alarm feature back on before hastily walking to a small cooler next to the jet's folding steps. He grabbed a cold bottle of water, reached inside a Velcro-secured pocket on the side of his pants, and snagged a quart-size Ziploc bag filled with four different kinds of pills.

The colonel had long since come to terms with the reality that he suffered from post-traumatic stress disorder. There had been a time, years ago—back when he was young and stupid—when he had stopped taking the meds, which cost him his marriage and almost his career.

Stark swallowed his daily dose almost twelve hours too late, chasing it with a gulp of water before stowing away the bag.

Resuming his patrol, he briefly shook his head at the thought of Kate, his beautiful ex-wife, who didn't want anything to do with him now and who had long ago divorced him and married some attorney in New York.

Kate had been the U.S. Navy doctor who treated Stark after an ill-fated mission with the Special Forces in Kuwait City in 1990. An Exocet missile hit his team while it was approaching a beach to remove obstacles ahead of the invasion force. A dozen operators—and close friends—had been killed instantly because some trigger-happy dumb-ass in some French missile cruiser in the Persian Gulf mistook Stark's Mark V Special Operations Craft for an Iraqi vessel. It was an unfortunate mistake made among a complex coalition of forces from thirty-five nations.

The whole episode went undetected for hours, as very few in the coalition were aware of Stark's black ops mission, leaving its sole survivor treading water with a mangled left leg until an Italian helicopter spotted him at dawn and fished him out.

Stark raised his brows and frowned at the irony of life. He would have never met Kate had it not been for that tragic wartime accident that nearly ended his military career. He had married her a year later in Virginia Beach, only to get divorced a short time later because of his extreme mood swings—because of the nightmares from that terrible night, compounded by a decade of giving and receiving violence. Last he'd heard via a mutual friend, Kate was still married, with a couple of kids.

He clenched his jaw.

Losing her and losing the life he could have had was the heavy price he had paid for arrogantly thinking that he could handle what no one ever has been able to handle without mental consequences: killing another human being.

Young and very damn stupid.

Now he simply took the meds while feeling damn lucky that the side effects were negligible enough to keep him and his contractor team in business.

He stared at the G-Shock again, annoyed at himself for forgetting to turn the alarm back on after the raid. The pills had to be taken religiously every twenty-four hours—no exceptions.

The access door built into the large hangar doors had a small window, and Stark peeked through it. The ramp beyond the glass was relatively quiet for KAF, just night crews driving fueling trucks around at this predawn hour, prepping planes, mostly A-10 Warthogs, F-16 Eagles, and a mix of Black Hawk, Apache, Cobra, and Chinook helicopters under the dim grayish glow of floodlights. And it was all backdropped by the jagged Sulaimans dominating the northwestern horizon, the distant peaks trying to stab a yellowish moon.

Stark stared at the peaceful sight, and for reasons he couldn't explain, his thoughts drifted to a similar moon rising above his hometown of Scituate, on the southern shore of Massachusetts. His father was a Korean War vet and retired army doctor and his mother a chief operating officer for a nearby four hundred–bed hospital. They had three boys, Stark being the youngest by several years. His older brothers followed in their father's footsteps and were deployed to Vietnam. Neither came back. Stark lost them before their twenty-second birthdays, while he was still in high school. That had marked the start of what was later diagnosed within the PTSD family of mental illnesses: suffering massive survivor's guilt. So he had joined the army after college, even though, with his degree from Penn State, he could have gone straight into officer training. But Stark had carried too much guilt, plus he had listened to his father, who said the best officers were enlisted men first. However, it didn't take long for the army brass to recognize his talent, and within a year he became a first lieutenant with the Army Special Forces.

And the rest is history, he thought, still staring at the tarmac as images of his many deployments flashed in his mind. Before he could stop himself, the horror returned. Visions of charred bodies, of flesh torn by bullets and shrapnel, momentarily filled his consciousness, bringing him back to Panama, Colombia, Bosnia, and Iraq. But it wasn't the dead bad guys that tore into his soul. Those he could handle even without the meds. It was the voices of his buddies, of his teammates, of his fellow soldiers bleeding out in his arms, that continued to haunt him. He had unleashed horror on his enemy but his enemy had paid back in kind, taking away so many men he loved as brothers. And mixed with those visions was the horror of that night near the shores of Kuwait City, when his team perished from 160 pounds of high-explosive death inside the warhead of that Exocet—

"Colonel?"

Stark blinked as Ryan Hunt pulled him out of the flashback. In an instant, the visions were replaced by tarmac and planes under a sky stained orange by the looming sun rising over the eastern rim rock.

"Yeah?" he said, without turning around. Checking his watch, he realized that he had been standing here frozen for over three hours.

Damn, he thought, silently hoping for the damn meds to kick in.

"Everyone's good to go, sir."

"Let's do it," he replied, angry at the realization that he had been standing there like a zombie while his team woke up and got ready.

Following Ryan to the same Tahoes they had used just the day before to return from their botched mission, Stark got in the front passenger seat of the first SUV, with Larson at the wheel.

"You okay, boss?" asked his go-to, electronics, and pick-up-the-sides-of-buildings guy. "We were worried about—"

"Did you get the pictures, Chief?"

Larson nodded and handed Stark a thumb drive.

"Good," he said, pocketing the device. "Now shut the fuck up and drive."

"Roger that," Larson said, turning the ignition and accelerating out of the hangar.

Five minutes later, and flanked by his contractor team all dressed in fresh tactical gear, the colonel stared at the caskets draped with American flags being loaded up to a C-17 carrier.

A breeze swept across the dusty airfield under a cloudless sky as temperatures soared into the nineties, even at this early hour. Jets, mostly Warthogs and Hornets, took off and landed in the distance, their exhaust plumes injecting the all-too-familiar smell of burned jet fuel into the air. The acrid scent always had a strange way of reminding Stark of his life, while the caskets symbolized just how quickly it could all end.

It never really got any easier, seeing American men and women who gave it all in the service of their country. Stark had seen these caskets in countless countries while fighting long-forgotten battles, some to be forever classified. But the feeling was always the same. It didn't matter if it was Colombia, Iraq, Bosnia, Afghanistan, or the waters off the coast of Kuwait. The ultimate sacrifice always looked like this in the end, with another American flag draped over another coffin going up the ramp of another transport for its final trip home.

A single tear managed to escape the corner of his left eye, and if Stark were to be completely honest with himself, he would have conceded that it had more to do with his survivor's guilt. It was at times like this that he would wonder which sacrifice was greater, being inside one of those coffins or walking alone on this earth shouldering the burden of those who had died under his watch—and that included Jones and the rest of his CIA team.

He watched as the former Delta, Sergeant Major Ryan Hunt, marched stoically in front of the contractor team. Although the colonel and his guys had been out of the service for quite some time, they came to attention as Ryan snapped the heels of his army boots and commanded, "Present arms!"

All brought their right hands up in the way taught to them at basic schools across the military. Once the caskets were carried by designated army personnel in front of his group and up the ramp of the C-17, Ryan said, "Order arms!"

Everyone brought their hands crisply down to their right sides.

"Ryan, get the team back to the hangar," Stark said, walking away from the closing ramp of the large jet and toward the Tahoes. "I have to go see someone."

"You want company, Colonel?" asked Ryan, flanked by Larson, Hagen, and Martin, who produced a watermelon lollipop and pulled off the wrapper.

"No, thanks," he said, before turning to Larson. "But if the chief is not too busy, I could use his large frame for a quick mission."

Feeling much better as the meds worked their magic, Stark snagged the keys from Larson and got behind the wheel of his SUV. Larson slid into the passenger seat while Ryan and the others left in the second SUV.

"So, what's up, boss?" asked the chief, sitting sideways, a black cap worn backwards, mirror-tint sunglasses reflecting Stark in matching black tactical gear.

Slipping on a pair of Oakley sunglasses, Stark cranked the massive 6.2-liter engine and put the Tahoe in gear. "We're paying a not-so-courteous call on a certain Canadian general."

The command center was a thing of beauty, designed to impress visitors. It wasn't necessarily the best arrangement to manage a war, but that was the direction NATO and the United States had drifted toward over the previous twenty years. Set up like an auditorium, with seats and desks rising from a center stage, the place was busy 24/7, always full of importance, most not justified.

Major General Thomas Lévesque, sitting in the commander's chair at the bottom of the auditorium, was the senior NATO officer in the room and the man responsible for ordering the drone attack on Compound 45.

It had been less than twenty-four hours since "friendly fire" came raining down on that mountainside, triggering a disaster that cost not only the lives of six CIA officers but also the job of the CIA station chief, who had taken the fall for the botched op and had been among the detail carrying the caskets into the C-17 to bring his team home.

Twenty-four hours had been plenty of time for Stark to figure out exactly what had happened, who was responsible, and then to decide what to do about it.

These command centers all had extensive audiovisual installations to project all manner of pictures, slides, and videos onto massive screens, like those at Houston's Mission Control. Large conference rooms lined the back of the auditorium, used for private staff meetings and briefing sessions.

When Chief Larson walked in, his size alone drew attention. Add to that the fact that he was all gunned up, with all his tactical gear on, which in these headquarters was highly unusual, and even more heads swung in his direction.

Stark put his large hand on a U.S. Army sergeant confined to a wheelchair, who was sitting at the video console system near the entrance. He was former Special Forces and had lost both legs in an ambush in Baghdad. Stark had helped him, the year before, get retrained as a video specialist and redeployed.

Sergeant Jimenez likely would have succumbed to alcohol or drugs or, worse, committed suicide like so many forgotten veterans did, at the appalling rate of twenty each day. Instead, he looked up from his console, bright-eyed and bushy-tailed, at the man who had given him a second lease on life.

"Colonel. Glad you guys made it out." Jimenez had been the guy who had given them the heads-up yesterday about the incoming strike.

"Thanks to you, buddy," Larson said while standing next to Stark, who gave Jimenez the thumb drive and told him what to do.

The sergeant went to work, downloading the files into the system and handing the drive back to the colonel.

It was not that Stark did not understand and respect the rank and room that he strode into. It was just that he did not give a shit. The brass at the bottom of this room, led by the moron sitting in the commander's chair, were responsible for what had happened the day before.

Stark thanked Jimenez and proceeded down the stairs to the center stage. Four guards—all wearing the uniform of the Canadian Army Military Police—walked up from where the general sat surrounded by advisors, reviewing a map of the region.

One of the MPs, a large blond man wearing the rank of corporal—the name Darcy stenciled over his left breast pocket—stepped in front of Stark.

"Son," Stark said. "Please . . . This is beyond your pay grade."

Darcy decided to hold his ground, his barrel chest blocking the way. "The general is busy and is not taking any—"

Stark grabbed him by the throat with his index finger and thumb.

The other MPs reached for their sidearms, but Larson's imposing seven-foot frame, glaring eyes, and weapons kept them from drawing them.

"Easy, gentlemen," Stark said, lifting his free hand at the MPs while gently shifting Darcy aside, releasing him to cough off the temporary shock to his larynx.

Slowly, the other MPs got out of their way.

By the time Stark made it to the bottom, all eyes were on him, including Lévesque's. He was a husky French Canadian, probably a descendant of lumberjacks, with orange hair and mustache and a face full of matching freckles. He was also larger than Stark, though nowhere near Larson's size.

In a commanding voice, Lévesque said, "Who the hell are you, eh? And what gives you the right to storm into my—"

"General, my name is Hunter Stark. I was on the ground at Compound Forty-Five with my men and my government's men when you and the staff in this room ordered a strike on the same compound."

The files that Stark had given to Jimenez now played on all the screens in the room. There were six pictures with dates and times and one message, "We killed them," running under each picture. Stark threw the thumb drive at the speechless general and then turned and left the room.

As Larson followed his boss out, Corporal Darcy, a hand still on his throat, mumbled, "Sorry."

Larson stopped and said, "You did not do this, son." Then, pointing at the general and his staff, he added in his booming voice, "*They* did." And he left the room, moving quicker than anyone of his size should be able to do.

His many years in the military had taught Stark a number of

things. One rather obvious lesson went something like this: when you piss on a two-star general's desk, all the yellow water eventually falls on your shoes.

So Stark knew that in the two weeks left on his CIA contract he was more than likely not going to get any new missions. But the seasoned warrior in him knew there was no way he and his men could sit on their butts for all that time in the middle of a war.

Stark drove over with Larson to the U.S. Marine headquarters across the airfield, easily recognized by the large round insignia up front sporting three palm trees. Colonel Paul Duggan commanded the 7th Marine Regiment out of 29 Palms, the Marine Corps Air Ground Combat Center in San Bernardino County, California. Duggan was on his fourth combat tour in Afghanistan, as were many of his staff, commanding more than two thousand marines. He was a tough, caring, lead-from-the-front type leader, admired by all. Stark and his team had fought alongside Duggan's marines three months prior to this latest incident, and all came away from that encounter with mutual respect.

Stark parked the Tahoe near the double doors, turned to Larson, and said, "Wait for me here, Chief."

The command and control space buzzed with activity and intensity. Close to fifty men and women worked on large maps, phones, or behind laptops spread across a dozen tables. Others walked about carrying documents or computer equipment. Everyone moved about with the mission-focus concentration required to manage a war in progress.

Stark found Colonel Duggan on a radio in the rear of the room, getting an update from one of his units operating at the foot of the Sulaimans, some forty miles away. The colonel was coordinating support and then calling his boss back at 29 Palms to keep him informed—something called "feed the lion," information being the food that the lion devours.

The 7th Marine commander was simply doing what he was trained to do, but he did it very well. Unlike the opulence that was NATO headquarters, everything here was Spartan and shipshape, which didn't surprise Stark. After all, 29 Palms was home to one of the largest military training areas in the United States. The base's elite Mountain Warfare Training Center for Afghanistan included a two-acre fabricated Middle Eastern village nicknamed Combat Town, complete with a mosque and native role-players.

Once the action abated, Stark approached Duggan, a craggy man and career officer who'd seen as much action as Stark. Completely bald, with sagging cheeks that reminded him of Marlon Brandon in the *Godfather* movie, and a pair of reading glasses hanging from the tip of his Roman nose, he looked up from a paper he was reading.

"Paul, good to see you again and hear that the Seventh is still doing well."

Duggan removed the glasses and yelled, "Hunter! Thought you would be dead by now, you mercenary son of a bitch!"

"True," retorted Stark. "I'm a whore . . . but I'm a well-paid whore. And speaking of whores, how's the ex-wife?"

"Which one?"

Stark laughed.

"That's why I stick to the Corps, Hunter. It hasn't screwed me over."

"Amen, Colonel."

"So, what brings you around my little piece of heaven?"

"Me and the boys are on a two-week stand-down and I was hoping you had some work. We're already being paid, and I figured no marine could refuse a free lunch . . . so how can we help?" Stark spoke quietly, realizing where he was and how outnumbered he was, yet he could not pass up the opportunity to give the marine colonel a little shit . . . even in his own headquarters.

"You checked with Lévesque?" asked Duggan.

Stark frowned. "No good. He's got that massive head of his jammed so hard up his ass he can't see daylight. Can't figure how you can work with the man."

"Easy," Duggan said, cracking his version of a smile, just a slight nudge at the edge of his sagging cheeks. "Treat him like a mushroom."

Stark narrowed his eyes as he said, "Feed him shit and keep him in the dark?"

The grin broadened as Duggan made a sound like that of a train leaving the station. He was laughing. "Gotta say, your sense and your timing are perfect, even considering you're an aging, broken snake eater."

"Takes one to know one," said Stark.

Duggan sighed. "Ain't that an ugly truth? Anyway, we're prepping a unit to hit a compound this afternoon, near where we first met. You and your guys would be a very welcome combat multiplier." Leaning closer to Stark and dropping his voice a few decibels, he added, "Plus, the platoon leader, Lieutenant Wiley, is green."

"Say no more, Colonel. We can provide overwatch and some guidance where needed."

"Out-fucking-standing, Hunter."

"So, where can we link up with this unit?"

7

Rules of Three

**COMPOUND 49. KANDAHAR PROVINCE.
SOUTHERN AFGHANISTAN.**

Several hours later, Stark sat by the side gunner of a Black Hawk helicopter, approaching a drop zone a mile south of Compound 49, another suspected IED factory. But unlike the last one, there were dwellings of various shapes and sizes forming a sort of sparse village surrounding the target, which was set up against a 1,200-foot hill that connected gradually to an 8,000-foot mountain.

Larson had already confirmed the topography, enemy intelligence, weather, and a host of other critical data with Lieutenant Peter

Wiley and his platoon sergeant, John Baxter. Both Wiley and Baxter had already been briefed by their company commander and should know well what they were getting into.

Hopefully, thought Stark, remembering what Duggan had said about Wiley being new. He scanned the village in front of the target with a pair of field binoculars as the Black Hawk circled the area.

People farmed and tended herds of goats. A dozen boys kicked a frayed soccer ball around a rusted goalpost near a large building that looked like a schoolhouse. A group of women wearing partugs, their heads wrapped in black burkas, washed clothes by a well just left of the school, on the outskirts of town. It all looked like your typical Afghan village scene postcard, except for the one-story structure surrounded by an eight-foot wall that U.S. military intelligence believed housed a Taliban bomb-making operation.

The issue that had not been worked out yet was how the platoon would approach the compound. There was also a serious question of how many Tallies were really in the compound, as the count varied by as much as ten insurgents in a twelve-hour period, assessed by a mix of satellite, drone, and human surveillance.

"Sir, did I already tell you I don't like this shit one bit?"

Stark turned to Larson as the chopper entered a hover prior to landing. Like the big chief, Stark's experienced internal danger sensors were all flashing red. He knew that only two things could explain the large discrepancy on the Tango count: either the intel was completely wrong or the Taliban had tunnels, and either answer made mission planning impossible. Without a clear picture of the enemy, any attack, already inherently dangerous, became exponentially more so.

The marines were huddled behind a rocky formation east of the target, but when he jumped off the helo, followed by Larson and the rest of the guys, Stark counted only about a third of the soldiers in the rifle platoon that Duggan had deployed. In the marines, a rifle platoon consisted of forty-three men divided into three rifle squads, each consisting of three fire teams, the latter being the basic element of a ground combat element made of four marines. Following the "rules of three," a rifle company was formed by three rifle platoons, and an infantry battalion formed by three rifle companies.

The chain progressed up to the infantry regiment commanded by a colonel and consisting of three rifle battalions, as was the case with Colonel Duggan commanding the 7th Marine Regiment.

"Where's the rest of your platoon?" Stark asked loudly over the noise of the helicopter, kneeling by a young marine crouching behind a boulder. "I need to speak to Lieutenant Wiley!"

"The LT and Sergeant Baxter moved out with two squads, sir!" the marine replied, as the departing Black Hawk's downwash kicked up sand and dust all around them. "Headed that way fifteen minutes ago!" He pointed in the direction of the kids playing soccer near the front of the village. The compound was behind several structures and farm fields. "I'm with the third rifle squad! We're standing by for orders!"

"What's Wiley doing? My team's supposed to run recon first! He has no idea how many hags are in that compound!" Stark shouted back, as the helicopter rushed off in the direction from which it had come.

The marine shrugged and pointed at his rifle squad leader a dozen feet down from him, in a crouch next to the radiotelephone operator.

"Talk about FUBAR," said Ryan.

"Is this for real, boss?" asked Larson.

"Tell me again how much are we getting paid for this one?" asked Martin, who had a camouflage bandanna covering his short blond hair and a lollipop sticking out from under his thick mustache. Hagen, the quiet one of the group, stood next to his SEAL brother and simply lit up a Sobranie Classic. He took a long drag and exhaled through his nostrils while slowly shaking his head.

Stark glared at his guys before going over to the pair of marines. The squad leader, which usually would be a sergeant, only had two stripes on his shoulder pads, meaning he was a corporal, probably on his second tour. The radio guy next to him was a private who looked fresh out of 29 Palms and scared out of his mind. By now the Black Hawk was a good half click away, so no need for shouting, but Stark did it for effect as time was of the essence. He had to get those rifle squads turned around. "Soldiers! Get me your lieutenant on the horn right now!"

The marines almost jumped when they saw Stark, with all his

gear, standing over them, flanked by his ominous-looking team. Their eyes drifted to Larson and his Browning.

"Yes, sir!" the squad leader said, reaching for the radio strapped behind his RTO, but Stark beat him to it.

"Lieutenant," he said into the unit. "Hunter Stark. Why did you deploy your men before I got here?"

Silence, followed by, "*I don't understand the question, sir. The gunny and I are keeping it simple. We're blowing the front gate, go to the corners, and overwhelm them . . . just like we've been trained as marines to do.*"

"Okay," Stark said. "Good for you. But do you see this as a hard fight? And what is your it-all-goes-to-shit plan? And are you confident in the intelligence you have been supplied, especially the Tango count?"

"*Hold on, sir,*" Wiley said. "*The gunny wants a word in.*"

Stark glanced at Larson, who just raised his brows.

"*Sir, this is Gunnery Sergeant Baxter, and it's been my experience that no plan survives the first round being fired. We may never have enough intelligence, and I don't recall being given a choice here. We have a mission to hit this place, and hit it we will, as best we can.*"

"Okay, Gunny," Stark replied. "We're here to support you in any way we can."

"*Good,*" Baxter replied. "*Then remain with the third squad and wait for our signal.*"

Staring at Larson, Stark handed the receiver to the RTO.

"So that's it?" asked Martin, removing the lollipop and waving it at Stark. "We just sit on our thumbs and wait for 'their signal'—whatever the hell that is?"

"Hey, they're getting what they're paying for," said Ryan.

Before Stark could reply, a blast echoed from the rear of the village, near the target, followed by screams of men, women, and kids, and then a second blast. Gunfire, a mix of AK-47s and American M4 carbines, the standard U.S. Marines rifle, echoed across the village.

Shrieks of pain and of anger reached them as the villagers scattered, some aboard weathered cars and pickup trucks, others on foot. Kids scrambled toward the schoolhouse, followed by a pair of dogs and several cackling roosters.

"Oh, God!" the radio guy screamed. "We're all going to die!"

For a moment, everyone just stared at the columns of smoke rising above the village.

"Ah, sir?" Martin said, leaning close to Stark, as if about to convey something important, using the lollipop to point at the commotion. "I *think* that's the signal."

"Dammit!" Stark shouted. "Chief, Danny, Mickey, on me! Ryan, cover us!"

Turning to the squad leader, Stark added, "Let them know we're coming in, then radio for air support, and get that helo and four more like it back here! Got that?"

"Yes, sir. Got it. Anything else?"

Stark nodded. The corporal definitely had some battle experience behind him, unlike the private, who looked as if he just pissed his pants. It went to show that no matter how many simulated scenarios they went through during basic back at 29 Palms, nothing came close to the real thing.

"Yes," Stark replied. "Tell your squad to keep their cool and conserve ammo. And watch what they shoot at! Don't feel like catching one in the ass today, okay?"

"Okay, sir."

"Good. We're going in there to help your guys!"

Ryan took off and began to climb up the closest and tallest rock mound while Stark took off in the direction of the village, where chaos suddenly reigned as the villagers, true veterans at this, had already almost dispersed, vanishing inside buildings or running across the field in different directions, along with their bleating goats. And in the middle of this chaos, he spotted three groups of marines, each carrying a wounded soldier. Several marines fired back at an enemy Stark could not yet see.

"Ryan! Get eyes on that!" Stark screamed, while charging with the contractor team, covering the few hundred yards separating them from the retreating soldiers in under a minute.

Stark let those carrying the injured get past, noticing that one of them was a second lieutenant and another a staff sergeant, both missing their legs below their knees, medics tending to them on the run. The third wounded soldier had been shot in the gut.

"Who's in charge, soldiers?" he shouted at the eight marines covering the retreat.

"Well, that's the LT and the gunny over there!" shouted one of the soldiers, a corporal with the name Gomez stenciled on his uniform, as he pointed at the men screaming and bleeding. "So I guess that's you, sir!"

"All right, Gomez, what are we looking at?" Stark asked as Larson, Martin, and Hagen took up defensive fighting positions, DFPs. The chief set up his Browning behind what was left of an old Suzuki SUV chassis while Hagen and Martin crouched behind the stonework surrounding the village's hastily abandoned water well.

"A trap, sir, and we walked right into it. The LT and the gunny stepped on IEDs. Then all hell broke loose. We were taking fire from rooftops, windows, and street corners. There's a large posse right behind us. About fifty Tangos, and they're—"

"You said *fifty*, as in *five zero*?"

"Yes, sir, and they're fucking nuts, sir! We keep blasting them but they just keep coming! They're right around the corner!" He pointed at the street-like space between two compounds five hundred feet behind them, left of the abandoned soccer goalpost.

"Anyone missing?"

"We're marines, sir! No man left behind!"

"All right. All right. Pull back to the rocks! We'll be right there! Make sure the helos and the air support's on the way and that everyone is dug in a DFP!"

"Yes, sir!" and the marines were gone.

Stark huddled next to Larson and got his MP5A1 ready. "Talk to me, Ryan!"

But instead of a reply, the distinct sound of a .50-caliber round parted the air toward the incoming wave of insurgents looming in the street. Corporal Gomez had been correct. It was quite the posse, the muzzles of their AK-47s flashing, their shouts mixing with the rattle of their Russian guns.

Larson opened up the Browning on them while Hagen worked an M32 six-shooter grenade launcher and Martin used his MP5A1 with devastating accuracy.

Stark watched the half dozen XM1060 thermobaric shells thumping out of the launcher, arcing over the space between his team and the posse of screaming men. They went off just over the initial wave of rebels, in overlapping blasts of pressure waves that ruptured their lungs and eardrums while the high-temperature fuel deflagration burned through their clothes and fried the skin off their bodies.

It was a cruel weapon, and in an instant a dozen rebels collapsed, screaming in agony. But its worse effect hit the second wave of men as they inhaled the toxic propylene oxide fumes of the shells' overlapping fifty-foot kill radius, burning the lining of their lungs.

Still the rebels kept coming, leaping over their fallen comrades while shouting and firing.

Stark quickly did the math and realized that there were just too many hags too damn close for the four of them to keep from being overrun, even with Ryan exploding heads with his rifle and Hagen's thermobaric shells. It didn't matter how much his men fired at them, the zealous bastards would not seek shelter, would not stop running, screaming, and firing like a crazed and unstoppable mob.

But just as he was about to give the order to pull back to the rocks, the distinct shape of an A-10 Warthog zoomed overhead, its twin turbofans scorching the air, probably no higher than twenty feet.

A blink of an eye later, as he smelled the burned fuel from its engines, its 30mm Avenger Gatling-type cannon burst into life with the sound of a thousand thunderclaps, vomiting rounds at the incoming threat at the rate of 2,100 per minute.

Even someone as battle hardened as Stark was momentarily taken aback as the enemy, less than two hundred yards away, vanished in a cloud of sand and blood kicked up by the Warthog's massive display of force. He could feel the ground tremble like an earthquake as the rounds transferred their energy, pounding the ground, drowning out even Larson's Browning.

And for an instant, as the A-10 dropped over the enemy, decimating it, and Stark prepared to call the marines back to go secure the damn compound, he couldn't help but wonder how the hell that pilot got there so damn fast, all the way from KAF.

8

Red One One

Many called it a flying tank, but U.S. Air Force Captain Laura Vaccaro called it a bad motherfucker. The A-10, hated by many in the air force as it was designated solely to support ground forces and not for air-to-air combat or bombing runs, earned it the nickname "Warthog."

To Vaccaro, however, the armor-plated ugly duckling was her baby, and she brought it in low and fast, preparing to open the massive Avenger on the designated target along the sixty miles of mountains and ridges between the towns of Lashkar Gah and Kandahar City.

"Red One One, Zulu Six Eight. Position marked. Confirm," said the marine on the ground, professionally and accurately providing his men's location and the area where the Taliban was holed up.

"Roger Zulu Six Eight. Confirm. Purple smoke. Rolling in hot," she responded, surrounded by metal, the smells of oil and perspiration always prevalent in the cockpit despite the air-filtering system. All this Vaccaro was used to. What she would never get used to and never forget was the excitement, the pride, and the fear of combat—something that few would ever experience.

The platoon was in trouble and there was no time to make confirming passes or send a marking round at the target to adjust for a second pass. The late afternoon sun was getting too close to the top of those mountains, meaning she had little time to get those marines cleared up for exfiltration before nightfall.

She had to get the first run right and follow up with more until she ran out of gas or bullets or the marines were safe.

The last point being the most important to the air force captain.

No pilot in any war ever got used to the feeling of flying in combat, coming to the aid of guys on the ground, putting rounds on bad guys, dropping bombs, pulling out, and circling back, doing it again.

Nothing like it, Vaccaro thought.

However, it did become, if you were not careful, a little too routine. Perhaps it was the way our psyches work to protect us. Perhaps all who experienced combat were made a little nuts. The issue was that there was no such thing as "routine combat." Nothing in combat *was* routine—nothing about someone trying to kill you should lull anyone into complacency. But it happened to many. The trick was to survive your own shortcomings, as it was certain that the assholes trying to kill you would take advantage of any and all mistakes that you made, physical, emotional, or mental.

"*Red One One, Red One One, Bravo Niner Six. SitRep.*"

Vaccaro frowned at the controller at KAF, Kandahar Airfield, call sign B96, requesting a situation report while she was clearly in the middle of a damned strafing run.

Where do they get these guys?

The A-10's fuselage, built around the Avenger, trembled the moment she squeezed the trigger, thundering across the mountain while vomiting 1.5-pound rounds at the rate of sixty-five per second. The depleted uranium armor-piercing shells tore through the enemy lines, vaporizing dozens of insurgents before continuing on to the compound, slicing it open.

The cannon carved a twenty-foot-wide track down to the basement, liquidating men and equipment. Doing so, however, drew the attention of Taliban machine gun emplacements east of the compound, their tracers arcing up toward her.

"*Red One One, Red One One, Bravo Niner Six. SitRep.*"

For the love of . . .

She pulled the control column, her jaw tight as g-forces piled up on her while shooting up to five hundred feet—just missing the compound as it went up in bursts of secondary explosions.

IEDs, she thought, ignoring the cross fire striking the 1,200 pounds of titanium aircraft armor layering the cockpit and critical flight systems.

She threw the close air support jet into a wickedly tight 180-degree turn, a few rounds pinging off the armored canopy and windshield just as the sun touched the distant western rim rock. Turning her head to inspect the damage, she completed the turn and zipped back for a second pass in the opposite direction.

This high up, the Sulaiman Mountains were thick with towering pines—unlike the stereotypical landscapes of Afghanistan in the movies. For a moment, as the sun's waning burnt-orange light touched the tip of the ocean of pines, it reminded her of Colorado Springs, where she had trained at the Air Force Academy.

It all sure looks the same, she thought, staring at the treetops swirling in the wind at dusk just before reaching the kill zone again. All except for the ground fire.

This time she directed the Warthog at the machine guns, diving cockpit-first into the swarm of enemy tracers, flying through the barrage hammering her leading edges, tearing into the armored skin before unleashing the Avenger.

Again, the mighty energy of a few hundred 30mm shells ripped through the Taliban enclave, cutting them to pieces. She cut hard left, performing another 180 turn and making a third pass using her complement of Hydra rockets.

The swarm of 70mm rockets blasted from beneath the wings and careered toward the surviving Taliban. Some raced for the cover of trees while others aimed their weapons at her in sheer defiance.

Good luck with that.

She pulled up just as the Hydras reached their target, detonating in dozens of bursts of orange flames. But in the same instant, two rocket-propelled grenades managed to shoot up from the flames.

She cut hard left before pushing the A-10 into a steep climb, watching one RPG rush past her cockpit, losing it in the turn-climb evasive maneuver. But the second shell exploded near the tail, the shrapnel blasting through a section of the elevators and rudder.

The A-10 trembled, the jolt severe as alarms went off in her helmet, and the heads-up display blinked crazily.

"Damn!" Vaccaro screamed, trying to control it, both hands now on the stick as she strained to level the wings. But the Warthog didn't respond; the flight controls froze on her last set of commands: a tight right turn and steep climb. Basically, she had locked the Warthog in an upward spiral.

What the hell? she thought, staring at the first stars appearing in the darkening heavens while whirling as if in the middle of a tornado. The control column suddenly trembled so wildly that it got away from her. A high-pitched metal grinding noise behind her sounded almost as if the plane was screaming in protest of whatever damage it had just sustained.

What is happening?

Airspeed began to bleed off as the heavy jet shot past five thousand feet, and the dual turbofans failed to sustain the near-vertical rate of climb. Unlike fighter jets such as the Falcon and the Hornet, which could climb vertically to twenty thousand feet, the Warthog decelerated quickly. Unless she acted quickly, that would lead to a stall.

Work the problem, she thought, managing to grab the control column as it quavered from side to side, before forcing it forward and to the left, trying to kill the climb and level the wings.

But the jet did not respond.

And that's when she realized that the hydraulics connecting her computerized cockpit systems—the stick and the rudder—to the Warthog's control surfaces were not responding. She found that amazing, indeed, as the A-10 had double-redundant hydraulic flight systems to prevent precisely this type of situation.

Instinctively, she switched to manual mode, bypassing the hydraulics and computers, engaging the backup mechanical flight system. It consisted of old-fashioned stainless steel wires and pushrods connecting her control systems to the elevators, ailerons, and rudder of the A-10 through a system of pulleys.

Push, Laura.

Loosening the harness securing her to the ejection seat, Vaccaro wedged the control column between her thighs and sternum, using her entire body to press it forward and to the left. Slowly, the array of wires transferred her commands to the control surfaces and the A-10 pitched down while killing the turn.

Taking a deep breath as the horizon reappeared in her windscreen and the spinning stopped, Vaccaro also noticed she was losing pressure on her left turbofan, which began to spew smoke. But even operating on one and a half engines and on manual bypass, she still had full control of her bird, and she rolled left to go back and finish her job.

She grinned under her mask, realizing what a sight it would make on the ground, with smoke pouring out of her engine, the tail damaged, and deadly rounds spewing out of the Avenger.

The dusky sky broken only by her ominous presence, she made the pass quickly, squeezing the trigger, tearing up anything that may have survived the initial passes, before pulling up, tapping the mike, and saying, "Zulu Six Eight, Red One One. That should do it, over."

"Red One One, Zulu Six Eight, you saved our dirty marine asses. Over."

"Zulu Six Eight, you're buying the drinks. Watch your sixes while you RTB." Return to base.

"You've got it, Red One One."

Turning back to Kandahar, Vaccaro decided it was time to talk to the controller. Tapping her mike she said, "Bravo Niner Six, Bravo Niner Six, Red One One lost hydraulics and also losing pressure on left engine but still operational. Flying manually. Requesting priority handling."

"Copy that, Red One One. Loss hydraulics and left engine problems. Flying manually," the KAF controller replied, before adding, *"Need a helo?"*

Keeping both hands gripping the quivering control stick while continuing to exert her muscles to keep the wings leveled and the nose straight ahead, she frowned at the KAF controller. Prior manual landing attempts at KAF on the Warthog had resulted in disaster. The plane was difficult enough to keep airborne without hydraulics, much less trying to land. So the air force had long briefed A-10 pilots in such circumstances to reach friendly lines before bailing out.

And that was all fine, except she flew in Afghanistan at dusk, meaning unless she could actually pull the ejection handles right over the damn airfield, she risked starring in her very own YouTube video after a short canopy ride. No way she could last long down there, especially after dark, which was minutes away.

Although she didn't think that often anymore about being a female military pilot, it was at moments like this that the thought of what the Tallies would do to her if she were captured momentarily entered her mind.

Quickly pushing that image aside, she said, "That's a negative, Bravo Niner Six. Red One One requesting priority handling and permission to land. Clear out the airspace."

"Red One One, standby."

She shook her head and decided to just follow the GPS to give herself vectors to final, but the Warthog fought her all the way back, especially the crazy control stick. It continued shaking the moment she eased pressure, forcing her to keep her thighs taut against it as she struggled to maintain level flight or make shallow turns while holding 250 knots. Plus there was that steady metallic screech from the tail that sounded like nails on a chalkboard on steroids.

In situations like this her training commanded her to focus on what was actually working, like the electrical system lighting up her cockpit, radios, and navigation equipment, and also her right turbofan, which she used to help her keep her wings leveled and her nose on the horizon.

If the A-10 began to dip, she added rear pressure on the control column while also advancing the throttles, using forward thrust to bring the nose back up. If the Warthog started to bank in the wrong direction, she added a dash of power to the opposite engine, using the asymmetrical thrust to assist her stick and rudder work, canceling out the unwanted turn.

Vaccaro did this on automatic, feeling the plane, the wire tugs, the subtle changes in pitch and roll, hands and feet working in conjunction with power settings, mile after mile, minute after minute, breath after breath.

You can do this.

Fueled by trained focus and an iron will, determined to bring her wounded bird back in one piece, she concentrated on holding a thousand feet while slowly adjusting her heading. Her eyes never stopped scanning, reviewing her instruments, the darkening horizon, her flanks, and making minute adjustments; always correcting, always tweaking, countering the aerodynamic forces playing against her. She slowly eased the throttles to bleed off airspeed while making a final shallow turn.

"Red One One, Bravo Niner Six. SitRep."

"Bravo Niner Six, Red One One. Six-mile final. Two Three."

"Roger, Red One One. Clear to land, Runway Two Three. Winds light and variable but there's a storm coming in from the west. Should be no factor. Altimeter two niner niner three."

"Red One One cleared to land. Two Three," she read back, as the lights of Kandahar grew visible through the haze and the last of the day's heat rising from this scorched land. To the west, as the controller had indicated, she could see lightning flashes from incoming storm clouds, but it was indeed too far away to matter. One way or the other, this Warthog would be on the ground in a couple of minutes.

For a moment she wondered if she should listen to the controller, eject, and take her chances with a rescue helicopter. But an instant later some asshole in a village rushing beneath her took a dozen pot shots at her, the muzzle flashes of what was likely an old Russian Kalashnikov reinforcing her decision to stay the course. A single round pinging harmlessly off what remained of her armored skin served as a constant reminder that, while in-country, she was always one decision away from getting brutalized by these bastards.

No way in hell, she told herself again, deciding that she had not graduated from the Air Force Academy at the top of her class and then gone on to fly A-10s in countless sorties through five rotations—three in Iraq and two at KAF—just to end up in the hands of these medievalists.

I'll end it before that happens.

The thought made her think of her father, U.S. Navy Lieutenant James Vaccaro, an A-6 Intruder pilot in Vietnam who got shot down over some forgotten jungle and chose to fight to the end, taking as many Vietcong with him as he could rather than letting the bastards capture him alive.

She exhaled heavily in her oxygen mask, decelerating as much as practicable as runway lights became visible against the many square miles of this well-illuminated metropolis in the middle of Taliban country.

Her textbook final approach speed stated 150 knots, but today she held her airspeed at 175 knots, concerned about getting too close to the stall speed of 120 knots, given the uncertainty of the damage she had taken. Those published airspeeds assumed a healthy fuselage, and at the moment her squealing Warthog was anything but.

However, if there was one thing this tank of a plane could take it was punishment. Its designers built it to fly with just one engine, half its tail section, and while missing up to 30 percent of its wing surface.

At least on paper.

Vaccaro doubted the good people at Fairchild actually flew such a variant.

So she decided to play it on the conservative side, and given the damage the wings had endured, she wasn't sure if she should risk lowering the flaps—or even if they would work. At the moment, in her current configuration, as much as the stick shook and the overall frame wailed like a stuck pig, she could still control her descent while keeping the nose aligned with the runway.

Using throttles to manage her sink rate, she held her course and speed while slowly losing altitude, lowering the landing gear the moment she flew over the perimeter wall and the adjoining water treatment plant.

That's how KAF greeted you: with a large pond filled with shit.

But to Vaccaro it was a welcome sight as she crossed it and approached the long paved strip, exhaling in relief when the gear-down indicator confirmed that all three were down and locked.

Deciding she could use every last inch of the 10,500 feet of runway, Vaccaro restricted her commands to minor adjustments, focusing not on the inevitable landing but simply on flying the plane while maintaining a slow but steady rate of decent.

The runway lights rose up to meet her as she floated in the ground effect for several seconds—the laws of aerodynamics resulted in increased lift the instant she got within twenty feet of the asphalt. And again she only made minor corrections.

The wheels touched down with just a slight skid one-third down the runway, and she cut back throttles to idle, gently applying the brakes before taxiing onto the flight line under massive floodlights.

She followed the directions of the ground crew marshal wearing a reflecting vest, acoustic earmuffs, and handheld illuminated bea-cons, guiding her to her tie-down spot.

The canopy swung out of the way and she shut the jet down, re-leased the seat belt harness, and removed her helmet, running a hand through her auburn hair. It was several inches longer than regula-tion, but as long as she continued shooting bad guys, her commander at KAF continued overlooking the peccadillo.

As she stood in the cockpit, her gaze landed on the ground crew, which was staring as if she had landed some alien spacecraft.

That bad?

Walking down the side ladder, she reviewed in silence the mess the Taliban had made of her bird. With missing sections of armored skin on the tail and fuselage, it looked as if a pit bull had bitten off quite a few chunks of her Hawg, exposing its complex innards. Plus, what remained of the empennage was charred and scarred. There were countless pockmarks under the wings from small arms fire, like hail dents, and a couple dozen quarter-size holes where larger rounds had punched through. The leading edges as well as the underside were also heavily scored from ground fire.

Damn, she thought, realizing that this had to be just about the most mangled Warthog ever returned to the flight line.

As a small crowd of pilots and more ground crew gathered about her, she shrugged, shouted, "You should see the other guy!" and headed to her squadron to get debriefed before getting some chow.

9

Battlefield Promotion

It was at times like tonight that Bill Gorman wondered what the hell he was doing in this fucking country.

For a moment he even wondered if he should have followed in his late father's footsteps and stayed in the New York City Fire Department, like Victoria, his younger sister, an FDNY paramedic.

Gorman had gone through the training and had just received his probationary status with FDNY Company 10, also known as the Ten House, when September 11 changed his world. Gorman's young wife, Jeannie, worked on the 104th floor of the North Tower and could not be evacuated. In addition, several members of his team clearing the towers never made it out.

As he watched his world collapse, Gorman swore to dedicate his life to fighting terror and headed to Fort Benning, Georgia, the army's Officer Candidate School. He served one tour in Afghanistan and two in Iraq—the last one connected to the Defense Intelligence Agency, the military counterpart of the CIA. And in a bizarre turn of events, the CIA recruited him after a successful DIA–CIA joint mission in Baghdad. Gorman then spent a year at the Farm, in Williamsburg, Virginia, and was assigned to work the New Delhi CIA station before Islamabad.

Gorman checked his watch and inhaled deeply, wincing in painful memory while staring at the stainless steel Rolex, a surprise present from Jeannie at his FDNY graduation. To this day he wore it as his version of a wedding band, a reminder of the wonderful woman he had lost to the same bastards he'd vowed to fight to his dying breath.

And speaking of bastards, he had tailed the men who'd left that compound for almost twenty-four hours, using whatever assets he had at his disposal, including one of their getaway RAV4s hidden on the side of Darband Road. He had also used his encrypted satellite phone to signal the Islamabad CIA station of the events that had taken place the night before.

Gorman had expected to be summoned into the vault—the CIA secure basement room at the embassy—for a heart-to-heart debrief with Langley that probably would have lasted far longer than normal, given the abnormal circumstances. But the reply he had received an hour later had actually surprised him. Instead of the typical anal probe, especially after a botched op, Langley had just appointed him interim station chief, since he was now the senior-most officer in Islamabad.

He shook his head at the bizarre turn of events while munching on a peanut-flavored PowerBar in the front seat of the RAV4 and peering through the darkness with a pair of Zeiss compact night vision binoculars. In addition to the bars and the bottles of water, Gorman had also changed into his stash of civilian clothes—a pair of black jeans, a black T-shirt, and sneakers. But for effect, he had kept the tunic and the pakol.

He had selected an ill-lit parking spot near the intersection of Shaheed–Millat Road and Street 58, located across the street and halfway down the block from his mark—and ironically just over a mile from the U.S. Embassy. The pair of white vans had gone through the automatic gate of a chain-link fence enclosing a small compound and had driven straight to a two-story, stand-alone warehouse in the middle. The place appeared newly built, at least relative to the surrounding one-story structures, a mix of private homes, stores, and other businesses. The chain-link was topped with barbed wire angled outward, meant to keep intruders out, as opposed to prisons, which angled the wire inward to keep inmates from escaping. Combine that with the electronic keypad by the gate, the security cameras atop the building, and the lack of lights inside and out, and Gorman felt certain the place was some sort of safe house or staging area.

At least a dozen men had gone inside. Unfortunately, the vans had blocked the warehouse's front door, preventing Gorman from seeing whether bin Laden was among them.

That was three hours ago, and in that time Gorman had issued his first set of instructions to his new team, which consisted primarily of a half dozen analysts. Although only thirty-three years old, he was the only officer with any field experience left until Langley could replenish the men lost in that poppy field—meaning he was alone in this surveillance job.

Well, not completely *alone.*

He lifted his gaze at the star-filled sky over Islamabad. Unlike his predecessor, Gorman had no qualms about contacting some of his former Army Intelligence buddies with the DIA in Bagram to request Predator coverage for the next forty-eight hours. And in the spirit of asking for forgiveness rather than permission, he had not consulted Langley on the decision to bring in its competitor. It was no secret that both intelligence agencies constantly tried to outdo each other to maximize their respective congressional funding.

And his military pals had come through. His analysts had signaled thirty minutes ago that they now had eyes over him in the control room adjacent to the vault, fed by a lone UAV from Bagram circling the area at ten thousand feet.

And now we wait, he thought, focusing the binoculars on the vans, which he now recognized as Ford E-350s, and inspecting the metal brackets bolted to the front and rear fenders. That also typically meant composite run-flat tires, transparent armor instead of windshields and side windows, plus ballistic nylon and Kevlar bolstering the chassis and interior surfaces, including the engine compartment. And it all gave even more credibility to Shaw's claim of having spotted bin Laden. Bulletproofing a pair of Ford vans was expensive business, even for al Qaeda. Heck, not even the CIA had such vehicles at the Islamabad station. The only vehicle with any level of protection belonged to the ambassador, who was currently on holiday somewhere in southern Italy.

And that all further meant that Gorman's RAV4 with its sheet metal paneling, tempered glass, and stock Yoko tires would never stand up to those tanks in a gunfight or a street chase. And to put a cherry on his shit cake, the men exiting those E-350s had carried enough weapons—a mix of AK-47s and Russian RPK light machine guns—to start a small revolution.

Unfortunately for him, all Finkle had approved to bring on this mission were sidearms—his idea of keeping it low-key. Most operations officers in the Clandestine Service preferred guile to weapons, believing that theirs was the business of doing without being seen, changing outcomes without being noticed. Weapons, they believed, were for the military and the police. Intelligent professionals were not afraid of using them; it was just not their first choice.

Gorman had objected, of course, claiming that pistols against automatic rifles was only marginally better than bringing a damn knife to a gunfight. But he was just told to get with the program.

So the CIA officer had done the only thing he could: remain within the parameters specified by his boss—sidearms only—while locating the largest pistol he could find in the embassy armory.

He was basically alone, with the closest experienced backup at the Kabul station or at Bagram, while tailing what could very well be Osama bin Laden aboard armored vans inside a compound defended by guys armed to the teeth.

For a moment he wondered if Bagram had deployed the Predators with missiles. But even so, no way he could stretch his DIA friendship to release a Hellfire into a populated area in the middle of Pakistan's capital—and a mile from the embassy. Hypocrites or not, the Pakistanis were still America's allies, at least on paper—even if Washington strongly suspected that they were harboring the terrorist mastermind.

So to make himself feel better, Gorman sought solace in the cold and black Desert Eagle pistol, which he wore on his left side with the handle facing forward for an easy cross draw with his right hand.

The Israeli-made semiautomatic came in three different calibers, .357 Magnum, .44 Magnum, and .50 Action Express. Gorman had opted for the latter, the beasty .50-caliber version, meaning he at least had the ability to discharge in rapid succession seven massive Remington jacketed hollow-point slugs. Each round had enough energy to go through an engine block and *then* do real damage to any jihadist foolish enough to believe that Allah would protect him from 325 grains of American steel traveling at 1,500 feet per second. And Gorman had also raided the armory to confiscate every spare .50-caliber AE magazine in sight—three of them. Loaded with seven cartridges each and secured upside down and backwards, the backup ammo weighed down the right side of the thick military belt he wore under his loose T-shirt, ready for a quick exchange.

As he handled the heavy pistol, thumbing the safety off and automatically checking that he had a chambered round, his phone rang in his left ear, where an earpiece coiled down to the vibrating unit on his lap.

Gorman stared down at the distraction while holstering the Desert Eagle. He had given his analysts strict instructions to hold the chatter unless there was blood or broken bones.

The caller ID was blocked, which meant that the caller was also on an encrypted satellite phone.

Sighing, he picked it up.

"Yeah?"

"Hey, buddy. How're you holding up?"

He dropped his eyebrows at the familiar voice. "Glenn? What the hell are you doing?"

Glenn Harwich was an old hand at the Agency, having cut his teeth working with the mujahideen in the late 1980s. Almost fifteen years Gorman's senior, Harwich had mentored Gorman after he'd joined the Agency following his tours in-country. Rumor at Langley was that Harwich had actually trained bin Laden in the use of the Stinger missile system. But very few people—Gorman included—knew that it was actually quite a bit more than just a rumor.

"Living the dream, Bill. You?"

"Where are you calling from? It's almost five in the morning," Gorman asked, hearing a lot of background noise.

"Army transport. Middle of nowhere, headed to the middle of nowhere."

"I thought you were living it up in Paris."

"Yeah. I was, and now I'm not."

"*Why* are you calling?"

"Had to check in on my favorite understudy after he made station chief."

"Interim. And how did you know?"

"I know everything. Definitely on the fast track, you young piece of shit."

Gorman frowned at the Fords, at the warehouse, at the danger within while he was armed with just a pistol and no backup—and at the fact that he'd lost his entire team, and almost his own life.

"Don't feel that lucky at the moment. I had to blow up Finkle and his operators last night after the Tallies shot off their heads in a botched op. A hell of a way to get promoted."

"*What?* Bill . . . I had no idea that—"

"And now there's a chance I may be tracking your old mujahideen pen pal in lovely downtown Islamabad."

"Who?"

"Elvis . . . He might just be in the building across the street."

"Stop screwing around."

"I thought you knew everything."

"Okay. Back up. Tell me *everything*."

Gorman did, taking a couple of minutes to bring his former superior up to date.

"Okay, listen. First, don't do anything stupid."

"Like tailing twelve armed Tallies in their own backyard with just a handgun and no backup?"

"Keep your distance and just watch and report, okay?"

"I can handle that."

"Remember that when you're in-country you're only one decision away from starring in your own YouTube video."

"Thanks for that."

"Anytime. I'll make some calls. See if we can get you help *pronto*."

"Glenn . . . where the hell are you? Really."

"Headed to KAF. Long story. Just lost the entire CIA team there. KIA. Blown up by our own NATO, and I'm their sole replacement."

Gorman sighed again. "Yeah, a lot of that going arou—"

"Gotta make some calls, Bill," Harwich said. "Just watch and report. Got it?"

"Yeah, I—"

Harwich terminated the call and Gorman frowned, staring at the phone before resuming his watch, sensing it was going to be a long night and an even longer day ahead.

10

Hunch

Glenn Harwich had pretty much kept to himself the entire flight, his only distraction being that short conversation with Gorman a few hours after leaving Frankfurt. But he could sense the eyes of the young GIs packing the sides of the army transport jet glancing in his direction, likely wondering what that bald-headed civilian was doing among troops that for the most part appeared to be on their first rotation.

Harwich could almost always pick out the rookies from the veterans. The veterans, like himself, wished to be left alone, unwilling to engage in a conversation that could lead to a friendship. Those veterans had likely already lost more than their fair share of friends, and the pain stemming from those losses—combined with their survivor's guilt—had a way of stripping any desire to make new friends.

He frowned, finding it hard to believe he was actually back in this country—and at his own request.

But what choice did I have? he thought, accepting the bitter reality that he'd had to step away from his relatively easier assignment as deputy chief of the Paris station to come to this shithole—at least until he sorted this out.

He remembered the intercept from an Agency bot patrolling the ISPs in Islamabad. The image, and the short note—useless to anyone but those who had been in that clearing in the Sulaimans that cold September night in 1988—had been reason enough for him to make a priority call to the deputy director of operations at Langley.

"Are you shitting me, Glenn?" the DDO had blurted. "Is this why you woke me up in the middle of the night?"

"It has to be, sir, and we're partly responsible."

"Okay. Okay. What do you need?"

"A ride to KAF and a good enough reason for being there. This has to be kept need-to-fucking-know until we actually fucking know something."

"Well, we won't need to think too hard to find you a cover story, unfortunately."

"What do you mean?"

"We just lost our team there to a misplaced Hellfire."

"Jesus."

"Not Jesus. NATO. Big screwup, and we need a guy there representing the Agency until we can work out a replacement plan."

And less than twenty-four hours later Harwich found himself boarding a C-17 cargo headed to Kandahar Airfield, staring at the image on his phone that had started it all: an old Soviet ring.

11

DFAC

KANDAHAR AIRFIELD. SOUTHERN AFGHANISTAN.

Tired, thirsty, and damn hungry, Laura Vaccaro finally finished her debriefing and walked up to one of the base's noisy dining facilities—the DFAC—near the end of the ramp. She still wore her flight suit, zipped down to the middle of her chest, exposing a pair of dog tags over a white T-shirt.

The smell of jet fuel mixed with the stench from the water treatment facility, plus whatever they were cooking in the kitchen this evening, hovered in the air like a bad joke. Thunder rumbled in the distance, but not from artillery or bombs. The storm system was almost on top of the base. With luck, it would bring much-needed rain to this desolate and dusty place. Of course, that meant the ground turning to thick red mud, but it was the lesser of the evils.

There were a number of creature comforts at KAF. Good food, unfortunately, wasn't among them. But Vaccaro didn't care. She had grown up poor on the outskirts of Colorado Springs, where she taught skiing for room and board, giving her an appreciation for three square meals a day—even if they were of the deep freezer to deep fryer variety.

Sometimes the brown trays, paper plates, and plastic cups could seem like fine bone china after coming back from a mission. The food was not as important as sitting down with some sense of normalcy, surrounded by those doing and feeling the same way.

The sound of hundreds of conversations mixed with the clanging of plastic trays and cups under an ocean of fluorescent lights, but after the long day she'd had, it was also a welcome sight.

Vaccaro grabbed a tray and got in line, her cheeks still sore from the oxygen mask.

Ignoring the looks from a handful of grunts at a nearby table, she focused on the hot choices this evening, selecting chicken nuggets and fries, balancing it with a cup of fruit and a chocolate milk—plus two bottles of ice-cold water.

She walked past several rows of tables packed with an eclectic mix of military personnel and civilian contractors, noticing the heavyset Colonel Paul Duggan of the marines sharing a table with five harsh-looking soldiers. A pair of small, rectangular reading glasses on black wire frames hung at the tip of Duggan's nose as he glanced at some report while the warriors flanking him pointed out something on the sheet of paper.

There was sameness to the U.S. military: short hair, mostly fit, same uniform look, same language, rank displayed, and similar weapons. Talk was the same, and they all ate the same way—like someone was trying to steal their dinner. But the guys sitting with Colonel Duggan were different. They had nonstandard and mixed uniforms, longer hair, and a *fuck you* attitude. She had seen the type before on other tours. War certainly made for strange but necessary friends and coworkers.

Probably SEALs, she thought, momentarily locking gazes with the bald and rugged one sitting to Duggan's left. She wasn't sure what it was that made her look in his direction only to catch him staring at her.

He stood abruptly to face her as she walked by and said, "Captain Vaccaro?"

"Yeah?" she said, shifting her gaze between this stranger and the men at the table, who continued their conversation with Colonel Duggan.

Leaning forward while dropping his voice a bit, he said, "I'm Hunter Stark. That was great shooting this afternoon. Brave move coming back with your engine hit. You saved a bunch of marines *and* my guys. Thank you."

"And who exactly are you and your guys?" she replied, staring into his blue eyes, the ends of which sagged a bit.

Stark smiled. "Just some guys who owe you their collective ass. Thank you again, Red One One. I hope to someday repay the favor." And with that he turned around and rejoined his table.

As she stepped away, Vaccaro noticed Stark leaning closer to Duggan and whispering something in his ear while pointing at her. The colonel looked at her departing figure over the rim of his reading glasses.

She kept walking, going straight to the rear of the hall and settling at one end of an empty table. She drained the first water bottle in thirty seconds, before sitting back and sipping the second one while contemplating her fried dinner choice.

"Is this seat taken?"

Vaccaro looked up at a smiling Captain John Wright, U.S. Marines, pointing at the spot across from her. He was just a bit taller than her, and muscular, with a narrow, clean-cut face, short blond hair, hazel eyes, and a strong neck and chin—the portrait of a Semper fi recruitment ad.

As Wright sat, the side of his boot reached inconspicuously under the table and brushed against hers.

"Captain," he said, with a slight grin.

"Captain," she replied, returning the grin.

"How was your day at the office?"

"You don't want to know."

Wright frowned at his burger and fries and grabbed one of her nuggets.

She narrowed her stare as he winked, popped it in his mouth, and chewed it slowly before saying, "Heard the one about the crazy air force jock who landed a Hawg at night held together by duct tape, wire, and a prayer?"

"Nope."

He tilted his head, cut his burger in half, and took a hearty bite while she nibbled on a fry.

"You saved lives today," he said.

She shrugged.

"I mean it."

Another shrug.

"We lost three guys, one of them a Peter Wiley, LT. Marines. We would have lost more had you not shown up when you did."

"It's what I do, John."

"Yeah, and you do it better than anyone I know."

She was about to reply when Colonel Duggan walked up to them and put a hand on Wright's shoulder, the reading glasses now hanging from his neck at the ends of a black leather cord.

Wright tried to stand and salute, but Duggan kept the hand in place and said, "At ease, soldier." Then, turning to Vaccaro, he added, "Good shooting today, Captain."

"Thank you, sir."

"Now," Duggan said, shifting his attention back to Wright, "a word in private, Captain?"

12

Simply Irresistible

Wright followed his commanding officer outside the mess hall, out of earshot of everyone. The tip of the storm was almost over them. A light mist shadowed this part of the base, the wind had picked up a bit, and lightning rumbled overhead.

"So, the air force captain, huh?"

Wright momentarily looked away.

It was frowned upon to fraternize with members of the opposite sex while on rotation, but everybody did it. And besides, there was something about Laura Vaccaro that had gripped him from the moment he'd set eyes on the red-haired pilot during his last R & R weekend in Qatar, four months ago. And it wasn't just because she had looked absolutely stunning in that tiny bikini. There was an aura of strength about her that the jarhead in him had found simply irresistible.

"Sir, I—"

"Relax, son," Duggan said with his craggy version of a smile. "I'm not here to bust your balls, though speaking on behalf of the Seventh Regiment . . . *Ooh-rah*."

Wright grinned. "*Ooh-rah*. Now, what's going on?"

Before Duggan could reply, the dark clouds above them opened up and the two marines stepped back beneath the overhang in front of the DFAC.

Wright noticed that the rain wasn't splashing. It was bouncing off the ground.

"It's hailing," he said.

"Yeah," Duggan mumbled, briefly putting on the glasses to look at the ground, before letting them hang again from his neck. "Fucking Afghanistan. It can't just simply rain around here. Everything has to be so fucking difficult."

"Roger that, sir," Wright said.

"Anyway," he said, as pea-size hail peppered the aluminum roof and skittered around the front of the dining facility while dozens of soldiers caught in the open ran for cover, vanishing inside various buildings. "I'm running short of rifle platoon leads, so until I can get more rotations, I'd like to transfer one out of your unit to cover the loss of Lieutenant Wiley."

"Will get right on it, sir."

"Appreciate that, son."

Wright liked him. A different commander would have simply grabbed one of his guys and sent him an email after the fact. But Duggan was considerate enough to ask, though in the end it still meant that Wright would have to step in and lead a rifle platoon if called upon before a replacement arrived.

"Semper fi," Duggan said, walking back inside.

"Semper fi," Wright replied, before glaring at the sky and also heading back into the mess hall.

When he reached his table a moment later, his dining companion was already gone, though she had left a chicken nugget on top of his burger.

13

Janki Mishka

"With all due respect, sir, I'm not moving a damn finger for the Agency until we get paid."

Colonel Stark chewed on a chicken nugget while he regarded Larson, sitting across from him in the mess hall. The chief had a valid point, of course, and his sentiment was certainly reflected in the stern gazes held by Ryan, Martin, and Hagen, sitting next to him. The CIA owed his team fifty thousand dollars for the last op, plus ten thousand each for the captured techs.

They had just finished briefing Colonel Duggan on the events at Compound 45. Now Stark had just received an introductory text from the new CIA chief at KAF, someone named Glenn Harwich, and the mere mention of it had triggered this dinner table mutiny.

He looked over at the table in the rear, where Duggan had marched off a moment ago to have a word with one of his guys having dinner with the pretty air force pilot. Her red hair reminded him of someone he had worked with a few years ago—in Russia of all places. Vaccaro was still there, eating alone now, and for a moment he thought about walking over there and joining—

"I mean, you think I'm being unreasonable?" Larson pressed.

"No, Chief," Stark replied, turning back to his guys, reaching for his bottle of water and taking a sip. "Not at all. But I still think we should meet the man. Who knows? Maybe this Harwich guy can get us paid."

"Yeah," Ryan decided to add to the conversation, sipping from a can of Sprite. "Those techs were alive and cuffed when we passed them over to the spooks. Not our fault NATO decided to blow the place off the map with little warning. Right, Mickey?"

The quiet Navy SEAL looked at the Delta sniper and nodded before returning to his brown tray next to a pack of Sobranie Classics and a lighter.

"And if not, then fuck them," said Martin, running a hand through his blond hair and smoothing his mustache with two fingers before unwrapping a watermelon lollipop. "The Agency ain't the only show in town."

Stark nodded to himself and set his phone down without returning the text. Maybe silence was the best way to get the Agency's attention. Besides, there were indeed other employers out there, whose contracts had taken them all over the world, and not just in support of Uncle Sam. In his decade since retiring from the Special Forces, Stark had accepted jobs as long as they met his simple criteria:

Will the mission make the world a better place?

Did the employer have cash in hand, and was the retainer enough to cover initial expenses?

Did all team members agree to go?

That philosophy had landed him deals across the Americas, Europe, certain African nations, as well Korea, Japan, and even China and Russia.

Russia.

Stark stared at Hagen's cigarettes before glancing over at Vaccaro and shaking his head, returning to his food. To this day he couldn't believe his team had actually run a joint operation with the GRU Spetsnaz in Moscow, back in 2002. But they had been in between jobs and his criteria were certainly met by the request from the Russian government to assist the GRU after forty armed Chechen rebels seized the crowded Dubrovka theater, taking 850 hostages.

What a logistical mess that was, he thought, recalling how any force entering the theater would have had to fight through a hundred feet of corridor before coming up against a well-defended staircase leading to the hall where the rebels held the hostages. And on top of that, the Chechens had planted explosives everywhere, including on the captives themselves. Working closely with a senior GRU Spetsnaz operative named Kira Tupolev, they had devised the idea of pumping a chemical agent into the building's ventilation shaft before commencing the rescue operation. When it was over, all rebels were killed without a single casualty on their respective teams, but at the cost of losing 130 hostages due to adverse reactions to the gas. Over the coming days and weeks, the use of the gas was viewed as heavy-handed, though not by the White House, which deemed the decision justifiable.

The alternative would have been much worse, he thought, staring at the bottle of water next to his tray, the clear liquid reminding him of the two liters of Stolichnaya vodka Kira had brought to his hotel on the eve of his departure. She had worn black jeans and a low-cut black T-shirt that exposed part of a compass rose tattoo hugging her neck and dropping into her cleavage. It was embellished by the most beautiful red roses mixed with pristine snow.

"I teach you to drink like a Russian, my *Janki mishka*, yes?" she had told him, uncorking the first bottle and pouring them shots while nicknaming Stark her "Yankee bear."

Kira had endured a cut across the right side of her forehead from shrapnel during the final assault. But the fine scar and even the stitches had only enhanced her appeal. And when combined with that mysterious body art . . . well . . .

Stark filled his lungs, recalling that amazing red hair—along with those hazel eyes and that smile—as they laughed and drank, Russian style, eating pickles in between shots.

Before long his clothes had come off as she forced him onto his back.

"Do not forget me, Janki mishka," she had whispered, hovering over him while guiding him inside her, the very intricate and colorful compass rose extending over her breasts and midriff.

Stark had been unable to reply as the Russian woman took him whole, managing to do what no other woman had to that point: help him forget Kate—if only for a little while.

Blinking the flashback away, Stark glanced over to the rear of the dining hall again, but Vaccaro had already left.

"Too young, Colonel," said Larson.

"And too pretty," added Ryan.

"Like we say in Brooklyn, sir," said Martin, "fuhgeddaboutit."

"Won't be able to keep up, sir," said Ryan.

"Keep up or keep *it* up?" asked Martin, curling and stretching his index finger. "I heard PTSD meds mess with your winky."

Stark just closed his eyes.

"Oh, yeah," Ryan added. "And a pretty red thing like that probably needs it every day."

"And twice on Sundays," Martin said.

"I'd listen to the porn star, Colonel," Ryan said.

"Plus, you saw the way she was looking at that jarhead captain," Larson chimed in again, glancing over at Ryan. "Pure lust, wouldn't you say, Romeo?"

"Pure," said Ryan.

"Think the curtains match the drapes?" asked Martin.

"Only one way to find out," Ryan said, while Hagen grinned and Larson laughed.

Stark slowly shook his head and quietly returned to his meal.

14

WASP

KANDAHAR AIRFIELD. SOUTHERN AFGHANISTAN.

Laura Vaccaro sat at the edge of the tarmac under a sea of stars. In the distance the Sulaimans rose up to meet a moon just hovering above their jagged peaks. The range looked majestic, mysterious— even peaceful.

From a distance.

Up close and personal, however, she knew that dark forces were constantly at work against NATO. The jihadists, relentless in their quest to exterminate every last nonbeliever in their zealous cause, had a very simple strategy: kill every last soul inside these walls. To them it was a war of complete annihilation of the enemy at all cost, and that included dying in the process, which made them so damn dangerous.

Vaccaro frowned while staring at various jets, cargo planes, and helicopters taking off and landing. Off to the right, the ground crew towed her crippled Warthog from the spot she had parked it earlier that evening, by a long line of tied-down A-10s on the ramp, and into a hangar for repairs. Her eyes moved to the adjacent Warthog, her new ride as of two hours ago. Someone had even already stenciled her name on the side of the cockpit.

She contemplated it while reminiscing about the hundreds of combat hours she had flown in the formidable air support jet standing larger than life under the yellow glow of floodlights bathing a tarmac the size of dozens of football fields. To this day it amazed her that a plane that entered service in 1977 not only was still in business but also was kicking ass and taking numbers. And last she'd heard, this beast of a machine was going through a number of improvements, primarily in avionics, precision weaponry, and improved armor, to extend its service life to 2028.

But improvements aside, the Warthog was still the same basic robust platform she first flew in 1991, shortly after Congress lifted the restriction on women flying in combat.

Hugging her knees, Vaccaro stared at the large Laco Trier pilot's watch on her left wrist while thinking of the female aviators that had come before her, trailblazers of yesteryear who had paved the way for her generation.

And it had all started with the WASP.

The legendary Women Airforce Service Pilots was formed in 1942 by pioneering civilian female pilots employed to fly military aircraft under the command of the U.S. Army Air Forces, the predecessor of the modern U.S. Air Force.

She filled her lungs with pride at the courage displayed by those pilots, who logged more than sixty million miles during the war years under the unflagging leadership of legends like Jackie Cochran and Nancy Love. The WASP flew every type of military aircraft of the time, from P-51 Mustangs to Spitfires, P-47 Thunderbolts, and all bomber models—in noncombat roles, but certainly in combat-type conditions. Their job was to relieve male pilots for combat duty in Europe and the Pacific, and it included test pilot duties, handling the delivery of airplanes from factories to airfields, training new male pilots, and running simulated strafing missions. The WASP even towed targets behind their fighters to train B-17 gunners using live ammunition. Of the 1,074 women who earned their wings to join the WASP ranks, thirty-eight lost their lives during World War II— eleven in training and twenty-seven in active duty.

As she thought of this, Vaccaro noticed a truck pulling up to the ramp a few hundred feet from her. It was filled with caskets draped in American flags.

She stared at the Stars and Stripes for a good minute or two, until a Boeing C-17 Globemaster III cargo jet caught her attention as it taxied from the runway. Its air force gray was dull in the floodlights as it stopped near the truck.

Probably from Dover, she thought. Dover Air Force Base, in Delaware, was home to the 512th Airlift Wing.

Shortly thereafter a long line of young men and some women, a mix of U.S. Army 82nd Airborne and U.S. Marines 7th Regiment, marched single file out of the rear ramp, hauling their standard-issue duffel bags. They headed to their respective branch's welcoming committee, which included NCOs and some officers.

From high school proms to Afghanistan in as little as six months via Fort Benning or 29 Palms plus an air force ride, she thought, wondering how many of those kids were having sex in backseats this past spring.

She stared at their baby faces, most of them in their teens, innocent eyes gawking about after being cooped up in that jet for fifteen hours. She dropped her gaze to an older guy in civilian clothes walking among them down the ramp, hauling a backpack.

Probably another civilian contractor, she thought. The man certainly stuck out among the young GIs with his bald head and salt-and-pepper beard, breaking ranks with them on the tarmac to meet up with someone in a dark sedan with tinted windows. He threw his stuff in the rear, climbed in, and drove off.

The line of newcomers continued for another few minutes, quieting down when the large truck backed toward the ramp and the detail started to unload the coffins—a sight guaranteed to strip any notion of romanticized war from their minds.

"Yeah, kids," she mumbled. "Welcome to hell."

"Talking to yourself again?"

Vaccaro looked up and stared at John Wright in his running shorts, sneakers, and a Semper fi T-shirt. Perspiration filmed his face. He had two bottles of water and offered one to her.

They sat there awhile in silence, drinking and watching the soldiers deplaning, before she pointed toward the caskets. "You know, back in World War Two, the army did not allow the U.S. flag to be placed on top of the coffin of any female aviator because they were not considered part of the military."

"Are you talking about the WASPs?" he asked.

"Yeah."

"I had no idea," Wright said. "I thought they received equal—"

"In your dreams. But it gets better. Because they were *not* considered military personnel, all fallen WASPs were sent home without traditional military honors—and at their family's expense. How's that for the ultimate *fuck you* from your country?"

"Oh my God."

"Yeah . . . and we still haven't bottomed out. After the war, the chauvinistic brass wanted to sweep the whole WASP thing under the rug, so WASP records were sealed for thirty-five years."

"Are you shitting me?"

"I wish. It wasn't until 1977 that accounts of their amazing accomplishments were made public, but the military still didn't allow the deceased WASP to be buried in Arlington until 2002. I mean, think about it, John, I was already out of the academy and flying A-10s in Iraq and Afghanistan, but those pilots who paved the way for me to do just that were not allowed a military burial."

"Looks like we're slowly getting there," he said.

"Yeah," she replied, pointing at the A-10 at the end of the line. "It took the military over six *decades* to bury female pilots at Arlington, but it took the same military less than—" she paused to glance at luminous dial on her watch "—four *hours* to find me a new bird. They even got my damn name on it already."

And unlike her last Warthog, this one had a mouthful of sharp teeth painted across its nose.

"Well, it does fit your flying style."

She chuckled. "I'm wondering what Mrs. Clark would think of me now?"

"Who's Mrs. Clark?"

"Fifth-grade teacher. We had to stand up and tell the class what we wanted to be when we grew up. So I said I wanted to be a fighter pilot. After the class stopped laughing, Mrs. Clark told me it was against the law for a woman to be a fighter pilot."

"That's cold."

She shrugged. "True stories usually are."

"Well, sweetheart, *technically* you didn't become a fighter pilot. You fly Hawgs."

"Go fuck yourself, Captain."

"Roger that, Captain."

"So, what did the good colonel want?"

He frowned. "Took one of my LTs to backfill the LT I told you about at dinner who bought the farm."

"Wiley, right?"

"You were listening. Yes. Him."

"Ah," she said. "And who's backfilling *your* team?"

"New rotation."

She stretched a finger at the deplaning soldiers. "Fresh meat?"

"Nah," Wright said. "Should get here in a week or so."

"And until then?"

He grinned and raised his brows at her.

"Dammit, John! You've done your stint in a rifle platoon—longer than anyone I know who's still in possession of their legs *and* their balls! I thought the whole fucking point of getting fucking promoted was to get you off the fucking field and on to Central Command to *coordinate* raids, *not* lead them!"

"Honey, please tell me how you really feel."

She punched him on the shoulder.

"I guess Duggan should have checked with you first," he said.

She punched him again. "Don't screw with me, soldier."

"You didn't mind it so much in Qatar," he said, running the tip of his index finger across her palm.

She pulled her hand away. "Perv . . . and don't change the subject."

"Look . . . my unit isn't due out for at least another week, maybe longer, so chances are I'll have a replacement by the time we have to head out again."

She turned back to the newcomers still deplaning.

"Besides," he added, "leading a rifle platoon isn't that much different from what you do, and you don't hear me complaining when you pull stunts like the one this afternoon."

"It was textbook *and* safe. And we wouldn't be having this conversation if I had a penis."

"Bullshit. It *wasn't* textbook and it *certainly* wasn't safe, penis *or* vagina. And besides, I thought we decided in Qatar that we weren't going to do this."

She sighed. He was right of course. Somewhere during their R & R week they had almost taken vows not to get in the way of each other's careers. Until they rotated out, they had a job to do, and it did involve a significant degree of risk. For this thing that started after a slow dance barefoot in the sand under the stars to have any chance of being anything more than . . . a *thing*, they had to respect the fact that their jobs were inherently dangerous. They were, after all, in the middle of a terrible war.

"Look, I just don't want to lose you, like I lost my dad," she said.

"I know," he replied. "But remember, I also lost my father *and* my grandfather in wars. And while I'd like to believe I'm going to beat the odds, we still need to respect our chosen profession, at least until we get stateside."

Vaccaro nodded, remembering their first conversation over beers at that beachside bar in Qatar. Their similar pasts, the pain and the pride of growing up knowing their fathers had paid the ultimate price for their country, had certainly played a role that evening.

"I know what we said, John," she finally replied. "But that was . . . well . . . before."

"Before what?"

"Really, John?"

Reaching for her hand and interlacing fingers, Wright said, "Qatar was . . ."

"Textbook?" she said, grinning.

"Yeah," he replied, also smiling. "Definitely textbook . . . But not very . . . safe."

She rested the side of her head against him while remembering their postdance activities in that beachside cabana.

"Safe is overrated."

"Sounds like something you would say."

"It's too bad indeed we're not in Qatar anymore, Captain Wright," she said, tightening her hand, "or I'd show you just how overrated it is."

"Yeah, that's too bad indeed, Captain Vaccaro," he said. The various military organizations at Kandahar had strict rules against fraternizing among soldiers. And while some chose to take the chance, and to risk their careers in the process, Vaccaro and Wright had agreed to stick to the rules.

Pointing at the caskets as the arriving soldiers vanished inside buses and the ramp ceremony began, he added, "We're *definitely* not in Qatar anymore."

They stood and watched it in silence.

15

Reversal of Fortune

ISLAMABAD. PAKISTAN.

The warehouse's door swung open at dawn and a dozen men poured out, single file, into the big E-350 vans. They were holding weapons, primarily AK-47s.

Tired and sleepy, his mouth dry and pasty, Gorman forced himself fully awake, focusing the Zeiss binoculars on the narrow gap between the door and the E-350s, but the angle was wrong, preventing him from seeing their faces.

The Fords drove off the compound and accelerated up Shaheed–Millat Road. Gorman put the RAV4 in gear and went after them just as dawn broke across the Pakistani capital, allowing him to keep his headlights off and maintain a respectful distance while dialing his team.

"Sir?" came the tired voice of Karen Barns, one of his senior analysts, a career CIA woman of around fifty with a face lined by two failed marriages. She had been around the Islamabad station longer than anyone and had taken charge of the monitoring of UAV imagery from inside the vault at the embassy.

"Tell me you have eyes on them."

"Two white Ford vans heading north on Shaheed–Millat Road."

Gorman eased off the gas and let them get a bit farther ahead in the semidarkness, but without losing sight of their taillights as they went east on Jinnah Avenue and around Fatima Jinnah Park, turning north on Agha Shahi Road.

"Looks like they're headed for the university," Karen reported in her matter-of-fact monotone voice.

Gorman turned to follow them, the heavily wooded park now to his left while he cruised past row after row of private residences on his right. After a mile or so, the woods to his left opened to reveal the main campus of the University of Islamabad. Work and school traffic started to pick up in the form of small cars, mostly Kias, Suzukis, and Toyotas, plus an assortment of bicycles, motorcycles, and tons of mopeds—many spewing crazy volumes of exhaust smoke. But Gorman actually welcomed the toxic haze hovering in the morning air. It helped obscure his presence from those he followed.

He remained focused, scanning his quarry plus his surroundings through the light of early dawn, keeping a buffer of five or six vehicles to avoid getting burned, especially since he was conducting this tail solo. The Agency would usually dispatch at least four cars to conduct a proper surveillance, each shadowing for a few blocks before another chase car took over, in overlapping sequence.

Gorman almost laughed at the surreal—and even ironic—nature of his situation, especially if the master terrorist was indeed aboard one of those vans while he followed them in an old Toyota with no backup. Meanwhile, his country had sunk hundreds of millions of dollars into scouring the globe for his whereabouts.

"Yeah," he mumbled while steering the weathered RAV4 and wondering where that money was being spent. "Any-fucking-where but here."

"Sir?" Karen streamed through his earpiece. "Say again. We didn't catch that."

Gorman frowned. "Disregard that last—"

"Targets turning right on Khayaban-e-Iqbal, heading northeast, away from the university."

Spotting them just as the taillights disappeared around the corner, he accelerated and swerved past a couple of mopeds and a truck.

Ignoring the driver of the truck honking at him, Gorman reached the intersection and cut right, continuing on the wide street for a couple of miles.

The E-350s approached the cutoff for Damin-i-koh, the long and winding road connecting the north section of Islamabad with the southern part of Haripur—the same damn road he had taken the night before, coming the other way.

But the armored vans remained on Khayaban-e-Iqbal for another four miles, until it dead-ended on Fourth Avenue, by a fruit and vegetable market. Its street-side kiosks showcased heaps of colorful produce—from mangos, dates, and apricots to squash and turnips. Turning left, they slowed when entering a suburban neighborhood in the northeastern section of the capital city.

Ignoring vendors screaming by the sidewalk while holding up handfuls of ripe tomatoes and pears, Gorman steered the Toyota onto Fourth, flanked by woods to his left and several rows of houses to his right. The sun was just breaking over the rim rock of the mountains skirting the eastern edge of the city, bathing the capital in wan orange light. Streetlights flickered and went off.

As he was about to ask where the hell they were headed, Karen reported, "They've stopped across the street in front of the fifth house on the next block. Two-three-seven Fourth Avenue."

"Whose house is that?"

"We're checking the housing database now."

Gorman pulled over on the residential side of the street, by the corner, a safe couple hundred feet from his mark, settling in the space between two parked cars, a black Kia coupe and a blue Suzuki minivan. This offered a diagonal vantage on the vans parked down and across the street while providing an acceptable level of concealment.

A tall woman wearing a dark *shalwar kameez* robe, her features hidden beneath a *dupatta* headscarf and a veil, appeared in the middle of the street, carrying an empty basket, probably headed to the market.

He focused on her arms, which moved freely, meaning no hidden weapons beneath the gown. He shifted from her to the vans as two men got out of the lead Ford, clutching AK-47s, and approached the lone female.

Gorman fingered the focusing ring of the Zeiss binoculars, resolving their images. Neither man was bin Laden. A conversation ensued, involving a lot of hand gesturing that could suggest concern—or nothing at all, given the high-strung nature of these people. But the discussion ended abruptly when the woman pointed toward the market down the street.

The men waved her off, and the woman walked away briskly as four men poured out of the second van and joined the first two, approaching the front of the house.

Focusing on the men, Gorman ignored the veiled woman as she rushed past his parking spot and continued down the street. He shifted the binoculars from face to face, hoping to catch a glimpse of bin Laden, but none belonged to the master terrorist.

"They're going into the residence," he said. "Got a name yet?"

"Negative, but we have a visual. Still checking local records."

Gorman frowned while staring at what might be a kidnapping in progress.

But who are they after?

"Keep looking. I'll be right back," he told Karen, removing his earpiece and tossing it and the phone onto the passenger seat.

He paused before reaching for the door handle, Harwich's words echoing in his head.

Keep your distance and just watch and report, okay?

He frowned, getting out of the RAV4 and stepping around the space between his front bumper and the back of the Kia, peering past the Kia's rear quarter panel for a better view.

While half the men stormed the front gate, crawling over it before opening it from the inside, the rest kept watch by the vans.

Gorman zoomed in to check the faces of the lookout team as the grabbing team vanished inside.

He was about to double back to his vehicle when one of the lookout men screamed, pointing at him.

Shit!

He tried to get into the RAV4 but never made it past the fender before a volley of rounds tore into the Toyota's grill, hood, and windshield, tearing it up in seconds. The staccato gunfire reverberated down the sleepy street, its thunder marking the start of just another day of violence in Islamabad.

Gorman rolled back to the sidewalk, surging to a deep crouch and running away from the Toyota while using the parked vehicles as a temporary shield. His right hand instinctively drew the Desert Eagle, the web of his hand pressed snug against the top of the grip. He thumbed the ambidextrous safety while his left hand automatically came up for support and stability. Tucking his wrists against his right pectoral, he kept the muzzle pointed slightly down, shooting finger resting on the trigger casing.

The firing stopped as he raced past five or six vehicles, dropping into the narrow space between an old Nissan truck and the front of a brown car he could not identify. Lying flat on his left side, he peered under the truck, spotting three pairs of legs running toward his hiding spot. They looked to be about forty or fifty feet away.

Taking a deep breath, he aimed the Magnum at the closest set and fired multiple times.

The .50 Action Express rounds made a hell of a racket, flashing under the truck and certainly telegraphing his position, but not before one of the jacketed hollow-point bullets vaporized someone's foot.

Gorman fired twice more and dropped the spent magazine, listening to the shrieks as his victim collapsed on the asphalt. He reloaded while switching targets, shooting rapidly at the next set of legs, the reports deafening, a shell taking off a leg at the knee with ridiculous force and a cloud of blood, flesh, and bone.

He dropped his second magazine and loaded a third while jumping back to the sidewalk as a volley of rounds pounded the truck and the brown car in a blaze of sparks.

Spinning away, he again rose to a deep crouch, his operative mind weighing the choice of keeping this fight in the street—especially after the grabbing team emerged from the house—or taking it to the thick woods across the road.

Making his decision, Gorman did what he hoped the Taliban soldiers would not expect: he left the protection of the parked cars and ran straight onto the road, in plain view. But he did it while emptying the Desert Eagle, aiming it at the third man he had seen running toward him, catching him kneeling down by his wounded comrades.

Shooting sideways while sprinting greatly reduced Gorman's accuracy. Still, a slug tore into the man's chest, pushing him in the direction of the other lookouts, who dove for cover when a couple of stray rounds struck the rear of the trailing Ford van.

Temporarily out and lacking the time to reload, Gorman pounded the pavement while pointing his momentum at the tree line. The soldiers abandoned their assigned posts and went after him, swinging their weapons in his direction.

Gorman reached the edge of the trees and dove headfirst behind a wide trunk as the fast rattle of AK-47s hammered the blacktop and then the woods. Bark exploded in a shower of mulch.

He landed on his side and once more rolled away. The leaf-littered ground and the thick canopy overhead swapped places as he pushed his body while clutching the Desert Eagle against his chest.

He hit something hard, which stopped his momentum. It was a group of moss-slick boulders a dozen feet from the spot where he'd entered the forest. His shoulder stung from the impact, but he ignored it, wincing in pain while managing to get back up as bark splintered to his immediate right.

Gorman sprinted left, zigzagging deeper into the woods, where darkness shrouded him. He rushed past towering trees and rock formations, ducking under hanging vegetation and low branches, hoping to lose his—

He tripped on an exposed root, crashing headfirst into knee-high shrubs while tightening his right hand, keeping his grip on the Desert Eagle.

Struggling to regain his footing, he pawed on all fours, finally staggering up and looking over his right shoulder while hurrying behind the protection of a wide trunk. He caught a glimpse of the silhouettes of the incoming trio, backlit by the sunlight from the street, which made them easy targets. By going into the murky woods first, he had given himself an edge. The men after him could not see him as clearly as he could see them.

In the darkness, he tugged with his left thumb and middle and index fingers at the final upside-down magazine in his military belt. Freeing it from its holster, he inserted it into the Desert Eagle, dropped the slide catch, and chambered a round.

Knees bent, his back pressed against the bark, Gorman slowly peeked around the trunk, but to his surprise he only saw one figure.

What the hell?

As he aimed the Magnum at its center of mass, probing the forest around the silhouette's flanks, he heard a noise behind him. But he never got a chance to turn around.

The blow to the side of his face made him drop the pistol, and the kick from an unseen boot to his solar plexus bent him over.

Falling on his side, Gorman coughed, feeling the urge to vomit as three figures loomed over him, clutching AK-47s.

He stared at his executioners in silent defiance as more of Harwich's words echoed in his mind.

When you're in-country you're only one decision away from starring in your own YouTube video.

But the men didn't seem to be in a cinematic mood as they pointed their muzzles at his head.

So this is how it ends, he thought, before multiple reports whipped the woods, thundering in his ears.

He cringed, shrinking back, hands shielding his face, his body tensing for the impacts that never came.

Momentarily confused, taking a deep breath, he looked up, probing the darkness.

The men had fallen, their limp bulks littering the ground by his feet. In their place stood the tall woman in the black shalwar kameez, whom he had seen minutes ago talking to the al Qaeda soldiers. She kept her feet spread apart for balance, hands clutching a dark pistol, her features still veiled by the dupatta. Behind her stood two men holding MP5s and dressed in the black tactical gear of Pakistan's Special Service Group.

Gunfire erupted on the street, mixed with shouts and the sound of engines roaring and tires screeching. Everyone, Gorman included, turned toward the racket, made by a mix of AK-47s and MP5s.

The woman looked at the SSG pair and tilted her head toward the street.

The operators took off while she approached Gorman, clutching her weapon, which he recognized as a 9mm Beretta 92FS. Gazing in both directions and behind her, the woman took a knee in front of him.

The face now materialized as a she pulled back the headscarf, dark hair falling to her shoulders, framing high cheekbones on a narrow face. Her catlike brown eyes glinted with recognition, and Gorman remembered that Sunday reception at the American embassy a month ago. His mouth recalled the taste of the bottle of Maker's Mark she had brought, along with a proposal for cooperation between the CIA and her agency, Pakistan's Inter-Services Intelligence. Gorman had agreed to think about it and let her know when he might be ready to have a follow-up conversation. Finkle had squashed the idea.

"Hiya, Mr. Gorman," ISI officer Maryam Gadai said in her British accent. "We meet again."

As Gorman quickly came around, breaking her stare to peer at his dead would-be assassins, and while the firefight intensified in the street, Maryam added, "Do you fancy another chat?"

16

Tribal Warfare

SULAIMAN MOUNTAINS. SOUTHERN AFGHANISTAN.

Nasseer Niaz moved through the predawn darkness like a shadow, swiftly and quietly, with practiced ease, the cool, dry air filling his lungs. Perspiration filmed his body, sticking to his dark *khet partug*, the combination tunic and pants made of cotton that he wore beneath a charcoal nylon vest keeping grenades and extra ammunition within easy reach.

Turning his sweaty, bearded face to the sky as a light breeze swept down the mountain, refreshing him, Nasseer briefly closed his eyes, thanking Allah for this simple pleasure.

His younger and much larger brother, Hassan, followed closely, holding a weathered AK-47, as did the rest of his small band of warriors.

But not Nasseer.

Although of average height and quite slim, he operated the intimidating twenty-pound Russian PK machine gun. He also carried another twenty pounds of 7.62×54mm cartridges in twenty-five-round connectable aluminum belt lengths. For this mission, Nasseer had linked four segments to create a continuous hundred-round belt inserted into the PK's right-side feedway, wearing the rest of the five-foot-long belt wrapped over his shoulders bandolier style.

Nasseer was the group's leader, but more than that, he was Shinwari, from a Pashtun tribe numbering four hundred thousand that had declared war on the Taliban for the atrocities committed by its regime in the 1990s—among them, the murder of Nasseer's parents.

His mission tonight: steal weapons and explosives from an enclave rumored to be also holding three captured Canadian soldiers from an ambush the day before.

He paused when reaching the edge of the forest, wincing in pain as another molar fell to neglect in the back of his mouth. Clenching his jaw, Nasseer dropped to one knee by the waist-high vegetation leading to the small clearing, aiming the Kalashnikov machine gun at the pair of armed men by the fissure-like entrance to a cave formed in a towering rocky outcrop.

The guards, AK-47s slung behind their backs, knelt by the remnants of the prior night's fire, which was barely glowing orange by the side of the cavern, palms facing the dying embers, trying to absorb what remained of their rising heat. Off to the right, Nasseer spotted a set of four rectangular solar panels connected to wires bundled into a thick cable running along the side of the rocky wall, disappearing inside the cave.

Nasseer ran the tip of his tongue over the latest abscessed tooth while assessing the enemy, swallowing the bitter taste that told him an infection had set in, which also explained his swollen neck glands.

It will have to come out, like the other ones, he thought, grimacing at the reason he'd lost so much weight in the last two years, after his dental problems began.

Pointing three fingers to his right and then to his left, he prompted his well-trained team to split, to spread along the edge of the woods while Hassan stayed put, kneeling next to his brother.

Nasseer crawled to the edge of the brush before extending the

PK's integrated bipod that was hinged to the front of the weapon, resting it softly on the ground, the muzzle parting knee-high blades of tall grass. He uncoiled the ammunition belt off his chest and piled it to the right of the forty-seven-inch-long weapon before settling behind it in the brush.

Pressing the skeletonized buttstock against his right shoulder, right hand on the pistol grip, he sank his left elbow on the ground while spreading his legs behind him for balance and recoil support, ankles flat on the ground, toes pointing outward.

He tilted his head slightly to align his right eye with the square-notched rear-tangent iron sight and the front sight assembly near the end of the long barrel. Then, slowly, he shifted the weapon to bring the rightmost guard into the center of his sights.

Hassan crept by him, resting his elbows on the ground while aiming his AK-47 at the cave.

Swallowing a mouthful of tangy saliva, Nasseer flexed his shooting finger off the trigger casing and touched the trigger. Deciding that his team had had enough time to reach their respective vantage points, he squeezed.

The PK thundered against his shoulder as the feed mechanism pulled the rimmed cartridges from the back of the ammunition belt, dropping them into the feedway, allowing the bolt to strip and feed the rounds into the chamber for firing.

He released only a short burst, five or six rounds, easing off the trigger when the guard's midriff exploded. Nasseer shifted his aim to the left, catching the second guard still crouched over the fire, staring at his dead comrade in apparent shock, and ripped through the guard's head and shoulders with a follow-up volley.

The man collapsed over the sizzling coals, kicking up a cloud of glowing ashes.

His team rushed onto the kill zone but remained clear of the entrance while Nasseer paused, centering the sights in the middle of the dark and wide natural fissure in the rock formation. Almost ten feet wide at the base, it gradually narrowed as it rose to a height of almost twenty feet.

Seconds ticked in his head as he waited patiently, familiar with Taliban tactics. Smoke wafted from beneath the guard crumpled over the embers, coiling across the camp, the smell of burned fabric and flesh tickling Nasseer's nostrils.

Nasseer grinned. The fanatical Taliban soldiers didn't disappoint, streaming out of the cave to make their stand, screaming and shooting blindly. He picked them off easily, unleashing quick bursts while Hassan also fired his AK-47. Within seconds seven men lay dead by the entrance to the cave.

Nasseer looked over at Hassan and nodded. His brother stood, giving the signal for the team in the clearing. Two men immediately jumped into action, rushing to the entrance, leaping over dead bodies, and tossing a pair of old Russian Model 1914 concussion grenades before retreating.

Two blasts later and three more insurgents stumbled outside, also firing blindly. Nasseer also took them out with single shots, before one of his men went inside the cave and exited a moment later, giving the "all clear" signal.

Nasseer picked up the Kalashnikov machine gun, slung the remaining belt over his shoulders, and approached the entrance, stepping over the dead Taliban. Before going inside, he ordered four men to perimeter duty in case the gunfire drew enemy forces in the area.

The interior was damp and murky, smelling of body odor, gunpowder, and something else he couldn't place. Several flickering oil lamps hung along the left wall, washing the interior in dim yellow light.

Nasseer eyed the stash of weapons lining the left wall, mostly AK-47s, assorted ammunition and grenades, plus several IEDs. But his attention shifted to long tables along the right wall. The first three were packed with IED hardware in various states of assembly, plus two explosive vests wired to handheld detonators—dead man's triggers.

He exhaled, thanking Allah that the Russian grenades had not set off any secondary explosions, with so much volatile material. Or that the surviving fanatics had not blown themselves up, especially given the contents of the last table: a pair of laptops tethered by long wires to cell phones hanging by the entrance to maximize reception. Three car batteries provided the necessary electricity through a DC/AC power inverter. The solar panels outside fed the hardware during the day while also charging the batteries for night operations. It was very simple and also very efficient, easy to move around.

He cruised past the weapons, explosives, and computer gear, guided by what he now recognized as the coppery smell of blood. And that's where he found them. Two soldiers, boys really, much younger than Hassan, hanging by their wrists from hooks hammered into the rock wall, their entrails, genitals, and eyeballs piled below them among pools of coagulated blood.

"We are too late, brother," said Hassan, stepping up to him. "The Ba'i wanted them alive."

Nasseer frowned. "I thought there were supposed to be *three* soldiers, not two,"

"That is true."

They ventured deeper in the cave, weapons ready, following a slight bend in the hideout, the coppery smell of blood pungent.

They found her tied to a table just beyond a makeshift kitchen and several cots.

"What in Allah's name have they done this time?" Hassan mumbled, while Nasseer simply looked at the bloody mess the Taliban had made of a girl not older than his youngest sister back in—

The woman suddenly shifted on the table, trembling, eyes gouged, her front teeth and tongue missing, as she coughed up blood and tissue.

"She's alive!" Hassan shouted.

"Cut her loose. Hurry," Nasseer said, rushing to her side as she writhed in pain, dropping her hands to her mangled groin the moment Hassan sliced off her restraints.

One of his men produced a blanket, wrapping the woman in it before placing her in one of the cots. They did what they could for her, but the internal damage had been extreme, and she bled out in minutes.

And mercifully so, Nasseer thought, before turning to Hassan, who was visibly shaken. "We're taking all three with us. They still have value, as do the computers and phones."

Hassan steeled himself and gave the order. The Shinwari cut down the dead soldiers and carried them outside along with the woman, before gathering the computer hardware.

"What about weapons and ammo?"

"Take anything we can carry."

"And the rest?"

Nasseer contemplated the large cache of explosives. "Torch it."

17

The Enemy of My Enemy

**INTER-SERVICES INTELLIGENCE HEADQUARTERS.
ISLAMABAD. PAKISTAN.**

"We lost them right . . . *here*," Gorman said, pressing an ice pack against a throbbing cheekbone while stabbing at the map spread out on the large conference table, where the now familiar Damin-i-koh snaked northwest of the capital, toward Haripur. "Bastards changed vehicles before we could reposition surveillance. Our best guess is that they were making a run for the border . . here . . . or here." He shifted his index finger northwest of Haripur, the starting point of the legendary Khyber Pass, a dangerous mountain pass between Pakistan and Afghanistan in the heart of the Federally Administered Tribal Areas. FATA was controlled by a number of warring Pashtun tribes, and it was also a mecca for opium smugglers.

"Surveillance? As in American drones inside Pakistani airspace?" mumbled Maryam with amusement, while sitting across from him in a basement conference center. "I'm going to pretend I didn't bloody hear that."

"Who said anything about drones? I said *surveillance*, though I thought you and I were past that," he replied.

Maryam twisted her lips at him. She had shed the shalwar kameez along with the dupatta and just wore tight black jeans, a black T-shirt, and one hell of an admonishing stare, which Gorman found quite irresistible. In his years running ops for the Agency, he had yet to come across someone like Maryam, figuring that beautiful female operatives were the stuff of novels and movies.

But then again, the Pakistanis were legendary for training women for the sole purpose of honey-trapping guys like him. So while Maryam had indeed saved his life—and while she certainly looked like she'd just stepped out of a South Asian beauty pageant—the trained operative in him called for caution. He was, after all, deep inside ISI land, surrounded by hidden cameras. Anything he said could be used to blackmail him in the future.

"But in the spirit of interagency cooperation," he added, "I had my people position two Predators circling the Afghan side of the mountain pass, just east of Jalalabad. Maybe we'll get lucky."

"I don't believe in luck, Mr. Gorman."

"Well, I was *damn* lucky you showed up when you did. And please, call me Bill."

Gorman and Maryam had made it back to the street after their unscheduled but quite fortunate rendezvous in the woods. The place had resembled a battle zone, with Taliban and SSG operators sprawled everywhere. One of the vans was long gone, along with the surviving Taliban soldiers, plus one Dr. Ali Khan, professor emeritus of nuclear engineering and board member of the Pakistan Atomic Energy Commission. That was the name Karen Barns had claimed belonged to the owner of the residence, when Gorman returned to the RAV4, where his satellite radio had survived the fusillade that had rendered the Toyota undriveable.

"Yes," Maryam said. "About that . . . *Bill*. How did you say you happened to be there?"

"I didn't. How did *you* happen to be there?" he replied, setting down the ice pack and massaging the side of his face.

Maryam sat back, crossed her arms, and hissed, "Bugger. Are we going to play more bloody games? This is why those cheeky bastards are winning."

And that was precisely the question, of course. How much could he really confide in a member of an intelligence organization that had been at odds with the CIA for as far back as Gorman could remember? Finkle's reply, when Gorman had asked the question following that embassy encounter with Maryam, had been zero. Nada. Zip. And that was part of the reason why they were inside ISI headquarters and not inside the vault at the U.S. embassy. He'd figured that it was safer to come here than to bring an ISI officer inside CIA sacred ground.

But Gorman had also learned from Harwich, long ago, that Agency rules were more like operational parameters. They were not meant to be broken. But if the situation required it, they could certainly be . . .

Tested?

Nodding to himself, he decided to do a little tit-for-tat tradecraft test and see how far he could get.

"Are you harboring the big boss of those . . . what did you call them? . . . 'cheeky bastards' somewhere in Pakistan?" he asked.

Maryam just stared at him.

"All right," he added. "Then tell me, why would they kidnap a guy whose expertise is in building nuclear bombs?"

More silence.

Raising his brows and lifting his hands, palms up, Gorman said, "Now *who's* playing games? Are we doing this or not?"

At her continued silence, Gorman stood and said, "Appreciate the save, Maryam. Really. I owe you one. But I've got work to—"

"I was there because we got a tip."

He remained standing. "A tip?"

She motioned for him to sit down. "Please, Bill."

Gorman complied, slowly, resting his forearms on the conference table. "I'm all ears."

Maryam looked up at the clock on the wall, which probably hid a wide-angle high-definition camera and a microphone, before locking her gaze on Gorman and saying, "I handle an asset in the cartel . . . goes by Zameer. He signaled last night that our . . . cheeky bastards needed safe passage into Afghanistan for one of our nuclear scientists in Islamabad. They will be assisted by Adnan Zubaydah, one of the drug cartel bosses controlling the Khyber Pass."

Leaning forward, Gorman said, "You expect me to believe that the ISI gets word that the Taliban is after one of your esteemed nu-clear scientists and all it sent for his protection was—"

"Zameer didn't give us a name, Bill. There are over twenty nuclear scientists living in this city, many working at the university, like Dr. Khan. So we had to divide our forces, and did so very care-fully to avoid telegraphing our presence. I was assigned to Dr. Khan eight hours earlier, and as soon as I spotted the vans, I ringed our team. The plan, however, was to follow them, not to intercept."

"So you were hoping that they would lead you to whatever it was that the professor was meant to work on?"

"Something like that."

"But I crashed your little party."

"Forcing our hand."

"But they got away all the same."

Maryam dropped her gaze to the map. "Aye . . . they bloody did."

"And this . . . Zameer . . . Any chance he can get us new intel on their whereabouts?"

Shrinking in her chair, Maryam said, "He has gone silent. Has not replied to our bloody messages since the shooting."

Gorman looked at the clock on the wall, and then at his Rolex. "And that was three hours ago."

"Fancy your watch," she said, stretching a finger toward it.

"Ah, thanks," he said, staring at it again while wondering if she was trying to work him. Before he could help himself, he added, "It was a . . . gift."

She tilted her head. "Very special gift."

"Yeah. Very special person, too," he mumbled, before realizing he was about to cross some line. "I take it that is not normal," he added quickly.

"*What* isn't?"

"Zameer going silent."

"Bloody right that's not normal."

So that meant this Zameer character was either burned—and killed—or, worse, like everything else in this damn country, he was playing it both ways, just as the government of Pakistan played it both ways with the United States and al Qaeda.

"You realize, Maryam, that the assholes who kidnapped the professor are led by the asshole *my* country has been after—the *same* asshole that *your* country is harboring?"

Gorman knew she could neither confirm nor deny that. The Agency had long suspected the government of Pakistan of sheltering Osama bin Laden. But apparently that same government wasn't crazy about the master terrorist being associated with anything that smelled nuclear.

"And now you need my help," he added.

"Aye."

Gorman sat back and stared at her. She represented the ISI, the enemy of the CIA. Heck, as of late, more resources were spent combating the ISI than Putin's GRU. But their agencies now faced a larger and common enemy: nuclear terrorism. If there was even the smallest chance of preventing al Qaeda from going nuclear through a little off-the-books interagency cooperation . . .

"All right, Maryam," he finally said. "What do you have in mind?"

18

No Honor Among Thieves

LANDI KOTAL. NORTHWESTERN PAKISTAN.

Pasha Baqer drove for his life.

And for his mission.

The journey from Islamabad to Peshawar had been uneventful, even a bit boring, and the Pashtun warrior had welcomed the boredom after nearly failing in his operation before it had even started, at the home of Dr. Ali Khan.

But his men had reacted well, creating a defensive perimeter, sacrificing themselves to fend off the SSG contingent long enough for him, Dr. Khan, and two of his men to get away in one of the vans. Osama bin Laden, always anticipating trouble—and always full of surprises—had a fresh team waiting just outside the capital city. Qadeer, one of bin Laden's cousins and personal bodyguard, had been among the men ordered to assist him in this most critical of missions.

Pasha had embraced his older relative before dumping the van and transferring to three Goats for the treacherous haul across the Khyber Pass.

Downshifting into second gear, Pasha tapped the brakes on the lead Goat before turning left at the intersection of two unnamed streets somewhere in the middle of the unpaved guts of this war-torn town. He was being directed by the man in the passenger seat, Adnan Zubaydah, a cartel lieutenant who was guiding the convoy through the Khyber Pass under orders from bin Laden.

Qadeer, aboard the last Goat and in charge of protecting the rear of the caravan, had spotted the enemy five minutes ago while they were driving from Peshawar on the N-5, also known as Grand Trunk Road. A black Land Cruiser had emerged from a bend in the road near the outskirts of town and was gradually gaining on the slower Goats.

Sliding into the turn, Pasha shifted up to third and floored it, the 4×4's fat tires spinning, kicking up dust and dirt as he accelerated down a side street that ran parallel to the N-5. Adnan held a radio to his lips, conveying the evasion plan to the other two Goats, who also negotiated the tight turn at speed, falling in line behind him, keeping the caravan tight. In the rear seat, two of his men flanked Dr. Khan, their tall and muscular frames contrasting sharply with the scientist's diminutive stature. But what the professor lacked in size he more than made up for in lung capacity and attitude.

"Are you kidding me?" the scientist shouted. "I thought you guys actually controlled this region!"

Pasha ignored him, just as he had since the nearly failed kidnapping attempt. Dr. Khan had not really minded being abducted to assist the Taliban, but he had been livid when his family was placed in the line of fire by the rebel group's miscalculation.

"Is this why I was taken? So I can get killed? You guys are a joke! A joke! Do you hear me? I demand to speak to the sheikh! Where is the sheikh?"

"Somebody shut him up!" Pasha shouted, barely keeping control of the Goat as it dashed past one- and two-story dwellings with mud and stone facades charred and pockmarked from decades of fighting.

He worked the gears, accelerating up the unpaved street. People, dogs, goats, and vendors scrambled out of his way. Pasha ignored the chaotic scene ahead of him. Left hand on the wheel, right hand alternating between the horn and the gear lever, feet working the pedals, he was stressing the military utility vehicle to its limit.

Adnan, a harsh man roughly Akaa's age, his face heavily lined and leathery under a stained Peshawari turban, divided his attention between the road ahead and the team behind them while chatting on the radio. His motion was abrupt but focused, in control, conveying the experience of having done this before.

Risking a glance at the rearview mirror, Pasha looked past the wide-eyed glare of Dr. Khan with one of Pasha's men's hands wrapped over his mouth, spotting the pair of green off-road vehicles within the cloud of dust behind him. He also caught a glimpse of the darker and taller Land Cruiser as it finally emerged from the turn roughly a block behind them.

They were getting close.

But according to Adnan it would not matter.

"Take this left!" the gruff cartel chief shouted, his deep voice booming over the roaring engine as they reached the next intersection.

Pasha tapped the brakes again before cutting left and easing into second gear, ignoring the perspiration rolling down his forehead. The Goat protested the sudden shift in direction, its chassis vibrating, the wheel trembling under his grip, but its low center of gravity kept the tires biting the gravel the moment he released the clutch.

Debris sprayed onto a pair of street vendors, veiling them in a cloud of the fine clay soil that layered the terrain in this region, as he pointed the nose of the Goat straight down another nameless street.

Accelerating, the 4×4 jolting over the harsher surface of this side street, Pasha tightened his grasp on the wheel to keep from bouncing on his seat while Adnan grabbed the dashboard for stability. Chickens cackled out of the way, wings flapping amid dust and the screams of running pedestrians.

And once again Pasha ignored it all, focusing on the picture beyond the grimy windshield as the houses ended in another two blocks, the narrow street suddenly opening to a makeshift soccer field.

He drove right onto the field while Adnan continued working the radio.

Another glance at the rearview mirror. The second Goat also made it to the field, tagging along behind him. But the last 4×4 had stopped, its green chassis sliding sideways, blocking the end of the street. Dust and debris shrouded it as Qadeer leaped out, Kalashnikov aimed at the incoming Toyota SUV.

Multiple reports resonated behind them as Pasha reached the end of the soccer field and steered onto a trail that wound down the side of a long hill, toward Grand Trunk Road.

The steep grade, combined with a coarse terrain meant for foot traffic, made Pasha wonder whether the sacrifice made by Qadeer, one of Akaa's most trusted warriors and a blood relative, had been necessary. Their military version of the Russian 4×4s had over a foot of clearance, easily managing the rocky and jagged track winding down the incline. No way that Land Cruiser and its lower ground clearance could handle the narrow switchbacks.

Still, the racket echoing down from the town, now a mix of AK-47s and other small arms, told him Qadeer was holding the line, forcing the enemy in the chase SUV to pause and engage him, buying Pasha the required time to get away.

Akaa's cousin was doing his job so Pasha could do his.

And if Allah wills it, perhaps Qadeer will survive this, he thought, easing into first gear to face the grade of nearly thirty-five degrees, according to the inclinometer on the dash. Pasha wound his way deliberately down the southern face of the hill, going over boulders and fallen vegetation.

The Goat lived up to its nickname, negotiating fissures and out-crops for the thousand feet of hillside from the edge of the soccer field to the shoulder of Grand Trunk Road.

Pasha entered a bit of a rhythm, guiding the vehicle back and forth on snug hairpin turns, disregarding the firefight while occasionally glancing in the rearview mirror to confirm that the second Goat remained behind him.

It took just a couple of minutes to reach the shoulder, and Pasha pulled off to the side to wait for the second 4×4, which joined him a moment later.

They continued on the N-5, leaving the town behind, while Adnan communicated with his people on the Afghan border just four kilometers up the mountains.

For the first time since spotting the surveillance, Pasha eased his hold on the wheel. The 4×4 accelerated up the winding road, flanked by steep walls of reddish-brown rock and clay rising up a gorge carved through the range millennia ago.

His mind transitioned from survival mode to assessing his situation, the sound of gunfire giving way to the whistling wind channeling through the meandering canyon.

Slowly settling down, his logical mind could not help but question how the hell the enemy had ambushed them twice in less than twelve hours, given all the precautions bin Laden had taken.

His eyes on the snaking road, Pasha frowned. It simply made no sense.

Unless . . .

Several buzzards rode the thermals high above the chasm just before the next bend, sweeping overhead in wide, lazy circles. But as he steered the Goat across the final stretch of Pakistani soil, a different kind of vulture filled his senses, a much more repulsive creature than the circling carrion birds.

A *ghadar*.

A traitor.

Filling with rage, Pasha swore on the souls of the warriors who had this day fallen to protect him that he would find this traitor and peel the skin off his face.

But until he did, his mission would be in constant danger.

Whoever it was that had interfered twice already would certainly try again.

Let them, he thought. *Let the bastards try to stop me!*
Whoever they are!
Wherever they are!

19

The Tip of the Spear

LANDI KOTAL. NORTHWESTERN PAKISTAN.

"I'm using an RPG!" shouted Zameer over the noise of another volley of rounds hammering the titanium and Kevlar plates of the Land Cruiser.

Mossad officer Aaron Peretz had just parked the 4×4 sideways for cover, and now he jumped behind the rear wheel while Zameer, his local asset, set down his UZI on the dirt road, by his boots. The short and skinny Pakistani, who reminded Aaron of a rug peddler, reached into the rear seat for the green and silver launcher. It was already loaded with a rocket-propelled fragmentation grenade.

"*No!* He's alone, and I need him *alive!*" replied the burly Israeli operative, his barrel chest pressed against the rear quarter panel as he knelt and aimed the UZI down the street. He briefly glanced at his informant, giving him an *I mean it* glare before returning his attention to the damn Russian 4×4 blocking the street.

"But sahib," Zameer countered, using the Urdu word for "boss," since Mossad tradecraft rules did not allow an asset to know the name of a handler, "the others are getting away with the scientist!"

"They already *got* away!" replied Aaron, releasing a 9mm burst, shattering the front windows of the Goat.

Visibly frustrated, Zameer picked the UZI back up, aimed it at the threat, and shot off a volley of rounds, which went all over the place, striking the Russian vehicle as well as the mud walls of the houses flanking it. He also hit a passing rooster, which collapsed in a cloud of dust and flapping wings.

Aaron sighed. His asset may have found a way to infiltrate the opium cartel and also gain the trust of the ISI, but he was a terrible shot.

"Are you certain we just can't take another street?" Aaron pressed. "Maybe go around him?"

"Too narrow, sahib. This is the only one on this side of town, and the bastards know it," Zameer replied.

Aaron forced control. This should never have gotten this far. In fact, the kidnapping should have *never* taken place, given Zameer's connections inside the ISI. But his informant had apparently not known which scientist would be taken, forcing the ISI to spread out its resources around Islamabad. And that, in turn, had forced the Mossad's hand in the form of this last-minute damage control circus to prevent al Qaeda from taking the professor across the border into Taliban country.

Aaron was the eyes and ears of the Mossad in the region, tasked with locating and terminating Osama bin Laden. And that meant recruiting and running assets such as Zameer while operating without an embassy, unlike the Americans, the Russians, and the British.

But Aaron was also Kidon, a member of an elite group of expert operatives and assassins recruited from Israel Defense Forces, his country's equivalent of the American Special Forces. Originally known as Caesarea, the mysterious assassination unit within the Mossad changed its name to Kidon in the mid-1970s. Meaning "tip of the spear," it became one of the most guarded secrets in the Israeli intelligence community, reserved only for missions deemed critical to the survival of the Jewish nation.

Like al Qaeda kidnapping a nuclear scientist.

As such, Aaron was expected to improvise and to prevent this unfortunate situation from getting any worse by devising a way to tip the scales, to change the odds in his favor. If al Qaeda was indeed trying to get into the nuclear business, then bin Laden couldn't be too far from the action. The Kidon viewed the kidnapped professor as just the means to achieving his ultimate goal: cutting off the head of the snake.

Aaron exhaled, staring at the green 4×4 before scanning both sides of the narrow street, now completely devoid of people. The moment he saw what he sought, he turned to his informant and said, "Keep him engaged with the UZI!"

"Wait, sahib . . . where are you going?" Zameer asked, as Aaron crawled to the front of the vehicle, crouching behind the tire, ready to spring into action.

"To do *my* job!" he shouted, loading a new magazine into his sub-machine gun before pointing at the Russian Goat. "So do *your* job and cover me! And shoot straight and on my mark!"

Zameer nodded, dropping the spent thirty-two-round magazine and inserting a fresh one while keeping his aim downrange, right eye glued to the reflex scope, ready to provide covering fire.

"Now, Zameer!"

The Pakistani agent fired a barrage of 9mm rounds across the two hundred feet separating the warring parties, peppering the side of the Russian vehicle, forcing the lone man behind it to temporarily seek cover.

The Kidon raced away from the Toyota and shot across the street and into a narrow alley off to their right, hiding in the long corridor formed by two rows of houses. Although he was large, like a body builder, Aaron was also quite agile, with powerful thighs and calves that he used to propel his 270-pound bulk with the speed and grace of a world-class soccer player.

His tight black clothes blending him with the shadowy passage-way, Aaron dashed down the width of the block to the next street, past piles of fetid garbage buzzing with flies. The refuse lined back patios strung with cords draped with swirling laundry.

His movements were deliberate, his eyes flicking in every direction, checking his chosen path as well as his flanks. This was, after all, the very heart of the volatile Federally Administered Tribal Areas—a fancy name for the most dangerous armpit of the world. Any moment any one of the dozens of warring tribes, or even opium smugglers, could show up in pickup trucks loaded with armed men to get a piece of whatever it was they thought was going down here.

The Kidon needed to wrap up his business here and get the hell out of Dodge before that happened.

Right hand on the UZI's pistol grip, shooting finger resting on the trigger casing, left hand under the barrel, he paused at the edge of a street too narrow for anything but foot traffic.

He nodded to himself.

Zameer, for all his shortcomings, was actually right. They could not have turned the Land Cruiser around and chosen another side street to follow the other Goats.

Verifying that the street was clear, he turned left, ignoring the stares of men, women, children, a donkey, and even two damned goats—all scrambling out of his way as he reached the dusty soccer field.

He stopped, risking a peek around the corner.

Satisfied that he held the element of surprise, Aaron ran across the width of the block, stopping at the end and once more risking a glance beyond the corner.

He stared at the one-on-one battle still raging, reminding him of a tennis match.

Zameer's staccato gunfire pounded the Goat while the al Qaeda man huddled behind the rear tire, waiting for reloading pauses from Zameer to return fire with his AK-47. Then it was his informant's window to fire back as the lone al Qaeda man restocked. Muzzle flashes came alive from the Land Cruiser, tearing into the Russian 4×4, flattening tires, shattering windows, and hammering sheet metal. The bulletproof Land Cruiser, however, had stood up to the attack quite well—its run-flat tires were still inflated, the transparent armor grazed but intact. He could only hope that the Kevlar protecting the engine and other vital components was also holding up, because the Toyota was his only ticket out of this hellhole.

He took a moment to assess his mark. The man seemed a bit on the older side and was dressed in the clean and darker clothes typical of al Qaeda commanders. And if that was indeed the case, and if he could capture him alive, perhaps Aaron could get the opportunity to—

A stray 9mm Parabellum round from Zameer's UZI punched the mud wall behind the Goat, near the corner, inches from Aaron's vantage point.

Aaron reacted fast, jerking his face out of the way as bursts of debris shot by like a shotgun blast.

For the love of . . .

His back against the wall, eyes settling on the wide mud tracks cut across the soccer field by the Goats that got away—and while Zameer's near misses continued buzzing by wildly—the Kidon considered his options. Approaching his mark during one of his reloading pauses would certainly minimize the chances of the bastard welcoming him with a loaded weapon. But doing so would expose Aaron to Zameer's imprecise fire, which nearly tore off his head a moment ago. On the other hand, approaching during the middle of an al Qaeda counterstrike meant all gunfire would be directed away from him— plus the noise would minimize the chance of the rebel hearing him.

Making his decision, he waited for the latter, stepping off the corner the instant Zameer paused to reload and the al Qaeda soldier surged from behind the Goat to return fire.

Peretz sprinted with tenacity, covering two hundred feet in fifteen seconds while assessing the enemy, knowing he would only get one chance at this.

Bringing the UZI up, he aligned the front and rear sights on the back of the man's left knee, putting a single round through it at a distance of a dozen feet.

The firing stopped abruptly, replaced by the screams of the very surprised survivor, who dropped his weapon and collapsed, hands on his wounded limb.

The Kidon was on top of him before the al Qaeda soldier could react, kicking away the assault rifle while shouting at Zameer to get the hell over there.

Aaron worked quickly, turning the man over and flex-cuffing his wrists behind his back. Unsheathing his old and trusty Israeli combat knife, a seven-inch ferro-blackened D2 stainless steel blade, he sliced into his captive's partug trousers near the left knee, exposing the wound, which did not appear as severe as he had feared.

The round had only nicked the right side of the joint, causing minimal bleeding. But just to be sure, he used the blade to slice material off the bottom of the partug to make a field tourniquet, which he applied tightly right above the injury.

"Kill me . . . infidel!" the man hissed in Urdu while Aaron stanched the blood flow. "I'm not afraid to die!"

"And you'll do that soon enough," the Kidon replied fluently, as he heard the Land Cruiser coming around and he stared in the direction that the other Goats had gone. "But not yet. Definitely not yet."

20

The Ba'i

KANDAHAR AIRFIELD. SOUTHWESTERN AFGHANISTAN.

A jolt of pain shot down his jaw, but Nasseer ignored it. His steady gaze was on the new Ba'i sitting across from him, inside the dark tent pitched just past the entrance to the NATO base.

Outside the sun had yet to rise over the eastern rim rock, leaving the base in the yellowish haze of floodlights. But the Ba'i's tent was off to the side, in the shadows of a towering perimeter wall, and he limited light inside to a single candle burning between them, its flickering flame unable to pierce the darkness of the surrounding canvas walls.

He is older than the last one, the Shinwari warrior thought, staring at the man's bald head, salt-and-pepper beard, which he kept short, and a pair of dark eyes under thick brows. He used a small flashlight to inspect the seized laptops and cell phones.

The American's rugged and heavily lined face—like his own—suggested a lifetime of fieldwork. Nasseer liked that.

"Exactly *where* did you find this?" the Ba'i asked in fluent Pashto. Nasseer also liked that; the last Ba'i had required a translator.

Still wearing the linked ammo belt slung sash-style over his shoulders, the standing end feeding the large PK resting against the table, the Shinwari chief leaned forward. Inspecting the map for a moment, he extended an index finger with a missing fingernail and pointed at a spot halfway up the Sulaimans. The place was a two-day ride from the base. "There is a cave . . . here. We killed eight of theirs, but yours were already dead." Nasseer didn't see the point of explaining that the woman had been alive when they found her.

The Ba'i shifted his gaze to the soldiers in desert fatigues who were carrying the remains off one of Nasseer's trucks and depositing them in black body bags.

Returning his attention to the Shinwari warrior, he said, "My predecessor spoke highly of you."

Nasseer considered the compliment. But in his world, compliments usually tagged along with requests.

The American added, "He said that your information was always reliable."

Nasseer shrugged while looking about the tent, his eyes drifting to what looked like three six-shot, revolver-style Milkor M32 grenade launchers next to four boxes of assorted 40mm shells, behind the folding table, though it was hard to see clearly behind the Ba'i. Finally he said, "We fight a common enemy."

The American, dressed in light clothes and army boots, grinned at Nasseer when he caught him staring at the promised goods.

Revealing two rows of glistening white teeth, the Ba'i asked, "Do you like what you see?"

Nasseer stared in silence at the man's healthy mouth while the tip of his own tongue grazed the rotten molar stabbing his nervous system again. He wondered if the Ba'i would be willing to throw a few hours of work from the base's dentist into the bargain.

But he could never ask for such personal favor, nor could he admit publicly to the pain. Instead he just replied, "As long as the weapons and shells are good."

"Factory-new gear and ammo, Nasseer. It's a fair deal."

Nasseer didn't reply. He just stared at the American. The thing about fairness was that it typically meant "fairness" to the party *claiming* it was fair. Still, he had to admit that three M32s plus lots of shells—irrespective of the information stored in those computers and phones—did look quite fair to him.

"I like to trade."

"So do I," the Ba'i said, taking the laptops and cell phones and depositing them inside a large rucksack by his feet, acknowledging acceptance. Then he reached behind him to place the launchers and the shells on the table to complete the trade.

And that's when Nasseer noticed the figure standing just beyond the hardware, dark clothes blending in with the shadows hiding the canvas walls.

Nasseer didn't like that. His prior trades had been private. His men had to wait outside, as did anyone the Ba'i brought along. But perhaps the new American wasn't accustomed to the one-on-one trading rules of his country.

Deciding to let it go this time, Nasser opened a box of nine 40mm shells arranged in a three-by-three pattern, a combination of M381 high explosive, XM1060 thermobaric, and M576 buckshot variants. The latter housed twenty-four-grain metal pellets that burst outward during detonation, shredding anything in a twenty-foot radius. The high explosive round represented the more traditional fragmentation grenade, wrecking vehicles, buildings, or humans in a fifteen-foot radius. But it was the XM1060 that impressed him. Its kill mechanism combined a pressure wave, the subsequent vacuum that ruptured lungs and eardrums, the high-temperature fuel deflagration that burned to the bone, and the lethal propylene oxide gas.

"That's one mean shell," the American observed, while Nasseer inspected it.

Nasseer nodded, having seen all three types in action over the years. The XM1060 was certainly the deadliest—and the cruelest—of them all.

"Now," the American added, "while we appreciate the computers and cell phones, and also the chance to bury our own, I hope my predecessor explained to you the value of delivering *live* soldiers. It translates into even better weapons than these . . . perhaps Javelins."

Nasseer blinked at the mention of the advanced rocket system. He had seen it in action, used by the U.S. Marines against Taliban positions, and was impressed by its range, accuracy, and deadly punch—hundreds of times more powerful than any 40mm shell.

He tightened his jaw at the thought of getting his hands on those missiles, but in doing so he inadvertently ground his upper teeth against his rotten molar and the stinging pain nearly made him lose control of his bladder muscles.

The American's expression changed a bit in response to his inability to control his own facial muscles, if only for an instant. But before the Ba'i could say something, Nasseer replied, "I know. But Allah did not will it this time."

Locking down the pain while swallowing a gulp of bitterness, he replaced the shells in the carrying box, closed it, and picked up one of the launchers. He had never handled an M32 before, and it must have been obvious, because the American said, "I will be happy to provide training."

Nasseer considered the offer but said, "Thank you, Ba'i. But training will come."

"As you wish," the Ba'i replied, before producing a phone and tilting the screen toward him. "I do have one small question."

"Yes?"

"Have you seen anyone wearing this ring?"

Nasseer leaned forward to get a better view, inspecting the image of what looked like an old Soviet ring. Slowly, he shook his head.

"If you do," the American said, "any information would be worth a *lot*." Putting the phone away, the Ba'i lowered his voice and added, "Even *more* than live soldiers. Understand?"

"I understand," replied Nasseer. He then spent a minute inspecting the shoulder-fired weapon with its six-round revolver-style magazine. He extended the stock and wedged it against his right shoulder, right hand on the pistol grip and left on the handle beneath the muzzle forward of the magazine, feeling the launcher's balance.

Setting it back on the table, Nasseer decided that, all things considered, the raid two nights ago had yielded plenty, including newer AK-47s and ammunition for his team and, now, reliable grenade launchers, which provided him with a tactical advantage. The M32s would enable him to take on a larger force with confidence, and that alone was plenty fair to him.

Standing, Nasseer bowed respectfully and said, "*As-salamu alaykum.*" *May peace be with you.*

The American also stood, returned the bow, and said, "*Walaykum as-salamm.*" *And peace be upon you.*

Nasseer called Hassan and two other men inside to carry the weapons and shells. Per their unwritten protocol, no one spoke while they took possession of the gear and headed back out to their weathered pickup trucks.

As Nasseer turned to leave, he caught another glimpse of the figure standing in the background. He shifted his gaze between it and the American while also slightly shaking his head, hoping the Ba'i was smart enough to understand the subtle message.

And then he walked away, got in one of the 4×4 vehicles, and drove off the airfield.

21

Piss and Vinegar

KANDAHAR AIRFIELD. SOUTHWESTERN AFGHANISTAN.

"Well, boss, hopefully Pancho Villa there and his banditos won't blow themselves up to kingdom-fucking-come. There's more to those M32s than just loading, aiming, and shooting."

Harwich turned around, suppressing a heavy sigh as a tall, young

Hispanic woman materialized from the shadows in the rear of the tent. He took a moment to contemplate Langley's answer to the current shortage of CIA field officers at the base: interagency cooperation in the form of breaking in FBI Special Agent Monica Cruz.

He settled for a shrug while wondering if "babysitting" was the more appropriate descriptor. "Well, Cruz, in case you haven't noticed, this is a simple tit-for-tat gig. They brought back our guys so their families can bury them, and I give them something in return that they didn't already have."

Monica was thin but muscular, wearing a pair of standard-issue army camouflage pants, boots, and a black FBI T-shirt. A holstered Glock hung from her army belt, within easy reach of her right hand, opposite an SOG knife. She wore her hair longer than regulation but kept it in a ponytail that reached between her shoulder blades and whipped behind her as she walked briskly around the table and sat in the empty chair left by Nasseer.

Leaning back and resting the soles of her boots against the side of the table, she resembled more a rebellious teenager than the professional described in the CIA brief. United States Marine Corps scout sniper with four tours, two in Iraq and two right here, where she earned a Purple Heart and a Silver Star, followed by three years with the LA SWAT team and now the Bureau.

Harwich kept his poker face on while trying to match the brief he had read on the way here to this woman unsheathing an SOG knife and using it to trim and clean her short fingernails. She was supposed to be thirty-one but didn't look a day older than his daughter, Samantha, currently a senior at NYU. As opposed to him, who was supposed to be forty-five but looked deep in his fifties, especially with his bald head and salt-and-pepper beard that lately had more salt than pepper.

"All the same, boss," she said, eyes on the field manicure as he heard Nasseer and his men driving off. "It takes the average marine a couple of weeks of training to become proficient—and safe—with that launcher. You ask me, I sure hope our guys are nowhere in the vicinity when the bandolier mullah decides to light one up."

"He's not a mullah."

"Whatever."

Harwich silently thanked Langley for the wonderful surprise that had been waiting for him when he had deplaned that C-17 two nights ago.

"So, indulge me," she said at his silence using the shiny knife as a pointing device. "How do you know that skinny little bastard didn't just kill our guys and then brought them here to trade?"

"Unlikely." He looked at the iPad in front of him, which contained the classified brief on Nasseer, who had provided solid intelligence to his predecessor for the past two years. "They're the good guys."

"Sure," Monica said, twisting her lips into a frown. "*This* time around."

"Not sure what you mean," Harwich said. "Nasseer has—"

"Gotta admit, boss," she interrupted, "we have this nasty little habit of arming tomorrow's enemies. And in my book, I call that a tit-for-*fuck-you*-tat gig."

Harwich couldn't suppress a sigh this time, letting it out while frowning and also nodding. Feisty or not, the young agent certainly had a point—one he unfortunately happened to have firsthand knowledge of. America did have such history, dating back as far as he could remember.

It had armed and trained Vietnam's Ho Chi Minh during World War II to fight the Japanese, just to turn back and engage him in that bitter war during the 1960s and 1970s.

It *heavily* armed Joseph Stalin during World War II to fight the Germans, just to turn around and have to deal with a formidable Soviet Union in the decades-long Cold War.

It armed Saddam Hussein in the early eighties to fight the Iranians, just to turn back around and overthrow him years later.

It armed Panama's General Manuel Noriega, just to turn back around and depose him years later.

It even armed, trained, and defended Saudi Arabia from a Saddam Hussein it too had armed and trained to fight the Iranians, just to have the Saudis fund, arm, and train ISIS in its fight against the United States and its allies.

Hell, Harwich even had the unenviable honor of having armed and trained Osama bin Laden back in the day, as part of America's fight against the very Soviet monster it had helped create during World War II.

And look where that got us, he thought, pained by the irony of having played a part in the creation of al Qaeda in a world that was truly upside down.

Harwich regarded this unexpectedly insightful woman, who had gone back to filing and shaping, working the serrated blade glistening in the candlelight. Her decadelong experience had not left even a single wrinkle on that smooth honey-colored face, while he was starting to resemble the Shar-Pei his ex-wife grabbed during their divorce five years ago.

"Good try on the ring, though."

"Yeah," Harwich replied. "Worth a shot."

"Any word yet from this mysterious CIA contractor team of yours that's supposed to be at KAF?"

Harwich dropped his gaze at his phone. Since his arrival here he had been unable to connect with this Colonel Hunter Stark that his predecessor had on a retainer. The man had ignored his multiple text messages and phone calls. But then again, he wasn't sure what he could have the man and his team do, as Harwich had been unable to unearth one ounce of intelligence on the damn image of the old Soviet ring.

And he was beginning to wonder if he ever would. Which made him question his decision to leave his plush post at the Paris station to come to this shithole of a—

An explosion rocked the base, followed immediately by the rattle of automatic weapons.

"What the—" Harwich began to say, in the time it took Monica to leap from her chair and dash out of the tent with her Glock already drawn.

22

Operators

Monica moved quickly, racing down the side of the towering concrete wall toward the smoke spiraling skyward beyond the main gate, less than five hundred feet away.

Behind her, Harwich screamed for her to wait for him.

Keep up, boss, she thought, as the airfield's floodlights flickered in the twilight of dawn, the looming sun splashing streaks of orange and yellow across the indigo sky.

A dozen marines guarded the main gate, where perimeter walls gave way to waist-high concrete barriers staggered fifty feet in front of the first level of base security. Their M4 carbines, aimed at an enemy she still could not see, flashed a deafening, stroboscopic barrage of 5.65×45mm hell into the boiling inky cloud shrouding the gate.

Suicide bombers.

She looked about her without breaking her stride, searching for Nasseer and his team, but the Shinwari clan was long gone.

How convenient, she thought, as alarms blared across the compound. Before long the base's fast-response team would reach the gate to reinforce the marine contingent.

But Monica beat them to it, running up to the closest three soldiers, their stances firm, legs spread apart, rifles aimed at the dozen or so figures dressed in white who were emerging through the smoke screen beyond the barriers. The rest of the gate detail also swung their weapons toward them, firing as one, cutting down the threat.

And that's when she noticed three shadows clad in black, shifting in the haze off to her right, a couple hundred feet away, rushing up the side of the perimeter wall in a deep crouch, chests wrapped in explosives. She saw the wires dangling under their right arms, rigging the charges to detonators in their right hands.

Monica yelled while aligning the closest figure, but the gunfire drowned her voice, the diversion achieving its desire effect, drawing the attention of the marines away from the incoming trio.

Harwich ran up to her, clutching a SIG Sauer P220 in his right hand.

"It's a fucking Kansas City Shuffle, boss!" she screamed, recalling the scheme of misdirecting the mark to look in one direction while sneaking up to it from the opposite side.

Harwich understood immediately, shouting back, "Taliban style!"

Standing shoulder to shoulder with her CIA superior, Monica fired multiple times, the Glock recoiling, ejecting spent cartridges, then sliding in fresh ones from the ten-round magazine. Harwich did the same with the SIG.

One of the rebels went down, then another. But the moment they did, she realized her mistake, and she yelled even louder as she saw, almost in slow motion, the insurgents' right hands releasing dead man's switches.

Harwich must have noticed it too, because he spun back to get behind the wall just as she did. They bumped into each other as they scrambled to put some reinforced concrete between them and the—

Deafening and blinding, the blast engulfed all three insurgents in a ball of flames and smoke that mixed with the thick haze from the initial blast. Even with the towering wall providing partial cover, the shock wave slammed her chest like a fist from God, tossing her back several feet.

She landed on her side, hard, the pain arresting, her ears ringing, her vision blurred.

Blinking, Monica looked up with considerable effort, shaking her head before sitting up and checking her limbs, exhaling when she saw everything still attached where it should be. She also noticed that she still held the Glock.

Staggering to her feet with difficulty, a headache forming in her temples, a powerful ringing in her ears, and feeling light-headed and nauseated, she noticed Harwich slowly rolling on his back a few feet away.

He looked as stunned as she felt, his wide-eyed stare glaring about, trying to get his bearings. Beyond him, barely visible through the dust and smoke hovering over the fortified entrance, she recognized the shapes of several marines sprawled about. Unlike Harwich and her, the soldiers had experienced the full force of three explosive vests from a distance of one hundred feet.

And beyond them, skirting the blistering smoke, several silhouettes materialized from the darkness and the pitch-black haze, advancing toward the temporarily unguarded gate with obvious haste and determination. A few hundred feet to their right and left, two additional groups of armed men raced toward them.

"Get up, boss!" she screamed, though her voice seemed distant, removed, a result of the explosion. "We're about to be overrun!"

Headlights loomed in the distance from multiple points across the base as a detachment of soldiers raced to the rescue. She could also hear the *whop-whop* sound of helicopters taking flight on the airfield at the opposite end of the base. But they were still at least a minute away, while the insurgents were seconds from breaching the perimeter.

Mustering strength, ignoring the mounting headache and her aching body, and not waiting for Harwich, Monica did her best to face the incoming threat. Holstering the Glock, she took a knee by a fallen soldier and grabbed the M4 next to him.

Her fingers moved automatically, verifying a chambered round. Remaining in a kneeling position, she aimed the M4 at the closest wave of assholes and fired seven rounds before the rifle ran dry.

As she cursed and snagged a fresh magazine from the marine's ammo belt, a line of bullets from the threat now less than a hundred feet away ripped through the dirt a foot from her.

Shit!

She rolled away on instinct while swapping magazines. But she never got the chance to fire another round. Her shoulder struck something hard, like a log, breaking her roll.

It was the right boot of the largest man she'd ever seen, with arms

as wide as her thighs, wielding an air-cooled .50-caliber M2 Browning machine gun. His features were hidden with camouflage cream
beneath a Stars and Stripes bandanna. Dressed in a Special Forces
black uniform under body armor, the giant aimed his cannon at the
insurgents.

"Stay down, little miss!" he shouted in a baritone voice, opening
up his monster of a gun, which was fed by an ammunition belt stowed
in a large rucksack hanging from his right shoulder.

He did not just fucking call me "little miss"!

Monica was momentarily taken aback by the reverberating noise
and awe of this weapon, and she grimaced while getting showered
with hot spent cartridges. But before she could get out of the way, the
man had leaped over her, running toward the insurgents while mowing them down.

Three more men followed Goliath and his mighty cannon,
running around her and Harwich. One was completely bald and quite
husky, built like a pit bull and clutching a suppressed Heckler &
Koch MP5A1. He was followed by a similarly built man sporting a
full head of dark hair and by a short and wiry man with ash blond
hair, a thick mustache, and a damn lollipop in his mouth. Both were
also armed with MP5A1s.

They dashed past her like ghosts, cruising through the haze and
the pungent smell of cordite from the explosions while firing their
submachine guns.

Who are these guys?

The blond soldier glanced down at her while firing. The lollipop
shifted as he shouted over the noise of the reports, "This ain't no
place for skirts!"

Monica stared in disbelief.

He did not just say that!

Anger made her surge to her feet, clutching the M4 and scrambling after them as the foursome tore into at least thirty insurgents
with a mixed-caliber barrage.

Monica joined in the fight, ignoring the side stares from the chauvinistic assholes, focusing her fire on the right flank, near the charred
concrete marking the spot where the suicide trio had detonated their
vests. Several insurgents emerged through the smoke veiling the

lower section of the perimeter wall. She limited her shooting to single rounds, making each count, but doing so made her momentarily ignore her left flank.

Her peripheral vision caught, at the last minute, two dark figures materializing through the haze. But before she could shift targets, she felt the unambiguous energy of two .50-caliber rounds whooshing overhead, ripping through the air just before both insurgents vanished behind clouds of crimson.

Sniper, she thought, as Harwich stepped up to her and covered her open flank with another M4 carbine and she returned her attention to the men trying to sneak in by the wall.

The force of six worked in unison with overlapping arcs of fire, cutting down the threat with synchronized accuracy. Then some of the insurgents began to fall forward, shot from behind and from the side by an unseen ally.

As the Humvees reached the front gate and a pair of Apache helicopters zoomed overhead, dispersing the smoke, Monica spotted Nasseer and his clan off to the right of the main gate, laying down suppressive fire from behind their 4×4s, tearing into the Taliban lines with multiple volleys of surgical destruction. The Shinwari boss held his Russian PK machine gun in his right hand while holding the belt feeding it with his left in an impressive display of strength and control.

Harwich waved at the Shinwari warriors, who continued flanking the Taliban rebels.

Two weathered coupes raced up the main road from the center of town, less than a mile away, drawing the attention of the Apaches. The attack helicopters banked toward the fast-moving threat while unloading a dozen Hydra rockets and 30mm fire from their underside M230 chain guns. It was a brief but fiery, and even synchronized, show that dwarfed the suicide vest explosions and pretty much vaporized the incoming cars before they got anywhere near the base.

But during the middle of the attack, as everyone stared at the Apache's massive display of force, another wave of insurgents mounted a last-ditch effort. Monica spotted them first, taking aim at two rebels armed with RPGs and approaching a concrete barrier. A half dozen rounds struck the insurgents in the chest. They dropped their

launchers while collapsing—and while the four soldiers, plus Harwich, stared at her.

"Good shooting, little miss!" the big guy with the big Browning
shouted in his booming voice.

"Not bad for a fucking skirt, huh?" Monica retorted, while the
blond soldier grinned and winked, a lollipop protruding from the
corner of his mouth, fingers playing with one end of his ridiculous
mustache, which reminded Monica of porn stars from the 1980s.

It ended as quickly as it had started, especially after a hundred marines set up M2 and M240 machine gun defensive fighting positions
around the gate and four Apaches patrolled the field leading to the
road into town. Units deployed in and around the city of Kandahar
were pulled back to protect the airfield. In addition, all aircraft, armored vehicles, and NATO divisions participating in Operation
Mountain Thrust, fighting insurgents in the Sulaimans, were recalled as KAF went into lockdown mode.

Monica inspected the carnage they had inflicted on the enemy
while ambulances hauled away wounded marines who had miracu-
lously survived the attack. Harwich thanked Nasseer and his team
for a timely intervention, before he went on to find any survivors
among the Taliban and bring them to the detention center for interrogation. Before Monica joined him, she watched the four nameless
soldiers disappear in the controlled chaos of a base recovering from
an attack. She then stared at the line of machine gun emplacements
set amid new concrete barriers shielding them from the cruel and
unpredictable land that was Afghanistan.

But beyond the smoke and war equipment, beyond the vast poppy
fields leading into town—past the mud-and-brick skyline of bazaars,
mosques, and markets—two UAZ-469 Goats reached the eastern
edge of town after a nonstop journey south from Jalalabad.

The two-car caravan turned west on highway A1 and crossed the
city without disruption, going around checkpoints and roadblocks
abandoned in haste moments ago by direct orders from NATO High
Command at Kandahar Airfield.

The tired and weary travelers continued west for another fifty miles, following the foot of the Sulaimans, before turning left on Southwest Road 2 and then right on an unmarked trail that eventually led them up steep switchbacks carved into the side of the mountain to a compound nestled in the dense wooded gradients high above Lashkar Gah.

23

A Pound of Flesh

JALALABAD. NORTHERN AFGHANISTAN.

It had taken the Kidon a couple of hours to break the al Qaeda man.

He could have done it sooner, but he had to pause twice to let Zameer vomit.

In the end, Aaron had asked his informant to just wait outside the Mossad safe house on the outskirts of town, where they had driven the Land Cruiser after exiting the Khyber Pass.

Strapped to a table, writhing in inconceivable pain, the insurgent continued begging for a bullet—anything to end a treatment no prisoner could endure, few interrogators could dispense, and most could not witness without getting sick.

"Please," Qadeer mumbled. "Please . . . end this . . ."

"Soon, my friend," he whispered. "I just need to be certain."

So he waited, leaving the needles in place at specific spots in the man's body to amplify the pain he had inflicted with a scalpel while also keeping Qadeer in a state of hyperawareness, preventing his body from shutting down. In a way, the technique was the opposite of Chinese acupuncture.

Qadeer had not budged when Aaron cut him, but he could not

tolerate the way those needles stimulated his nervous system, smothering all semblance of resistance.

"That is . . . where they are . . . going . . . I swear," he mumbled, before once more begging for it to end.

Aaron examined the deliberate damage he had inflicted on this man, removing just the right pound of flesh from just the right places before letting the needles do their magical work.

"But there is nothing there," Aaron replied, looking at the location north of Lashkar Gah where the man claimed there was an old Soviet compound from the 1980s.

"There . . . is . . . I swear . . . Oh, please . . . kill me."

Aaron stared into the man's surviving eye. "I believe you," he finally said. "Now, tell me more about this bomb."

Drenched in sweat, Aaron stepped out thirty minutes later and found Zameer sitting by the railing around the front porch, a cigarette in his right hand, which was still trembling.

The Hindu Kush mountains rose sharply while traversing the nation from the northeast to the southwest, becoming the Sulaimans near the middle of the country.

"Are you okay?" he asked his informant.

He nodded slowly, his eyes on those distant snowcapped peaks. "Yes, sahib. I've just never seen . . ."

"I know. Dirty business. But necessary."

"Did you . . . learn what you needed to?"

Aaron nodded, his eyes shifting south. "I did. And I need to leave right away."

"Where?" Zameer said, making a face.

The Kidon tapped the informant on the shoulder. "Take the Land Cruiser. Head back to Pakistan. I'll be in touch."

Zameer narrowed his stare. "But . . . how are you going to—"

"I'll manage. Now get out of here. Someone is coming to clean up in there," he said. "And you don't want to be anywhere near here when they arrive."

24

RN-40

COMPOUND 57. SULAIMAN MOUNTAINS.
SOUTHERN AFGHANISTAN.

The brothers embraced after nearly five years apart—since Akaa had fled the country in the wake of the American invasion following the September 11 attacks. Pasha had gone with him while Akhtar remained behind to lead the holy resistance movement in Kandahar province.

They cried, laughed, and cried some more. Their journey from those early years of battling the Soviets in the mountains alongside Osama bin Laden had been violent, turbulent, and intensely unpredictable. They fought the invasion force with everything they had, from Chinese automatic weapons and mortars to hit-and-run attacks in the middle of the night to car bombs. They buried IEDs along all Soviet access roads and launched rocket strikes against their garrisons. They were outarmed and outnumbered, but the mujahideen believed they had Allah on their side—plus the Americans. Areas like the Panjshir Valley, the Sulaiman Mountains, and Jalalabad turned into killing fields, with the death count on both sides rising to insane levels.

But the rebels persevered through a war of terror, instilling fear in the heart of the enemy, shooting down their aircraft with Stinger missiles, making them pay dearly for every town they took, every road they secured, and every hill they controlled. The Soviets could defeat the insurgents in any given region, but they could not keep them defeated. Sooner or later the mujahideen would strike back, frustrating the Soviets' best efforts to achieve control of any given area for very long. They kept up the pressure, using their iron will against Soviet technology, until the pain level was too hard for Moscow to stomach. And in May of 1988, Moscow began a ten-month-long withdrawal from the embattled nation.

After the invading force returned home, the communist government left in place held on to Kabul for almost three years, supplied by Moscow.

Akhtar remembered the day when the mujahideen finally liberated the city, though the intense fighting had left it in ruins. But they had done it. The underfed mountain goats had repelled the mighty bear. He had been just a boy when Kabul fell, and so had Pasha. But boys or not, Akaa had made sure they had done their part in the fighting. He had made sure their pesh-kabz blades were stained with Soviet blood.

But those glorious days following their victory were short-lived.

Soon—and much to bin Laden's detriment—Pashtuns, Tajiks, Hazaras, Uzbeks, and a host of other rival factions that made up the mujahideen turned on one another for control of the government. And the civil war didn't limit itself to Kabul. Herat, Kandahar, Mazar-i-Sharif, Lashkar Gah, and other cities also became embroiled in chaos as tribes attacked each another viciously, without regard for civilians caught in the cross fire.

The fighting was no longer about jihad. And it certainly wasn't about the good of the Afghan people. It was about power, about control. And it was bloodier and crueler than the war against the Soviets.

So Osama bin Laden had to step in.

By then he had already founded al Qaeda, an organization global in scope, seeking to reinstate an Islamic caliphate around the world. When word got out that gunmen at militia checkpoints in Kandahar and other cities had begun raping women, Akaa forged an alliance with Mullah Mohammed Omar, leader of the largest group of former mujahideen, the Taliban. The alliance between al Qaeda and the Taliban had been quite natural, since both believed in a strict interpretation of Islamic law. But while al Qaeda maintained its focus on global jihad, the Taliban concentrated on restoring order inside Afghanistan.

The Taliban declared holy war against rapists, thieves, and

murderers. The madness—the violations of Sharia law—would not be tolerated.

It had not been the Taliban's intention to take power or to rule the country, at least not in the beginning. They had been simply trying to restore order. But to do so, they had to be ruthless about enforcing the law.

Akhtar remembered the executions outside Kabul's Olympic soccer stadium, where he and Pasha had been among the young warriors tasked with carrying out sentences handed down from Taliban tribunals. They cut off the hands of those guilty of theft, shot rapists, beat men failing to comply with Sharia dress codes and beards, and stoned to death women accused of adultery.

It had not been easy.

But it had been necessary to unite a nation.

By 1996, the Taliban controlled Kabul, and by 1998, most of the country.

Until the Americans came.

Akhtar stared at his brother. As with him, the long war had been harsh on Pasha, lining his once smooth face.

"I have missed you, brother," Akhtar said, as they stood in the small courtyard just past the fortified entrance to a compound built by the Soviets back in the 1980s as a mountain headquarters. It was located almost nine thousand feet up the Sulaimans, on a wooded plateau overlooking Lashkar Gah.

Moscow had spared no expense. The place was a citadel. Reinforced concrete walls, instead of mud and stone, rose two stories high against a steep wall of granite. It included a basement bomb shelter with an escape tunnel into the opposite face of the mountain. Watchtowers at every corner overlooked the rectangular property, and a twelve-foot wall surrounded it all. Given the altitude, large conifers, primarily towering *Cedrus deodara* and stone pines, cast a permanent shadow beneath their wide and overlapping canopies, shielding the compound from the scorching sun. But more importantly, the trees hid Akhtar's headquarters from American UAVs.

A cold breeze swept down the snowy peaks capping the mountain range, rustling branches and chilling his face. Pasha, wearing camouflage pants under a long cashmere tunic, a round woolen pakol hiding his short dark hair, slowly nodded while regarding his older brother with eyes that sagged at the ends.

"It has been a long and treacherous journey. But Allah was merciful." He pointed at the scientist getting out of the car, a short and wiry man with salt-and-pepper hair, a wispy mustache, and round wire glasses.

"Allah *and* our beloved Akaa," Akhtar added. "Plus the warriors we had to sacrifice." At the last count, the attack on Kandahar had cost him more than thirty-five men.

"I hope it is all worth it, brother," Pasha said. "We lost a lot of good men, including Uncle Qadeer."

Akhtar didn't know that, and he grimaced when a pain stabbed his gut. For a moment he wasn't sure if it was the need to opiate or the loss of a blood relative, but in the end it didn't really matter. It had to be done.

"The Americans, the Russians, the British, and the French have them," Akhtar said, turning to face the man Pasha had introduced as Dr. Ali Khan. "The Chinese, the Indians, the Pakistanis, and even the damn Jews have them. And now you will help us add Afghanistan to the list of states with nuclear weapons."

"And in return you leave my family alone?" Dr. Khan asked.

"You have my word," replied Akhtar.

"So far I have not been impressed." The scientist crossed his arms and just glared at Akhtar through his little glasses.

"Come again?" Akhtar said.

Stretching an index finger up to Akhtar's face, Dr. Khan said, "You put my family in danger with that firefight outside my home, and then you almost got me killed in the pass."

Akhtar looked at Pasha, confused.

His younger brother shrugged. "Somebody betrayed us and sent the SSG to the professor's house. We had to fight our way out."

"Like I said," Dr. Khan said, "*not* impressed."

"Professor," Akhtar said, working hard at measuring his words, "it would be wise not to test my patience."

"Then stop testing mine."

Akhtar looked at Pasha, who just shrugged again and said, "The balls on this guy, huh? See what I've been putting up with, brother?

Maybe I should cut them off and see if his attitude tempers, like the goats?" Pasha placed a hand on his pesh-kabz.

"I will do *my* job," Dr. Khan retorted, stabbing himself in the chest with an index finger. "The question is, can you do yours properly so I can do mine?"

Akhtar fought the urge to reach for his own pesh-kabz and peel the skin off his face while Pasha gelded the little bastard. But bin Laden had sent the man, and they did need his expertise.

So he took a deep breath, counted to ten, and just grinned and said, "Then *show* me, Professor. Show me by taking a look at what we have."

They descended to the basement, where the Russian weapon rested on a lab table. It was just under ten feet in length and almost two feet in diameter, painted silver and green.

Anticipating the needs of the scientist, Akhtar had arranged two tables packed with an assortment of tools, mostly stolen from various raids. He had also set up two video cameras to record the disassembly process. The air conditioner controlling the temperature and humidity in the room hummed quietly, powered by the same refurbished Soviet diesel generators that were providing electricity to the compound.

Dr. Khan, now dressed in a white lab coat, as were three men designated to assist him, stood in front of the weapon. He spoke slowly into a lapel microphone connected to a waist transmitter slaved to one of the cameras.

Akhtar and Pasha stood to the side, out of the range of either video recorder. The scientist took his time eyeballing the bomb before perusing the tools on both tables, settling on a small adjustable wrench.

"The Russian RN-40 tactical nuclear device exterior appears in good condition," Dr. Khan began in a forensic, monotone voice. "We are dealing with a gun-type fission nuclear device designed to detonate at a preprogrammed altitude for an airburst, or via a nose contact fuze for a groundburst. It gets its name because of its gun barrel shape. At one end conventional explosives fire a projectile made of stacked uranium-235 rings down the length of a bore gun tube, sliding over a second set of smaller-diameter U-235 target rings, achieving the required critical mass to trigger a fission event. In the case of the RN-40, the yield is estimated to be in the thirty-kiloton range, or twice the size of the Hiroshima bomb."

One of the guards standing next to Akhtar began chanting to Allah, and Akhtar quickly slapped him on the back of the head.

Dr. Khan frowned at the guard, who was quietly rearranging his turban, then said, "We will start disassembly by removing the front nose locknut, which attaches to the main steel rod holding the nose contact fuze, altimeter radar, batteries, and U-235 target rings."

The professor's hands moved with expert ease. It was obvious to Akhtar that he had done this before during his years helping to build Pakistan's land- and air-based nuclear warheads, which numbered close to 130.

"Well, he seems to know what he's doing," Akhtar whispered to Pasha.

"Yeah, and that's too bad," Pasha replied.

Akhtar gave him a sideways glance.

Pasha shrugged. "I was looking forward to dragging him outside by his dick before feeding it to him."

"Oh, how I've missed you, brother," said Akhtar.

The locknut came off easily, allowing the professor to slide off the heavy steel nose plug forging, which resembled a gym weight. Two assistants carried it to a fourth table, set up for disassembled components, where the third assistant measured the component, weighed it, and tagged it.

Dr. Khan then slid off the impact-absorbing anvil and the tungsten carbide tamper plug, both resembling thick metallic cylinders. The contact fuze was next, and the professor took extra care in its removal, unplugging the wires connected to the trigger mechanism. This was delicate work, especially given the state of uncertainty about the weapon. Like everything else, the removed components were tagged while the cameras recorded the process for future reassembly, for propaganda, and for any other purposes Akaa might devise.

Akhtar watched the proceedings with interest and anticipation, finding it difficult to keep quiet, wanting to ask Dr. Khan about the state of every component. But he held back, choosing to lead by example, allowing the scientist to do his work.

It took all three assistants almost an hour to remove the outer shell, which came off in a dozen sections attached to a steel skeleton, finally exposing the gun-shaped mechanism. He also removed the tail fins, the parachute, various explosive bolts, lift lugs, and two layers of armor plating.

By the time Dr. Khan stepped back to inspect the actual weapon, he had detached almost three hundred pounds of material from the device.

He worked on the back of the bomb next, inspecting the electric gun primers, primer wiring, and conventional explosive charge designed to shoot the U-235 projectile rings down the gun tube. A protective steel back and a tungsten carbide disk insulated the delicate U-235 projectile rings from the explosives. Dr. Khan removed and inspected everything, making notes before passing them to his assistants.

Three hours into the process, they sat by the disassembled components while reviewing his notes and handling various sections, especially the trigger components.

At the end of the fourth hour, Dr. Khan stood and walked up to Akhtar and Pasha.

"Well?" Akhtar asked.

Dr. Khan looked at the guards, and Pasha said, "Out! Everyone!"

The assistants and the guards mustered out single file, closing the door behind them.

Alone with the professor and Pasha, Akhtar asked again, "Well?"

"The device is in good shape . . . for the most part."

"What does that mean?" asked Akhtar.

"The actual gun system, including the U-235 rings and the explosive charge, are good. This is good news, as they are the most critical components."

"But?" Pasha asked.

"But I can't say the same for the electric gun primer," the scientist continued, removing his glasses, cleaning them with the sleeve of his shirt, and slipping them back on. He held up a small printed circuit board. "It will need to be replaced. Also the primer wiring is no good."

He picked up a strand of green wires, disconnected them from the circuit board, and flaked off the insulating plastic with his thumb. "No good."

Akhtar and Pasha exchanged a look of pure disappointment before the latter asked, "Anything else?"

"The projectile tungsten carbide disk."

"What about it?"

"Too brittle." He tapped the four-inch-thick disk with the edge of a screwdriver and a chunk shattered off. "It's meant to protect the stacked U-235 rings of the projectile from the explosion of the conventional charge by cushioning the ensuing shock wave, allowing for a smooth acceleration of the projectile to the other end of the gun barrel. It also needs to be replaced."

"What else?" asked Akhtar, his voice beginning to show an edge.

"The battery pack." He pointed at a small shoebox-size container housing six cylinders resembling sticks of dynamite. They were encased in greenish, powdery battery acid. "There are six cells in the battery pack. Only three are needed to power the system. The other three are for backup. But all cells are dead, as you can see from the spilled acid. Fortunately, the desert heat kept the acid from damaging any components. They will need to be replaced with the exact type."

The brothers sighed in unison, and then Pasha said, "That's all?"

"I think so," he said. "I will have to spend another day checking everything else closely to make sure, but at the moment I think the rest just needs some cleaning and lubrication before reassembly. How soon can you get me the replacements?" He tore off a sheet of paper from his notebook and handed it to them.

Akhtar took it and read the short list, which included detailed descriptions, critical dimensions, and serial numbers. He had, of course, no idea where or how to get such components. But then again, he'd also had no idea what to do with the device after bringing it here. He was a warrior, not a scientist. Unlike Akaa, he lacked al Qaeda's international connections. All he could do was send the information to Akaa and hope for the best.

Handing it to Pasha, he stared at the scientist with far more confidence than he felt, saying, "I'll pass on the request to our people. It shouldn't be very long."

As he left the basement to give the professor time to check his work, Akhtar couldn't help but wonder how in the hell Akaa would be able to secure components for a seventeen-year-old Russian nuclear bomb.

And without raising any suspicions.

25

Second Fiddle

BAGRAM AIR BASE. NORTHERN AFGHANISTAN.

Bill Gorman wasn't new to the art of interrogation.

Freshly out of the Farm, he had gone on to spend an introductory month at the United States Naval Station Guantanamo Bay, Cuba. It was in this place, nicknamed "Gitmo" after the airfield's designation code, GTMO, that the young CIA officer was exposed to the most controversial forms of this tradecraft, honed to near perfection in the wake of the September 11 attacks.

The methods, lumped under the term "enhanced interrogation techniques," included waterboarding, sleep deprivation, rectal infusion, walling, chaining, and nudity. Used independently or in combination as part of a strategy to coerce confessions, EITs were regularly administered to a large population of detainees.

Although he was not necessarily a fan, Gorman was painfully aware that the intelligence gained through those nightmarish sessions had helped thwart attack plans, capture more terrorists, and save lives. Critical to the Agency's understanding of al Qaeda, EITs still ran in full force at more than fifty black sites across twenty-eight countries, including Gitmo in Cuba, the Temara Interrogation Center in Morocco, and the Salt Pit in Kabul.

Which was later moved right here, he thought, as he stood in the rear of a holding room in the heart of Bagram's Parwan Detention Facility.

But tonight Gorman wasn't applying any of the interrogation practices he had either used or seen used. Tonight the CIA officer played second fiddle to Maryam Gadai, who approached the recent detainee, who was zip-tied to a sturdy wooden chair bolted to the middle of a reconfigured metal shipping container.

Unlike the containers used as living quarters for the nearly ten thousand troops stationed at Bagram Air Base, this one lacked creature comforts. A single fluorescent bulb washed metallic green walls with the same grayish light that glinted in the defiant eyes of Adnan Zubaydah.

Gorman sighed. The captured cartel boss served as testament to what could be achieved with a little interagency cooperation by the two most powerful intelligence services in the world. The ISI had kept tabs on Adnan and other cartel chiefs for years, so they had on file recent photos of the rugged drug lord and al Qaeda sympathizer. The images had been uploaded to the CIA database, where facial recognition software had compared them to the high-resolution images captured by the Predators circling the border over the Khyber Pass. It had taken just a couple of hours before a UAV camera returned an 87 percent match. The elusive drug lord had been spotted near a poppy field on the Afghan side of the border, a mile off of the N-5, which changed names from Grand Trunk Road on the Pakistani side to Jalalabad–Torkham highway in Afghanistan.

Two dozen marines aboard a pair of Black Hawk helicopters and a fierce one-hour battle had yielded the wounded but quite alive man who now was staring with contempt at Maryam. Unfortunately, by the time the troops had secured the field and seized Adnan, there had been no sign of Dr. Ali Khan or of Maryam's asset, Zameer.

She had shed her traditional clothes the moment they'd reached the airfield, and Gorman took her to the co-op. She now wore a pair of army camouflage pants, a sleeveless dark green T-shirt, and standard issue boots. The tighter-fitting clothes revealed a figure that belonged to a Marilyn, not a Maryam, and Gorman had difficultly not staring. Plus she had let down her hair, which reached the middle of her back.

"I will tell you nothing," Adnan said in Urdu, sitting up proudly before spitting saliva and blood at her new boots. The man had taken a bullet in the shoulder and another one in the left thigh, but luckily they had gone through clean, missing major organs or arteries, and a medic had patched him up on the ride back to the base.

"I just got these," she said, looking down at the red slime on the insteps.

"I am ready to die, *whore*," he said, arms visibly straining against the restraints.

Gorman couldn't see her expression as she faced their captive, who had been shaved and dressed in a white prison jumpsuit. But Maryam didn't reply. She simply reached into her back pocket and produced two photographs, which Gorman had printed from the images her agency had transferred to the CIA a couple of hours ago.

Adnan's heavily wrinkled face shifted as his stare dropped to the four-by-six-inch photos she held in each hand, his eyes narrowing in obvious curiosity before widening in a mix of surprise and fear.

"I know you don't care what happens to you," she said. "But I know you *do* care about them."

The man shrank back in his chair when presented with photos of his wife and children, taken just last month in Peshawar. "Over thirty thousand people go missing each year in Pakistan, Adnan," she added. "No one would notice six more."

"You are bluffing. You do not even know where they are."

She set a photo on each of his knees, facing him, and then removed a piece of paper from her right pocket, unfolded it, and said, "Your two daughters are on their lunch period at the Fatima Jinnah Public School in Asya Park. Your two youngest boys are in math class at the Iqra Public School on Warsak Road, and your oldest boy is walking in between classes at the Khan Academy of Business and Technology. Your wife is helping your mother shop at the Jinnah Market."

"How . . . can you *possibly* know that?"

"It's our business to know everything about everyone, especially persons of interest such as yourself."

"You . . . you wouldn't dare," Adnan mumbled, nostrils flaring, the veins on his forehead and neck pulsating.

Maryam produced a satellite phone. "Try me. One call and it's over. We pull your roots."

It took a moment, but Gorman just stared in awe as Adnan began to talk, slowly at first, with hesitation, his eyes shifting between the photos and Maryam. He conveyed the location of a compound in the southern section of the country, high above Lashkar Gah, where Pasha Baqer had been ordered by Osama bin Laden to take the nuclear engineering professor.

At Gitmo it would have taken several sessions of waterboarding, combined with sleep deprivation and other techniques, before coming close to breaking a tough detainee.

Maryam, armed with the right intelligence, had done it in under minute.

Gorman handed Maryam a tablet computer showing a map, and Adnan pointed to a location not marked on any NATO map.

"There is nothing there," Maryam said.

"There is," he said. "Hidden from view. An old Soviet bunker. I promise."

"Well see," she said. "But why, Adnan? What's there? Why are they taking him there?"

The drug chief shook his head. "I . . . I do not know this."

"You understand," Maryam said, "that if you lie to us . . ." She waved the sat phone at him.

Fierce determination flashed in his stare as he said, "I swear to you. It is the truth. My job was only to get them across the pass. That's how they operate. I do not know the reason for the kidnapping."

She turned around, faced Gorman, and raised her eyebrows.

He stretched a thumb toward the door.

A minute later they sat across the hall, inside another container outfitted as a conference room.

"You think he's telling the truth?" he asked.

"Aye. He will not risk his family. Now the question, Bill, is what are you going to do with this information."

Gorman considered that for a moment, then said, "I know a guy . . . in Kandahar."

26

Spooks, Feds, and Grunts

KANDAHAR AIRFIELD. SOUTHWESTERN AFGHANISTAN.

Accompanied by Evan Larson, Colonel Stark met the new CIA station chief, Glenn Harwich, outside his hangar. He remembered the intelligence officer, and also his companion, standing next to him, an FBI agent named Monica Cruz, on loan to the CIA.

"Hey, little miss," said Larson.

"It's 'Agent Cruz' to you," Monica blurted back.

"Got it," Larson replied. "Little Miss Cruz."

"Knock it off, Chief," Stark said, without taking his gaze off the CIA man, recalling the attack on the airfield yesterday. He was a bit shorter than Stark and also a bit older, at least based on his bald head, salt-and-pepper beard, and dark bags under his eyes. The man looked spent, tired, in sharp contrast with the fed, who looked fresh out of Quantico. Slim and muscular, she wore her long, dark hair in a ponytail and had a harsh stare of brown eyes over high cheekbones, a fine nose, and full lips. Add radiant honey skin from an in-country tan, plus the tenacity and skill she had displayed in putting down those insurgents, and Stark had a difficult time not doing a double take on her. But as was the case with the pretty air force captain, Stark didn't want his guys reminding him that Monica was also too young for him.

"So, Mr. Harwich," he finally said. "You wanted to talk? Talk."

"Need to run surveillance here," he said, showing a spot on the GPS map on his tablet computer. "Five days ago, a professor of nuclear engineering was kidnapped in Islamabad by the Taliban, with assistance from al Qaeda, and we believe he was taken . . . to this location."

"What's in there?"

"Not sure. Trees cover the area, but we did a focused infrared and it could be some sort of facility, which is why we need the surveillance to figure out what the hell it is. We've just labeled it Compound Fifty-Seven. The officer on the case, Bill Gorman, is en route from Bagram with one of his local assets and would like eyes on the ground before he arrives."

"Do you have a field report with the details?"

Harwich tapped away on his tablet for a few seconds, looked up, and said, "Just transferred it to your op folder. We're calling it a high-threat target for now. U.S. eyes only."

Stark frowned. "Meaning NATO doesn't know about this?"

"For the moment. Until we know more."

"Now, Mr. Harwich, do I need to remind you what happened the last time the CIA and NATO didn't compare notes?"

Harwich dropped his gaze briefly. "Yeah, I'm aware of that. But we're dealing with . . . well, a missing nuclear engineering professor—*nuclear* being the key word. So until we know more, Langley wants to keep it under wraps. And the *nuclear* thing isn't in the report, by the way."

"Of course," Stark said. "Just a 'high-threat target.'"

"Right. And there's something else . . . something that's also not in the report."

Stark just stood there while Harwich produced his phone, fiddled with it for a few seconds, and turned the screen toward him. "I need to know the instant you find anyone wearing this."

The colonel and Larson leaned forward to get a better look.

"Looks like some sort of Soviet graduation ring," Stark observed.

"Correct. From the Gagarin Air Force Academy, the Soviets' version of—"

"I know what that is, but I don't understand what this has to do with your request. And if the FBI knows about it"—Stark pointed to Monica—"then the Agency for which we both work needs serious help. So how about we stop all the bullshit and you just tell us what we need to know to help you."

Exchanging a glance with Monica, Harwich said, "You're right, of course, and old habits die hard, so here comes the *if you tell anyone, my career is over* kind of information."

"Shoot," Stark said.

Harwich spoke for just one minute, enough for Stark to understand.

"So you think the hags found the Soviet nuke and they've kidnapped the scientist to get it operational?"

Harwich tilted his head. "That's the working theory. So, get ready for—"

"Happy to do it," Stark interrupted.

"Great, Colonel. I'll let Gorman know that you—"

"As soon as we get paid for the last op.'

The CIA man narrowed his stare. "Excuse me?"

Stark took a moment to explain.

Harwich looked away, then at Monica, and back at Stark, and just said, "I'll take care of it."

"Just like that?" Stark asked.

"Just like that," Harwich replied.

"Yeah," Larson replied. "I want to see that."

Just then, Ryan stepped outside the hangar, followed by Martin and Hagen, who lit up a Sobranie and remained to the side.

"I thought I told you guys to remain inside," Stark said, looking over his shoulder at the trio.

"What ya gonna do, sir? The man's gotta smoke, and he ain't doing it in the hangar," Ryan said, walking casually up to Stark before stopping abruptly, pointing a finger at Monica, and adding, "Hey! Arizona, right?"

Stark noticed how quickly Monica's expression softened. *"Ryan? What the fuck?"*

"Yeah," Ryan said, his face broadening into an ear-to-ear grin. "What the fuck? How *you* doin'?"

"*I'm* doing fine," she said, pointing at her chest before redirecting her little index finger at the former Delta sniper. "But *you* never called . . . asshole."

"I meant to . . . really . . . but—"

"Whoa," Martin interrupted, pulling the lollipop out of his mouth and using it to point at Monica. "Hands off, Romeo. I'm calling dibs on the skirt."

"Go fuck a goat, little man," Monica said to Martin, prompting Larson to laugh while Hagen grinned, took another drag, and exhaled skyward.

Returning her stare to Ryan's rapidly reddening face, Monica added, "And as for you—"

"Sorry," Ryan said. "I really meant to—" "

"Yeah, sure."

"No, really, I'll make it up to—"

"Okay, knock it off," Stark interjected, staring Ryan down while Harwich frowned at Monica. Shifting his gaze back to the CIA man, he added, "Ball's in your court, Mr. Harwich. You now know where to find us." And turning to his team, but really glaring at Ryan, he added, "Guys, with me. Inside. *Now*."

Everyone moved, except for Ryan, who gave Monica a little wave and a wink, which she returned, and Martin, who also waved at Monica, who just ignored him.

"All right, let's go, you little goat fucker," Larson said, planting a massive gloved hand on the back of Martin's neck and steering him into the hangar. "And you too, Romeo," the chief added, grabbing Ryan by his dog tags and dragging him away while Harwich tugged Monica by the shoulder to head back to their building.

Hagen closed the hangar doors behind them, and Larson released Ryan, who simply tucked his dog tags under his shirt.

"Ryan? What the hell was that?"

"Monica Cruz, sir," he said with an innocent shrug.

"Don't screw with me, Sergeant Major."

"Remember that sniper seminar I took in Scottsdale last summer?"

"What about it?"

"She was there too, sir. One evening after class, we were all hanging out at this watering hole at the edge of town when these bikers came in and started harassing her. She took out the leader in solid hand-to-hand—mind you, the bastard was *twice* her size, so look out, Chief. But then the rest of the gang started to surround her, so I . . . well . . . took care of them, and afterwards . . . well, we sort of hit it off and—"

"All right, fine," he said, though he wasn't sure if he was more annoyed at Ryan's lack of professionalism or at the fact that twice in the last day he'd been attracted to someone just to realize they were already taken, and this one by a member of his own damn team. "Just remember my rules when you're on my clock."

"Sorry, sir. She just happened to be the hottest and most badass girl I've ever—"

"Chief, pull up the file from Harwich and review it with the team," Stark said. "I'm going to make some inquiries about these Harwich and Gorman characters. Make sure their heads are actually attached to the correct part of their anatomies. I'm not having a repeat of the last op."

"But, Colonel," Larson said, "I thought we're not dealing with those Agency assholes until they do right by us and pay what we're owed."

"Oh, Chief. They will pay. They will most *certainly* pay."

27

Light My Fire

"What the hell was that, Cruz?"

Monica shrugged, still not believing Ryan was actually here. The sight of him brought her back to that dusty saloon, back to those rowdy bikers and their haphazard attempt to scare her outside the ladies room. She had taken out their Alpha with a roundhouse to the side of the man's right knee, but the rest of his gang had caught up to her by the bar while intimidated patrons parted like the Red Sea. In the time it took her to reach over the counter and grab a half-empty bottle of Cuervo Gold by the neck, Ryan had already swirled through the group and—

"Cruz!"

"Yeah, boss?"

Harwich exhaled. "What's wrong with you?"

"Why? What did I do?"

"Really?"

"Don't want to talk about it."

"That shit doesn't fly with me. Try again."

It was Monica's turn to exhale. "Fine, boss. Fine. Name's Ryan Hunt. Former Delta sniper. Met him a year ago at a shooting class in Arizona. Caught me by surprise seeing him here is all. All right?"

He shook his head. "Not all right, Cruz. I don't give a shit who you bang or don't bang, just don't mix business and pleasure on my watch again. Clear?"

"Crystal," she said. "What are you going to do about their request to get paid first?"

"What I always do, Cruz."

"And what's that?"

"Light a fire under someone ass."

28

A Pinch of Luck

KANDAHAR AIRFIELD. SOUTHERN AFGHANISTAN.

Stark grabbed a bottle of water from the cooler next to their C-21A jet and walked to the far end of the hangar while producing his daily dose of PTSD meds. He downed them with a few swigs before dialing Colonel Duggan's private number.

"Bored already, Sierra Echo?"

Stark grinned. "Negative, sir. I've been assigned another mission by my civilian contractor."

"Oh. So you're back whoring for the Agency. What's your pimp having you do now?"

"Ah . . . sorry, Colonel. Not allowed to talk about it."

A pause, followed by "Hunter . . . are you stupid or just pretending to be stupid?"

"Probably both, sir, with a side of crazy."

"That Agency secrecy shit is *precisely* what almost got you killed a couple of days ago."

"I know that."

"Then, and pardon my French, why the *fuck* are you calling me?"

"Because I don't trust them . . . sir."

Duggan laughed. "Well, at least you haven't gone completely stupid. So, speak."

Stark frowned, hating to ask for a favor. "Could you run the names of my new handlers through your system?"

"What are you after?"

"Making sure they're not dumb motherfuckers that will put my team in harm's way . . . like their predecessor. I kind of like my balls and my head where they are."

"I see."

"I would appreciate it."

A pause, followed by, "Well, hell, you did save some of our guys yesterday. So . . . names?"

Stark gave them to him.

"Call you back."

Hanging up, Stark sipped his water while staring out the window at the activity on the ramp and the runway behind it. Planes of all shapes and sizes, from UAVs, A-10s, and F-16 Falcons to C-5 Galaxy transports took off and landed in this metropolis that America had chosen to plant smack in the middle of the most hostile country on the planet.

But it is places like this that keep you in business, he thought, looking back at his guys hanging out by their jet. Ryan and Martin flanked Hagen as the three of them looked over the shoulders of Larson, who was working his laptop on a table next to the nose landing gear. As much as those four joked around, they were all business when it came to reviewing the details of a potential new mission.

And that was exactly what it was: a potential new mission. In addition to Harwich finding a way to get them paid for the last op—including their bonuses—each member of the team had to accept the new mission. They either all agreed or they passed.

Stark truly believed that it was this one hundred percent buy in, plus the fact that everyone received equal shares of the take, that kept the team hungry and frosty—and also alive.

That, plus a cup of guts, a teaspoon of wild, and a pinch of luck, especially after that first shot was fired and all carefully crafted plans went straight to hell.

But what Stark would not know, at least until it was too late, was that Harwich's predecessor had left a digital link between the contractor team's operational file and Major General Lévesque's daily

intelligence brief. The intent was to prevent another left hand–right
hand disaster by keeping the NATO chief aware of Stark's activities
while at KAF. For reasons that might never be known, Harwich's predecessor had failed to include the existence of the link in his brief.
So the moment Harwich loaded the information on Compound 57
into Stark's operational file, calling it a high-threat target, it made it
to Lévesque's desk within the hour. And knowing little more than
the compound's coordinates and the fact that it was . . . well . . .
deemed a high-threat target, NATO assumed it had to mean an IED
factory.

29

Sharia Law

DIYARBAKIR. SOUTHERN TURKEY.

Zahra Hassani floored the black Kawasaki Ninja motorcycle, accelerating from the airport on Akkoyunlu Bulvari, the wide boulevard
cutting through the center of this shithole of a town on the banks
of the Tigris River.

A town she never thought she'd see again.

Shops and restaurants along the popular thoroughfare, already
closed at this late hour, blended into a blur as she pushed the bike,
twisting the throttle while working the gears with the toe of her
riding boot.

But that didn't matter to the petite Kurdish woman dressed in a
black riding jumpsuit and matching Skully helmet.

She wasn't in the mood for shopping or eating or socializing.

Zahra was hunting.

Familiar streets rushed past as she headed toward the red-light district on the south side of town. She had been just a child the last time she lived here, recovering from the circumcision performed by her radical Muslim uncles, who had maimed her with a razor blade.

After raping her.

Her father had found her beaten and bleeding in the alley behind their house, about to be stoned to death, accused of adultery by the same men who had cut her.

She had been fourteen years old.

Zahra tightened her grip on the Ninja's handlebars while narrowing her gaze at the quiet surroundings beyond the Skully's antifog visor, which superimposed video captured by the ultra-wide-angle camera mounted on the rear of the polycarbonate helmet.

A small window opened on the upper right-hand side of her field of view. It was her employer, Saudi Arabia Prince Mani al Saud, calling her phone, which was interfaced to the helmet via Bluetooth. They had landed just an hour ago aboard his Cessna Citation X business jet for a clandestine meeting with senior members of the Partiya Karkerên Kurdistanê, the Kurdistan Workers' Party. The PKK controlled the major heroin staging areas and transportation routes between Afghanistan and Europe. But the meeting was postponed until the following morning, giving Zahra an operational window of a few hours.

Plenty of time, she thought, ignoring Mani's call as she reached the edge of Diyarbakir's red-light district, a mecca of clubs, brothels, and countless streetwalkers, all under the glimmer of neon lights and the bass of American rock music.

Zahra slowed down as traffic thickened, as car windows rolled down to negotiate with the mix of Arab, Turkish, and Armenian girls, most in their late teens, dominating the sidewalks of Toplukonut Street. She contemplated this sea of stilettos, miniskirts, tank tops, and makeup, all for sale at thirty Turkish lira—around ten dollars— for thirty minutes. And the debauchery continued inside the many licensed and state-regulated brothels lining both sides of the street, where a customer could rent a private room that came with the girl of his dreams for little more than a hundred dollars per hour. Legalized in 1923, when Atatürk founded the modern republic, Turkey's prostitution industry had a current registered workforce of three thousand girls.

Her mother had been one of them.

Zahra was born in the Kurdish slums of Istanbul to her father's mistress, a girl not much older than the long-legged and scantily dressed creatures presently stepping inside SUVs and sedans. Her father had been a high-ranking officer in the People's Defense Forces, the paramilitary wing of the PKK, a left-wing militant organization based in Turkey and Iraqi Kurdistan. When her mother died from tuberculosis when Zahra was only eight, her father took her in to help the maids. Years later, when her father was away on a mission, his zealous brothers changed her life forever.

Her father moved Zahra to a clinic in Diyarbakir, not far from the airport, to help her recover from her wounds before enlisting her in the PKK's Free Women's Units. Zahra trained in southern Turkey and northern Iraq, where she turned her suffering into anger, applying herself to the cause with mind, body, and soul. Over the following decade, she rose in the ranks, leading her own group of female assassins against high-profile Turkish officials. Her assassination methods, executed with cold precision using a Ruger Mark III pistol fitted with a Gemtech sound suppressor firing subsonic .22-caliber ammunition, made Zahra a legend in the PKK. It also put a price on her head, decreed by the Turkish government. Realizing that the best assassins also made the best bodyguards, the PKK leadership appointed Zahra to the security detail of the president of Iraqi Kurdistan. During an official visit to Riyadh, Saudi Arabia, in 1997, Zahra met Prince Mani al Saud, who exposed the petite Kurdish operative to the wealth she could attain by becoming an independent security consultant. She resigned her government post in 1998 to manage security for the prince.

And now I'm back in this hellhole, she thought, throttling the Kawasaki to get around the line of vehicles, accelerating up the bustling avenue, before turning right onto Oztas Street and continuing for four more blocks.

The noisy boulevard gave way to a quiet neighborhood. She checked the address plugged onto her phone's GPS, displayed on the Skully's visor, and pulled over in front of a two-story corner building.

Was the informant wrong?

She gazed up and down the tree-lined street and was about to check the address again when two men dressed in black suits and guarding the entrance shifted their stances ever so slightly. But it was enough for Zahra to notice their silhouettes, barely visible against the dark double doors.

Hello.

Dismounting and removing her helmet, she shook her head to loosen her shoulder-length hair, as dark as her eyes and makeup. Setting the Skully on the handlebars, she walked up to the men while offering a smile that was not returned by either man. They were tall and broad, their muscles pressed against the fabric of their silk suits. One was bald, with a goatee, and the other clean-shaven under a full head of brown hair. Their eyes followed her while they kept their arms to their sides, relaxed, confident in their size—and probably in their training and concealed weapons.

But it would not matter.

Nothing would.

"You lost, lady?" one of them asked in the Common Turkic language she had not heard, or missed, in some time.

But it would be the last thing he would ever say.

Zahra reached behind her back with a gloved right hand and produced the suppressed Ruger, shooting finger already caressing the trigger as she aimed and fired a 22LR subsonic round. The Gemtech absorbed the powder burn while propelling the forty-two-grain lead bullet through the aluminum cylinder and straight to the middle of his forehead.

Although the slug's mass wasn't nearly as large as a 9mm, it tore through his frontal lobe and lodged itself in the middle of the parietal lobe, robbing the guard of dozens of brain functions, including the ability to stand, hold a gun, or even scream. The Ruger's blowback mechanism ejected the spent cartridge and extracted a fresh one from the ten-round magazine, sliding it into the firing chamber.

His associate tried to react, but the laws of physics played against him. In the time it took him to reach inside his jacket for his holstered pistol, Zahra had already shifted targets and pulled the trigger again, just as the first man collapsed by her feet.

It was over in four seconds. Stepping over both guards, who were now seized by spasms, she reached the foyer, quiet at this hour. But the peaceful setting, the pastel walls, dark hardwood floors, and crystal chandelier, couldn't hide the fact that this brothel saw as much activity as the loudest one back on Topluxonut Boulevard.

The only difference being price and quality.

The luxurious and discreet establishment offered the most beautiful—and disease-free—women in town, catering to a clientele able to afford the equivalent of one thousand dollars for an unforgettable night.

And the irony of it all was that this business was owned and run by a pair of brothers from Istanbul.

The Hassani brothers.

She didn't bother going upstairs to the suites, where patrons were either already asleep or still getting their money's worth. Shoving the Ruger behind the small of her back, pressed against her spine, Zahra turned right, toward the office, where she found two more guards.

Like the ones up in front, this pair sported more muscles than Olympic weightlifters, all packed inside tight black suits. And just like before, her small stature and looks bought her a few precious moments.

She waved and smiled as she approached them. The men exchanged a puzzled look before one of them walked up to meet her halfway. Zahra shot him through the left eye before pushing him toward his surprised partner, who made an attempt to reach inside his jacket.

Pivoting on her left foot, Zahra brought her right foot up and around, striking the side of his temple with the toe of her right boot.

The guard staggered back but didn't fall. He was tall, almost a foot taller than her, and strong, able to grab Zahra's shooting hand by the wrist.

But it also would not make any difference.

She drove her right knee up in between his legs, crushing his testicles, but before he could scream, she chopped his larynx with the edge of her left hand.

The guard dropped to his knees, a wide-eyed stare looking almost straight at her in sheer disbelief. And that's how she left him, gasping for the air that could not get through his collapsed windpipe.

She inched the door slowly open, wary of having been heard and of walking into the wrong end of a pistol. But all she came upon were two men sitting on a sofa to the right of a pair of desks and a minibar. Two girls wearing nothing but stilettos knelt in front of them, their faces buried in the men's groins. Zahra had caught them literally with their pants down. They had drinks in their hands, eyes closed and heads tilted back while the girls did their thing. A small table with opium pipes and a white powder that looked like cocaine stood between them.

One of the girls turned around, smiled, and mumbled hello in Urdu, her eyes half-open with the stupor of drugs, her nose smudged white, confirming that the powder was cocaine. She was a pretty Pakistani in her early teens, with breasts barely developed. The noise got the attention of the other girl, who looked Arab, like Zahra, and also quite stoned. They started giggling, and then the Pakistani girl stretched a hand toward Zahra, asking her to join in.

Seriously?

"Get out," Zahra said. "Now."

The girls exchanged a puzzled look, shrugged almost in unison, and staggered to their feet, somehow managing to balance themselves on those four-inch heels. They stumbled out of the room and chuckled some more when nearly tripping over the bodies of the guards in the hallway.

The Hassani brothers slowly came out of their trance, eyes also half-closed. One of them, Khalid, tried to reach down for his trousers while his brother, Walid, closed his eyes again, and his head bobbed sideways.

"Don't," she warned, standing in front of them, her weapon held close to her chest, harder to grab and easy to point and shoot.

Khalid leaned forward and blinked, apparently not realizing until that moment that she was even in the room. His eyes widened when he noticed her holding a gun. Then, slowly, his dark eyes measured her and blinked again, this time in recognition, as he whispered, "Zahra?"

"Hello, Uncle."

Before he could reply, she shot him twice in the groin, and as he started to scream, shot him once in the larynx. As he collapsed, trembling and gasping for air by Walid's feet, Zahra also shot his brother twice in his genitals and once in the throat.

She remained there for a moment, watching them choke in their own blood as they stared in horror at their maimed genitals, then back at her. But for reasons she could not explain, the moment didn't seem as satisfying as she had envisioned for so many years. And a part of her even felt sorry for them, until she remembered her own journey after they had cut her, how she had dreaded the thought of anyone touching her. She recalled her long string of failed relationships because it was just too painful to become intimate. Her uncles had really hurt her for life—or so she had thought, until she met Prince Mani, who fell for the feisty assassin-turned-bodyguard. And as had been the case in the past, Zahra had turned down his advances, until Mani had figured out why, one late evening during a stopover in Monaco, after both had had a bit too much to drink. The alcohol haze had momentarily made her forget, until his fingers slid under her panties and she had screamed as pain shot up from her mutilated genitalia.

"Are you okay?"

"It . . . hurts . . ."

"Oh, baby, why?"

"I'm so embarrassed."

His hand still on her, Mani had felt the butchery and had simply hugged her as she cried, whispering softly in her ear.

"You will always be safe with me."

The surgery had actually been relatively minor. Just a couple of hours in the hands of Europe's finest surgeons, and a month later Zahra had felt like a woman again.

When the Hassani brothers finally stopped moving, Zahra spat on them, walked right out of the building, and rode the Kawasaki back to the private hangar at the airport, where she found the prince pacing in front of the Citation.

Unlike other Saudi royalty, Mani preferred Western clothes, and tonight he was dressed in a pair of linen pants, a white polo shirt, and loafers, no socks. And also unlike the glamorous royalty, he wore no jewelry, except for a Breitling pilot's watch hugging his left wrist.

"Where the hell have you been?" he snapped, an iPhone in his right hand. He was a handsome devil, with a perfect tan, a perfect haircut, and perfect teeth, and he smelled of lavender, which she would never admit was her favorite smell. His soft features hardened a bit as she approached him, gray eyes glinting in frustration. "I've call you several—"

"Can't a girl go sightseeing?"

"You do realize you work for me?" His lips pressed into a hard admonishing line.

She rolled her eyes and actually wanted to laugh. "What's the rush? The meeting isn't until the morning. We still have time to—"

"Change of plans," Mani said, checking his watch. "We're leaving immediately."

"Oh . . . where?"

"If you'd answered the damn phone I could have—"

She just cupped his face with a gloved hand, pulling him down and brushing her lips over his before whispering, "That attitude isn't going to get you *anywhere* with me."

He gave her his devilish half-smile, hands on her back as he pressed her against him and said, "Moscow, Zahra. We need to go to Moscow . . . tonight."

"Moscow? Why?"

"I just got a most urgent request . . . from the *sheikh*."

30

Military Intelligence

"Are you shitting me, Romeo?" said Chief Larson over the secure frequency while he knelt next to Stark, who remained in a crouch between two boulders high up in the rocky hills north of the coordinates provided by the first Agency handler the colonel actually liked.

Stark wasn't sure how it had happened, but within a couple of hours of his meeting with Harwich, the funds had posted in his team's account in the Cayman Islands. And it had happened just as Duggan had called back to inform him that, as far as military intelligence was concerned, Harwich was quite the legend in the intelligence world and Gorman was one of his understudies.

"Nope," Ryan replied. Perched three hundred meters up on a hill in overwatch, the former Delta master sergeant had just reported that a U.S. Marines rifle platoon was marching single file toward the compound from the south, and their approach had alerted the guards. *"Jarheads are about a click away."*

"Goes to fucking show you," Chief Larson cursed.

"What's that?" asked Martin.

"That military intelligence is truly a contradiction in terms."

"For once the chief is right," replied Martin.

"Well, even a broken watch marks the correct time twice a day," Ryan chimed in.

"Twice a day would be an upgrade for NATO," said Martin.

Stark sighed, lacking the energy to tell his team to zip the chatter, especially when they were right on the money. NATO intelligence kept sending United States Marines into unwinnable situations.

The colonel tightened his grip on his MP5A1 while observing a large force of Taliban soldiers gathering outside the heavily fortified, fortress-like compound. Stark was tempted to call the marines off, but doing so would telegraph his position to NATO. And this being a CIA-sanctioned mission, there was no telling what the Agency had shared or not shared with Major General Lévesque— or with Colonel Duggan for that matter. All he knew was that this job—which paid quite handsomely—called for complete radio silence unless he had something to report, and then he could only use this one encrypted radio to do so.

Grimacing at the nature of his mercenary work, especially when it placed American servicemen in unnecessary danger, he picked up the radio to alert Harwich.

31

Need-to-Know

**COMPOUND 57. SULAIMAN MOUNTAINS.
SOUTHERN AFGHANISTAN.**

"You've got to be kidding me!" Harwich exploded, storming out of his supposedly secured communications building and marching off to NATO headquarters.

"I thought this was strictly Agency need-to-know," Monica said, catching up to him.

"Yeah," he said. "Tell me something I don't *fucking* know!"

Monica drove while Harwich just stared out the window in silence until they reached the large structure in the middle of the base, cruising past rows and rows of stacked shipping containers converted into living quarters and offices.

They were able to talk their way into NATO headquarters, but reaching Major General Lévesque, who was holed up in one of the conference rooms in the back of the auditorium-like building, proved unexpectedly difficult, even with their combined credentials.

"I need to see the general!" Harwich insisted, trying to get past a pair of oversize corporals from the Canadian Army Military Police who were blocking the way into a conference room.

The one in charge, a Corporal Darcy, cleared his throat and said in a rather raspy voice, "Later, eh? He's in a staff meeting with the heads of the various armed forces and has ordered no interruptions."

"Listen," Harwich insisted, "he's about to send another platoon of United States Marines into an ambush!"

"Like I said, the general is—"

"Hey, *Canuck*, this is beyond your pay grade," Monica broke in, stepping right in front of the large soldier while noticing the bruises on his neck, which gave her an idea. "Get the hell out of our way."

Darcy looked down at her and blinked in surprise before exchanging what looked like a borderline amused glance with his partner, who shook his head.

"Look, whoever the hell you are," Darcy began, after clearing his throat again. "There is a protocol to see the general, eh? Go see his aid and he'll fit you in—"

"Go," Monica told Harwich, after grabbing Darcy's throat right over the bruises, bringing the man to his knees while side kicking his partner in the balls.

Harwich burst through the double doors while Monica released the throat grip on the corporal, leaving him coughing next to his partner, who was curled up on his side, moaning, both hands on his groin. As she entered the room behind the CIA man, Monica expected to see the usual entourage of high-ranking officers from various countries in their military uniforms. Instead, just Major General Lévesque and Colonel Duggan occupied one end of the conference table, and they both turned to the intrusion.

"Who do you think you are to burst into this special brief, eh?"

Lévesque asked, standing at the end of the conference table, the freckles on his face shifting as he frowned. Colonel Duggan from the U.S. Marine Corps sat next to him, regarding them over the rim of his reading glasses.

"You've misused our intelligence, General," Harwich said. Turning to Duggan, he added, "Your marines are about to walk into another ambush."

The marine colonel leaned back slowly and lowered his glasses before pointing at the screen.

Monica and Harwich turned to take a look, and suddenly froze. She was staring at the image of three men sitting at one end of a conference room.

The first was George Tenet, director of Central Intelligence. The second was Donald Rumsfeld, secretary of defense. And they flanked the forty-third president of the United States, George W. Bush.

32

Straight From The Horse's Mouth

THE WHITE HOUSE. WASHINGTON, DC.

President George W. Bush thought he had seen a lot, first as governor of Texas, where he served after defeating incumbent Ann Richards in 1994, followed by his bid for the presidency in 1999 and his controversial victory over Al Gore in November of 2000.

And then came the unprecedented strikes on September 11, 2001.

On my watch, he thought, forever changing America—as well as his vision for his first term in office.

The nation had been attacked in the most cowardly and infamous of ways, and President Bush made it his life's mission to bring those responsible to justice while setting up the covert and overt mechanisms to prevent another such attack.

Ever.

And certainly irrespective of how the media or the public viewed those decisions.

His job was to protect America through any means possible, clandestine or otherwise, even if part of the population criticized the very manner in which he protected them from another September 11.

But doing so had required some thinking outside the box. After all, the last time America had been attacked that way was in Pearl Harbor, on December 7, 1941.

President Roosevelt had taken painful but necessary steps to ensure our nation's survival, entering World War II. And so had President Bush, taking unprecedented, bold, and quite controversial measures, blazing new trails—this was the reason the United States Secret Service had given him the code name Trailblazer.

The past four years had been some of the most tumultuous in American history, with the wars in Afghanistan and Iraq Plus, there was that search for those nonexistent weapons of mass destruction and the creation of agencies such as Homeland Security the enactment of the Patriot Act, and the bolstering of military forces, law enforcement, and intelligence services domestic and abroad. Names like al Qaeda, the Taliban, and Osama bin Laden suddenly became known to every American as the face of the enemy in his administration's well-publicized war on terror.

President Bush thought he had indeed seen quite a lot in his years, until he regarded the two individuals who had apparently crashed the closed briefing that Secretary Rumsfeld had set up for him this morning.

That's definitely a first.

Leaning back, legs crossed, hands on his lap, the American commander in chief actually didn't mind the break in the monotony of his day, especially if what the bald-headed man with the unkempt beard said was true. The last thing his White House needed was more dead marines to feed the media frenzy against him during his second term, as his ratings continued to drop.

On the other hand, those two characters had interrupted a very critical meeting that strongly indicated, for the first time since he took office, that there might actually be a weapon of mass destruction somewhere in that region. Granted, it wasn't Iraq, as he had announced as his reason for invading that country and deposing Saddam Hussein in 2003.

But I'll take it, Bush thought.

Director Tenet leaned over and whispered, "That's the guy who put it together, Mr. President, CIA officer Glenn Harwich."

The president glanced over at Rumsfeld, who slowly nodded.

Although he was born in Connecticut and educated at Yale and Harvard, President Bush considered himself a Texan through and through. And as such, he'd spent more than his fair share of years among ranchers and horses. One of the key life lessons he'd learned while growing up didn't come from either of those Ivy League schools. It came from an old hired hand at a west Texas ranch who showed him the best way to tell a horse's age: by looking at the animal's teeth.

Straight from the horse's mouth.

He had heard the term before, of course, but never gave its origin much thought until that day. The advice, however, stuck, serving him well through the years, as he made a conscious effort to dig through the layers of bureaucracy—as governor and then as president—to get to the truth of an issue. By going to the source, to the horse's mouth, he could bypass levels of interpretation and "spin" before reports reached his desk. Whenever someone like a military or intelligence chief briefed him on an issue, the president had the habit of picking up the phone right there and then and speaking directly with the individual responsible for the report. Oftentimes he'd even summoned that source for a private chat, to stare directly into the horse's mouth. And the times when he had been unable to do so, such as with the reports of weapons of mass destruction in Saddam Hussein's arsenal, the very same horse had kicked him hard in the ass.

But this morning, and thanks to the unscheduled interruption, the president was staring directly at one such horse: Glenn Harwich.

"General Lévesque?" Bush said.

"Yes, Mr. President?"

"I don't wish to keep you from doing whatever it is you need to be doing right now to prevent another ambush of my marines."

The NATO chief blinked, realizing he was being excused.

"I'm on it, Mr. President," Lévesque said, and promptly left the room.

The president didn't dislike the KAF leader appointed by the NATO secretary general, but he didn't like him, either. If he had his way, however, he would have appointed the man still sitting at the table, Colonel Paul Duggan.

"Well, Mr. Harwich," Bush continued, staring at the surprised eyes of the CIA man in the high-resolution image, who was standing next to a feisty-looking Hispanic woman wearing an FBI T-shirt and desert camouflage pants. "Please tell us what it is that you need to find that damn Russian bomb."

33

Let Them Come

COMPOUND 57. SULAIMAN MOUNTAINS.
SOUTHERN AFGHANISTAN.

"How am I supposed to fulfill my obligation when you can't seem to keep me safe long enough to do so?" Dr. Khan asked, his hands holding a pair of probes connected to a digital oscilloscope as he took measurements from one of the printed circuit boards he had removed from the weapon.

It was a very fair question, but one that Akhtar did not feel like answering at the moment.

"This is a project of *immense* technical finesse. It's not one of your stupid machine guns!" the scientist added, the steady drone of the air conditioner and recirculation unit mixing with the heavy breathing of Akhtar's men as they made the final preparations to leave.

"We don't have a choice. Pack what you need. My men will haul it." Akhtar turned away to catch up with Pasha at the other end of the lab, by the hall connecting to the stairs leading to the main floor. The Americans were coming. Despite all of his precautions, despite the altitude, the thick canopy of stone pines, and the camouflage scheme painted on all roof surfaces, the enemy had somehow located this long-abandoned Soviet bunker.

It was time to go higher and deeper into the mountain.

To a place beyond the reach of their planes and helicopters.

As he walked off, Akhtar was pleasantly surprised to hear the professor ordering his men to crate up the device, minus three hundred pounds of armored plates and other unnecessary components. The technicians responded immediately, moving about the lab efficiently, gathering all of the required gear to secure the bomb to a carrier resembling an ambulance stretcher, easily carried by four men.

Akhtar approached Pasha, who was gearing up.

Placing a hand on his shoulder, he said, "Hold them back, brother."

"They have no idea what's coming their way," Pasha replied, staring at Akhtar's narrow and heavily lined face beneath a dark turban.

Grabbing his Remington sniper rifle, he rushed outside the compound, where his force of 150 well-trained and heavily armed men waited for his command. Another eighty men protected the compound and would escort Akhtar through a system of tunnels and hidden trails up the mighty Hindu Kush mountains, where the Taliban had a secret headquarters nestled in its snowy peaks.

There, Akhtar would wait for bin Laden's courier.

There, at an altitude over twelve thousand feet, his brother would be safe, beyond the reach of NATO helicopters and troops operating primarily in the Helmand River valley.

But to *get* there, Akhtar first needed to get away from *here*.

And that's where I come in.

Pasha stepped beyond the protection of the heavily fortified gate. His plan was simple: hit the incoming force hard and fast from the front while killing any escape route. Keeping two-thirds of the warriors with him, Pasha ordered the rest to move quietly around the advancing American soldiers and take offensive positions by the clearing a mile down the mountain, where one of his scouts had observed a pair of Chinook helicopters unload precisely forty-four soldiers an hour ago.

Let them come, he thought, confident that the math was in his favor this afternoon, climbing up the nearest stone pine to get a clearer picture of the incoming team marching single file up an old trail rigged with IEDs.

Settling on a wide branch and breaking up his silhouette with a camouflage poncho, he brought the front end of the American platoon into focus on his Leupold scope. Below him and spreading across the front of the compound, a force of almost one hundred battle-hardened warriors prepared for battle, the business ends of their mixed weaponry pointed at the enemy.

Let them come.

34

Six Six Zulu

COMPOUND 57. SULAIMAN MOUNTAINS.
SOUTHERN AFGHANISTAN.

The only sound Captain John Wright could hear was that of his boots crushing leaves and fallen branches, and the ever-present crickets chirping in the midday sun, which was broken into jagged streaks of light by the canopies of towering stone pines. He filled his lungs with the pine resin fragrance infused in the cold and dry mountain air.

Wright, like his father and grandfather before him, believed in leading from the front. And as such, he was with the point element today, carrying on the distinguished military legacy of a family defined by their actions, not their words.

First Lieutenant Elias John Wright had led a platoon through the killing fields of France and Germany in World War II, before falling during the winter of 1944–1945 at the brutal Battle of the Bulge, in the Ardennes. Surrounded by a German division making a last-ditch effort in the waning months of the war, Lieutenant Wright had made the ultimate sacrifice, choosing to remain behind to man a machine gun emplacement. In doing so, he gave his retreating platoon enough time to reach Allied lines so a counterattack could be mounted. But by then it had been too late for the twenty-three-year-old officer, whose frozen body was found a week later, bayoneted to death, overrun after firing his last bullet.

Lieutenant Wright never got to see the baby he had fathered during his very short married life in Manhattan, Kansas, before his deployment. But the boy, Samuel John Wright, grew up staring at the folded American flag on the mantelpiece, next to a shadow box housing his father's ribbons, a Silver Star and two Purple Hearts. So he had followed in his father's footsteps, graduating from West Point as a second lieutenant before getting deployed to Vietnam, where he distinguished himself in the Battle of Binh Gia in December of 1964. Like his father before him, the young lieutenant found himself and his men cut off from their infantry division as the Vietcong closed in for the kill. The hot jungle of Binh Gia may have been a world away from the frozen Ardennes, but the fight was the same, as was the determination of the young Wright to honor his oath to his country.

Shot in the leg, unable to move without help, and realizing he was just slowing down his platoon, Lieutenant Sam Wright had also made the ultimate sacrifice. Remaining behind while armed to the teeth, he had made one hell of a last stand, a dogged defense, Custer style, fighting to his last round while keeping the enemy away from his retreating team. Days later, a recon platoon found his mutilated remains surrounded by more than thirty dead Vietcong rebels—the last dozen blown up with his final grenades.

Captain John Wright also had grown up staring at those military awards, on that same mantelpiece in his Manhattan, Kansas, hometown. The American flags folded side by side, the numerous medals and ribbons, had fueled his desire to join in his family's military tradition. Graduating first in his class at 29 Palms, Wright had jumped straight into the fray, twice in Iraq and now on his third tour in Kandahar.

Wright forced the images of his ancestors to the back of his mind, surveying the terrain ahead on this goat trail while providing cover for three specialists trained in the use of IED detecting equipment. He would rotate back to the platoon, checking as he went, accomplishing two things: he could let his men see him sharing the danger, and he could see how they were holding up.

Two of his specialists were armed with the Vallon VMC1 "Gizmos," extremely lightweight pulse induction metal detectors, similar to those people use on the beach, but on steroids. They flanked a third technician, who was using the larger Vallon VMR3G Minehound, basically a Gizmo enhanced with a powerful ground penetrating radar. The GPR feature was the U.S. military's response to the insurgents constructing some IEDs with less metal by using plastic containers, foam rubber, and wooden boards, challenging traditional metal detectors. The trio swept the path immediately ahead of Wright, who was followed by the rest of the rifle platoon, forty men marching single file.

Armed with a Heckler & Koch UMP45 submachine gun in .45 ACP, Wright scanned the winding path along the side of a mountain, which the intelligence briefing claimed led to Compound 57.

According to Duggan, the intel had reached Lévesque's desk a few hours ago via some link between the CIA and NATO, and the general had then assigned the job to the U.S. Marines.

The target, a well-hidden compound and suspected IED factory, stood a few miles north and almost nine thousand feet above the vast fields of poppy fields surrounding Lashkar Gah.

And since Wright had not yet been able to replace the lieutenant he had loaned to another rifle platoon, he'd had to step in and lead this mission—something he had not done in a couple of months. Feeling a bit rusty, he was relying heavily on Master Gunnery Sergeant Jim Bronkie, a three-tour veteran, who was following right behind him, also armed with a UMP45.

As he watched the specialists sweep their gadgets over the rocky terrain, Wright momentarily thought of the late Lieutenant Wiley and looked at his own two legs. Sighing, he shifted his gaze back to the trio working their combined gear in a low and precise manner designed to detect metallic or low-metallic IED components in the ground.

What made the Gizmos and Minehounds special was their portability and adaptability to any type of soil. The units shared a feature called Mineralized Mode, an automatic soil compensation that adapted the detector to soil conditions anywhere in the world. But for it all to work properly, for the detector heads to detect metal, the detectors had to be in motion—thus the name "dynamic detector" and the constant back-and-forth action of the operators. And while the pulse detectors scanned the ground, the Minehound's GPR provided additional value, with its color screen displaying everything hidden in the ground, irrespective of composition.

One of the Gizmo operators suddenly stopped, an action that made Wright pause and lift his left hand to signal the platoon.

Slowly, the Minehound technician shifted his unit to the left and just ahead of the Gizmo specialist pointing at the ground in front of him. Upon looking closer, Wright noticed that the color of the soil on that spot was a dash darker than the surrounding dirt. And he would have never noticed it if it weren't for the specialist, who now swept his unit in a circle to help the GPR paint a crisper picture on its seven-inch LED display.

"IED," the Gizmo tech said. "Metallic."

After thirty seconds, the Minehound tech confirmed it with his GPR and produced a can of bright orange spray paint. He circled a suspect area about five feet in diameter before marking it on the GPS map of a small tablet computer. The system was linked to the U.S. military's explosive ordnance disposal unit, who would eventually deploy technicians to confirm the presence of an IED and either unearth it or detonate it on site. But for now the problem area was identified for the platoon.

The trio stepped around the potential bomb and continued their sweep. Wright gave the signal to move forward, after passing down the line the order to keep clear of the orange circle. But about a hundred feet later, all three specialists stopped again when the Mine-hound GPR began to beep wildly near a section of terrain flanked by two walls of moss-slick boulders.

Wright paused again while the Minehound tech checked his screen several times. Pinging the area with the GPR to obtain a full image, he turned and said, "Nonmetallic mines. Four, sir. Daisy-chained."

"What do you think, Gunny?"

Bronkie, a strapping man in his midthirties from Hyannis, Massachusetts, said, in an accent and a voice that reminded him of John F. Kennedy, "Go around the boulders, sir. Safer that way."

"All right," Wright said, while the Gizmo guys marked off the path. "We go around."

The technique was becoming more popular with the Taliban: setting up an easy-to-find metallic IED followed by the difficult-to-detect nonmetallic mines.

A mind fuck and frustratingly slow, but necessary for sound tactical movement, thought Wright, going around the narrow path for roughly fifty feet before returning to the goat trail, where they continued up the side of the rocky hill until they reached a vantage point directly east of their target.

Wright produced a pair of binoculars and focused them on the large facility. Unlike the mud and stone buildings down in the valley, this place was quite the citadel, with tall walls of reinforced concrete surrounding a two-story concrete and steel building. A pair of faded red stars on the far corner of the wall signaled that it was built by the Soviets during their occupancy in the 1980s. He counted at least a dozen men up on watchtowers, four of them armed with Russian RPD light machine guns. The site, built into the side of a rocky mountainside and shaded by a thick canopy of stone pines, explained why the only surveillance available had come from infra-red imagery.

Which means the intel is probably shit.

Even when provided with satellite and drone imagery, and eyes on the ground on a site, as had been the case with Compound 45 the day before, the insurgent count was always questionable. And the discrepancy had to do with the fact that the insurgents just loved their damn tunnels. For all he knew, there could be a hundred Tangos behind those walls.

As Wright decided to call a halt when they were within two thousand yards of the objective—as close as he would ever dare approach, given the unknowns—his AN/PRC-148 MBITR, strapped to the side of his vest, came alive through the earpiece coiling into his helmet.

"*Six Six Zulu, Bravo Niner Six.*"

Wright tapped the mike just below his chin and whispered, "Bravo Niner Six, Six Six Zulu, go ahead."

"*Six Six Zulu, be advised of increased reported threat at your target. Do you have visual?*"

No shit, he thought, looking over at Bronkie, also equipped with an MBITR. He tapped the mike. "Affirmative. Six Six Zulu has visual. Place is a fortress. Four RPDs and at least a dozen Tangos so far. Probably more."

"*Copy that, Six Six Zulu. Hold position.*"

Wright slowly shook his head. "Copy that. Six Six Zulu holding."

What in Allah's name is he doing? Pasha thought, adjusting the Leupold scope of his bolt-action Remington M24, observing the captain call a halt a half kilometer from the compound, just shy of the kill zone Pasha had set up for the marines.

Reaching for his radio, he whispered, "Wait for my signal."

Adjusting for the breeze, and also for distance, Pasha let the front of the platoon reach the center of his crosshairs as he readied to deliver that American captain a little message.

Wright dropped to one knee and pulled up his binoculars again, saying, "Screw this, Gunny. Get everybody back one click into DFPs."

"Yes, sir," Bronkie replied, motioning the minesweeping trio to the back of the line so they could lead the thousand-meter pullback.

But as the three guys walked past Wright, and just as Bronkie started to convey the order to the squad leaders via their MBITRs, a report thundered down the mountain.

Wright stared in disbelief at the face of his gunnery sergeant as the impact sliced it cleanly off his head. The large man just stood there, a mess of muscle tissue, ligaments, and shattered bones pulsating beneath his helmet, hands still clutching his rifle.

One of the Gizmo guys, splattered in the sergeant's blood and facial tissue, started screaming. It happened precisely six seconds before another report blasted in Wright's head, deafening, crushing, as if a sledgehammer had just pounded his helmet.

Colors exploded in his mind before everything went suddenly dark.

Pasha had put a 7.54×51mm round through the face of the man wearing several stripes on his shoulder pads. He knew from experience that gunnery sergeants were typically the most experienced soldiers in a platoon, more so than the officers.

Pasha shifted targets while manually ejecting the spent round, working the bolt action to load another one to take out the captain kneeling on the ground. He wanted to cut off the head of the snake before unleashing his men on the approaching team.

Akhtar's orders were clear: under no circumstance should those soldiers be allowed inside the compound before he could move the bomb and the scientist to a new location.

But as Pasha squeezed the trigger a second time in three seconds, a spark flashed in his eyes. The M24 rifle shook violently with the impact of what he recognized as a suppressed round fired by an enemy sniper who had obviously spotted his initial muzzle flash.

The round tore the Leupold scope cleanly off its mount, along with a chunk of wood from the top of the bolt-action mechanism.

Tossing the damaged Remington to the ground, his hands trembling from the impact, Pasha rolled off the branch and scurried down the pine tree before the hidden sniper could adjust his fire.

Landing on his side on a thick cushion of leaves, he silently cursed leaving his prized M24 behind and reached the rear of his fighting force, where he gave the order to move on the enemy.

It was time to finish this.

35

Rules of Engagement

"*Missed him, Romeo,*" said Larson over the squadron frequency. "*But saved that captain's ass.*"

"*His head, actually,*" corrected Ryan.

"*Not bad given he only had six seconds' warning after that first muzzle flash,*" commended Martin.

"Dammit. Kill the chatter," ordered Stark, hiding his annoyance toward Ryan for releasing that suppressed round, even if no one could tell its origin—and even if it probably resulted in keeping that captain's face attached to his head, unlike that of the gunnery sergeant. It was still a violation of his CIA-funded mission's rules—and of his own rules of engagement. His team's survival depended heavily on stealth, on their ability to remain hidden, especially when facing such formidable enemy.

"And nobody makes another move," Stark added. He'd already warned Harwich, who indicated he would contact Duggan immediately, though apparently "immediately" meant a different thing at the Agency. "Let the marines take care of themselves. They're trained for this."

But as the Taliban contingent that had been amassing outside the compound's wall broke into a full-blown attack, Stark began to reconsider his contractual obligation to his employer versus his loyalty to American troops.

36

Bounding Overwatch

**COMPOUND 57. SULAIMAN MOUNTAINS.
SOUTHERN AFGHANISTAN.**

"Sir! Enemy contact straight ahead, eight hundred yards, small arms and light machine guns!"

The helmeted face of one of his rifle squad sergeants, a three-tour guy from Louisiana named Eugene Gaudet, backdropped by swaying branches blocking the sun, materialized in front of John Wright as he lay on his back. Eons ago, during basic training, he had gotten kicked in the head during hand-to-hand combat drills. It had nearly knocked him out and given him a concussion.

This felt worse.

"What are your orders, sir? Sir!" the man shouted in his thick Cajun accent. His brown eyes, positioned a bit too close, flanking an aquiline nose with flaring nostrils, narrowed in obvious concern on a face tight with urgency.

Standing with considerable effort, his ears ringing, Wright blinked while staring at Gaudet, then at his faceless gunnery sergeant lying dead next to him, then back at Gaudet, who said, "Your helmet, sir! It deflected a—"

"Get Chinooks to the LZ and call air support!" Wright shouted through the dizziness. He had to get helicopters to the landing zone.

Gaudet got on his MBITR. "Bravo Niner Six, Bravo Niner Six, Six Six Zulu."

Static, followed by, *"Six Six Zulu, Bravo Niner Six. Go ahead."*

"Six Six Zulu taking fire. Tallie ambush. Need relief and immediate exfil. LZ hot. Repeat. LZ hot. Need a Hawg."

"Six Six Zulu, Bravo Niner Six understands you're taking fire and need exfil and Hawgs. Confirm."

"Bravo Niner Six, Six Six Zulu confirming. Exfil and Hawgs. Hot LZ. Be advised Six Six Zulu has casualties."

"Roger that, Six Six Zulu. Two Hooks on the way. Grunt in the air," the operator at KAF reported, referring to the Chinook helicopters and an A-10 Warthog, respectively.

Wright heard Gaudet's conversation, hoping like hell that KAF did not deploy Vaccaro, given her close call less than twenty-four hours ago.

His training overshadowing the crippling pain, he ordered a leap-frogging withdrawal to the landing zone.

Leapfrogging, also called "bounding overwatch," allowed for one squad to take an overwatch position, laying suppressing fire on the enemy while another squad bounded to a new covered position. This way there was always an overwatch team engaging the enemy directly while the rest of the platoon withdrew to a more favorable location, before swapping roles, in leapfrogging fashion. The tactic had the added benefit of confusing the enemy, who would fire in the direction where the overwatch team had just been, only to realize they were no longer there.

The well-trained force deployed as ordered. Wright and Gaudet remained with Rifle Squad A. They set up an overwatch defense perimeter behind trees and boulders along the expected frontal attack while Squad B pulled back one hundred feet to get ready to leapfrog. Meanwhile, Squad C rushed back to protect the LZ a mile away.

Armed with a mix of Heckler & Koch UMPs, M-32 grenade launchers, M4 carbines, and M249 light machine guns—and as the large Taliban force from the forested mountainside materialized three hundred yards away—Wright gave the order to fire.

The speed and nimbleness of the enemy's reaction surprised even someone as battle hardened as Pasha. Four of his men failed to react in time and seek cover. The incoming volleys cut them down, their backs exploding with rounds punching through before they fell in the thicket.

Dammit, he thought, aiming an AK-47 at the center of the muzzle flashes while turning left, then right, leading his men in a zigzagging pattern, emptying the forty 7.62×39mm cartridges housed in the curved magazine.

But as he reloaded, he noticed that the enemy was no longer there, a realization not yet made by the dozen men flanking him and still firing at nothing.

"Hold your fire!" he shouted, wondering where the hell they had gone.

But an instant later, two men a dozen feet from him perished as a new fusillade materialized from a spot ten meters off to the right and at least fifty meters behind the original enemy location. Their muzzle flashes illuminated the woods in stroboscopic fashion. Then twenty seconds later they were gone, but another set of muzzle flashes sparked almost immediately to the left and again fifty or so meters behind.

There are two teams! Pasha finally realized. The American force had split up into two teams that covered each other during their retreat, so there was always suppressing fire, which effectively forced his team to constantly seek shelter instead of charging.

Ordering his men to lay low and advance with caution, Pasha waited for the right opportunity to attack again.

37

Into the Fray

KANDAHAR AIRFIELD. SOUTHERN AFGHANISTAN.

"Six Six Zulu taking fire. We need relief and immediate exfil. LZ hot. Repeat. LZ hot. Need a Hawg."

The afterburners kicked Laura Vaccaro in the back as she listened to the call sign of Wright's platoon, shooting her off the runway like a rocket and leaving KAF behind in the wake of the A-10's twin turbofans.

Blue skies, desert, and the distant Sulaimans filling the armored canopy of a her new A-10, Captain Vaccaro turned the stick to a heading of 230 degrees, placing the Warthog on a direct intercept course with the provided coordinates almost eighty miles away, holding five hundred feet at three hundred knots.

"Red One One in the air. One six minutes out. Repeat, One six minutes out."

"Red One One, Six Six Zulu. Tallies north and east of LZ."

"Roger that," Vaccaro replied, trying to make out if that was Wright on the radio, but the accent was wrong. It sounded . . . *Cajun?*

"Red One One, Bravo Niner Six. Traffic twelve o'clock. Five miles. One thousand five hundred, two Hooks. Hooks Six and Seven. Traffic six o'clock. Five miles. Five hundred, a Hawg."

Vaccaro spotted the twin dots just over the horizon as she closed the gap on the Chinooks. "Red One One has traffic in sight."

"Hook Six looking," replied the pilot of the lead Chinook.

It took twenty seconds to catch them, and as she rushed beneath and to the left of the dual-rotor helicopters, Vaccaro added, "Hookers, Hookers, Red One One will clear things up for you."

"Red One One, Hook Six. Copy that."

"Red One One, Six Six Zulu standing by. Smoking your target in ten zero."

Vaccaro clicked the mike twice to acknowledge that the marines would use grenade launchers to lob smoke shells onto Taliban positions in ten minutes, though she figured that enemy muzzle flashes alone would be enough for her to spot the bastards.

Twelve minutes.

The terrain changed from desert and rocky hills to light vegetation as she inched back the control stick to follow the sloping terrain at the foot of the mountain range, keeping the jet dead on five hundred feet above ground level as measured by the A-10's radar altimeter.

Nine minutes.

She scanned her instruments as trees dominated the landscape above four thousand feet, confirming proper operation of every system, in particular the massive 30mm Avenger nose cannon.

Five minutes.

A quick diagnosis of her underside ordnance, the primary 70mm Hydra rockets, returned nominal as she tried to perform another radio check with the marines on the ground, but all she heard was the deafening noise of full automatic fire.

Two minutes.

She came up from the southeast, skimming the treetops at three hundred knots, her altimeter shooting past nine thousand feet, eyes on the LZ just ahead, a mountainside clearing she could not yet see while flying nap-of-the-earth. But she could see the bluish smoke rising above the trees.

"Red One One coming in hot and fast."

"Red One One, Six Six Zulu. Roger, hot it is."

"Roger that," she replied, climbing a thousand feet over the terrain while briefly throttling back, getting a bird's-eye view of the clearing and the coiling blue smoke.

Dropping the nose and advancing the throttles, Vaccaro headed cockpit-first into the fray.

38

Fire and Movement

**COMPOUND 57. SULAIMAN MOUNTAINS.
SOUTHERN AFGHANISTAN.**

Distant explosions and the unmistakable thunder of an Avenger 30mm cannon marked the unmistakable arrival of a Warthog. But Wright was too busy to check who was piloting it.

The marine captain and his team were developing a rhythm, leap-frogging back across the goat path every thirty seconds, one squad covering the coordinated getaway of the other. Once the bounding squad settled in their new position, it assumed overwatch, firing their weapons for just twenty seconds while the other team began its bound. And leading the way ahead of both squads, working at a faster clip than recommended, the trio of minesweepers combed the wider track of hillside required by the infantry tactic.

Wright and Gaudet remained in the overwatch, constantly switching squads, firing their .45-caliber UMPs at the large mob of screaming and shooting rebels closing in on them while getting reports from the battle in progress at the LZ, among their team, an A-10, and a second contingent of Taliban.

Bastards are trying to cut us off.

Wright frowned, picking his targets carefully, the fire selector lever on semiautomatic mode, allowing him to fire single shots, like real operators. Fully automatic fire on a weapon like the UMP45 was the stuff of movies.

Still, after four minutes, the marine officer was running dangerously low on ammunition while the enemy continued coming at them strong.

Removing a spent twenty-five-round magazine and inserting his last one, Wright got ready to shift squads while retreating to a new vantage point, firing next to Gaudet and another soldier, a young corporal named Franklin.

"Stay with me, Corporal!" Wright shouted, noticing shadows off to their left. The Taliban was trying to flank him. Pointing in that direction, he ordered, "Hit them over there!"

The kid, on his first tour and justifiably agitated, took a stand next to his captain and his sergeant, laying down suppressing fire with his M4 carbine for several seconds before switching magazines and shooting another volley.

"I'm out, sir!" Franklin screamed.

"Pull back to your squad!" Wright ordered, dispatching Franklin to rejoin his buddies while he and Gaudet brought up the rear.

The kid took off, and Wright saw the mistake a moment before it happened.

The corporal's squad had gone around the corridor formed by the parallel wall of boulders, where the minesweepers had marked off the nonmetallic daisy-chained IEDs, and it had already returned to the goat trail on the far side of the pass. Franklin, in his hasty attempt to catch up, and getting a glimpse of his team already past the fifty-foot-long rocky passage, completely missed the orange markings on the ground and plunged straight into the kill zone.

The image of the kid running in between moss-slick rocks, M4 carbine in hand, vanished in a sheet of fire and shrapnel as he triggered the mines.

The blasts, shaped by the rock formations, shot out of the channel in both directions, punching Wright in the chest while hammering the rear of the retreating force on the other side of the pass. His body armor absorbed the brunt of the shock wave, tossing him back several feet. He landed by Gaudet, who somehow managed to keep his footing, remained standing, and—

A late detonation flashed on the forested hill on the other side of the rocky pass. Even in his altered state of mind, Wright realized what it was: the first IED the minesweepers had identified, likely triggered in the aftermath of the daisy-chained blast.

For an instant the world went black, then gray, before the canopy of trees resolved, followed by the cries of Corporal Franklin.

Staggering to his feet, the UMP45 still in his hands, and actually amazed that the kid was still alive, Wright heard himself scream, "Claymore mines, Gaudet! And suppressive fire! And get Franklin to the LZ! Now!"

Then he almost fainted, and dropped to his knees, before adding, "Move, soldiers!"

Two soldiers knelt by Wright, covering him with their M249 light machine guns, unloading a wall of full metal jacket at the enemy less than two hundred yards away, forcing their dark silhouettes, visible against the side of the hill, to seek shelter.

Wright and Gaudet worked quickly, setting up three M18A1 Claymore mines. Each packed seven hundred one-eighth-inch steel balls behind a shaped charge. They positioned the charges linearly every twenty feet down the goat path, facing the enemy. Hidden behind fallen branches, the Claymores provided three layers of defense.

Wright had Gaudet help him run the Claymore wires down to the entrance to the boulder path. But the dizziness returned, and he nearly collapsed.

Gaudet helped him reach the long crater formed by the IED blasts, still warm to the touch. The two corporals walked backwards toward them while firing their M249s, reaching the rocky formation, keeping the enemy at bay as the sergeant connected the wires to a single detonator with three buttons.

"Get your men back to the LZ, Sergeant!" Wright said, coming back around, trying to hold it together, breathing deeply, forcing his eyes to focus on the sloping terrain beyond his DFP.

As images of his father and grandfather loomed over him, he added, "Hurry! Get the hell out of here! I'll hold them back!"

All three marines stared at him as if he had two heads.

"What about you, sir?" Gaudet finally asked.

"Leave me your ammo! And go!"

"But, sir! That's—"

"An order, Sergeant! A *direct* order! Now go!"

Several insurgents loomed in the distance the moment the suppressing fire stopped, and the distant sound of helicopters echoed down the mountain. Wright shouted, "It's the only way, guys! I can barely stand and will slow you down! Now go! Get everyone to those helos!"

"No man left behind, sir!" Gaudet shouted. "You're coming with us!"

"And whose going to cover us from that?" Wright insisted, pointing at the threat. Twice as many insurgents were visible now, almost as if the forest was birthing them in real time. One of the corporals emptied his M249 and most heads ducked for cover.

"There's no more time! Go!" Wright said.

"But, sir, we can't leave you—"

"Now, soldier!"

Gaudet put a hand on Wright's back and said, "Semper fi!"

"Semper fi!" Wright hissed under his breath.

They left him three magazines for the UMP45 plus the other M249 connected to a two-hundred-round M27 linked belt of 5.56×45mm NATO cartridges.

Fighting the growing wooziness from the round to his helmet plus the IED blast, Wright gutted up, dealing with a likely concussion while lying flat inside the shallow trench carved by the IEDs.

Setting the M249 on its forward bipod, the stock pressed against his right shoulder and shooting hand on the pistol grip, the marine captain aligned the enemy from the entrance to the corridor. His flanks were protected by the boulders rising to either side of him, stained red with American blood—blood he intended to avenge.

He readied to defend his line in the sand for the sake of his men, just as his father and grandfather had done in distant lands long ago, taking as many of the bastards with them as possible.

Wright waited as the enemy materialized, their loose clothing fluttering in the breeze, turbans shifting as they broke into a run, AK-47 muzzles flashing.

But he waited still, letting them get closer.

Up close and very fucking personal.

Before reaching for the detonator.

Pasha heard the multiple IED explosions and grinned. The buried mines had broken the Americans' coordinated retreat, interrupting their fancy tactic by forcing them to rush their wounded to the landing zone, giving his men an opening.

The marines had had their chance to show off their warring skills, and it was now time for Pasha to show off his—and finish them off.

He had divided his men into progressive waves of ten to fifteen warriors, each one more experienced than the preceding one, and better armed. The concept was simple. Deploy the newbies first to give the enemy a false sense of confidence, before hitting them harder and harder with each subsequent wave, confusing them while breaking them.

And I will break them, he thought, as the first wave, composed of eleven newly trained recruits—hormonal teenagers promised eternal life for fighting with the Taliban—took off toward the rocky pass.

They left in a blur of AK-47s, khet partugs, and war cries.

Pasha watched their figures dashing down the hill toward—

A terrible explosion rumbled just ahead of his men, the blast blinding, shredding them with the force of a hundred shotgun blasts, the shock wave slamming into the next wave of jihadists standing a dozen feet from him.

Wright blinked as the outermost charge, designed to strip the determination of the most committed enemy, swallowed the incoming silhouettes in a fan-shaped pattern of steel balls that momentarily blocked all sunlight.

The Claymore was overwhelming in its destructive force. Men vanished if they stood within its sixty-degree horizontal arc and maximum height of six feet, cut to pieces by this ridiculously powerful weapon.

But the marine captain had been around the block enough times to know this particular enemy would be simply temporarily set back by the Claymores, never deterred.

These fanatics simply didn't know how to quit.

An instant later, as a new wave of warriors emerged through the forest, running toward him, Wright pressed the second button on the detonator.

39

A Fair Fight

**COMPOUND 57. SULAIMAN MOUNTAINS.
SOUTHERN AFGHANISTAN.**

"Hardly a fair fight, Colonel."

Stark observed the events unfolding down the hill from his vantage point and had to agree with Chief Larson. Although it was admirable that the marine captain had chosen to stay behind to cover his platoon's retreat, there was no way he could handle the violence heading his way. Even with the Claymores and the solid DFP, the math just didn't work.

Checking his Casio and realizing that the CIA contingent—a Bill Gorman—wouldn't be here for at least another four hours, Stark said over the secured frequency, "Chief, Ryan, Mickey, get in there and provide suppressing fire. Danny, keep eyes on that compound."

"What about Agency rules, sir?" Ryan asked from his sniper's perch.

"This one is on me, boys. Get busy."

"Where are you going, Colonel?" asked Larson, as Stark stood and checked his MP5A1.

"To make it a fair fight."

40

Jarhead Justice

Pasha kept sending them, wave after wave, their boots stomping across the uneven terrain, marching right over the disfigured and bloody remains of their fallen comrades.

The first and second waves never made it past a hundred yards before the explosions consumed them or the machine gun emplacement near the mouth of the passage cut down the few that escaped the shower of steel.

The air stank of cordite and the coppery smell of blood and burned flesh, replacing the pine resin fragrance of just moments ago as the third wave scrambled ahead. Its ranks were filled with more seasoned warriors, though they were still mostly kids, just a few years older than he and Akhtar had been the first time they drew blood.

The men charged ahead without fear, confident in their cause, certain that Allah was on their side. They fought for their homeland, for their beliefs, just like their fathers had fought against the Soviets, with an iron will.

But they still didn't get far. A third hidden charge ignited the hillside, the burst deafening, ripping through cloth and flesh.

41

Sweet Point

The trick to the Claymores was patience. And that last blast had truly taxed Wright's discipline, waiting for the rebels to get close enough while he was taking fire, while rounds peppered the ground around him, sparking off boulders.

But he had waited, aware of the Claymore's optimum effective range, the sweet point between lethality and area coverage of 160 feet with a hit probability of over 40 percent on a man-size target, though fragments could travel as far as seven hundred feet.

The rest he handled with the M249, keeping his fire low and limited to short bursts.

A fourth wave of rebels emerged on the hillside, screaming and firing their Kalashnikovs, advancing toward him like a maddened horde.

John Wright, fresh out of Claymores, knew that it would take a miracle to survive another minute.

But as he steeled himself to face the same fate as his ancestors, while cutting down as many of those bearded devils as possible, the miracle happened.

What in Allah's name is happening? Pasha thought, as his fourth wave of men, ten of his best warriors, was decimated. But not by American mines or that lone soldier firing his light machine gun from the mouth of the boulder pass.

His men were not falling on their backs from taking rounds to their chests. Instead, they succumbed to large-caliber shots shrieking down the hill.

Someone had flanked them—someone on higher ground and armed with a much louder and much more powerful weapon.

That's a fifty-cal, he thought, its dismembering rounds wreaking havoc on his men, turning his warriors into a mangled mess of bloody parts bursting in the forest.

Wright was confused. His men were supposed to be on their way to the LZ. But someone had joined in this fight—someone unseen and also unyielding, obliterating that last wave with a brutality matching the Claymore carnage.

And though he was confused, his veteran sense could discern at least three weapons being fired against the enemy from their left flank. A Browning M2 certainly dominated the well-orchestrated action, but in between the synchronized beat of the heavy machine gun he saw the surgical strikes from individual .50-caliber shots, probably from a sniper.

To Wright, the single shots tearing off heads and chests resembled disruptive silent notes to the unchained melody of the Browning. And although he also could not hear the third weapon, he could see the impacts from a smaller-caliber weapon than his own M249, perhaps from a suppressed UZI or MP5.

Wright was indeed confused, but he was also out of ammo. Firing his final machine gun rounds, still feeling groggy from the headshot and the IED shock wave, he managed to stand.

And as he did so, he had the sudden desire to make a run for the landing zone.

42

Come Back to Me

Muzzle flashes sparked to life, followed by tracers rushing up toward her.

"No you don't," Vaccaro mumbled, unleashing a torrent of 70mm Hydra rockets, their bright contrails swarming toward enemy positions threatening to overrun John Wright and his marine rifle platoon.

In the blink of an eye, more than a dozen men vanished in sheets of orange flames.

She pulled back and circled the calculated mess she had created, before aligning the Avenger and squeezing the trigger.

The nineteen-foot-long cannon thundered to life, demolishing with a few hundred 1.5-pound rounds anything that had survived the Hydras. But just as she was about to pull back up, the fuselage trembled with the sound of a dozen hammers.

"Damn," she thought, catching a glimpse of the muzzle flashes to her right, a pair of machine gun emplacements where the insurgents had managed to flank her. Pushing the throttles to get herself out of range, she watched as warning lights from her left turbofan accompanied a loss in thrust.

"Bravo Niner Six, Bravo Niner Six. Red One One is hit. Lost port engine."

"Red One One, Bravo Niner Six. Hooks thirty seconds away. RTB. RTB."

"Negative, Bravo Niner Six," she replied to KAF's order to return to base. "I'm staying with my boys." Then she added,

"Hookers, Hookers, stand by. LZ not secured. Repeat, LZ not secured. Acknowledge."

"Red One One, Hooks Two and Three holding two miles south."

She made a wide circle before dropping right over the machine guns and opening the Avenger. Ground fire peppered her left wing, tearing into the armored skin. Airbursts of antiaircraft fire ignited in small dark clouds around her nose as she worked the control stick, rudders, and throttle to guide the cannon straight across the enemy positions.

The massive gun cut a track of terrain ten feet wide that reached the threat, the two machine gun nests, each manned by three men. For an instant, she saw their muzzles pointed directly at her, men in turbans at the controls while others fed ammo belts into the sides of the weapons.

And then they were gone, swallowed by the river of explosive death roaring over them. The colossal energy deposited over the course of five seconds cut men and machines to pieces, disintegrated them.

She pulled up at the last moment, banking hard left while climbing, reaching two thousand feet and entering a tight holding pattern while verifying that she had put down all resistance.

The first marines stepped tentatively into the clearing, weapons in hand, before turning to the skies and waving. She tried to see if Wright was among them, but with their helmets, they all looked alike from three hundred feet.

Vaccaro rocked her wings. "Hookers, Hookers, LZ cleared. Customers waiting."

"Roger that, Red One One. Thanks for your help."

"Red One One, Bravo Niner Six. RTB. RTB."

"In a moment, Bravo Niner Six. Circling overhead until they're cleared," she replied, entering a shallow holding pattern while fighting the urge to contact the marines for a SitRep, in the hope that Wright would reply.

Come back to me, John. Fucking come back to me.

43

Ghosts

SULAIMAN MOUNTAINS. SOUTHERN AFGHANISTAN.

Wright lacked the energy to run, but he ran anyway, fueled by adrenaline and sheer willpower, fighting the dizziness and the ringing in his ears. He left the puzzling battle behind, too tired and groggy to care who had interceded on his behalf.

The rattle of mixed gunfire behind him gave way to the deafening double rotors of the Chinooks biting the air just ahead, hovering beyond the edge of the tree line, where he could also hear the thunderous sound of an Avenger cannon.

Wright ran as fast as his body allowed, his vision blurring, his mind growing foggier, his senses numbing. But as he neared the tree line, and through the cacophony of sounds, he heard his men shouting as they boarded the choppers, as they got the wounded aboard, as they prepared to leave the area.

They've made it, John. They've made it, thanks to you.

The thought preceded a wave of nausea that dropped him to his knees just a few feet from the edge of the clearing, bending him over in uncontrollable spasms as he gagged, then vomited, eyes veiled in tears, ears ringing, legs turning to putty.

Collapsing on his side, he began to tremble, the abuse finally catching up to him. And in this altered state of body and mind, he saw the forest come alive in front of him, watched the figure of a helmeted soldier rushing toward him in the snow.

The snow?

The man knelt by him and smiled.

Pops? What are you doing here?

Taking you home, kid.

Wright stared, dumbfounded, at the image of his grandfather as snow fell around them, alongside the reverberating pounding of artillery, followed by the rounds whistling overhead. The ground shook around them, explosions of shrapnel, frozen dirt, and snow.

But another figure emerged through the explosions, a tanned and wiry man in jungle fatigues and an unbuttoned army vest, hauling an old-fashioned M-16. The sweatband around his helmet held a pack of Marlboro 100s and a book of matches. Sweat dripped down his face, dog tags hung from his neck, swinging across his chest.

Wright remembered those dog tags.

On the mantelpiece, next to the flags and the—

Hey, Johnny.

Dad?

But the figures grew transparent in the forest, their vintage uniforms replaced by a large soldier clad in body armor, holding a suppressed MP5A1. He materialized behind them, emerging from the surrounding woods like a ghost, prompting Wright to press his right palm against the grip of his holstered SIG P220.

"Easy, soldier," the stranger said, taking a knee and placing a hand over Wright's to keep him from drawing his service sidearm. "I don't know about you jarheads, but us snake eaters only shoot the bad guys."

Wright wanted to laugh, but his head and belly ached too much. Instead, he relaxed his shooting hand, surrendering to the Special Forces warrior, who picked him up with ease and threw him over his right shoulder.

Staring at the back of the soldier's boots as they rushed out of the forest and into the clearing, Wright tried to thank him, to express his gratitude. But his mind was spinning, propelling all thoughts to the periphery of his consciousness. In this whirling world, as the ground, the boots, and the Chinooks swapped places in his blurry field of view, Wright felt many hands on him, heard the distant voices of his platoon, and above them that of Sergeant Gaudet.

"Bravo Niner Six, Six Six Zulu, we've got him!" Gaudet shouted into his MBITR. "We've got the captain! Getting out of Dodge!"

But Wright didn't care. His head turned toward the open side door of the Chinook as it left the ground. He caught a glimpse of that mysterious warrior, rushing back into the woods, vanishing from view just as he had appeared, like a damn ghost.

Ghosts.

For an instant, Wright thought he saw two other figures by the tree line, one drenched in sweat, the other caked in snow.

Before he passed out.

44

Doer of Deeds

SULAIMAN MOUNTAINS. SOUTHERN AFGHANISTAN.

Pasha ran with a handful of men to the clearing, making a wide circle around whoever it was that had opened fire on his soldiers. He'd left a small contingent behind to keep that hidden force busy while focusing his energy on the landing zone.

In his hands he held not an AK-47 but a fully armed FIM-92 Stinger missile system, a leftover from the days when the Americans had armed the mujahideen.

The forest thinned as he approached the wide mountainside clearing, the smell of cordite and burned flesh pungent from the air support that had demolished the team he had deployed earlier to cut off the enemy retreat.

He cringed at what he saw left in the wake of that A-10 attack. It looked apocalyptic, with entire tracts of forest cut down and mixed with turned-up soil, rocks, broken rifles and machine guns, and body parts—lots and lots of them.

Entrails were splattered everywhere, some still smoking. He stared at carnage on a level he had never seen, even in his worst battles, and the sight fueled his anger, his determination to find a way to exact revenge for this abomination.

By the time he and his men reached the clearing, however, the rescue helicopters were long gone.

But not the jet, he thought, watching it circle overhead. *Not the doer of this terrible deed.*

Shouldering the launcher and holding its pistol grip with his right hand, he went through the steps required to ready the weapon—steps he had memorized eons ago when fighting a different enemy. For an instant he even recalled practicing with a wooden mock-up alongside his older brother.

Unfolding the antenna and removing the front-end cap, he raised the sight assembly in front of his right eye while ignoring the steps related to the IFF system. He did not need a machine to tell him whether the circling Warthog was friendly or foe.

Releasing the Stinger's safety and actuator, he activated the battery coolant unit while listening to the gyro spin-up noise telling him the weapon was operational. Using his left hand, Pasha put a finger over the Uncaging button while the index finger of his right hand caressed the trigger.

Aiming the launcher at the circling Warthog, he waited for the system's high-pitched, steady sound, signaling that the missile's infrared seeker had located the A-10's superhot exhaust plume.

45

Narrowing Choices

**RED ONE ONE. SULAIMAN MOUNTAINS.
SOUTHERN AFGHANISTAN.**

She remained circling at two thousand feet while the Chinooks completed their extraction run and headed back to KAF at full speed.

"Bravo Niner Six, Red One One. RTB," she said, deciding that she had pushed her luck probably as much as she should for one day. Plus, she had gotten confirmation that Wright was aboard one of the choppers.

She stared as their distant silhouettes vanished while she followed a bend in the mountains.

"Red One One, Bravo Niner Six. Copy. RTB."

But as she began to turn the Warthog to an easterly heading, a new alarm screeched in her cockpit, and unfortunately it wasn't another malfunctioning system.

It was a missile warning.

Someone had achieved a lock on her bird.

She pushed the throttle, but the A-10 responded sluggishly on one engine.

The alarm's pitch increased.

"Red One One under attack. Missile," she said calmly while working the problem, cutting hard left, heading in the direction opposite from the Chinooks' course. The last thing she needed was to draw the missile to one of those helicopters already safely out of sight.

Heading straight west while dispensing flares, Vaccaro shoved her single engine into full afterburners and dropped the nose.

Airspeed shot to three hundred knots as the ground filled her windshield. She pulled up and turned right, following the contour of the mountain for nearly a minute.

The missile was momentarily distracted by the flares but quickly reacquired her, due to her relatively slower speed, locking on to her single exhaust plume.

"Dammit."

"Red One One. Bravo Niner Six. SitRep. SitRep." KAF came on the radio asking for a situation report.

"Hold on, boys. A little busy here," she replied, the rugged terrain rushing beneath her as she shot diagonally up the face of the mountain, her altimeter reading ten thousand feet. She released more flares, before swinging the control forward and to the left, now accelerating down the side of the mountain at a ninety-degree angle to the incoming missile.

She watched her airspeed inch past 430 knots, dangerously close to the never-exceed speed of the Warthog, shooting away as fast as possible with one engine, assisted by gravity.

But even that wasn't fast enough to distance her bird from the countermeasures.

Thirty seconds later, the missile detonated twenty feet from her tail.

The cloud of shrapnel expanded radially, tearing into the armor plating protecting her surviving turbofan. The blast pierced through, riddling the skin with dozens of dime-size holes, damaging the arrays of stainless steel blades rotating at thousands of rpm.

Warning lights and alarms warned of her starboard engine losing pressure and overheating.

"Lost second engine. Repeat. Lost second engine and—"

The turbofan detonated behind her in a cloud of fire, spewing flames and smoke, narrowing her choices.

"Red One One, Red One One. SITREP."

For a moment, Vaccaro thought of her father. Then she reached for the ejection handles that would activate both the canopy jettison system and the ACES II seat ejection.

Replying with more calm than she felt, she said, "My fun meter's pegged, boys. Punching out. Would like a helo and a driver ASA—fucking—P."

The instant she pulled on the handles, Vaccaro initiated the miniature detonation cord embedded within the armored canopy, shattering it milliseconds before the first stage of the ejection seat ignited.

The windblast took her breath away as the solid propellant shot her out of the dying Warthog like a cannonball before the second stage took over, sending her on a parabolic flight away from the flaming wreck.

The last thing she saw before passing out from the g-forces was her Warthog in a steep bank, caught in a death spiral to the ground, until its right wingtip struck the side of the mountain and it exploded.

Pasha stared at the distant canopy blossoming over the western rim rock as he lowered his empty launcher tube.

His men cheered in unison.

But he didn't. His eyes followed the parachute being carried away by the mountain's prevailing westerly winds, and in his mind he saw a similar parachute on this very mountain long ago.

Pasha remembered the tactics employed by Akaa to reach the fallen pilot, and he recalled in particular the calculated damage he and Akhtar had inflicted on that Soviet—not to kill but to horrify, for a lifetime.

The canopy may have been of a different color and the pilot of a different nationality, but the enemies of Islam all bled and cried the same way when subjected to the steel of a pesh-kabz.

Pasha stared at the enemy pilot, who couldn't be more than a few miles away.

I am not through with you yet.

46

Lady Luck

RCAF CHINOOK 06–03765. SULAIMAN MOUNTAINS.
SOUTHERN AFGHANISTAN.

"Where the hell is she?"

Wearing a green David Clark headset he had taken from Gaudet, Captain John Wright had stumbled into the cockpit the instant he had come around, fueled by pure adrenaline and anger after hearing from Gaudet that Vaccaro had been shot down.

"She went down about four miles west of the compound, sir," replied the copilot, a lieutenant with the Royal Canadian Air Force, briefly turning his helmeted head to look at Wright over his left shoulder.

Staring at his own reflection on the mirror tint of the man's visor, and ignoring just how bad he looked—he felt even worse—Wright said, "So? Go get her!"

The pilot, another RCAF lieutenant, shook his head while the copilot pointed at the fuel gauges. "No can do, sir! We're halfway to KAF already with a full load of soldiers, plus wounded, and very low on fuel. Barely have enough to make it back!"

"You don't get it!" Wright replied, struggling to find the right words, since he couldn't make this personal. "That woman saved our bacon out there! How the hell you think you were able to reach that LZ? We *all* owe her!"

"We know that, sir! But we can't go back! Another helo is being dispatched!"

"She's neck deep in Tallie country! There's no time for another fucking helo! We need to turn this bird around and get her the hell out of there *now*!"

"And I'm telling you we don't have the fuel for that!" shouted the pilot. "Take it up with General Lévesque, eh?"

"Dammit!" Wright said, yanking off the headset and heading back to the cabin, with Gaudet in tow.

"You gotta sit down, sir!" the sergeant said over the noise of the dual rotors.

"I don't have time to fucking sit down!"

Gaudet just stared at his face and frowned.

"What the hell are you looking at, Sergeant?"

"Your eyes, sir! They're so dilated . . . I think you have the mother of all concussions!"

"What I have," Wright retorted, the dizziness forcing him to sit down before he stretched an index finger to the west, "is a downed American pilot who just saved our ass and who is about to be taken by those mother—"

Wright paused when his vision narrowed and he saw dark spots.

He took a deep breath. He couldn't pass out. Not yet. Not now, when she needed him to fight for her, to find a way to get her out of there.

"Speaking of saving your ass, sir!" Gaudet said. "Who was that guy that brought you back?"

"Hell if I know, Sarge," Wright said, shaking his head at the mysterious .50-caliber suppressing fire that had allowed him to make a run for the LZ, and at the ghostlike figure that had scooped him up from the forest floor as if he weighed nothing.

"Well, I'll take it, sir. Sometimes lady luck's on our side. Hopefully some of it will rub off on that pilot."

Lady luck.

Wright stared at the mountains projecting to the west, fighting the increased light-headedness that made him close his eyes, thinking of his platoon's "lady luck"—currently some twenty miles away beneath the canopy of pine trees.

Fighting for her life after saving their lives.

The dizziness rocketed, kindled by the physical abuse he had endured combined with the horror sweeping through him at the thought of Laura Vaccaro in the hands of those barbaric assholes.

As his vision continued to close up, as his eyelids became unbearably heavy and the deafening rotor noise faded away, he prayed that somehow—*some-fucking-how*—someone found her before the enemy did.

Somehow.

Then he collapsed. But Gaudet caught him, laying him on the floor.

The last thing he heard as everything went dark was his sergeant screaming for the medic.

47

Trading Value

SULAIMAN MOUNTAINS. SOUTHERN AFGHANISTAN.

Nasseer Niaz ignored the jolt of pain stabbing his jawline as he reached the edge of the gorge in time to see the parachute blossom after the ejection seat's short parabolic flight. A moment later, a blast echoed up the mountain, a column of smoke billowing skyward, marking the crash site.

Massaging the swollen gum around his diseased molar with the tip of his tongue, Nasseer observed the camouflaged canopy as it veered in the breeze along the southern face of the mountain, its pilot motionless, perhaps injured, or worse. And just above the crash site, an eastern imperial eagle searched for prey while contemplating the havoc below, its massive wingspan riding the thermals in wide, lazy circles.

The Shinwari warrior considered the opportunity, weighing the risks against the benefits. This was, after all, Taliban country, and though his soldiers were battle hardened, any unnecessary exposure could telegraph his presence.

Like going after a downed American pilot.

On the other hand, delivering that pilot to the Ba'i meant advanced weapons, like the Javelin missile, certainly a cut above the M32s he had negotiated for the laptops, smartphones, and the dead Canadian soldiers.

As Nasseer made his decision, Hassan and the rest of his team reached the wide ledge, followed by his trainer wielding one of the new grenade launchers.

"Will you help us, Aaron?" Nasseer asked. "Will you help us secure that pilot?"

"That's not your kind of war, Nasseer," Aaron replied, loading shells into one of the M32s and walking up to the edge of the plateau. He was a tall man, and as broad as Hassan.

Nasseer didn't respond.

"See that smoke?"

Nasseer turned to see the distant haze coiling high above the trees.

Aaron used the M32 as a pointing device. "That area will be crawling with Taliban within the hour. Why on earth would you want to be anywhere near it and risk getting burned?"

Nasseer gave him a slight shrug.

At his silence, Aaron added, "Your strength comes in your ability to operate without being seen, using the intelligence that we provide, yes?"

Nasseer couldn't disagree with his trainer's logic, but he chose to ignore him, turning to keep an eye on the descending canopy, which looked about three or four miles away, an easy hour's hike, or less.

"Look," Aaron continued, "this is the best time to hit their hideouts, especially the rebel camp marked on our map—while they're away chasing a lone pilot for bragging rights."

Nasseer almost laughed. That was certainly no rebel camp. It was a very large and well-protected Soviet concrete bunker from the 1980s that would require much planning and firepower to breach.

But Aaron always lived up to his promises, providing training and intelligence on enemy positions, which made Nasseer's raids much more effective—and safer, given his much smaller and nimbler force. Their arrangement was a win-win for both Aaron—wherever he was from—and the Shinwari, using their combined skills to put a significant dent in the Taliban.

Aaron had arrived yesterday after traveling nonstop from Jalalabad aboard one of Nasseer's supply trucks. He was claiming to have broken one of Osama bin Laden's own cousins, who had pointed him to that old Soviet compound.

"Besides," Aaron added "that pilot looks dead."

"Maybe . . . maybe not," Nasseer finally said, tilting his head while massaging his bearded jaw, working a thumb into the base of the damn molar. "Either way, the Javelins are worth the risk."

With a heavy sigh, Aaron looked at Nasseer, then at the parachute, then back at the Shinwari fighter. "Fine, but we're taking the pilot with us. We need to hit our objective *first*—and as soon as possible. *Then* you can go back to the base and trade, okay?"

Nasseer considered that for a moment. Aaron was always fair, and he could tell that this mission was of high importance to his people, and it was apparently time sensitive.

With a single nod, the Shinwari chief gave the order to his men, and they headed single file down the incline as the parachute sank beneath the trees.

48

Flash of Destruction

COMPOUND 57. SULAIMAN MOUNTAINS.
SOUTHERN AFGHANISTAN.

He opiated before leaving the headquarters that had been his home for nearly two years. Feeling the burst of alertness that always swept his mind following chemical absorption, Mullah Akhtar Baqer gave the compound a final glance, anger boiling in his gut.

He really didn't want to leave. This was not only his center of operations but also the perfect location to nurse the device back to health as soon as the replacement parts in Dr. Khan's list arrived from bin Laden. The basement lab was ideal, with its clean room and all the necessary tools for the feisty professor to fulfill his obligation. On top of that, his leaving added a complication to the delivery of the replacement components. The plan called for the courier to head here so the professor could get the bomb functional before taking it to a predetermined location, where a plane would fly it out of the country.

However, he didn't know if the message he had already dispatched to bin Laden would allow for a change. And that meant that Akhtar would have to leave a party in the area to meet up with the courier, in case the courier showed up here, to get the replacement components up the mountain to his new hideout.

But the immediate priority was to move the bomb. NATO knew of the existence of this place, and soon it would likely become the target of Hellfire missiles, though he hoped for a ground assault instead. Betting on the ground assault, his men were rigging enough daisy-chained charges outside the compound to deter anyone foolish enough to come near the place.

Down the mountain, Pasha had been successful in turning back the initial assault, though not without taking heavy losses. The Americans were at least temporarily out of his way, airlifted back to their walled base at Kandahar, opening a window of opportunity for his escape.

"All set?" the mullah asked Dr. Khan, who knelt by the device secured to the makeshift carrier resembling an ambulance stretcher.

The professor was tweaking and adjusting, his skinny face buried in the guts of the weapon. Without lifting his head, he said, "In a moment."

"Professor, we do not *have* a moment."

That prompted the man to look up from his work. "Then make one, yes? It isn't ready to be transported yet."

Akhtar sighed. The scientist continued to test his patience, but then again, the man had his priorities straight, placing the welfare of the weapon above all else—if for no other reason than the sake of his family back in Islamabad.

Just as I demanded of him.

"Five minutes, Professor," Akhtar said, holding up the fingers of his right hand, walking away before the professor could protest.

He reached for the encrypted Russian radio clipped to his partug pants and brought it to his lips while depressing the Talk button and asking, "Do you have him?"

After a moment of static, Pasha's voice crackled through the handheld device. *"We're in pursuit."*

"And we're moving out."

"Copy that. Out."

Akhtar put the radio away. Keeping chatter to a minimum was key to survival in this region, where American planes flew constantly, monitoring the airwaves. With luck, anyone listening and able to break the encryption would get nothing from the brief conversation. And with even more luck, his brother just might be able to catch the American pilot for interrogation before rescue crews reached the crash site. Aviators were typically privy to tactics and even to strategy, which his thousands of fighters in the Kandahar region could use.

He neared the entrance, where a dozen men who had volunteered to remain behind to ensure the safe passage of the weapon readied their Russian RPD machine guns at every watchtower and other defense emplacements around the compound. They were young, fearless, and most importantly, willing to make the ultimate sacrifice for Afghanistan—though Akhtar didn't share their religious conviction. If Allah truly existed, he would not have allowed his people to suffer back-to-back invasions by the two most powerful nations on the planet.

But just as we killed the Soviets' will to fight, we shall also strip the determination from the Americans.

And the weapon under his care could do just that: inflict enough casualties in a brief flash of destruction to test the invaders' will.

Who needs Allah when I have thirty kilotons of wrath in my possession?

Technicians finished rigging various types of mines just beyond the outer wall before joining the professor and the rest of the team, who were gathering at the secret entrance to the tunnel in the rear of the basement.

Akhtar remained outside for another minute, glaring at the skies beyond the canopy of trees. He silently cursed the technology that allowed the enemy to deliver death to his men from the comfort of drone control systems often located a half world away.

But he was now in possession of even deadlier technology, which soon, with the assistance of Axaa and the professor, would allow him to unleash hell on the enemy.

In a brief flash of destruction.

49

Delivery Service

**DOMODEDOVO INTERNATIONAL AIRPORT.
MOSCOW. RUSSIA.**

Zahra Hassani remained in the back of the room. Hands always by her sides, free, she oversaw the negotiations, looking at everyone and no one, assessing the potential threat level of each player at the table, and especially of the bodyguards stoically parked behind them.

Three Russians in their tailored business suits, wearing gaudy rings and watches, sat across from her principal, Prince Mani al Saud. Twice as many protectors stood behind them.

Plus the woman, Zahra thought, glancing at the tall Slav with the auburn hair and pale skin standing just to the right of the bodyguards. She spoke on a cell phone, out of earshot of everyone, while monitoring the proceedings with the calculating hazel eyes that crowned her high cheekbones. She also had the most peculiar tattoo—an elaborate compass rose surrounded by red roses and snow—covering the base of her neck and disappearing inside her shirt.

As had been the case in the past, Prince Mani was clearly in charge, controlling the meeting even when heavily outnumbered by players and bodyguards, laying out his terms to the Mafia bosses. It didn't matter if the prince was dealing with the PKK, the Russians, the Sicilians, the Americans, the Iraqis, the Iranians, the Pakistanis, the Taliban, or even bin Laden himself. The man was always in control, always dictating nonnegotiable terms, always getting the other side to conform to his requests. And he did it with the finesse of a veteran diplomat, his confident smile and demeanor putting everyone at ease, including the man sitting directly across from him: Vyacheslav Ivankov, one of the richest, most feared, and best-connected crime bosses in Russia, with an estimated net worth of nearly $700 million.

Pocket change, she thought.

It didn't hurt the prince's negotiating position, of course, that he always arrived with suitcases full of cash, bonds, and diamonds. It also didn't hurt that, having done this for nearly a decade—first for Saudi Arabia and then for himself—the man had friends in high places across two dozen governments and twice as many militia groups. And tonight the situation wasn't much different from previous meetings.

With two exceptions.

One, the last-minute nature of this assembly, as it usually took weeks to set up these sessions.

Two, the damn Russian woman.

Unlike the stereotypical bodyguards remaining close to their principals, hands free and ready to reach for their concealed weapons, the redhead seemed far more interested in her conversation than in the proceedings. Which, of course, raised the obvious question.

Why the hell is she here?

But Zahra was a pro, and she did what pros were paid to do: she kept her cool while handling the immediate task at hand with maniacal focus—which in her case was protecting her mark. And while keeping a pragmatic eye out for anything suspicious beyond the horizon. This, however, kept pointing her operative compass to the woman's ornate compass.

She continued scanning Ivankov and his two associates, the bodyguards, the two access points into a building adjacent to the hangar currently housing the prince's Citation X, and of course, the redhead.

But although she stood alone behind Prince Mani, Zahra wasn't quite on her own. A tiny lapel microphone and a flesh-colored earpiece and matching wire coiling into her black shirt connected her to the prince's copilot, the chef, and two flight attendants—all armed and standing by in the adjacent hangar.

Zahra felt confident that she and her backup could handle the row of overfed clowns with their bull necks and barrel chests who were standing behind the Mafia bosses, should the negotiations break down. But she wasn't so certain about the woman. She was too relaxed, too at ease. And that level of tranquility—in sharp contrast with the tense faces of the bodyguards—telegraphed the presence of a real operator.

But so are you, she thought. *And so is Mani*.

The prince, a graduate of the prestigious United States Air Force Academy and former fighter pilot with the Saudi Air Force, ran his international smuggling business with the same cold and calculating precision with which he flew jets. And in true form, Prince Mani had arranged for the location of this clandestine meet to his convenience.

They would remain in the international section of the airport for their entire stay, beyond the reach of customs agents. Getting the goods, obtained from a military warehouse outside of Moscow, past airport security checkpoints was Ivankov's problem. The Mafia boss had to deal with customs to smuggle the small box of components on the left side of the table. And he would also have to deal with customs to bring into the country the large Louis Vuitton case next to Zahra, packed with a ridiculous amount of cash and uncut diamonds from one of Mani's mines in Africa.

All Russian eyes—even the woman's—had gravitated to the iconic pattern on the leather suitcase the moment Zahra had rolled it into the room, following the prince. The bodyguards in particular had struggled the entire meeting, furtive eyes breaking their training for another glance at the riches inside a case that, even empty, cost as much as a Rolex watch.

But before anyone could lay hands on its soft leather handle, the technical contents inside the cardboard box required a technical inspection. Mani looked over his right shoulder at her, and she in turn tapped her lapel microphone three times.

The door connecting the meeting room to the hangar swung open and two men wearing Russian Army uniforms walked in the room. Both captains, they carried black duffel bags filled with gear, and an empty padded rucksack.

The bosses exchanged a nervous glance. The bodyguards sensed their superiors' uneasiness and shifted uncomfortably.

The captains belonged to the Rosatom State Atomic Energy Corporation, the regulatory body of the Russian nuclear complex—ironically, the same institution that the Mafia had raided to obtain the components.

"What is the meaning of this?" asked Ivankov.

Zahra hid her amusement at her principal's ability to hold all the cards, even with someone who was known to have connections with Russian state intelligence organizations. Ivankov had made a name for himself first in Russia, in the 1980s, and then in the United States, where he arrived in 1992 and grew a powerful crime organization from New York to Los Angeles. The FBI finally caught up to the man, arresting him and then deporting him to Russia in 2004 to face murder charges over two Turkish nationals shot at a Moscow restaurant in 1992. But he had been acquitted of all charges the previous July when the state witnesses to the crime—one of them a police officer—mysteriously changed their stories.

"They're with me," said Prince Mani with an innocent smile, legs crossed and hands on his lap as he tilted his head at the Russian officers. "Technical check."

Ivankov rubbed his white goatee while staring at the two captains through the light tint of his round glasses.

And Zahra knew precisely why: the Mafia boss had tried to recruit the Russian officers for years but they had seemed incorruptible. Now they did as instructed by the Saudi smuggler, using the hardware in the bags to inspect each component.

Zahra looked at the woman, the only one on that side of the table who had not reacted, continuing her side conversation while the captains performed their checks. But, for a brief moment, Zahra thought that one of the captains gave the Russian woman a subtle nod.

Did I just imagine that?

"You do not trust me, old friend?" asked Ivankov, leaning forward and resting his forearms on the table, his diamond rings glittering under the fluorescents. He had known the prince for over a decade.

"I certainly do trust you, just as I'm also certain that you believe the components are good. But please understand that my client . . . well, it's very unhealthy to disappoint him. I need to be absolutely sure they are in perfect working order. There will not be a second chance."

Ivankov considered the answer for a moment before exhaling, glancing at the Louis Vuitton case, and finally leaning back, gesturing agreement with his right hand.

The inspection took another twenty minutes as the parties sat quietly checking their cell phones, except for Zahra, who never stopped her disciplined scan.

The captains connected each piece of hardware to various testing devices, reviewing the results in a handheld LCD screen. Satisfied, they slipped the hardware inside a bubble-padded sleeve, labeled it, sealed it, and placed it inside the rucksack.

They checked the voltage in the battery pack and the integrity of various metallic rings. The double thumbs-up from the captains came after inspection of the final component, a bundle of colored wires, which they also bagged and stowed with the rest of the gear.

And that was Zahra's cue to roll the suitcase around the table, where one of the bodyguards hefted it in between Ivankov and the prince.

The Mafia boss did the honors, unzipping it and taking almost fifteen minutes to inspect the $5 million in mixed currency—mostly U.S. dollars, euros, and British pounds—plus another $3 million in diamonds.

"You do not trust me, old friend?" asked Prince Mani with a grin. "It's all in there."

Ivankov looked up from the stash and also smiled, his face relaxing, before halting his review, zipping up the suitcase, and saying, "Old habits." He then nodded at the same bodyguard, who removed it from the table and kept it by his side.

As the group stood and the principals shook hands, the Russian woman promptly walked away. Zahra stared at her long red hair swinging across her back as she vanished beyond the hangar door, the phone still pressed against her right ear.

Fifteen minutes later, Zahra knelt between Prince Mani and the copilot as they taxied out of the hangar under an overcast afternoon sky.

"Who was that woman?"

Prince Mani shrugged. "The pretty one? I'm guessing one of Ivankov's bodyguards?"

Zahra shook her head. "More than that, I think."

"Oh, like us?" He shifted his right hand from the dual throttles and placed it on her thigh. Zahra promptly moved it back.

"I'm serious. She was an operator."

"Okay . . . so, how does that change things? It was still a clean trade."

"I'm not sure. How good do you know those two Russian officers?" she asked.

"Two hundred thousand euros good. *Each*. Why?"

"Because I think one of them looked at her and gave her a nod."

"I don't blame him. She was hot, especially with that tattoo."

"Dammit, Mani. I'm serious."

"If you want to be serious, then worry about what's coming next."

"What's that?"

"Karachi."

"Why? I hate Pakistan."

"Change of planes. A business jet is not conducive for the run we need to make." He patted the rucksack.

"Run? Where?"

"Southern Afghanistan."

"I hate that even more. Who is doing the delivery?"

The Prince looked over his shoulder, smiled, and said, "You are."

50

Every Last One of Them

DOMODEDOVO INTERNATIONAL AIRPORT.
MOSCOW. RUSSIA.

Senior GRU officer Kira Tupolev left the meeting between the Russian Mafia and the smugglers and walked straight to the Mercedes sedan parked across the street from the hangar.

"Where to?" asked Sergei Popov, her driver and second-in-command of her Spetsnaz squad.

Settling in the rear seat, she found his eyes in the rearview mirror and steeled herself for what needed to be done.

Her country had waited nearly seventeen years for the opportunity to right a terrible wrong.

She had waited seventeen years for the opportunity.

Contrary to popular belief, the Russian Commonwealth of Independent States and its predecessor, the Union of Soviet Socialist Republics, fell in the category of "anal" when it came to accounting for its nukes. And while she conceded that the Kremlin leadership was far from perfect, Kira had seen firsthand the lengths to which her nation had gone to prevent the proliferation of its nuclear weapons. There had been incidents, of course, where audits of weapons-grade uranium or plutonium counts at various warehouses had not matched official reports, especially back in the days when Ukraine had its own arsenal. And there was the ever-present Western media and its relentless desire to amplify every incident, however insignificant.

Losing an entire tactical nuclear weapon, like the RN-40 in 1988, fell in the category of unprecedented, and her nation had been damn lucky that the same Western media never got wind of it.

Unfortunately, all efforts to recover it before pulling out of Afghanistan had been fruitless.

The Afghan desert swallowed it. Those had been the closing words in the official report that reached the Kremlin in the final days of September 1988. But to Kira, at the time a freshly minted KGB officer working in East Berlin alongside the Stasi, the East German secret police, the report had a personal repercussion.

"Kira?" Sergei asked again. "Where do you want to—"

"Novo-Ogaryovo," she responded.

Ignoring Sergei's wide-eyed stare when she mentioned the private residence of President Vladimir Putin, she added, "But first, I need to see the colonel."

"But . . . it is not visiting day."

"It is now, Sergei."

They left the airport via the Moscow–Domodedovo highway, turning east on the MKAD loop, then south on Route E30. They continued for three kilometers, taking the exit for the Moscow Hospital for War Veterans.

"Wait here," she told him, as they pulled up to the modern annex adjacent to the old hospital, a dilapidated seven-story white and gray structure left over from the Soviet Union era. She slowly shook her head at the poor bastards who lacked the appropriate connections to be transferred from that large facility to the newer medical center—even *it* was a depressing place, but at least the equipment worked.

Still, she had pulled every string she could to get the colonel moved here five years ago, where he received better care, but that didn't ease the sting of her weekly visits.

Nothing could, short of . . .

Taking a deep breath, she glanced at a late afternoon sky the color of gunmetal that reflected her mood and walked briskly up the concrete steps and through glass double doors. A bald man in his sixties, wearing a dark blue uniform and manning the security desk off to the right of the small lobby, looked up from a newspaper. It was Andrei, the afternoon shift guard.

The sound of ruffling paper mixed with her heels clicking hollowly over polished floors under a dozen recessed lights.

"Kira?"

"Need to see him," she said, heading for another set of double doors leading to the patients' rooms.

"But it is not—"

"It's important, and it will be quick," she said.

Andrei considered that for a moment.

"Or I could have my boss call your boss. Remember how that worked out last time?"

Andrei stood and shook his head. "Go ahead. Make it quick."

Kira went through the second set of doors and faced a long and wide hallway with more recessed lighting, freshly painted walls, and pristine floors. It even smelled good. But it still ranked at the very top of the most disheartening places on earth—at least for her.

She walked straight for the fifth door on the left and slowly inched it open, finding him in his usual spot. The recliner faced a large window overlooking an assortment of concrete statues of various Greek gods embellishing a rose garden. And it was all backdropped by a memorable view of the heavy rush hour traffic on E30, under that miserable Russian sky.

Though it didn't really matter, since he was blind.

Colonel Mikhail Tupolev had recently turned fifty-eight, but he looked twenty years older.

Afghanistan would do that to a man.

Kira remembered his last visit, in 1982, on the eve of his deployment. They had celebrated her letter of acceptance into the KGB academy and had toasted her upcoming trip to Minsk to begin training. He had promised to return for her graduation, but the increasing shortage of pilots had prevented him from rotating home. And when that dreaded country finally released him from its grip, the shell of a man that had reached the intensive care unit at the top floor of the weathered building next door, in the fall of 1988, had been too much for his wife, who left him and moved to Saint Petersburg.

But Kira couldn't abandon him, even if he couldn't recognize her. The mujahideen had taken care of maiming his mind as much as his body. And on top of it all, the insurgents had even robbed him of his right to an honorable death by his own hand. According to the account from the rescue crew, the colonel had experienced the same treatment as so many other captured soldiers who had tried to end it with their sidearms rather than . . . this.

The bastards had shot off his hand and taken his Makarov—the same pistol his father had used in Stalingrad, decades earlier—and also his beloved Gagarin class ring.

She pulled up a chair and sat next to him. His gaunt face was fixed on the highway even though he lacked eyes. His hearing was good—according to the doctors—though he seldom reacted to anyone, due to a combination of the PTSD and the drugs. But he loved listening to that highway traffic. It was almost like a magnet to his damaged soul.

Her eyes dropped to his left hand, the one he kept shaped as if he were holding a pistol, index finger constantly twitching, squeezing the imaginary trigger in his PTSD-induced nightmare.

"He's still back there," the doctors had told her at the beginning, when she had managed to peel away from her first KGB post in East Berlin to visit him. "He's still reliving the hell he went through."

And that was the primary point of the meds: to stave off the nightmare, tempering the gunslinger action. But today he had not yet gotten his dose, which also meant he was in his most responsive state, before he succumbed to the lethargic effects of the PTSD drugs.

"Daddy," she said. "It's me, Kira."

No response, just the index pulling that damn trigger.

"I found it, Daddy," she added, fingering her cell phone and staring at the message from a few days ago, which her people in northern Pakistan had intercepted.

The image of a class ring from the Gagarin Air Force Academy, followed by,

FOUND WHAT WE LOOKED FOR THAT NIGHT.

NEED ASSISTANCE TO ASSESS ITS CONDITION.

The year of his graduation, 1971, was clearly visible in the JPEG file, and Kira had spent the better part of the past day tracking down every graduate from that year. The only one missing his ring was her father.

Kira was convinced that the bomb had surfaced. She was also

certain that, after so many years, the weapon would be in need of re-
pair, and in the case of a device as sophisticated as the RN-40, that
meant original replacement parts. So she had done what the KGB,
and later on the GRU, trained her to do: use deception as a weapon.

She had contacted Vyacheslav Ivankov to help her set up a sting
operation, using the only language the Russian Mafia boss understood: money. When the request for the RN-40 spare parts arrived
from one Prince Mani al Saud, who was acting as broker, Kira and
her Russian Mafia asset had been ready to set up the exchange in the
hangar. In addition, her agents inside the Rosatom State Atomic
Energy Corporation had incorporated a miniature encrypted GPS
transmitter in the battery pack included with the components.
Ivankov and the Rosatom captains had played their parts perfectly,
so Kira had let the Mafia boss keep the contents of the suitcase as
his fee while the Rosatom captains were paid directly by the Saudi
prince.

"Daddy, I found the bomb," she said, "and I'm going to get it back."

For a moment he ceased moving his index finger, and Kira thought
she saw his eyelids, sewn shut years ago, quiver ever so slightly.

But a second later the imaginary firing resumed.

Kira forced savage control of her emotions, keeping her voice
steady as her gaze landed on one of those weathered Greek statues,
the one depicting Nemesis, the angel-like goddess who exacted ret-
ribution.

"I'm going to Afghanistan, Daddy. I promise I will bring back
your ring . . . and I'm going to kill the bastards who did this to you."

Leaning over to hug him, her wet stare fixated on the sword
clutched in Nemesis's right hand, she added, "Every last one of them."

51

Muy Caliente

THE WHITE HOUSE. WASHINGTON, DC.

President Bush sat behind his desk at the Oval Office, munching on one of his favorite midmorning snacks: a grilled cheese sandwich made with plain Kraft Singles, white bread, and a touch of Tabasco, personally prepared by White House chef Walter Scheib.

The president smiled when thinking of one of the few positions he hadn't changed during the transition from the Clinton years, though he did pretty much revamp the chef's menu from hummus, quinoa, and other such foods to down-home American dishes. The list included Texas beef, pulled pork sliders, chicken potpie, a variety of Tex-Mex dishes, and of course, grilled cheese sandwiches.

But the president did find it amusing that his predecessor kept such a healthy menu at the White House, given his well-known addiction to the epitome of American fast food: McDonald's Big Macs.

As he considered whether Hillary might have had something to do with those heart-friendly choices, the phone rang. He recognized the internal extension from the kitchen. It was Chef Scheib, following up.

He pressed the Speaker button while glancing over at Counselor to the President Dan Bartlett, who was standing in the middle of the room getting the CIA and the DIA technical guys settled in the sofas, while CIA Director George Tenet and Secretary of State Condoleezza Rice stood in the background conferring quietly with Defense Secretary Donald Rumsfeld.

"What is it, Walt?"

"Good morning, Mr. President. Just wanted to check and see if—"

"It's hot, Walt," Bush said, his lips and tongue burning. Scheib had been a bit too liberal with the Tabasco today.

"Excuse me, sir?"

Taking a final bite and licking his fingers Bush added, "*Muy caliente.*"

Silence, followed by, "Oh, I'm so sorry, sir. I'll be happy to bring up another—"

"Already down the hatch, Walt, though I'll probably regret it later."

"Sorry again, sir. Cheeseburger pizza for lunch?"

"Nope. Huevos rancheros, Walt. Hold the Tabasco." He pressed the Speaker button again, wiped his mouth with a pristine napkin embossed with the White House seal, and walked over to this unscheduled meeting that was taking up the five minutes he insisted on having to himself and his snack every midmorning.

Rice, Tenet, and Rumsfeld, all wearing gray business suits, remained standing behind the sofas.

"All right, boys and girls. What's so important?"

Bartlett, also wearing a gray suit, said, "The punch line, Mr. President, is that the Russians also know about the nuke in Afghanistan."

Bush, who always insisted in hearing the ending first, nodded approvingly. "How's that, Danny Boy?" he asked, calling Bartlett by his nickname.

Bartlett turned to the techies, two guys and two gals who looked no older than Bush's twin daughters, Barbara and Jenna. The analysts tag-teamed each other for two minutes to explain that CIA internet robots, or "bots" as they were typically called, had intercepted a Russian bot hauling a data packet to a Moscow ISP containing an image of a Gagarin class ring. It was the same image, along with the same brief note, that Glenn Harwich had interpreted as meaning that the Taliban had found the missing RN-40.

When they finished, Bush turned to Director Tenet and said, "Brother George? You're good with this?"

"Yes, Mr. President."

"You too, Rummy?"

Secretary Rumsfeld, arms crossed while holding his reading

glasses between the index and thumb of his right hand, said. "The bastard knows."

Bush considered that for a moment. Rumsfeld probably had the best blend of political, military, and corporate experience of anyone in the room. He'd served his country as a naval aviator before representing the state of Illinois on Capitol Hill as a young thirty-year-old congressman. He then worked in both the Nixon and Ford administrations in cabinet-level positions that included chief of staff, ambassador to NATO, and secretary of defense. Returning to private business after Ford lost the 1976 election, Rumsfeld became president and CEO of G. D. Searle & Company and later of General Instrument before Bush tapped him to become his secretary of defense.

Rumsfeld added, "It is now a race, Mr. President. Gotta move fast."

Turning to Secretary Rice, he said, "Condi? Course of action?"

A Stanford University Fellow, Dr. Condoleezza Rice was one of the most educated individuals in his administration. She had degrees from a half dozen universities, in political science, Soviet studies, arms control and disarmament, and international security.

Rice stared at him awhile with her big dark eyes under fine eyebrows, an index finger over her lips while considering her reply. She finally said, "Direct, Mr. President. No screwing around."

Bush dropped his hands inside the pockets of his pants while contemplating the portrait of George Washington over the mantelpiece opposite his desk. "So mano a mano with Pootie-Poot?" he finally said, using the nickname he'd given to Russian President Vladimir Putin.

Rice tilted her head and smiled. "The only language the steely-faced motherfucker understands."

Bush chuckled and stretched an index finger at Bartlett. "Make the call. Let's get this over with."

Bartlett checked his watch and frowned.

"What is it, Danny Boy?"

"Congressman Boehner, sir," he said, referring to Republican House Majority Leader John Boehner.

"What about him?"

"He's been waiting outside for over an hour, sir."

"Well, tell *Boner* he's just gonna have to hold it a bit longer."

Rice glanced down and smiled while Rumsfeld and Tenet just shook their heads and the CIA analysts tried hard to hide their surprise at the president's laid-back attitude.

"Yes, sir," he replied, checking his watch again and looking into the distance.

Bush sighed. "What else, Danny Boy?"

"It's almost eight o'clock in the evening in Moscow, Mr. President."

"Good," Bush replied. "I hope I'm interrupting something *really* important."

52

Portrait of a Bully

NOVO-OGARYOVO ESTATE. ODINTSOVSKY DISTRICT. MOSCOW. RUSSIA.

He put on the ring and stared at it, grinning.

Of all the jewelry available to him, some dating back to the period of the czars, the Super Bowl XXXIX ring, which he had taken earlier in the year from Robert Kraft, owner of the New England Patriots, was his favorite.

And it wasn't the high quality of the diamonds adorning the American football that made it his darling. Nor was it the emblem of the Patriots, made from rubies and sapphires, in the center of the football, or the diamond-studded letters that read "World Champions," or the fact that the ring was priced at over $25,000.

Russian President Vladimir Putin couldn't get enough of the ring because no one else in his government had one—at least, not one obtained the way he had gotten his, by prying it from the fingers of Kraft himself during Kraft's visit to Saint Petersburg.

His colleagues in the government had their gold Rolex or Patek Philippe watches. They had their diamonds from Cartier and Tiffany's. They rode in the luxury sedans dressed in Armani, Kiton, or Dolce & Gabbana suits.

But no one had an original and very real Super Bowl ring like his, which made it special.

And Putin loved feeling special.

Dressed in a charcoal suit and a starched white shirt, no tie, the Russian President joined his dinner party on the first floor of his estate, which he had renovated in 2000.

It was always the same. All eyes converged on him as he stepped into the lavish hall adjacent to the dining room, under the soft glow of ornate chandeliers. Waiters in tuxedos waltzed about carrying trays filled with hors d'oeuvres and champagne flutes for the pleasure of two dozen men and women chatting amiably, laughing, and raising drinks to their host. A Borodin symphony flowed from unseen speakers.

Putin took a moment to take it all in, a scene in sharp contrast with his difficult youth. The youngest son of Leningrad factory workers, Putin was born in 1952, eight years after the World War II siege of that city. His older brothers died before he was born, one at birth and the other during the siege. His father was severely disabled and disfigured by injuries sustained in battle, and his mother nearly died of starvation. Putin was born into this atmosphere of hunger, disability, and profound grief. His childhood was marked by trauma, and with both parents working multiple jobs to survive, the young Putin spent a lot of time in the communal courtyard of his apartment complex, which was dominated by thugs, prostitutes, alcohol, and fistfights. He took special pride in having survived, and he even thrived in this setting, becoming one of those thugs. But he had also been book smart and earned a law degree from Leningrad State University, joining the KGB after graduation and rising through its ranks over the following fifteen years, exiting as lieutenant colonel.

His tough upbringing, combined with his education and intelligence experience, was precisely why he believed himself to be the only leader capable of fixing Russia's fragile political and economic system. Failing to do so could revert the country back to its dark Soviet past.

One or two missteps is all it would take to bring all of that back, he thought, as a waiter presented him with a box of Cohibas, shipped directly from the bundles rolled exclusively for Fidel Castro.

He selected one, clipped the end with an eighteen-karat cigar cutter, and held it up for his aide to light it, drawing multiple times and exhaling toward the chandeliers. Another server brought him a glass of Stolichnaya, straight up. Putin held the cigar between his index and middle fingers and the glass between the thumb, ring, and pinky fingers of his left hand, keeping his right hand clear to greet people.

Wetting his palate with his favorite brand of vodka before drawing again on the cigar, he briefly closed his eyes, the nicotine and the alcohol washing away the burdens of another sixteen-hour day running what he considered to be the toughest nation on the planet.

Especially compared to the Americans, he thought, shaking his head at the way its media focused on the stupidest things instead of real issues.

He walked among his closest friends, pumping men's hands, kissing ladies on the cheek, and exchanging greetings—all while drinking and smoking, which he accomplished with grace and elegance. They were mostly deputy prime ministers, as well as heads of various agencies, including defense, justice, and atomic energy. There were also generals from various service branches—plus their wives, girlfriends, or mistresses.

Just then, Anton, one of his new bodyguards, appeared at the other end of the room. Young and muscular, with a full head of dark hair and dressed in a dark blue suit, he cruised through the crowd swiftly but without drawing attention, slowing as he approached the president.

Putin used the cigar as a pointing device while saying, "I told you I did not wish to be disturbed, yes?"

"Sorry, sir," Anton replied, color coming to his face, before leaning closer and whispering, "It's GRU officer Tupolev. She's in the library."

Without excusing himself, Putin briskly walked away with Anton in tow and stepped inside the large rectangular room.

Old books, some dating back to the Czars, crowded the shelves lining three of the four walls under a pair of chandeliers. The last wall was reserved for portraits of prior leaders all the way back to Lenin, all in matching black frames. He had thought about taking them down, but for better or for worse, each of those men staring stoically down at him, chests full of medals and awards, had a part in shaping the country he now led.

A heavily ornate table, handmade from high-quality Russian birch, ran the length of the room. Hand-carved matching chairs on either side faced individual desk lamps. He had also thought about removing the furniture, since very few people aside from the resident librarian/historian had any interest in actually sitting down here to read the relics stuffed in those dark oak shelves. But as it turned out, the furniture itself was a relic from the Czar days, and quite priceless, according to an appraiser from Sotheby's, which made them special.

And speaking of special . . . Kira sat against the end of the table, arms crossed. Dressed all in black, which contrasted sharply with her porcelain skin, auburn hair, and those very light hazel eyes, she raised her thick brows at him before looking over at Anton. Her elaborate compass rose tattoo, amid lifelike red roses and snow, extended from the base of her neck to the top of her chest, disappearing in the cleavage exposed by her low-cut shirt. Although Putin had not seen her in a few years, they corresponded frequently.

Putin handed the cigar to Anton and said, "See to it that no one disturbs us."

"What about the guests, sir?"

He turned to stare at his aide, who promptly nodded, backed away, and closed the doors.

Slowly shaking her head, Kira said, "He doesn't look old enough to shave."

Putin took a sip of vodka while regarding the feisty operative whom he fell for in 1988, when they were both working the Dresden station. She had been on her first KGB post, collaborating with the Stasi to recruit young men enrolled at the Dresden University of Technology and send them undercover into the United States. Putin ran the Dresden KGB station and quickly took a liking to Kira, taking her under his wing and teaching her the kind of field ops that could only be learned in the *actual field*. The relationship soon became intimate, even though he had been married since 1983. After the fall of the Berlin Wall, in 1989, Putin got into politics in Leningrad— soon renamed Saint Petersburg—while Kira fell victim to the KGB purges of the time and was sent to prison.

Inmates used tattoos to identify their particular crimes and level of aggressiveness. The compass rose was reserved for a *suka*, a traitor, or bitch—the way extreme KGB personnel were perceived by the new world order. Kira spent two years in the gulag before Putin was able to locate her, pull her out and, at his recommendation, get her absorbed by the GRU Spetsnaz. She had spent the last decade and a half participating in and eventually leading ops in Chechnya, Georgia, and across the Middle East, where she distinguished herself and was even awarded the Duty, Honor Cross military intelligence medal as well as the coveted Medal for Valor. Putin had actually pinned the latter on her five years ago for her work against Chechen rebels. Although Kira had just turned forty, she was still an amazingly attractive woman—and an even deadlier operative.

He walked up to her, set the glass on the desk, and put a hand to her left cheek, narrowing his eyes while nudging back her hair to expose a fine scar traversing her right temple. He traced it with an index finger.

"That's new. Where did you get it?"

"Dubrovka theater. 2002." She tilted her head, letting her hair fall back over it.

Putin grunted and sipped his vodka while grinning with pride, eyes following the tattoo as it disappeared into her cleavage.

"I haven't seen the entire compass in a while."

"Seriously, Vlad? And please tell me that child isn't charged with protecting your life."

"Would you like the job?"

"I'm not a babysitter."

"Are you calling your president a *baby*?" He set the glass back on the table, embraced her, and tried to kiss her scar, which he found incredibly sexy.

She pushed him away. "We have a problem."

"But it's been so long. Can it wait until after—"

"The Taliban definitely has our bomb."

He narrowed his gaze, remembering her report from a few days ago. "You mean to tell me that—"

"It's the RN-40 that my dad lost in—"

"*Afghanistan*," Putin slurred, his face sobering as he looked away. His gaze panned over the endless volumes of fat and dusty tomes surrounding him. Then he glared at the portraits, stared into the lifeless eyes of his predecessors.

One or two missteps is all it would take to bring all that back.

Realizing that losing a tactical nuclear weapon to religious fanatics could easily turn into one of those missteps—especially if al Qaeda was able to get it operational and deployed—he added, "Is your plan—"

"Already in motion," she said, taking a moment to bring him up to date on the meeting with Prince Mani al Saud.

"The battery powering the GPS tracker is good for a month. After that we lose the signal, so we need to move fast," she added.

"What happens if we do lose track of it?"

"Our fail-safe is that the replacement gun primer circuit board will not trigger a pulse strong enough to ignite the conventional explosives, so the uranium projectile will not be fired into the uranium target."

"So the bomb will not detonate?"

"Correct," she said. "But with some expertise they can still turn it into a dirty bomb, thus the reason for the whole sting operation and the GPS tracker. We need to find it, Vlad."

"Dammit," he said, looking away. "We certainly do—and quietly. The world, and especially my enemies here and abroad, can *never* know."

"Agreed," she said. "It'll make Dubrovka seem like . . . child's play."

"Child's play," he repeated, remembering what a political mess that had been.

Reaching for the Stolichnaya, he gulped it down, and contemplating the empty glass he said, "Anything you need, Kira. And I mean anything you—"

A knock on the door, which inched open just enough for Anton's head.

"Speaking of child's play," Kira said, tilting her head toward the intrusion.

Putin frowned. "Dammit, Anton! I thought I told you that—"

Anton held out an encrypted satellite phone. "It's the president of the United States, sir. Says it's urgent."

Putin considered that for a moment before thrusting his free hand at his aide, who rushed in, placed the phone in it, and just as quickly left the room.

Kira pointed at herself and Putin motioned her to stay while pressing the Speaker button on the phone. He trusted very few people in this world, and Kira was among them.

"Good morning, *Kovboy*," Putin said, calling Bush by the nickname he had given him, meaning "Cowboy" in Russian, while also realizing it was midmorning in Washington, DC. "To what do I owe this unexpected pleasure?"

"Good evening, Pootie-Poot," Bush replied. "This one's about the nuke you lost in Afghanistan back in eighty-eight. Rumor's that the Taliban has found it. Know anything about that?"

Putin stared at Kira, who widened her stare.

"First time I'm hearing about it," he finally replied. "Back in eighty-eight, you said?"

"That's how you're gonna play it? 'Cause it's gonna bite you right in your Pootie ass."

"I'm afraid that happened well before my time"

"Before, during, or after, we're still talking about a Russian nuke, so it makes it *your* problem. And because it's in the hands of those camel jockeys, it also makes it *my* problem."

"I will have my people look into it," Putin said.

"Yeah, have your people call my people and then we can all do lunch while those bastards nuke one of our cities."

"*I said* I will look into it, and then I *will* get back to you, yes?" Putin said.

"Yeah. You do that. You do that, indeed."

The connection ended, and Putin used the phone's antenna to point at Kira while repeating, "*Anything* you need."

53

Family History

SULAIMAN MOUNTAINS. SOUTHERN AFGHANISTAN.

The headache awoke her.

Vaccaro sat up, feeling light-headed, her mouth dry and pasty, her back throbbing from the dozen-plus g-forces that had compressed her spine when she shot out of that cockpit like a damn cannonball.

Slowly, blinking rapidly, she tried to get her bearings, eyes shifting west, where the sun danced just above the rim rock, its dying burnt-orange glow giving way to a full moon.

Eyeing the glowing hands of the Laco Trier, Vaccaro frowned. She had been out for nearly thirty minutes—a lifetime in her situation.

Where the hell's my ride?

First she checked her emergency locator beacon, which should have gone active the instant she ejected, providing a homing beacon for the rescue crew. Satisfied that the small gadget integrated with her survival vest was broadcasting her position, she reached for her AN/PRC-148 MBITR, strapped to the side of the same vest.

"Bravo Niner Six, Bravo Niner Six, Red One One on the ground. Where's that helo and driver?"

"Red One One, Bravo Niner Six. Glad to hear your voice. Hook Seven Five en route. ETA fifteen minutes."

Vaccaro frowned, wondering if she even had half that time left when anyone within five miles probably had heard the explosion and saw her ejection booster and canopy.

Thirty minutes ago.

She gathered her parachute into a neat lump before reaching for her holstered Colt 1911, one of two that had belonged to her father. Lieutenant James Vaccaro had had the other one with him during his final stand.

The semiautomatic was made of polished stainless steel, which was frowned upon because it could be easily spotted at night, the reason most military personnel preferred the matte black semiautomatics offered by SIG Sauer and Glock.

She released the magazine, verifying it held eight .45 ACP rounds, plus one in the chamber. She stared at the last round in the magazine, the one at the bottom, wedged against the spring.

The one with her name on it.

If it ever came to that.

Sighing, and praying that history didn't repeat itself in the Vaccaro family, she reinserted the magazine, thumbed the safety, and secured it back in the chest holster of her vest with a Velcro strap.

The wind intensified, sweeping down the mountain.

She hugged herself, shivering, thinking of her survival training, which commanded her to seek some form of shelter while waiting for the rescue helicopter to arrive. At the same time, Vaccaro needed concealment, had to remain hidden from an enemy who thrived on capturing, torturing, and beheading pilots.

Plus whatever else the bastards might do to a woman.

Focus!

And that meant selecting a spot out of the ordinary that would not attract the enemy, which disqualified clusters of trees and caves.

The manual recommended using rocks or boulders for both shelter from the elements and as a hiding place. Fortunately, Afghanistan had plenty of both, so she selected an outcrop at the edge of the gorge that had a natural recess deep enough to disguise her presence while also shielding her from the howling wind.

She crawled down into it, beyond the ledge, careful not to miss a step and risk tumbling down the side of the mountain. She wedged the parachute into the hole, using it as a cushion as well as a blanket, before reaching for the Colt with her right hand and removing one of her two MK-13 flares from her survival vest with her left.

The clearing projected just above her head now, where she hoped a helicopter would come in time to get her the hell out of this place. The steep and rocky drop below her boots led to a canopy of trees bordering another ledge almost five hundred feet below her.

Staring at the second hand of her Laco Trier, Vaccaro did a quick mental check to make sure she had not overlooked any critical steps in her survival training.

Satisfied she had done everything by the book, the air force pilot did the only other thing she could do: she prayed that the Chinook helicopter found her before the enemy did.

54

Baaligh

SULAIMAN MOUNTAINS. SOUTHERN AFGHANISTAN.

Pasha never stopped running, cruising through the increased darkness with his dozen handpicked warriors, charging toward a single objective with unyielding determination. He pushed everyone to the breaking point, ignoring their labored breathing just as he ignored his own body, every step bringing him closer to the downed American pilot.

The goat trail narrowed as the grade increased while curving north, as the air progressively thinned—as temperatures dropped.

They rushed up the incline in a single file, armed with a mix of weapons, from RPGs to AK-47s, a Russian RPD light submachine gun, and even a new SVD Dragunov sniper rifle to replace his broken Remington.

They lacked night vision equipment, but Allah had been merciful this night, providing all the illumination they needed from the moonlight filtering through the trees. The vegetation thickened with altitude, in sharp contrast with the desolate and rocky terrain in the warmer valley leading to the sand dunes surrounding Lashkar Gah.

Pasha recalled the downed Soviet pilot when he was just eight years old. He could hear the man's screams as he and Akhtar had cut him with the curved steel of their pesh-kabz knives. Pasha could almost feel the blood in his hands, the pilot's body writhing in the calculated pain Akaa had taught them to inflict.

That night had been his initiation, his coming of age, becoming *baaligh*, reaching the age of maturity in Islam. Akaa had opened his eyes to the world through blood that glorious night long ago, as he crossed the bridge into Sharia-wise adulthood.

And so he ran, a hand feeling the holstered Makarov, his shooting finger resting on the muzzle, feeling the Russian pilot's inscription, confident it could not possibly be a coincidence that the winds had carried an enemy pilot to a clearing similar to the one seventeen years ago.

This was the work of Allah.

This was his fate.

They finally reached the location where the parachute had vanished less than forty minutes before, out of breath, having covered four miles in record time. He spread his men efficiently around the twenty-meter-wide ledge extending for nearly a hundred meters along the face of the mountain, shadows moving slowly now in the moonlight, silently shifting in the darkness, waiting for his order.

His eyes scanned the narrow clearing, bounded on one side by stone pines and other vegetation and on the other by the rocky outcrops at the edge of the gorge.

Where would you hide and wait for a rescue helicopter?

He remembered the Soviet pilot choosing an obvious spot near the edge of the woods. But his men found no one there.

No, he thought. *This pilot is smarter than that.*

But he didn't need to order his warriors to search anywhere else to flush out the hidden American aviator.

The distant sound of an incoming helicopter would do that for him.

55

Bait

SULAIMAN MOUNTAINS. SOUTHERN AFGHANISTAN.

"Red One One, Hook Seven Five. Two minutes out. Homing in on your beacon. Any hostiles?"

Vaccaro had lowered the volume of her MBITR to a mere whisper, hoping that the whistling wind would mask it from any approaching insurgent. She lacked the throat mike and earpiece accessories used by elite marine or Ranger units to maximize concealment.

She peeked beyond the edge of her cliffside hideout and saw nothing but moonlight dancing over the clay dust kicked up by the wind sweeping the clearing. And she heard nothing but the rustling of branches.

"Hook Seven Five, Red One One. Negative. Coast looks clear."

"Roger that."

The whistling gusts gave way to the sound of the Chinook's double rotors echoing across the mountainside, and a moment later she spotted its red and green navigation lights.

The MK-13 flare consisted of a cylindrical tube roughly ten inches long. One end of the flare contained red smoke for day signaling. The opposite end held a red flare for night ops.

Holstering the semiautomatic and securing it with the Velcro strap, she crawled out of her hideout and up to the edge of the clearing, where she pulled the rings at both ends of the MK-13 and tossed it a dozen feet downwind from her. The flare ignited, bathing the clearing in pulsating red light while smoke oozed from the other end, rushing away from her.

"*Red One One, Hook Seven Five has your flare in sight.*"

"Roger, Hook Seven Five. Great to see you guys."

Pasha set his new Dragunov rifle by his feet before inserting a PG-7VL HEAT grenade into the smooth-bored barrel on the front of the RPG-7 launcher one of his men had just handed him. He did this with practiced ease, making sure the shell was properly aligned with the firing mechanism. Shouldering the three-foot-long launcher, he held the pistol grip with his right hand and the secondary grip eight inches behind it with his left hand, keeping it taut against his chest.

Cocking the external hammer with his right thumb and lightly pressing his index finger against the single-action trigger, he positioned his shooting eye behind the PGO-7 telescope sight, which provided a 2.7x fixed magnification.

He brought the incoming helicopter's center of mass to the center of the sight's crosshairs before slowly shifting his sight to the left along the horizontal windage scales to adjust for what he estimated to be a ten-knot crosswind.

And he waited, aware of the weapon's limited range, especially in a crosswind. At fifty meters, he should expect a clean shot, but the probability of a first-round hit dropped to the vicinity of 70 percent at one hundred meters and to below 40 percent at two hundred meters.

He had already passed the word to his men: no one was to fire until he did. And no one was to make a move on the pilot, which he now recognized was a woman, standing tall, red hair swirling in the wind, waving her hands at the rescue craft while surrounded by matching reddish and pulsating smoke.

Like the devil she is, he thought, staring at her figure half hidden in the crimson haze.

One hundred meters.

He inhaled slowly as the helicopter, a Chinook, approached the clearing, its rotor wash swirling the smoke in overlapping wisps curling across the ledge.

Eighty meters.

Pasha exhaled slowly as the craft entered a hover, rotating away from him, positioning the tail section just off the edge of the ledge.

He was momentarily confused. But then, as the rear ramp lowered, he realized that the Chinook crew didn't intend to touch down but merely to bring the ramp to the edge of the gorge so that the woman could simply walk onto the craft. But in the process, the pilot had given him a clear line of sight directly into the interior of the massive helicopter.

At a distance of just under fifty meters, he made a final sight adjustment and exhaled before pressing the trigger.

A smokeless powder for recoilless-type launch thrust the grenade away from the shooter. RCL gun action allowed for the initial propellant blast to escape through the rear of the launcher instead of following the projectile out the barrel and potentially hurting the grenadier. Upon launching, the grenade unfolded its stabilizing fins, and at a safe distance of fifteen meters from Pasha, the built-in rocket booster ignited, accelerating the warhead toward its target.

Vaccaro watched the ramp lowering over the edge of the clearing and saw a helmeted crewman waving her over.

She took off toward the waiting Chinook, kicking hard, trying to close the couple hundred feet of separation quickly, ignoring the gusts of wind fighting the helicopter's powerful dual downwashes.

And that's when she noticed a flash of light reflecting off of the crewman's visor, and also just to her left, coming from the edge of the woods.

An instant later, a trail of light propagated toward the helicopter. It went right through the ramp opening, just missing the crewman, and shot straight into the cockpit.

Her last image of the Chinook was of the crewman kneeling by the ramp, turning his head when the RPG flashed by, a foot from him, but her mind was already screaming a single word.

RPG!

She shifted her forward momentum to the right, away from the helicopter and back toward her rocky hideout, running away as fast as her legs allowed.

The helicopter's windshield exploded outward a moment later and a column of flames shot out the rear ramp, licking the clearing and even reaching the tree line.

But she didn't stop. She couldn't stop. Her instincts pushed her away from the inferno, from those rotating blades that she knew would soon become deadly missiles.

She reached the outcrop where she had been hiding and dove feet-first into the recess still cushioned with the parachute as flames and debris engulfed the entire clearing above her.

But she lunged too fast, and instead of landing inside the recess, she bounced off the parachute and began to roll down the steep incline.

Shit!

The hill, the flames, the exploding helicopter, and even the damn moon and the stars swapped places as she tried to stop her fall, hands reaching wildly around her, fingers scratching at rocks, at dirt, at exposed roots, but nothing seemed to work.

Vaccaro caught a glimpse of the flaming wreckage also careering down the face of the mountain, off to her far left, as her shoulders, elbows, and knees stung while rolling out of control. The spinning increased in a dizzying whirl, her eyes losing focus, her vision darkening as she felt branches around her, above her.

The canopy of trees swallowed her, and she fell through it, until the side of her head hit something.

Hard.

And everything went black.

Pasha landed on his butt from the massive blast of his own creation.

The acoustic energy shook the entire mountainside as parts of the helicopter flew in every direction, some slamming right into the trunk of the stone pine where he hid in a crouch, hands over his head.

A massive section of a blade shot deep into the woods, impaling with ridiculous force a wide trunk a dozen feet from him, the noise deafening.

But the blast ended as abruptly as it had begun, except for the ruckus created by the flaming wreck vanishing from view as it slid down the side of the mountain.

Grabbing his Dragunov, he stood and raced around the side of the wide trunk, cruising past a couple dozen pieces of the flaming wreckage littering the clearing while the flare spewed the last of its smoke and crimson light.

Pasha dashed past it all as his men emerged from the woods with far more caution. He reached the spot where he had seen the woman jump just moments ago, peering beyond the bundled parachute and down the gorge, catching a glimpse of her figure landing on the canopy and disappearing below it.

The main wreckage had also crashed through the same trees, but some two hundred meters to her left, setting part of the narrow woods on fire.

He trained the powerful Leupold Mark 6 night vision scope of his new rifle on the spot where the woman had disappeared. The quality of the 18x magnification in its 44mm optics was simply outstanding, and he now understood why bin Laden favored it. He carefully scanned the crystal clear picture of the treetops, searching for any break in the canopy that would give him a clean shot.

Dammit, he thought, slinging the rifle a moment later while barking commands to his men. Pointing at the spot where the pilot had vanished, he ordered his four best climbers down the sharp grade while the rest of his men headed for the same switchback trail they had used on the way up.

Before he left, and as his rock climbers began their descent, he gave the spot where the pilot had disappeared a final glare, his hand reaching for the pesh-kabz.

I am not through with you yet.

56

Knife to a Gunfight

SULAIMAN MOUNTAINS. SOUTHERN AFGHANISTAN.

She hurt like hell.

That meant she was still alive, though she wasn't certain how.

Rolling off her side, Vaccaro sat up, cringing at the pain in her ribs, glancing at the Laco Trier, the luminous hands of which told her she had been out for just a minute or two.

Slowly, she flexed her arms and legs, but nothing seemed broken. Standing, while ignoring the scrapes on her knees and elbows, she reached for the MBITR strapped to her vest, but her fingers came in contact only with wires and broken plastic.

She pulled it free and sighed. It was crushed, and so was her emergency locator beacon, no longer transmitting her location. When she reached down for the Colt, her fingers sank inside an empty holster.

For the love of—

Scraping noises brought her eyes up, beyond the ragged treetops. Her gaze narrowed in the moonlit twilight, which was enhanced by red and orange splashes on the precipice from the burning wreckage off to her far left.

Slowly, figures materialized on the mountainside, four of them descending quickly, scaling with athletic ease down the rocky incline, roughly three-quarters of the way down from the ledge. AK-47s slung across their backs.

They would be here in under a minute.

Not much of a running start, she thought, realizing that they certainly had the upper hand by being familiar with the terrain—and armed—while all she had left was her SOG knife, still strapped to her left leg.

A knife to a gunfight.

Way to go, Laura.

If she had the Colt, she could pick them off while they were still away.

She looked down at her empty holster again, eyes shifting back to the spot where she had fallen.

It can't be far from here, she thought, remembering how she had secured it with a Velcro strap before working the flare.

She looked back up, keeping an eye on the incoming threat while searching frantically in whatever light filtered from—

There!

She spotted its stainless steel polish glistening in the darkness.

Thank you, Dad.

Reaching down for it and thumbing the safety, she aimed it at the foursome almost on top of her, about to reach the trees, lining up the closest one.

Realizing that the moment she fired she would lose her element of surprise, Vaccaro exhaled slowly and pulled the trigger. The report thundered across the range.

The man screamed and fell into the trees. The others swung their heads in his direction, but she had already switched targets, firing on the second climber and scoring a second hit.

As he dropped noisily through the trees, breaking branches before landing almost in front of her, Vaccaro shifted her aim, but the last two had already figured out her scheme and had taken their chances by jumping onto the closest trees. She could hear them up on the branches ahead of her but had no clear line of sight. And she knew that firing without a clear target would only telegraph her position, allowing the insurgents to train their AK-47s on her muzzle flash.

She sought the cover of a wide trunk while keeping her Colt out of sight. The same glistening steel that had allowed her to find it was now a liability.

Vaccaro hated her odds. Two against one, Kalashnikovs versus her Colt, plus the threat was likely battle-hardened warriors. However, neither had opened fire, meaning they didn't have a clear line of sight either.

And that gave her an idea.

Picking up a rock, she tossed it as hard as she could toward the other side of the ledge before swinging the Colt in the general direction of the noise made by the insurgents up in those branches.

A moment later the rock struck the ground and rolled noisily across it.

Fire erupted from the adjacent stone pine, the muzzle flashes clearly visible as they directed their aim to the origin of the noise.

But she was already pointing their way, and with a minor shift, she fired at the closest muzzle flash before switching targets and firing again at the second one, her reports lost in the rattle of the Russian guns.

An insurgent screamed and fell, crashing headfirst onto the ground. But there was silence from the last man as darkness once more shrouded the ledge.

She moved back, slowly, trying to use the whistling wind to mask her movements, the Colt held in her right hand but pressed against her chest and covered with her right arm, shielding it.

She came up to one of the men who had fallen through the trees, his Kalashnikov still behind his back. She knelt and pulled the weapon free while also noticing a transceiver radio strapped to his chest, stained in his blood. She snagged it and secured it in place of her MBITR.

Standing, she holstered the Colt and verified that the AK-47 was loaded and had a round in the chamber before deciding to move back, to get away from the clearing. Perhaps it was now best to cut her losses and—

The blow to the side of her face made her legs quiver, give, and she fell, dropping the Kalashnikov while rolling away and also reaching for the Colt, aiming it up at a threat.

She saw the boot at the last second, and her hand throbbed from the impact. She let go of the semiautomatic, realizing what that meant. The bastards would capture her alive—would do to her shit she couldn't even start to imagine.

Her right hand reached for her SOG knife, but a kick to her solar plexus killed that initiative and any other impulse she might have had to fight back. She curled up, trying to breathe, her mind growing—

Another kick lifted her off the ground, nearly bending her in half, sending her crashing against a rock. Punch-drunk, scourged, her body taxed to its limit from the ejection followed by the fall and now this beating. Her vision quickly tunneled as tears blurred the dark world around her, though not before she saw the toe of a boot swinging toward her face.

But the blow never came. Instead, Vaccaro thought she heard the mechanical sound of a suppressed weapon, followed by rounds striking flesh.

And then silence.

She curled up on her side, struggling to breathe, her thoughts pushed to the edge of her mind as darkness like none she had ever experienced swallowed everything.

57

Role 3

KANDAHAR AIRFIELD. SOUTHWESTERN AFGHANISTAN.

"Temp ninety-nine-point-six!"

"BP eighty over thirty-five! He's losing too much blood!"

"Pulse fifty-two!"

The screams and the wailing woke him up. And that light, very bright, and right over his face, stabbing his retinas.

Blinking, John Wright tried to avoid staring at the long fluorescents overhead as shadows walked past him in apparent haste.

What the hell?

Slowly, with effort, he raised his head, realizing he was on a gurney parked on the side of the trauma unit. All sorts of medical personnel, men and women wearing desert camouflage fatigues or green scrubs stained with blood, plus masks and blue gloves—also bloody—huddled over another gurney a dozen feet away.

Wright managed to sit up, eyes focusing on what he now recognized were members of the Kandahar Role 3 medical treatment facility, designed to tackle anything Afghanistan threw their way.

He took a deep breath, rapidly getting his bearings, noticing an IV pumping fluids into his right forearm. But it was the groaning and wailing that ripped his attention back to the man writhing in obvious pain while surrounded by doctors and nurses.

Their hands wielded a variety of tools, mostly scissors, as they cut off sections of the man's bloody uniform and removed field tourniquets. Finally, two nurses stepped away to grab wads of sterile pads from a nearby shelf, exposing what remained of the soldier's thighs, a mangled mess of shredded tissue, bone fragments, and dirt.

"Look at me, son!" one of the doctors shouted.

"Mama! Mama!" the kid screamed, eyes closed. "Home! I want to go—"

"Take a deep breath!" the same doctor shouted. "And keep your eyes on me! On me, soldier!"

Wright stood with difficulty and pulled the IV off his arm. A nurse, trying to keep the soldier's head down, shook her head at Wright, who recognized the kid trying to look down at his own legs, apparently not realizing he was also missing his entire right arm and part of the shoulder, still clamped taut by a field tourniquet. It was Corporal Franklin, and the last time Wright had seen him he was running straight into the daisy-chained mines.

Franklin turned his head and for a moment locked eyes with Wright.

"I'm sorry, Captain! I'm so sorry! I screwed up! Oh, God! I really . . . screwed . . . this . . . up . . ."

The anesthesiologist finally worked his magic and sedated Franklin, ending the jerky movements and the screams while three separate surgical teams went to work on what remained of his maimed limbs. Then a fourth team emerged to work on his mangled groin.

Wright fought hard to shake the anger boiling inside him. This could have all been prevented with better intelligence, and he planned to get to the bottom of this—

"Captain Wright! Over here, sir! Captain!"

Wright looked over and spotted Sergeant Eugene Gaudet walking toward him.

Working through the dizziness, he asked, "What's the damage besides Franklin and the gunny?" He stretched a thumb at the operating table.

A full head of dark hair covered most of Gaudet's forehead, and he ran a hand through it while taking a deep breath before saying, in his Cajun accent, "Two gunshot shoulder wounds. Not critical. The rest are mostly cuts and bruises, Captain. Besides Sergeant Bronkie, Franklin, and the two marines who got shot, you're next in line, sir."

Wright considered that for a moment while looking about the room and the adjoining hallways, which were lined with more gurneys filled with more GIs, most either unconscious or moaning. Equipment blinked and beeped all over the place. IVs fed fluids and other concoctions via clear tubes into arms, legs, and even necks, while a small army of men and women—a combination of doctors, nurses, and medics—moved about with purpose. Some pushed gurneys and carts, others wheelchairs, some discussed the information on their clipboards or tablets, and most wore stethoscopes around their necks. But everyone seemed one hundred percent focused on their respective tasks.

"You saved us today, sir," Gaudet added. "You got us out of that bloodbath largely in one piece. It's all in my initial field report."

Wright made a face. "You wrote it already?"

"Just some scribbled notes, sir. Nothing fancy. Colonel Duggan met us here, and you were . . . well, indisposed."

"How long have I been out?"

"About an hour, sir. Took them awhile to get to Franklin. The Tallies have been busy today on several fronts, and believe it or not, there were a few worse cases ahead of him."

"Christ Almighty," Wright whispered. "Let's give them some space," he added, stepping away from the trauma unit and into a hallway that led to the large front lobby.

The modern 70,000-square-foot facility with its thick, rocket-resistant walls, looked out of place in the middle of the dusty base. But given the number of wounded—and the severity of their injuries—NATO had decided to upgrade the Role 3 facility from its original plywood and canvas version and staff it with the best trauma equipment and personnel that money could buy. Once patched up and stabilized, the wounded streaming in from the field would be shipped off to Role 4 or 5 facilities in Germany or the United States for extended care and rehab.

"Assemble the rifle platoon by"—Wright checked his watch—"nineteen hundred. I want to have a word with the guys."

"Ah, sure, of course, sir, but shouldn't you ask a gunnery sergeant from one of your other rifle platoons? I'm just a squad lead."

Placing a hand on Gaudet's shoulder, he said, "Not anymore. Certainly not after today."

Before Gaudet could reply, Wright tapped his watch and added, "Nineteen hundred, Gunny. Ticktock." And he started to walk away.

"Where are you going, sir?"

"To have a word with the colonel."

Wright found Colonel Duggan behind his desk at Marine Corps headquarters, a pair of small rectangular glasses balanced on the tip of his nose as he browsed some document.

He looked up over the rim of his glasses, frowned, and said, "Your ass should still be on that gurney, son. I think you've seen enough excitement for one day."

"I'm good, sir," Wright replied, standing there while controlling a flaring headache and ignoring the ringing in his ears. He knew Duggan was right, of course. But that didn't make the situation any better. Vaccaro was still out there. On the way over here, he'd stopped at the communications building next door and had heard the final transmission from the rescue helicopter. He had also watched the short live stream feed from one of the Chinooks' rear-facing combat cameras. Although a bit grainy and hazy from the flares, the image of Laura Vaccaro running away from the RPG blast was clear enough to conclude she may have survived.

"Just would like an asset over the area, sir. She's out there. I know it."

"Please tell me that your request has to do with the fact that she was able to buy your team time to get the hell out of that mess, and nothing else, right? And now you want to pay her back?"

"Affirmative, sir. Absolutely *nothing* else."

"Good answer. I don't have to tell you that the whole thing was one giant clusterfuck and that General Lévesque is livid that we lost a whole Canadian crew and a helo in that rescue attempt. And I also shouldn't have to tell you that before we agree to deploy *another* helo her way we will have to make damn certain she isn't being used as bait again."

"Thus my request for a high asset, sir."

Duggan sat back and reached for a handwritten page, its edges smeared in dry blood. "Sergeant Gaudet's initial report. You did right by your men, son." Then, leaning forward and dropping his voice a bit, he added, "A bit stupid on the heroic side if you ask me, but still . . . you have some balls and rock-solid instincts."

"I still lost my gunny, and one of my men was hit hard by multiple IEDs in a confined area. Plus two marines got shot in the shoulder, but they'll be all right."

"Yeah," Duggan said, pointing at the piece of paper. "I read that. How's Corporal Franklin?"

"Just left him in the OR, sir. I think he's gonna make it, but lost both legs and an arm . . . and maybe his balls."

Duggan closed his eyes.

"He's *nineteen*, sir."

"Dear Lord," Duggan mumbled, before picking up Gaudet's note and waving it at him. "Your sergeant. He's a keeper."

"Yeah, about him. I'd like to bump him up to replace Sergeant Bronkie. Give him another stripe."

"Consider it done," Duggan said, making a note. "Just get me the paperwork. What else?"

"The intel, sir. It was . . . well . . . *shit*."

"Careful," Duggan said. "The best way to get a new assignment is to bitch about its current owner. How do you think I ended up in KAF in the first place?"

Wright knew the story. Hell, everyone at KAF had heard how Duggan had flown from 29 Palms to the Pentagon and stormed the office of the commandant of the United States Marines Corps to complain about reports of marines not being properly equipped in the field, resulting in several deaths and many more dismemberments.

Duggan had been on the next plane to KAF.

"All the same, sir. Intel was still shit."

"Yeah," Duggan said, removing his glasses and rubbing his face. "About that . . . The intel actually wasn't *all* shit. It just was . . . not managed quite properly."

"What do you mean?"

"Come," he said. "You've earned the right to know."

"Know what, sir?"

"There's someone you need to meet, and that should also take care of your high-asset request."

Confused, Wright followed the colonel out the back of the headquarters and into a large shipping container converted into an office of sorts. Duggan entered a code into the digital pad next to the metal door and pulled it open.

Inside was a balding man in civilian clothes. He looked in his midfifties, with an unkempt salt-and-pepper beard, and was standing behind a much younger Hispanic-looking woman. Dressed in desert camouflage pants and boots plus a black FBI T-shirt, she sat by the keyboard, facing a pair of large computer screens displaying what he recognized as UAV terrain imagery.

They looked in Wright's direction and then, without acknowledging him, returned to their work.

Duggan said, "Captain, meet my new—and largely *insubordinate*—intelligence staff."

"Sir?" Wright said, confused.

"You think our intel is *fucked*, Captain?" Duggan said, raising his voice a decibel, which drew the attention of the bald-headed man, while the woman kept working the keyboard, her eyes on the images displayed on both screens.

"Colonel, I—"

"Here is your chance to *unfuck* it."

Now the woman also looked their way.

"Sir, I didn't mean any disrespect by—"

"I'm briefing General Lévesque in one hour," Duggan said, checking his watch. "That's how long you have to work with these characters and get me a plan of action for Compound Fifty-Seven."

"Sir, what about getting a UAV over—"

"Ticktock, Captain. One hour. You're my new military intelligence liaison with the CIA and the FBI, so figure it the fuck out."

58

New Mission

SULAIMAN MOUNTAINS. SOUTHERN AFGHANISTAN.

Pasha stood over his fallen comrades in the clearing, gusts of wind shrilling across the wooded plateau, trees rustling, as temperatures dropped into the forties.

Wearing a dark cashmere tunic and a woolen pakol, the Dragunov in his gloved hands, he paced the killing grounds slowly, alone, after ordering his men to the wreckage, on the outside chance that any of the helicopter crew survived the RPG strike and subsequent crash.

But Pasha really just wanted time alone to inspect the bodies, the footsteps on the ground, the trail left behind by the pilot and whoever it was that had come to her rescue.

Did the Americans send ground troops along with the helicopter?

Pasha doubted it. The footprints did not match those of American boots, except for one pair: those belonging to the pilot. The others were a mix of desert sandals and hiking boots.

He slowly shook his head while following the path that several men had taken from the west side of the clearing, approaching the pilot while she had rolled on the ground at the feet of one of his men. But someone had shot the man twice in the back and he had collapsed face-first where Pasha had found him.

His eyes narrowed in anger as they followed the track left behind by whoever it was that had decided to make his job harder.

As he started to walk over to his men standing around the smoldering wreckage, his radio beeped.

"Brother, any survivors?"

Pasha stood by the remainder of his team and said, "Doesn't look that way."

"And the pilot?"

"Still at large. She got help."

"She?"

"Yeah. Female pilot. Someone interfered. killed four of ours, and rescued her."

A pause, followed by, *"Forget her."*

"What? *Why?* They left a trail for us to follow, and they can't be far."

"Because, brother, I need you to head west immediately, to a spot almost eight miles from our compound."

"Well, the good news is that I'm at least halfway. What's there?"

"Your new mission."

"New mission?"

"The most important of your life."

59

LALO

The Cessna 208B Grand Caravan fitted with tundra tires came in low and fast, its single Pratt & Whitney PT6A-140 turboprop propelling it to Formula One speeds.

Prince Mani al Saud sat at the controls while Zahra Hassani finalized checks prior to her upcoming low altitude–low opening insertion.

Developed during World War II for drops over hostile enclaves, the LALO technique minimized the time airborne troopers spent vulnerable to ground fire. But there was a catch: if the main chute failed to open, the low-altitude drop—typically from around four hundred feet—prevented the trooper from deploying the reserve chute.

So Zahra just didn't wear a reserve, confident in the way she had carefully folded her main canopy. Instead of the reserve chute, she carried the handful of components in a rucksack strapped to the front of her tactical vest, next to her suppressed UZI submachine gun.

Her hair tied in a ponytail, her features darkened with camouflage cream, wearing black tactical cargo pants made of a cotton/nylon/Teflon ripstop fabric and a matching long-sleeve shirt and boots, Zahra felt ready for business.

She flexed her gloved hands before checking the rest of her gear, including her suppressed .22-caliber Ruger, secured to her waistband, and spare magazines for both weapons. She rested her right palm on the rubber handle of her Israeli-made Dustar seven-inch fixed-blade tactical knife, her thumb feeling the Velcro strap that kept it in its sheath.

Satisfied that her gear was in order and secured, she sat in the copilot's seat as the desert rushed ridiculously close to the belly of the single-engine plane flying into Afghanistan twenty miles south of Chaman. The route would keep them 120 miles south of Kandahar, away from the fighting.

The nature of this mission meant that Zahra flew alone with the prince tonight, having left the rest of the crew with the Citation X at the Karachi airport.

Towering dunes, some two hundred feet high, rose above them as Mani wedged the Cessna through these canyons sculpted by the constantly shifting sand. The scene beyond the large Plexiglas windshield resembled some sort of video game as he steered the Cessna through these surreal and fluctuating channels.

The meandering and quite dangerous path took them in a fairly steady northwesterly heading, their low altitude and the seemingly endless pyramids of sand—barchans, as they were called—making their entrance into the NATO war theater invisible to radar. And their distance from Kandahar also made the likelihood of overhead UAVs quite unlikely.

But the catch was that they could not really see the horizon or even the very distant Sulaiman Mountains, due to the soaring dunes, which forced them to rely on the GPS to navigate through this rat maze to their destination.

She stared at Mani's profile—a fine nose, a strong chin, and a full head of very burnished hair under a Bose headset—as he maneuvered them across one of the most desolate and ravaged places on earth. Yet it looked peaceful, even dreamlike, as infinite silica crystals reflected the moonlight in a shimmering gleam hovering just a foot or two over the surface.

"You know, it's actually beautiful," she said into the microphone built into her helmet. It was connected to a Wouxun KG-UV6D transceiver just powerful enough to stay in communication with Mani, who wore a matching set connected to his Bose headgear. All other radios were off, per his agreement with bin Laden for complete silence, to minimize electronic detection.

"Yeah," he replied, eyes front as he turned the yoke and worked the rudder pedals to bank the Grand Caravan to the right, negotiating another turn in this powdery labyrinth. "That's Afghanistan for you. One moment charming and the next deadly . . . like you."

She hugged herself tightly without realizing it, her eyes on this man who'd had such a physical and emotional impact on her life.

You will always be safe with me.

She blinked the thought away and asked, "How much longer?"

Risking a glance at the GPS, he said, "Fifteen minutes. All set?"

"All good here."

"Say hi to Pasha for me," he said.

"Ha-ha," she replied, recalling the fiery nephew of bin Laden, with whom she had collaborated on the occasions when Mani met with the sheikh over the years. Pasha was head of the sheik's security, just as she protected the Saudi prince, meaning they had had to work together to coordinate their bosses' safety, though not without a degree of friction. Pasha was a firm believer in Sharia law.

They continued zigzagging, constantly banking to avoid the next sand dune, before continuing northwest, always northwest, the drop point looming closer as the Sulaimans slowly rose before them.

Mani maintained his altitude relative to the ground, even as sand turned to rocky terrain slanting heavenward, climbing steadily as the land rose.

"Two minutes," he said, without taking his eyes off the windscreen. "Got your GPS coordinates?"

"Yep."

"Remember," he said, "we're deep in no-man's-land. The GPS maps around here aren't that accurate. They're more like . . . guidelines."

"Got it," she said, standing, placing a hand on his shoulders, and squeezing gently. "I'll be right back."

"You know where to find me," he responded, turning diagonally toward the mountain range when the terrain became steeper. He kept his right wingtip thirty feet off the rocky southern face while approaching the coordinates provided by bin Laden.

She headed for the cabin and slid the side door open. In preparation for this jump, realizing they would be alone, Mani had had the door spring-loaded, so it would close after she released it.

The foot of the mountains and the desert projected below the rectangular opening. Somewhere off to her left she could barely make out the distant glow of Lashkar Gah by the foot of the Sulaimans.

Part of the plan was to jump off this side of the plane and into the gorge, giving herself maximum altitude without Mani having to increase his separation from the incline.

"Time!" he shouted.

Zahra kicked her legs and jumped while holding the rip cord, which she pulled the instant she cleared the tail.

The canopy blossomed with a sudden pop above her. The winds carried her slightly farther west than planned, but she still approached the ground less than a half mile from her desired touchdown.

She tugged the handles of her rectangular chute, guiding it to a relatively flat patch of terrain, landing with a short run the moment her boots touched the ground thirty seconds later.

"Made it," she spoke into her mike.

"Enjoy the hike."

"Enjoy the flight. See you."

"Not if I see you first."

And just like that, as the turboprop continued its northwesterly heading along the mountainside, she removed her harness and gathered her chute, hiding it under some rocks before moving the rucksack from her front to her back. Releasing the Velcro straps securing her suppressed UZI to the side of her battle vest, Zahra verified that she had a round in the chamber and then placed it in single-shot mode.

She turned off the transceiver to conserve battery and maintain radio silence before inspecting the GPS display on her wrist. It marked two locations.

The first was the planned rendezvous spot, which she had to reach by dawn, an old and secret Soviet bunker currently used by Akhtar as his headquarters.

The second marked her alternate location, where she would go if her primary target became compromised: a clearing eight miles west of the bunker.

Briefly closing her eyes while inhaling the cold mountain air and listening to the Cessna's engine fading in the darkness, Zahra began to make her way to the red spot on her GPS.

60

Heart of a Smuggler

SULAIMAN MOUNTAINS. SOUTHERN AFGHANISTAN.

It took a fair degree of patience, instinct, and perhaps even a smidgeon of fortune to locate this most secret of passes across the Sulaimans. But it took a hell of a piloting skill, a steady hand, and more guts than on a slaughterhouse floor to actually attempt to fly through it—and at night. On top of that, the navigation maps loaded into the GPS for this desolate part of the world were only accurate to around five hundred feet.

Less than twenty minutes after dropping Zahra, Prince Mani steered the Grand Caravan into what looked like a narrow crack between the mountains. Flying into the constricted and winding gorge without hesitation, he committed himself to following the dry ravines and rock-strewn riverbeds of this nameless and uncharted pass used by Afghan fighters for a millennium.

In doing so, he knowingly violated the cardinal rule in mountain flying: never enter a box canyon unless there is enough room to turn around. The logic behind the rule was simple. If flanked by towering walls that prevented a 180-turn and the terrain ahead suddenly rose beyond the airplane's maximum rate of climb, the pilot would be "boxed" inside the canyon with no way to avoid a crash.

The danger of being detected by NATO forces, however, more than justified flying this seemingly impossible and slender pass, which he followed slowly, bleeding speed to reduce the span of his turns as he gently tracked its contours.

But this had to be done carefully. Flying too slow was to risk entering a stall during a turn, resulting in a sudden loss of altitude, which, given his nap-of-the-earth flying, meant death. Flying too fast was to risk exceeding the width of the canyon's winding turns, which also meant death.

But Prince Mani never did anything—even flying a box canyon at night—without giving himself at least a sporting chance of surviving. That's where his oversize tundra tires came into play, allowing him to attempt a landing in the bottom of the gorge should everything else fail. But in order to be able to set the plane down in the event of a sudden rise in terrain, he had to manage his speed at every turn.

So, easy does it, he thought. The GPS provided him with a gross view of what lay just beyond the next bend, so he could prepare for it while also getting ready to react to errors on the same GPS map, which meant he had to trust the picture beyond the windshield more than the moving terrain maps on the Cessna's color screens.

But this wasn't Mani's first rodeo, flying through regions where GPS maps were not as accurate as in the civilized world. He was a graduate of the United States Air Force Academy, which he had attended by special invitation from the U.S. Department of Defense, earning a degree in finance in addition to becoming a proficient pilot. This was followed by an eight-year stint with the Royal Saudi Air Force, where his education and connections made him the ideal candidate to handle the covert physical transfer of $900 million to al Qaeda, between 1992 and 2000. And Mani had stepped up to the challenge, becoming the behind-the-scenes go-to pilot and negotiator of his government's top secret initiative to keep the terrorist organization from committing acts of terror inside Saudi Arabia. In the process of doing so, he became one hell of a bush aviator while also discovering an affinity for the smuggling business, which came in handy after September 11.

Saudi Arabia broke all relations with al Qaeda following that attack, and Prince Mani was blacklisted by the royal family, released from his government job and removed from his position as number eleven in line for the throne. The realization that his family had used him as a scapegoat only served to strengthen Mani's desire to use his experience to launch a trafficking operation. Among his customers were terrorist networks, militia groups, cartels, Mafia rings, and most wanted fugitives, including one Osama bin Laden. And to show how loyal he was to his clients, Mani even used $10 million of his own funds to pay off all the required Pakistani officials to secure the land in Abbottabad and kick off the project to build a long-term safe house for the elusive terrorist.

And the rest is history, he thought, recalling how he had risen to become the region's top smuggler, taking airplanes into spots that would make the best fighter jocks piss their pants. And he did it with the same cool hand and fingertip control with which he flew the Cessna tonight.

He continued traversing the range, becoming an indistinguishable black smudge following the bottom of a lost canyon, should a drone or satellite happen to be tasked directly over him. But Mani knew there wouldn't be any, not with Operation Mountain Thrust raging between Kandahar and Lashkar Gah, well east of him.

And that's why this just might work, he thought, marveling at the simplicity of bin Laden's plan, which called for him to continue through this meandering pass to a preselected dry riverbed ten miles away. But first Mani had to get through what locals called the "needle squeeze," a vertical rock formation near the middle of the pass, narrowing the gorge to just under fifty feet, which was two feet shorter than the Grand Caravan's wingspan.

As he approached it, Mani banked the wings thirty-five degrees to the right while applying opposite rudder to maintain a straight flight path. He also applied a dash of power and rear pressure on the yoke to offset the loss of lift due to the steep angle of bank.

The maneuver, called "slipping," often used to land in crosswinds, allowed him to momentarily reduce his horizontal allowance requirements to below forty-five feet, clearing the pass with room to spare.

The moment he flew through it, he cut back throttle and leveled his wings while approaching the dry riverbed, which looked a bit surreal, even for the experienced smuggler. Dozens of torches were held by still figures along the makeshift landing strip, washing their bearded faces and the towering canyon walls behind them with flickering orange light.

He applied thirty degrees of flaps while further reducing power, letting the Cessna settle naturally over the rock-strewn riverbed. The touchdown went fairly smoothly, just a slight vibration on the yoke and rudder pedals. This was due in part to the tundra tires and in part to the party waiting for him having removed significant obstacles—large rocks or fallen logs—in the reasonably lit thousand-foot stretch.

He turned the Cessna around at the end of his landing run, as directed by a man holding two torches, who guided him as an airport ground crew marshal would, leaving the Caravan's nose pointed straight into the landing strip, ready for a quick getaway. He would wait here until Zahra delivered the components and the bomb became operational, at which time he would fly back out of the canyon, at night, to a predetermined spot in the desert to pick her up, along with the functional bomb.

That was the plan anyway.

He took a moment to shut down the airplane and then stepped out, breathing in the cold mountain air. Figures surrounded the large Cessna, wielding more torches, resembling a mob, silent, dark eyes gazing at his airplane. Four of them walked closer, carrying a large dark canvas, which they proceeded to drape over the wings and fuselage. Then someone walked past the men standing in a circle. He didn't carry a torch, so his face remained in shadows as he stepped around the engine cowling, placed a hand on one of the blades of the large aluminum propeller, and then turned to the prince.

"Welcome to my land," he finally said in his British accent.

Mani just stood there in near shock as he stared at the bearded face of Osama bin Laden, who was smiling.

"But . . . you're supposed to be in . . . How in the world did you get here?"

Bin Laden's grin widened as he placed a hand on Mani's shoulder. "There's been a change of plans, my friend. The bomb is coming here."

Mani had to blink at that. "*Here?* But I just dropped off Zahra by the—"

"We know. There is a team waiting for her. And I'm here to personally see there are no more . . . mishaps."

Mani controlled his facial expressions while trying to process the change in plans, thinking of Zahra and the components, fearing he had dropped her into the hands of the enemy.

"It will work out," bin Laden added. "I'm seeing to it personally. Trust me?"

"Of course," he said. "But you, my friend . . . The Americans control this region. I have no influence to protect you, like I do in Pakistan."

Bin Laden laughed, then said, "I go where the cause takes me, Mani. Always have. Always will. I am needed here, not hiding in Pakistan, and there isn't a damn thing the Americans, or anyone else, can do to stop me."

61

One Good Point

KANDAHAR AIRFIELD. SOUTHWESTERN AFGHANISTAN.

"So," Wright said, sitting across the table from Harwich and Monica, a terrain map of the region around the suspect compound spread open between them. For the past thirty minutes they had brought him up to speed on the situation at Compound 57. While he wasn't necessarily a fan of intelligence types, given recent events, Wright had to admit that these two seemed to have an interesting dynamic going, one he found refreshing, because neither was afraid to speak their mind. "You guys think this compound where I nearly got my head shot off could be harboring a nuke?"

The CIA man nodded. "That's my assessment."

Turning to Monica, who sat next to Wright and who seemed more interested in cleaning her fingernails with the tip of her SOG knife, he asked, "And you concur, Agent Cruz?"

Looking up from her makeshift file, Monica said, "I concur that we need to stop talking about it and just blow it the hell off the map."

"And I *told* you," Harwich said, "not until we get confirmation.

We need to be *certain* that the nuke is there, and we're not going to get that by turning the place into a crater. For all we know, they may have moved it already."

She stood slowly, grabbed the knife by its tip with the index and thumb of her right hand, and flung it at the table. The knife swirled twice before the tip stabbed the red *X* marking Compound 57, quite loudly. Both men jerked back in unison and stared at the knife embedded in the table.

"Cruz!" Harwich exploded. "What the—'

"If you're that worried about those ragheads hauling the weapon on a fucking mule up the mountains, then define a search perimeter. It's been less than—what?—two hours since the good General Lévesque decided to do us all a big fucking favor and telegraph our intentions with *his* rifle platoon?" She pointed a finger at Wright before adding, "And there are no real roads up there, so my guess is that the camel jockeys can't be more than a few miles away, especially if they're hauling a nuclear weapon the size of an RN-40, which weighs, like, a ton, right? I mean, think about it. They can't be moving very fast."

Harwich regarded her for a moment before looking at Wright, who nodded and said, "She has a point, Mr. Harwich."

"Okay, okay," Harwich finally said. "So we define a perimeter. And *then* what?"

"Then . . . nuke it."

He sat back while Wright just stared at her.

"*That's* your suggestion? *Nuke* the side of the mountain?"

"Don't we have nuclear subs in the Indian Ocean? I think a ten megaton should handle a blast radius that large."

"Have you lost your mind, Cruz?"

She shrugged. "It's the only way to be sure, boss. Besides, it's just goats and goat fuckers up there. Nothing the world will ever miss."

Wright had a difficult time containing a grin.

"Well, Cruz," said Harwich. "Tell you what. You suggest it to the general at the next staff meeting, and then tell me how that works out for you."

"I just might," she said, working the knife off the table by rocking it back and forth until she yanked it out.

"Now," Harwich said, frowning at the inch-long tear in his map, and then at Cruz. "You did make *one* good point."

"Only one, boss?" she said, returning to her personal grooming. "You sure know how to flatter a girl."

"Captain," Harwich continued, turning to Wright.

"Yes, Mr. Harwich?"

"How many men would it take to seal off . . . say . . . a *five*-mile-radius area from Compound 57?" He made a circle with a red pencil to mark off the desired terrain.

The marine stared at the map, then his eyes shifted four miles to the west of Compound 57, where the Chinook had gone down, and that gave him an idea.

"I'll have to check to be sure," he said, "but off the top of my head, probably a couple of infantry battalions should do it. Around nine hundred marines."

"And we have that manpower ready to deploy?"

"Yes, sir. Ready and willing. Just have to get the colonel to approve the op."

"Okay. Knowing what you now know, what sort of force do you estimate would be required to *take* Compound 57?"

"Now that we have eyes on the ground, a rifle company should do it."

"How many men is that?"

"It's three rifle platoons, each with forty-three men, so around a hundred and thirty. We'd come at it from all angles and overwhelm it with suppressing fire before blasting our way in. Then it'd be a matter of going room to room."

"What about IEDs and suicide vests?" asked Monica.

"We deal with that every day, Agent Cruz," Wright said. "As long as the intel is solid, we can take them."

"Very well," Harwich said. "Let's go find Colonel Duggan and—"

"There's something else," Wright said, as Harwich and Monica were about to stand.

"What's that, Captain?"

Wright considered the best way to bring Vaccaro into this, and finally said, "A high asset over this area." He placed his finger near the edge of the red circle, where Vaccaro was last seen, on the side of the mountain where the Chinook went down.

"And what's there?" asked Monica, suddenly interested.

"Captain Laura Vaccaro, the pilot who saved our ass."

Harwich sat back down. "Yeah. I heard."

"You think she's still alive?" Monica asked.

"Until I know otherwise, yes, and she's on the ground close to our area of interest, so . . ."

"So she could actually be an asset," Monica said. "Eyes on the ground right here."

Wright slowly nodded, suddenly taking a liking to the FBI agent.

"All right," Harwich said. "Let's go brief Duggan, and then I'm going to see what I can do about Captain Vaccaro."

"And what would that be, Mr. Harwich?"

Before Harwich could reply, Monica stood and said, "What he always does: light a fire under someone's ass."

62

New Faces

SULAIMAN MOUNTAINS. SOUTHERN AFGHANISTAN.

The Avenger cannon exploded with an insane and blazing fusillade of depleted uranium rounds, each packing enough energy to rip apart a car engine. The river of fiery death shot across the clearing, shredding men and equipment alike, vaporizing everything in its path, gouging the hillside while pulverizing thousands of pounds of rock.

She banked to the west, toward the thick of the enemy training their weapons up at her as she released the Hydras. The volley of

70mm rockets shot out from under silvery wings, cascading toward the windswept mountain as tracers rained up from a barrage of antiaircraft fire, the opposing ordnance crossing paths in midair in the blink of an eye.

Metal-shredding bursts of flak engulfed her Warthog as insurgents vanished in a sheet of flames. Her control column vibrated off her hand while alarms filled her cockpit—while her turbofans detonated in a deafening inferno of sizzling metal that propagated toward the cockpit.

She reached for the ejection handles but they were too far. She tried again and again, fingers stretched desperately skyward as the flaming debris from the engines engulfed the canopy with an ear-piercing crescendo. Cracks formed on the armored glass as the blast swallowed her, as the A-10 spun toward the ground.

The canopy collapsed and flames pierced the cockpit, the heat overwhelming her, blistering the skin off her face as she writhed in unbearable pain, trapped in her seat, spinning toward the ground.

Vaccaro screamed, sitting up, hands on her face, fingertips feeling her skin—startling the men gathered by the campfire.

She filled her lungs with cold air as bearded faces washed in flickering red and orange light resolved, dark eyes under woolen pakols and turbans turning to her, hands wielding AK-47s.

No!

Raw fear gripped her gut as she bolted to her feet, reaching for her Colt, but her fingers once more sank into an empty holster. In the same motion, she went for her SOG knife, but it too was gone.

This can't be happening!

Vaccaro felt dizzy from having stood too fast, felt blood draining from her head as her world began to spin, just like in the nightmare—as her legs gave.

"Easy there!"

She heard him in the same instant that she felt his arms catching her from behind, setting her gently on the ground. Confused, she looked at the stranger dressed in Western clothes—black jeans, a dark pleated woolen shirt buttoned down below his sternum, and hiking boots. He was a big guy, strong arms and legs, barrel chest covered in dark hair, and strong features under a closely trimmed dark beard.

He took a knee by her side.

A lock of hair fell over his rugged, tanned face, green eyes narrowing as he smiled a smile of slightly crooked teeth that sported a gap between the front two and somehow seemed to fit well with his lumberjack-like persona.

"Welcome back, Red One One," he said, in a bit of a baritone voice.

"How do you . . . ?"

"We overheard your radio transmissions . . . and so did the bad guys who used you as bait for that Chinook."

The locals gathered by the fire approached her, and she recoiled against the stranger.

"It's all right, Red," he said. "They're with me."

"Name's *Captain Vaccaro*," she said, shifting her gaze wildly between him and the insurgents.

"Of course it is," he replied, his large face softening with dark amusement.

One of the locals stepped ahead of the group, a man of short stature, quite thin, dressed in the traditional woolen tunic, baggy pants, desert sandals, and turban. He held a ridiculously large machine gun fed by an ammunition belt worn bandolier style, evoking images of Mexican outlaws. A much larger man—the largest of the group—followed him, similarly dressed but clutching an AK-47. They stared at her with what looked like genuine concern.

"Who . . . who the hell are you people?" she asked the burly man kneeling by her side.

"Friends, Captain Vaccaro," he replied.

"And who are you?"

He considered that for a moment, then said, "Aaron."

"What are you doing in the middle of these mountains, Aaron?"

"Same thing you're doing. Killing Taliban."

Vaccaro took a moment to consider that, breathing deeply before pointing at the motionless insurgents standing like statues in the night, their baggy pants flapping in the breeze. "But they look like the . . ." she began, stretching a finger at the two in front.

"Shinwari," Aaron interrupted. "They've been at war with the Taliban for some time."

"And you?"

"I . . . help them . . . with their problems," Aaron said, rubbing his chin, before turning to the two warriors in front of them.

"You know what I mean," she said. "Who are you *with*?"

"I'm someone who was never here, following orders that were never given."

"Seriously?" she asked. "You need to work on your lines. Who do you work for?"

"That's Nasseer, their leader," Aaron said, pointing at the shorter man. "And the big guy is Hassan, his younger brother and second-in-command."

Vaccaro frowned at him before looking up at the men, trying to remember the Pashto from her survival manual.

She finally said, "*Salaam alaikum*."

Aaron grinned while the Shinwari exchanged a glance. Then, pressing hands over their chests, they replied, "*Salaam alaikum*."

Then Nasseer also knelt by her, adding in heavily accented English, "Peace be with you, Captain Vaccaro," and produced her Colt and the SOG knife. "I believe these belong to you."

She blinked at the man, not expecting to see her weapons or hear her language. She noticed his gums, red and swollen, as well as his rotting teeth. Sitting up, she put away the pistol and the knife. "Thanks, Nasseer. Could I have some water, please?"

Nasser reached for a dark waterskin strapped behind his back, made from some animal hide, and unscrewed a metal fitting at one end. He took a swig and then passed it to her. Without hesitation, and putting those diseased gums out of her mind, she also drank from it. The water was cold and amazingly refreshing, and she closed her eyes as it cooled her throat and chest.

"Thanks," she said.

"You should thank Hassan and Aaron," Nasseer said.

Vaccaro narrowed her stare at him, confused.

"We are almost two miles west from where we found you, Captain. How do you think you got here?"

"You guys . . . *carried* me?" she asked, realizing the feat, given the roughness of the terrain.

Aaron tilted his head and gave her a devilish grin. "We sort of took turns on you, Red. But you didn't seem to mind us manhandling you."

She frowned at him before making another attempt at standing. Aaron tried to help, but she refused him, gaining her footing while breathing deeply.

Slowly, she walked up to Hassan and placed the palm of her hand on the large man's chest as he dropped his big brows at her.

"*Tashakor,*" she said, smiling. *Thank you.*

The giant's face broke into a smile of brownish teeth and said, "*Hark ala rasha.*" *You're welcome.*

"Hey, Red, what about me?" Aaron said, also smiling, tapping his barrel chest, revealing that gap in between his front teeth, eyes narrowing with dark amusement.

She ignored him and turned to Nasseer, who was studying her with penetrating eyes encased in dark circles, reminding Vaccaro of a skinny raccoon. "I need to get in contact with my people," she said. "They're probably still looking for me after—"

"And we shall, Captain," Nasser said. "As soon as we finish assisting Aaron in his mission."

"What mission?" she asked.

Nasseer turned to Aaron, who looked away and slowly shook his head. "A mission that never happened," he mumbled.

"Really? Enough with that spy talk shit," she said. "*What* mission, Aaron?"

"Damn," he mumbled. Looking back at Nasseer, he said, "Might as well tell her, since we have to take her with us."

When Nasseer spoke, Vaccaro felt her legs trembling again.

63

Hunky-Dory

SULAIMAN MOUNTAINS. SOUTHERN AFGHANISTAN.

Moonlight-split clouds rushed past the side window of the Black Hawk helicopter as it shot down the side of the dark hill like a predator, its belly nearly grazing the sparse canopy projecting silvery ragged shadows over the wooded terrain.

Gorman fought the gut-wrenching maneuvers as the pilot flew this nap-of-the-earth shit, which was meant to keep them safe from ground fire but which wreaked havoc on his digestive system.

So he'd forced his eyes outside the cabin while breathing deeply, staring at the rushing landscape while Maryam slept peacefully, strapped in the seat next to him, wearing a green David Clark noise-cancellation headset.

How can she do that? he thought. Rotor vibrations reverberated through the large fuselage as the helicopter suddenly pulled left, then right, then up, rattling his mind, his stomach—even his teeth—forcing him to keep his jaw tight.

And Maryam slept through it all, her head tilting sideways, finally resting on his shoulder.

He looked over at her, with her eyes closed, seemingly at peace, in sharp contrast with the deadly operative who had saved his life in Islamabad or the cold and exacting interrogator who had broken the opium cartel boss at Bagram.

She squirmed, mumbling something incomprehensible, pressing her side against him, and breathing deeply, hands on her lap.

Lovely and deadly, he thought, eyes drifting from her hands to the Rolex hugging his left wrist, telling him they had been airborne for almost two hours now, and she had slept through most of it. But then again, the woman had slept through the majority of their stay at Bagram, until Gorman was able to secure a ride south.

The stainless steel watch, combined with her proximity, made him think of Jeannie, of a marriage cut short by—

"Three minutes, guys!"

Gorman blinked when he heard the pilot through his headset.

Maryam woke up, realized she was leaning into him, and quickly straightened, eyes finding his in the cabin's semidarkness.

"Sorry . . . I was really knackered," she said, before yawning.

"Knackered?" he said.

"Aye," she replied, reaching for a bottle of water and an energy bar. "But everything's hunky-dory now," she added, draining half the bottle before unwrapping the energy bar and taking a hearty bite.

Gorman closed his eyes and inhaled.

"You okay, mate? You look a bit iffy."

"I'll be fine once we get on the ground."

"Ah, dicky tummy?"

Gorman was about to reply, but the pilot tossed the Black Hawk into a steep right turn followed by an even steeper descent down the forested mountainside.

"Jesus!" he hissed under his breath, his stomach cramping, unable to control a loud belch.

"Are you going to chunder in here?" she asked.

"Chunder? Where the hell did you learn how to speak—"

"Two minutes!"

Shaking his head, feeling her eyes on him as she bit into the energy bar, Gorman reached for the massive Desert Eagle as a distraction, removing it from a hip holster, verifying it had a full magazine of .50 Action Express rounds plus a round in the chamber. At the Bagram armory he was able to locate six more spare magazines, which he had secured in the pockets of his utility vest, plus an assortment of fragmentation and concussion grenades.

"Are you compensating for something, mate?"

He chuckled before saying, "Yeah, Tallies armed with assault weapons. But nothing can stop these bad boys." He tapped the massive semiautomatic before pointing at his Kevlar vest. "Not even this. You all set?"

"Aye," she replied, placing a palm on her sidearm, a 9mm SIG Sauer, as well as on the suppressed MP5A1 strapped to the side of her Kevlar vest. "Like I said . . . hunky-dory."

Yeah, he thought, swallowing the lump in his throat. *Me too. Just hunky-fucking-dory.*

The pilot shallowed the angle of descent before transitioning to a hover, while a helmeted crew member came down from the cockpit to open the side door and toss a very thick rope into the darkness. *"Time!"*

"Blokes first!" Maryam said, removing her headset while shaking her dark hair loose, briefly exposing a pair of small silver earrings. She extended a gloved hand to the door as the crew member waved them over.

Gorman did a final check of his vest before slipping a pair of heavy leather metalworking gloves over his tactical gloves to protect him from the friction-generated heat of sliding down the rope.

Sitting at the edge and swinging his legs outside the helicopter, Gorman gripped the rope with both hands while also securing it in between his legs and feet. Glancing down at the narrow gap between two stone pines forty feet below him, he pushed himself off the edge and let gravity do its thing, controlling his rate of descent with his hands, legs, and feet.

Fifteen seconds later he was on a ground littered with pine needles while Maryam's figure emerged over the edge, slid in the darkness, and landed softly next to him.

The standing end of the rope had a Velcro-secured pouch attached to it. Gorman and Maryam deposited the heavy gloves in it before signaling the crewman.

A moment later, as the Black Hawk vanished in the darkness and they reached for their weapons, Gorman looked about him, scanning the rocky hillside beyond the edge of the woods. Maryam pressed her back against his while doing the same, so that they were covering each other.

"Are we in the right place, mate?"

"In theory," he said.

His eyes already adjusted to the darkness after being in the cabin, Gorman probed the surrounding vegetation, mostly stone pines amid rocky outcrops. And that's when he spotted the shadow detaching itself from a clump of boulders.

"Hey," Gorman whispered. "Over there."

Maryam turned toward him. They were now shoulder to shoulder, facing the lone figure materializing through the darkness just enough to wave them over before merging with the rocky hill, disappearing like a ghost.

They walked over to the boulders lining the edge of the path, and Gorman was actually surprised that he could not spot the man even though he had seen him hiding here a moment ago. It wasn't until they were right on top of him that he reappeared, motioning them down into what Gorman now realized was a recess in the rocks, where he had been hiding.

In the wan moonlight, kneeling next to Maryam, Gorman finally got a look at this ghostlike warrior. He was shorter than Gorman, and thinner, wielding an MP5A1, his narrow face darkened with camouflage cream, his hair hidden inside a dark bandanna, a thick mustache covering his upper lip, and a lollipop sticking out of the corner of his mouth.

"I'm Bill Gorman," he said, then pointed at Maryam. "This is my asset, Maryam."

"Hiya, mate," she said, with a short wave.

The warrior looked at Gorman, his face impassive. Then he turned to Maryam and the mustache straightened some as his face softened, the lollipop shifting in his mouth.

"Yeah . . . *hiya* to you," he finally replied, before looking them over, poking their Kevlar vests, which were similar to the one he wore. He nodded approvingly before producing a roll of black electrical tape and a small container, unscrewing the top. It was dark green camouflage cream. He handed both items to them while pointing at their faces, necks, the stainless steel Rolex, and Maryam's silver earrings.

"I'm Danny," he said to Maryam, ignoring Gorman. "The guy charged with keeping your pretty ass alive."

64

Revelations

"So you're telling me that the Taliban may have a nuke *there*?" Vaccaro asked, staring through Aaron's binoculars from the top of a ridge overlooking a compound fairly close to the hillside she had torched earlier that day. It looked to be around seven miles from their location.

"*Had*," he corrected her. "We think they moved it after your people spooked them by overtly trying to storm the place—and running straight into an ambush. I mean . . . what did you think you were attacking?"

She crossed her arms. "I was told a rifle platoon got ambushed while approaching a suspected IED factory."

Aaron sighed. "Of course. To NATO, every compound is a suspected IED factory. NATO's biggest problem isn't the Taliban. It's NATO. Everything looks like a nail to them, and so they bring in the big hammer—people like you. The problem is that sometimes, like in this case, a more surgical approach is required."

"Fine," she said. "So we screwed up and they moved it? Where?"

"Not sure. Probably deeper in the range."

"How do you know this?"

Aaron produced a transceiver.

"Hey!" she said, recognizing the radio she had taken from the dead insurgent. "That's . . . *mine*."

Aaron smiled. "Not really, Red."

"It's 'Captain Vaccaro'! And that *is* mine."

"You'll get it back soon enough, just not quite yet."

She was starting to lose her patience with this bear of a man. Hands on her waist, she asked, "Why? Afraid I'll call in the marines?"

He considered her comment and then said, "That's one possibility, though it would be unfortunate, given the way your marines—which work for NATO—handle delicate intelligence." He pointed at the compound.

She frowned and looked at the column of smoke and fire still rising from the clearing a mile from Compound 57, where she had cleared the way for the Chinooks. But the compound itself seemed to still be in one piece.

"You sure they moved it?" she said. "The place looks undamaged."

"They're gone, Red. That's why we headed west, away from the place, after we picked you up."

"How can you be so sure?" she asked, annoyed at this mysterious man insisting on using her call sign.

"This little radio," he said. His closely trimmed beard shifted as he grinned. "It has been . . . how should I put it? . . . unexpectedly productive."

"What do you mean?"

For the second time that evening, what she heard surprised her.

65

HALO

SOUTHERN AFGHANISTAN.

The Antonov An-72AT jet cruised at forty-five thousand feet over the desert, under an international flight plan to deliver oil refinery control systems equipment from the port of Karachi, in Pakistan, to the Basrah refinery, in Iran. Its current altitude and flight path kept it too high and too far south to be of any consequence to NATO operations out of Kandahar Airfield.

Still, since entering Afghan airspace thirty minutes ago, Kira Tupolev had kept a close watch on the radar, standing behind the navigator station. The midsize Russian jet, powered by twin Lotarev D-36 turbofans positioned high over the wings, utilized the engine exhaust gases blown over the wings' upper surface to increase lift.

The Coandă effect, she thought, recalling the short lesson in aerodynamics given by the pilot. The unusual design feature not only increased the jet's range by allowing it to cruise at a lower power setting but also improved takeoff performance. The An-72AT could land in short, unpaved fields typically reserved for small planes and some turboprops.

"Ten minutes!" the pilot announced over the earpiece secured inside her helmet.

Satisfied that no one from KAF would be bothering with them tonight, Kira patted the pilot on the shoulder and headed back to the main cabin. This version of the An-72 family was designed as a freighter capable of air-dropping up to ten tons from its hinged rear ramp.

But tonight it only hauled seven Spetsnaz operators and their gear.

Kira regarded her handpicked team occupying some of the folding side seats near the middle of the cargo area. They wore black one-piece wingsuits made of a mix of nylon and spandex fibers, black tactical helmets, new prototype powered boots, and a slim backpack housing a HALO chute and two canisters—the large one to power the boots, and a small one connected to the oxygen mask each had hanging from their neck.

She sat next to Sergei Popov, who was screwing a sound suppressor cylinder to the muzzle of his black Kalashnikov AK-9 fully automatic assault rifle. He was tall, slim, and muscular, like Kira and the rest of the group, a physical requirement to maximize aerodynamic efficiency in their upcoming high-altitude drop.

"All set?" she asked her second-in-command.

Sergei wore his wingsuit zipped to his waist, exposing the top of his one-piece Nomex and Kevlar battle dress. "Yeah," he replied, tilting his square chin at the group. "They are. Me? I'm just triple-checking things."

He secured the AK-9 to the Velcro straps on the side of his battle dress, which also held a half dozen spare twenty-round magazines, an encrypted radio, a Kizlyar titanium tactical knife in its nylon sheath, and a KBP P-96 9mm pistol along with three spare magazines.

Sergei's equipment, identical to everyone else's, was also hand-picked by Kira, along with the small rucksack packed with enough energy bars and drinks to see them through the first five days of their mission.

After that I need to reassess, based on where we are, she thought. A mission like this one could only be planned so much, and success relied on the initiative, ingenuity, and patience of its operators to see it through. The wishful thinking scenario would be for Kira to track the courier to the bomb within the first few days while remaining completely hidden and then to use her sat phone to call in a missile strike. Sukhoi fighters loaded with supersonic BrahMos cruise missiles were standing by in Iran, less than two hundred miles away. Then it would be a race to the exfiltration point before NATO or the Taliban figured out what had taken place.

But wishful thinking was for amateurs. The reality was that no plan survived the first shot; thus the reliance on the three pillars of a successful mission.

Initiative, ingenuity, and patience, she thought, as Sergei stood and zipped up his suit. A two-inch digital display secured to the front of his tactical helmet interfaced via Bluetooth with the altimeter hugging Sergei's left wrist and with a small GPS receiver on the back of the helmet—again, all standard equipment. As was the switch built into the palm of his right glove, which would activate the twin rockets in each boot. Only Kira wore an additional piece of hardware: a digital tracker tuned to the same frequency as the transponder embedded in the components provided to Prince Mani al Saud by the Russian Mafia.

Kira had trailed the RN-40 spare parts across two continents by tasking satellites from Russia down to Turkey, Iraq, and Saudi Arabia, then across the Indian Ocean and into Pakistan, then into southern Afghanistan.

And now it's less than a hundred miles away.

"You trust these boots?" Sergei asked, staring at them. They resembled ski boots, sporting a hard shell made of various heat-retardant composites meant to protect the wearer from the extreme temperatures inside the miniature combustion chambers.

"I trust our training and the laws of physics," she replied. "And they tell me we can't reach our target without them. So . . ."

"Yeah."

"But look at the bright side," she added. "We have a forty-knot tailwind helping us—"

"Five minutes!"

A red light came on in the rear of the cabin.

The team stood and formed a single line, with Sergei at the front and Kira bringing up the rear.

"Masks and goggles!" she ordered into the microphone inside her mask.

Everyone secured their masks and lowered their ZAO high-performance tactical goggles, made specifically for GRU Spetsnaz. They featured shrapnel and flame protection, fog resistance, particle filtration, and were incredibly comfortable, with full air circulation for extended wear. Plus, they were coated in a new-generation opto-electronic polymer that automatically amplified the available light for nighttime operations or transitioned to a UV-protective tint for daytime missions.

At the moment, they seemed completely clear, but as soon as she lowered them over her eyes and let them adjust, the cabin interior became a bit brighter, with a barely noticeable shade of green.

Her ears began to ring as the pilot slowly depressurized the cabin in anticipation of their drop and also throttled back, slowing the jet to the predetermined drop speed of 160 knots while starting a slow turn south to head back to Pakistan.

"One minute!"

The LED at the rear of the cabin switched from red to yellow, and a moment later the ramp lowered, revealing the silvery tops of a thin layer of clouds some ten thousand feet below them. And well above them, a moon hung high in the southern skies.

The LED turned green and the group immediately moved to the rear in silence.

Sergei led the jump, running somewhat awkwardly down the ramp because of the stiff boots. He extended his arms and separated his legs the moment he leaped off the edge, stretching the membranous surfaces of his tri-wing suit between his arms and torso and between his legs, transforming his human form into a full-body wing.

He vanished from view as the next jumper shadowed him, three seconds later, and the next, and the next, just as they had drilled this high altitude–low opening—HALO—insertion, to the point of obsession. The last two operatives were the least experienced of the group, which meant they each had more than a hundred night jumps like this one.

Kira followed almost a full twenty seconds behind Sergei, spreading her webbed wing surfaces the instant she stepped off the ramp.

Air rushed through the inlets of three sets of ram-air membranes— under the arms and between her legs—inflating them, instantly turning them into semirigid airfoils. This allowed Kira to relax, as she did not need to use sheer force to maintain the shape of the tri-wing suit. The aerodynamics of the suit design took care of that.

But as her combined altimeter and GPS map display at the top of her field of view indicated, at her current forward airspeed of sixty-eight miles per hour, the suit by itself could only achieve a glide ratio of 5 to 1, meaning five feet forward for each foot of lost altitude. And that further meant that, even with the tailwind, starting at forty-five thousand feet, or around 8.5 miles high, her team would glide for forty-three miles before having to deploy their chutes, placing them exactly thirty-eight miles short of the current location of the hardware.

Too far.

"Boosters in five," she spoke into her oxygen mask, before adding, "Four, three, two, one, fire!"

She threw the switch in her right palm, opening the valve that allowed the pressurized liquid rocket fuel to reach the small combustion chambers built into the sides of her boots.

The thrust was immediate and powerful, increasing her forward airspeed to ninety-four miles per hour while decreasing her angle of descent by nearly fifteen degrees.

A flash ahead and below her drew her attention from the display recalculating her new glide ratio.

The operative who had jumped behind Sergei had a malfunction. His legs were on fire.

Dammit!

She heard his scream as he tried in vain to jettison the booster system, dropping from the flight path as flames propagated up his waist, then his chest. Somewhere around a thousand feet below the group, his fuel tank detonated in a burst of orange flames.

"Fucking boots!" Sergei cursed over the secure channel.

"Steady!" she said, forcing her mind to focus on the display. "Stay the course."

Thirty-nine thousand feet.

The computerized system recalculated flight parameters after the booster increased the glide ratio to 9.7 to 1, extending her range to eighty-two miles. On paper, that should have been more than enough, but the boosters only had enough fuel to burn for roughly a third of their total glide time. The simulations back home had shown that, after taking into consideration the increased speed and glide ratio, she would be less than five miles from her target. But that didn't allow for the winds aloft, which worked in her favor, and other atmospheric conditions. And that all meant she would not know for certain until the boosters cut off and the system recalculated the new touchdown location.

So we wait, she thought, making minute adjustments to follow her team coasting slightly below and ahead of her, their paths marked by streams of light shooting out of their boots. The wingsuit and the battle dress she wore beneath it temporarily shielded her from the freezing temperatures as she breathed in slowly, trying to stretch her limited supply of oxygen.

Easy does it. And—setting aside an equipment malfunction—that was the key to a successful glide: being relaxed. It not only minimized the amount of oxygen she consumed but it also worked to optimize the overall stability of her high-altitude insertion, keeping her in the desired pipe.

Twenty-eight thousand feet.

The boosters cut off just as they reached the top of the clouds, and the system automatically jettisoned them to reduce weight. This also exposed the boots integrated with her battle dress, so she would be ready for action the instant she reached the ground.

They now approached the most critical phase, since she would lose the horizon for the thirty or so seconds it took to break through the clouds.

"Steady now," she spoke into her mask, as the team vanished one by one. "Remember your training," she added, which called for forcing oneself to avoid making any flight adjustments in response to the brain's natural tendency to compensate for the sudden loss of being able to tell up from down. The problem, experienced by pilots immersed in instrument conditions, was that the brain would lie. Pilots would enter deadly turns or descents while thinking they were just making corrections to remain in level flight. But unlike Kira and her team, pilots could rely on their instruments, especially the attitude indicator—also called the artificial horizon—to keep them out of trouble.

But she lacked such instruments.

When she finally broke through at twenty-four thousand feet, Kira had remained in proper glide attitude. But there was a problem. There had been five team members ahead of her when they entered the clouds. Kira now saw only three.

Risking a brief downward glance, she spotted two figures spinning out of control a couple thousand feet below. It was the two least experienced gliders, but they still knew better.

Dammit!

She followed their near-vertical trajectories as they jerked their suits to attempt to break the spins. However, the tri-wing suit's lack of a vertical stabilizer, like those used to apply opposing rudder in planes, made it quite difficult to counter a spin.

Realizing there wasn't a damn thing she could do for them, she maintained her profile while reviewing the new flight parameters, which had her touching down six miles from the current location of the hardware.

It'll do.

Now she could see the Sulaimans in the distance as she soared over the desert, which reflected the moonlight filtering through the clouds, creating a faint sheen across this war-torn land.

Afghanistan.

She cringed at the thought of what these bastards had done to her father, maiming his body and mind.

Focus.

Desert dunes became visible as they dropped below twenty thousand feet, as the distant lights of Lashkar Gah loomed over the eastern horizon.

Kira continued making slight adjustments, primarily moving her shoulders, hips, and knees, which changed the tension applied to the fabric wings, optimizing her overall glide angle.

Eighteen thousand feet.

They crossed the edge of the desert, leaving sand dunes behind and rushing over the agricultural plains surrounding the Helmand River as it flowed out of the mountain range before curving east toward Lashkar Gah.

The computer system now had her landing five miles from the target, and the only explanation had to be stronger-than-anticipated southerly winds.

I'll take it, she thought, following the winged formation as they broke below ten thousand feet, dashing through the air at almost seventy miles per hour, completely in control. Her mind stayed ahead of the tri-wing glider, making minute corrections while shifting her attention between the computerized real-time glide ratio, altitude, and speed and the picture in front of her as her team rushed toward their landing zone.

Fifteen thousand feet.

The mountains rose higher as she managed her flight efficiency with constant body-shape manipulation, optimizing her forward speed and fall rate.

Thirteen thousand feet.

The terrain began to rise as they officially left the valley and crossed over the foot of the range, initially rocky and desolate, its jagged features casting shadows in the moonlight. And for the first time she spotted her own shadow shooting over this rugged land, like a predator hunting for prey.

Eleven thousand feet . . . and now for the tricky part, she thought, realizing that the altimeter provided altitude relative to sea level and not to the rapidly rising terrain. Lacking a radar altimeter, which would have provided her with true distance to the ground, Kira would have to eyeball it.

And that's where HALO experience came into play, enabling her to determine what five hundred feet high looked like.

Sparse vegetation gave way to a sea of pine trees layering the mountainside, sporadically broken by rock-strewn ledges as they dropped below ten thousand feet. But the thick canopy below them appeared to be less than a thousand feet away.

Sergei led the way, almost a quarter mile ahead, pulling his rip cord just as he appeared about to crash headfirst into the side of the mountain.

His dark canopy blossomed a moment later, arresting his forward speed before he reached a small clearing between clusters of trees.

The rest of the team followed suit, rectangular parachutes deploying in short intervals just as a rocky precipice filled her field of view.

The parachute tug killed her momentum in the blink of an eye, the straps compressing her chest as she tightened her muscles, and she cringed while transitioning from a glide to a gradual descent. She pulled on the steering handles, guiding herself toward the same small clearing where Sergei now gathered his parachute.

She landed softly with a short run, pulling on the canopy as it lost tension, letting it fall behind her while she released the straps and worked the heavy-duty zipper of the tri-wing suit from neck to groin.

Walking out of it in her skintight battle dress, Kira tested the integrated boots, the spring-loaded heels cushioning her feet. They certainly gave her a nice bounce while walking, lessening the strain on her legs.

She removed her oxygen mask and took a deep breath of fresh mountain air strong with a pine resin fragrance.

Reaching for the sound-suppressed AK-9 strapped to the side of her utility vest, she verified a chambered round before setting the safety/fire selector lever to semiautomatic or single-shot mode.

She readjusted the goggles and the helmet, the latter made of layers of Kevlar and carbon fiber. She pulled up the long stretchable neck of her battle dress and connected it to the base of the helmet, forming a unified armored profile without losing flexibility.

The other two operatives made their way to the clearing a couple of minutes later, joining Sergei and Kira, who reviewed the information on her helmet display.

"Just under five miles that way," she said, pointing her AK-9's silencer to the east.

"What the hell is out here?" Sergei asked.

She shook her head, reading the GPS, which included any structure left over from the days of the Soviet Union's invasion.

"Well," Kira finally replied, "the closest thing besides our old bases at Kandahar and Lashkar Gah is a concrete bunker used to house forward deployments."

"Could the courier be going there?" Sergei asked.

She shrugged. "Anything is possible. Everyone set?"

Sergei and the two surviving operatives nodded in unison.

"All right. Single file. Five-meter spacing. Go," she said.

Not off to a good start, Kira thought, as Sergei led the way. Losing 40 percent of her team before the hard part even started had not been in any of her planning scenarios.

Initiative. Ingenuity. Patience.

Sighing, she fell in line behind her remaining operatives, hoping that a maniacal focus on the pillars, combined with their training—and perhaps a bit of luck—would be enough to achieve their objective and get them off this mountain in one piece.

66

A Bloody Mess

COMPOUND 57. SULAIMAN MOUNTAINS.
SOUTHERN AFGHANISTAN.

Stark knew it would be difficult, even with plenty of eyes on the ground, high assets, a U.S. Marines rifle company of three rifle platoons, and his own team playing quarterback by orders of Colonel Duggan.

But the money was good, and it was for a good cause.

"So, Mr. Gorman," he said, lying on the ground at the edge of a bluff with a clear line of sight into the front and right side of the compound, while Larson and Hagen were perched kitty-corner to cover the rear and left side. "You want us to clear the compound of hags but leave the building and its contents intact? And at three o'clock in the morning?"

The CIA man and his asset, some ISI looker named Maryam Gadai—who Gorman said could be trusted—flanked Stark at his vantage point. All three combed the compound with ATN DNVM-4 digital night vision monocular scopes. Martin stood guard behind them to cover their six while Ryan was off finding an adequate vantage point to set up his .50-caliber sniper rifle.

But the problem was that Stark could not get himself to trust a fucking new guy—much less when the FNG happened to be a CIA spook. And he could trust the *asset* of the FNG even less, *especially* when that asset happened to work for the archenemy of the CIA. And sure, Gorman had already given him the "enemy of my enemy" speech shortly after they arrived here a couple of hours ago, explaining his very valid reasons for this CIA–ISI joint op, but that didn't mean Stark had to like it. The place was a damn fortress, with a single access point beyond the fortified perimeter wall.

Gorman, who was built like him but much younger, with thick dark hair, a goatee, and the classic in-country tan, looked over from his Leupold scope and said, "Yeah, Colonel. And I get the difficulty level on this one. Only one way in or out, and the place is a damn Russian concrete bunker. But look, if it were easier, I'd have the CIA do it. As of late, though, we seem to be tripping all over our damned dicks. So . . ."

Maryam lifted her head and said, "You can actually trip on your tallywacker, Bill? Nice one, really."

"It's just a saying . . . Never mind," Gorman said.

"Oh, that's too bad, love," she replied, smiling before returning to her scope.

"I trip on my tallywacker all day long, *love*," said Martin, from behind.

"In your dreams, shorty," Maryam said.

Stark regarded her for a moment, in the silver moonlight filtering through the trees. She was indeed quite the looker, in an ethnic sort of way, even with the camouflage cream and hair tied in a ponytail. He could see how her fine nose and high cheekbones, leading up to large catlike brown eyes under thick brows, could warm the coldest man. For a moment he wondered if she was playing Gorman—or like they said in the trade, "honey-trapping" him.

But he at least had to give her credit for holding her own with his often-crude team. And to Gorman's credit—and that of his asset, or whatever she was—they had chosen to get their hands dirty instead of calling the shots from behind the walls at KAF, like Harwich and the other intelligence types.

"Delta One, Sierra Echo One. SitRep," Stark said into the mike connected to his MBITR, contacting Ryan, call sign Delta One for this op.

Stark was Sierra Echo One and Larson and Hagen shared the call sign Sierra Echo Two. The SE denomination was Duggan's way of having a little fun with him, since in soldier speak special operations guys were called snake eaters.

And speaking of soldiers, Captain John Wright had volunteered to coordinate the rifle company, call sign Six Six Zulu. They were standing by a thousand yards away, not far from where they were ambushed the day before, and had already dug in defensive fighting positions. He actually admired the man for getting back on the horse so damn quickly, though Stark had a feeling that Wright's decision may have had something to do with one Captain Laura Vaccaro, still MIA in the area.

"*Delta One in position,*" replied Ryan. "*Range comfortable. Five hundred yards. Wind five to ten, left to right.*"

"Sierra Echo One has PIDs," said Stark, shifting the monocular around to count the rebels posted at the four machine gun emplacements. "Positive ID four times insurgents atop watchtowers at each corner of perimeter wall armed with RPDs. Confirm."

"*Delta One confirms four PIDs, plus two Tangos on trees,*" Ryan replied.

"*Sierra Echo Two confirms four PIDs, but can't see Romeo's two Tangos,*" Larson said from the other side of the compound.

"Delta One, Sierra Echo One. Send them," Stark said, and a moment later the insurgents manning the RPD light machine guns bent over their hardware with sound-suppressed .50-caliber holes blown through their midriffs in five-second intervals. Then, somewhere west of the compound, a man fell off a tree, followed seconds later by another. Six perfect, silent shots in just over thirty seconds—and at night.

"*Sierra Echo One, Delta One. Six times insurgent engaged in center mass. No movement.*"

"Roger that, Delta One," Stark replied.

That was the beauty of using such a large caliber: no need for headshots, as it really didn't matter if the rebels were wearing vests. Nothing short of an M1 Abrams could stop a .50-caliber round.

"Stand by," Stark added.

"*Roger. Delta One standing by.*"

"Best bloody shooting I've ever seen," Maryam whispered to Stark. "I need to meet this Delta One bloke."

"He's got a girlfriend, love. I don't." Martin whispered behind them.

"I'm too much woman for you, shorty. You'll never survive it."

"You gotta die of something," Martin replied.

Gorman shook his head while Stark ignored them, scanning the compound and saying, "Sierra Echo One sees no other visible threat. Confirm."

"Sierra Echo Two. Confirmed."

"Delta One. Confirmed."

"Strange, Colonel," said Gorman.

"What is?"

"No other threat in sight. I thought the place was crawling with Tallies."

"Well, there's a pretty good chance they took off after NATO's FUBAR play yesterday."

"That was a real cock-up," Maryam said.

"Yeah," Gorman said with a heavy sigh. "There's that."

"Only one way to find out though," Stark said. "Six Six Zulu, Sierra Echo One."

"Sierra Echo One, Six Six Zulu, go ahead," replied Wright.

"Six Six Zulu, proceed."

"Roger, Sierra Echo One. Six Six Zulu. Moving up the peak and into forward DFP."

"Bollocks . . . Not so fast, chaps," said Maryam.

Stark looked over at her while Gorman said, "What's up?"

She had her right eye pressed against the rubber cup of the night vision monocular. "Something seems dodgy in that clearing."

"Where," Stark said, looking into his scope again, while Gorman did the same.

"Do you see those small patches of discolored soil along the front of the compound? There's quite a few of them. That's freshly dug earth."

Stark focused the DNVM-4 on the ground and slowly panned it back and forth across the long clearing a couple of times. It took a moment, but once he stared at it closely enough—and knew what to look for—he could make out the slightly darker patches of ground, each a couple of feet wide. It looked as if someone had turned the dirt over recently.

"Well. Fuck me," Stark said, not remembering those from yesterday, deciding that it must have happened while they abandoned their surveillance to assist the marines. "Looks like the hags buried some presents for our jarheads, and that certainly explains their absence outside the wall."

"Fuck me, indeed," Gorman mumbled, also realizing what it had to be.

"Easy, chaps. One shag at a time, and what about a pint of lager first?" said Maryam. "But before that you might want to ring your marines."

"I'll buy Miss Pakistan that beer," said Martin.

"Keep dreaming, shorty."

Stark said, "Six Six Zulu, Sierra Echo One. Stand by. Do not advance to forward DFP. Need to check something in front of the compound first."

"Roger that. Six Six Zulu holding current DFPs."

"Delta One, Sierra Echo One."

"Go ahead Sierra Echo One," replied Ryan.

"Do you see those patches of discolored dirt along the front perimeter?"

A moment later, Ryan replied, "Affirmative."

"Put a round in one."

"That won't work, love," Maryam said.

"Delta One standing by."

"Send it," Stark said, ignoring her, and a moment later a silent bullet punched the ground, stirring up dirt and rocks. But nothing else happened.

"Told ya," Maryam said.

"Delta One, try another patch," Stark ordered.

"Roger that."

A moment later another round stabbed the ground a dozen feet from the first shot. Stark ordered two more rounds fired at other smears along the front of the compound, but they all did little more than stir up the ground.

"Fancy a wombat?" Maryam offered.

"What's that?" asked Gorman.

Stark ignored him while doing a double take on her and nodding, actually starting to like this Maryam woman. "Which kind?"

"M576?" Maryam offered.

Stark spoke into his MBITR. "Delta One, Sierra Echo One. Try an M576."

"Roger."

"What are you guys talking about?" Gorman insisted.

Maryam looked at him and slowly shook her head. "What do they teach you at CIA school, love? 'Wombat's' what we call a grenade launcher."

Before Gorman could reply, Stark added, "Grenade launcher, Mr. Gorman, and we actually call them 'thumpers' because of the sound they make when firing a grenade. And the M576 is a buckshot forty-millimeter shell. It houses twenty-four-grain metal pellets that burst outward during detonation, shredding anything in a twenty-foot radius."

"Makes for a bloody mess," added Maryam.

"I'll second that," said Martin.

"I see," said Gorman. "So if there are IEDs buried there, the shock wave might set them off."

"That's the hope, Mr. Gorman," said Stark, before tipping his head at Maryam.

A moment later, Ryan came back through the op channel. *"Delta One in standby."*

"Send it."

The blast lit up the entire hillside the moment the shell detonated right over one of the patches, triggering a chain reaction and kicking up rocks and debris that propagated across the clearing as if it had been impacted by a meteor shower.

Even at a distance of a thousand yards, Stark felt the acoustic energy kick as the daisy-chained IEDs, meant to take out at once dozens of men approaching the compound, rumbled like overlapping lighting strikes, rattling him to the core.

Rocks and debris shot skyward, shredding anything in their path, though fortunately it was just tree branches and not a contingent of United States Marines. Dust and heat propagated through the forested hill, forcing Stark and his team to hit the ground as the shock wave blasted over them.

"Bloody mess, huh?" Gorman hissed, lifting his head while staring at Maryam through the haze surrounding them.

"Aye," she said, dusting off her face.

The perimeter wall's gate suddenly swung open and a posse of men rushed through, screaming while firing in every direction.

"Sierra Echo One, Delta One, you seeing this shit?" asked Ryan.

"Affirmative," Stark responded. "The hags think our marines tripped the IEDs, so they're scrambling out to finish the job. Six Six Zulu, Sierra Echo One reporting at least three zero Tangos headed your way."

"Roger that. Six Six Zulu engaging," reported Wright.

"Sierra Echo Two, engage," Stark said to Larson.

"Roger that," Larson replied.

Standing, he exchanged the monocular for his MP5A1, already fitted with a Firefield tactical night vision riflescope. As he heard the rumble of Larson's M2 Browning drowning out the rattle of AK-47s, Stark turned to Gorman and Maryam. "I'm assuming you two know how to shoot?"

Without waiting for a response, Stark added, "Then cover our back," and rushed down the hill.

Danny Martin took off after him, running past Gorman and Maryam while winking and saying, "Anytime, love."

67

Fire at Will

**COMPOUND 57. SULAIMAN MOUNTAINS.
SOUTHERN AFGHANISTAN.**

This time it was different.

Captain John Wright had set up his rifle company in three defensive fighting positions shaped like semicircles a thousand yards from the front of the compound.

Wearing USNV PVS-7 night vision goggles attached to his

helmet—as was his entire rifle company—Wright huddled next to newly promoted Gunnery Sergeant Eugene Gaudet, behind an array of large stone formations, with a clear line of sight on the Taliban force exiting the gate and spreading evenly across the clearing.

Just a little closer, he thought, finger on the trigger of his UMP45 as dozens of figures loomed above the bend in the trail, dark silhouettes wearing loose clothing and headdresses, holding AK-47s.

As he prepared to give the order to fire, the same deafening sound of an M2 Browning that he'd heard yesterday, during their retreat, reverberated across the hillside. The insurgents, who appeared momentarily confused, dove for cover as their left flank fell to a volley of .50-caliber machine gun fire.

Bastards think we stepped on their mines, he thought, before saying, "Light 'em up, boys."

The entire hillside came alive as the muzzle flashes of three rifle platoons, or almost 130 United States Marines, stabbed the sparse forest, cutting down the enemy.

Wright picked his targets carefully, lining them up one at a time, even the handful that turned around and started running back to the compound when they realized their mistake. And in the middle of what was quickly turning out to be a turkey shoot, he spotted four figures off to his far right, firing their way into the compound.

68

The Loo

**COMPOUND 57. SULAIMAN MOUNTAINS.
SOUTHERN AFGHANISTAN.**

Stark led the stack, followed by Martin and the Agency crew, the smell of cordite assaulting his nostrils, eardrums pounding, all senses on high alert. They snuck in behind the Taliban force that had exited the compound, leaving just two guards by the entrance.

Stark took the first one with an easy headshot, and Gorman demolished the chest of the second one with the Desert Eagle, which he clutched in both hands. Maryam held an MP5A1.

"Sierra Echo One inside perimeter," he said, shifting his aim to the right while Martin covered his left flank and, he hoped, Gorman and Maryam covered the rear. But Stark didn't like the idea of relying on a pair of spooks to keep from taking one in the ass, so he said, "Chief, where the hell are you?"

"Almost there, sir!"

Stark shook his head, not certain how Larson and Hagen would be able to get around to the front quickly enough, especially through the cross fire that the marines were laying on that clearing.

"Delta One, you still have eyes on us?"

"Negative, sir. But I have eyes on the entrance. No one is coming after you."

Stark scurried across fifty feet of dirt, reaching one side of the large metal door of the main building, pausing next to it, his back pressed against the concrete wall.

An explosion drew his attention to his left in time to see a blast on the perimeter wall, engulfed by smoke and dirt. An instant later,

Larson's bulky figure emerged through the haze, caked in white dust, followed by Hagen.

That's one way to get inside, he thought, as Martin also reached the front, resting his back against the concrete wall, shoulder to shoulder with him.

Gorman and Maryam joined them but on the other side of the door, remaining clear of the entryway.

Maybe they'll live through this.

While the battle waged down the hill, Larson finally reached them, hauling his large Browning and a rucksack with extra ammo, plus more of the same C-4 charges he had used to blow a hole in the perimeter wall. Hagen fell in line behind him.

Stark reached for the door and tugged on it, but as he had expected, it was locked.

"Chief, you mind?"

Larson scampered around him, taking a knee by the hefty door, working the explosives around the heavy-duty hinges and the latch and connecting all charges to a single detonator.

"Everybody back," Stark said when Larson finished and got out of the way.

"Fire in the hole!" Larson shouted just before the shaped charge tore the heavy door off its hinges and shot it into the entryway.

A moment later, Stark and Martin followed up by tossing a pair of concussion grenades.

Two blasts that sounded more like heavy thumps shook the entrance, and Stark once more led the way, MP5A1 up, scanning the hallway through the weapon's sights. "Sierra Echo One and Two inside the building."

"Delta One Roger. All clear outside."

"Six Six Zulu. Hags down. Moving up."

That was quick, he thought, as the hallway dead-ended in the middle of a long corridor that ran in both directions.

He stared at moldy concrete walls and floor with skepticism. The stench of urine and body odor was mixed with the smell of cordite.

"Chief, take Danny and Mickey with you and clear that side," Stark said, pointing to his right, before extending index and middle fingers at Gorman and Maryam. "You two with me."

Heading in the opposite direction, Stark reached the closest door and kicked it open, staring at a large room littered with dozens of cots and folding chairs, along with blankets and pillows strewn about.

"Clear," he said, going back in the hallway, where he met Gorman and Maryam, who had also checked the room across the hall.

"Dining room," said Maryam, returning to the hallway. "Empty. Looks like the blokes left in a hurry."

They made their way to the next pair of rooms. Stark cleared another dormitory while Maryam and Gorman stepped out of theirs.

"That was the loo," she said, making a face. "And it smelled terri—"

A figure dashed out of the next room, the muzzle of his AK-47 already pointed at Maryam's face. Stark had his MP5A1 aimed in the wrong direction. Before he could bring it around, the rebel fired twice, the rounds deafening inside the concrete structure as Gorman jumped in front of Maryam.

Two 7.62×39mm slugs struck him squarely in the vest.

Stark took out the insurgent with a headshot as Gorman crashed against the wall and landed on his back.

69

Good to Go

COMPOUND 57. SULAIMAN MOUNTAINS.
SOUTHERN AFGHANISTAN.

The blasts against his chest felt like the hardest hit he ever took in a football game, knocking the wind right out of him. For a moment everything went blurry, then dark, before his vision returned and he focused on a beautiful face hovering over him.

The face of an angel.

Jeannie. My beautiful Jeannie.

Bill!

She was calling out to him, but the voice didn't match. The accent was different.

Bill! Wake up!

Slowly, Jeannie's face dissolved, replaced by the face of Maryam Gadai, her large brown eyes wide open with concern.

"Bill!" Maryam screamed again, kneeling by his side, checking his chest.

Stark also took a knee, hands on Gorman's vest. He pulled out the slugs and showed them to him. "You're one lucky son of a bitch, Mr. Gorman."

"Don't feel . . . so . . ." he mumbled, grimacing as he sat up.

"That's the nicest thing anyone has done for me, love," Maryam said, putting a hand on his face.

"I owed you that one," he said, feeling color coming to his cheeks as she stared at him with those damn beautiful eyes.

"Rubbish," she said. "I won't forget this, love."

"Keep an eye on him," Stark told Maryam. "I'll be right—"

"No," Gorman said, breathing deeply. There was a stabbing pain on his chest, but nothing he couldn't handle. "You can't do this solo, Colonel. We're coming with you."

Grabbing the Desert Eagle, he gutted up, stood, and stared Stark in the eye. "Good to go."

70

Tunnel

COMPOUND 57. SULAIMAN MOUNTAINS.
SOUTHERN AFGHANISTAN.

Impressive, Stark thought, as Gorman worked through the pain and got to his feet, insisting on coming along.

"Very well, Mr. Gorman," he said. "Let's roll."

They continued, room by room. It was mostly dormitories, plus a couple of private bedrooms, a kitchen, and a nearly depleted armory—but not another soul in sight.

Their end of the corridor led to a set of stairs going down, probably to some sort of basement.

Stark decided to take a peek around the corner, and muzzle flashes immediately filled the dark stairway.

"Shit!" he screamed, jumping back as bullets peppered the opposite wall.

"You okay, Colonel?"

"Yeah . . . I think so," he said, checking himself, while Gorman reached for an M67 fragmentation grenade on his vest and pulled the safety pin, releasing the spring-loaded striker to initiate the delay fuze. Counting to three, he tossed it around the corner.

They heard shouts, mixed with the sound of the metallic object clanging down steps, before the 6.5 ounces of Composition B explosives detonated.

Stark went first again, weapon aimed low, firing into anything that moved, stepping over two bloody bodies and shooting into the backs of two more making a run for the basement. The rounds sent them tumbling down the stairs and into the stairwell landing.

He also stepped over them, but he stopped short of the next corner.

"I've got this, Colonel," Gorman said, moving around the dead rebels while reaching for another grenade, this time an MK3A2 concussion grenade, tossing it around the corner.

The blast in such enclosed quarters shook Stark to the bone, forcing him to take a step back, his ears ringing.

I'm getting too old for this crap, he thought, before looking at Gorman and Maryam, their faces nearly invisible in the twilight of the basement.

"You," Stark said to Gorman, "on me. And you," he added, turning to Maryam, "cover our back."

Without waiting for a response, he turned the corner, facing a short hallway of concrete walls leading to a pair of double doors. He moved directly to them, like a shadow, MP5A1 ready, finger on the—

Two suppressed rounds popped inside the concrete structure, coming from the stairwell.

Stark and Gorman pivoted in unison while dropping to a deep crouch.

Maryam stood to the side, just before the stairwell landing, legs spread shoulder width apart, MP5A1 aimed at two insurgents on the ground, each with a shot right between the eyes.

She stretched a finger at the hidden door built into the side of the concrete wall, where the men had been hiding. Peeking inside, she said, "Tunnel. Long one."

"Great," Stark said, then he tapped his MBITR. "Chief, anything?"

"Negative. Just empty rooms."

"Get back this way. We're in the basement. I need you to check the tunnel just beyond the stairs."

"Roger."

"And advise Wright that they may have left via a tunnel, so scrub the hillside for any sign of an exit."

"Roger that."

Turning to Gorman and Maryam, he said, "Let's see what's behind those doors."

Gorman led the way, followed by Stark and Maryam.

They stepped into a pristine room—clean floors and white walls under white ceiling tiles and fluorescents that actually worked.

Stark lifted his night goggles, squinting in the sudden brightness. They stared at multiple lab tables packed with IED-making hardware and walls lined with shelves also filled with explosives, timers, fuzes, wire, and metal casings of various sizes. The room was temperature controlled, the whirl of an air conditioner breaking the silence of the place. Somewhere in the background he could hear the hum of a generator.

Stark turned his attention to the contents of the large table in the middle, which Gorman and Maryam had already prioritized. It looked like the outer shell of a long, cylindrical bomb, including stabilizing fins and nose cone.

Stark ran a finger over the Cyrillic script adjacent to a red star on the wide ring joining the four fins.

"All right, Mr. Gorman, Miss Gadai. Looks like it's your show now," Stark said.

Gorman and Maryam went to work photographing everything, including various serial numbers stamped on the inside of the metal shells, before inspecting assorted disassembled components. One reminded Stark of a gym weight; the other was a thick metallic cylinder.

"This is the bomb's impact-absorbing anvil, as well as the carbide tamper plug," Gorman said, pointing to the cylinders, before adding, "and this is the steel nose plug forging. Definitely a gravity-type weapon."

"That's correct," Maryam said. "How do you know that?"

"CIA school," he said with a wink.

They continued cataloging each component and their stamped serial numbers.

Stark left them doing their thing while he stepped back outside and met up with Larson and Martin, who were already peeking inside the tunnel.

"Well?" he asked.

"Quite the escape route," said Larson. "Looks like it goes way out."

"All right. Take Mickey, check it out, and report back. Danny, with me."

They walked back into the lab, where they found Gorman and Maryam huddled over a strand of wires next to a four-inch-thick disk made of some dark stuff.

"What's going on?"

"Good news and bad news, Colonel," Gorman said.

"What's the bad news?"

"The *good* news," Maryam said, ignoring him, picking up the strand of green wires, and peeling off the insulating plastic with her fingernails, "is that these are the primer wires and they're rubbish. Also," she added, pointing at the thick disk, "this is the projectile tungsten carbide disk, meant to protect the U-235 projectile from the charge of conventional explosives. Also no good." She broke off a piece by tapping it with a pair of pliers. "And this . . ." she said, pointing at a box roughly the size of a shoebox, filled with cylinders and a greenish paste. "It's the battery pack. Also no good."

Stark nodded. "So I take it the bad news is the fact that we now believe that we're dealing with a nuke?"

"Not just any nuke, Colonel," Gorman said. "We'll have to check with Langley first—and Maryam will do the same with her people—but it looks like Glenn Harwich's suspicions were spot on. We're dealing with a Soviet nuke, and it also looks like it was taken apart by people who know what they're doing."

"Like our bloody Dr. Khan," added Maryam.

"Yeah," Gorman said. "And—"

Larson walked in the room.

"Colonel?"

"Yeah, Chief?"

"You're not going to believe this shit."

They followed Larson out of the lab and into the tunnel. An electric cable ran along the ceiling, feeding small bulbs every hundred feet or so, casting a grayish glow on a shaft that angled up slowly for nearly a mile and a half into chest-high vegetation, leading to a westward clearing.

Hagen stood in the middle of it, staring at a spectacular moon casting a silvery hue across the mountain range while smoking one of his Russian cigarettes.

Gorman inspected his handheld GPS. "Colonel, this is one hell of a shortcut. On the surface we're almost *eight miles* from the compound, if we were to follow the mountain to the other side."

"Well, Mr. Gorman, this is precisely why we can't seem to win this damn war. The enemy fights us in three dimensions while we waste our time dropping bombs on the surface."

Maryam stepped away from the group and walked to the west end of the clearing.

Stark motioned Martin to follow her and then tapped the mike of his MBITR. "Six Six Zulu, Sierra Echo One. SitRep."

"Six Six Zulu in compound. Three niner insurgents down," replied Wright. *"We also have the place surrounded. No one's coming in or out without us knowing."*

"Roger, Six Six Zulu. Our target escaped through a tunnel into west side of mountain. What's the radius of the infantry division on outer perimeter?"

"Ah . . . at the moment, around five miles. We have nine hundred men enclosing that area."

Stark turned to Gorman and Larson while Hagen continued smoking. "See what I mean? They're trained to think like—"

"Hey, mates!" Maryam screamed from the side, and Martin waved them over.

They gathered around the Pakistani operative and Martin, who remained on their knees, inspecting a collection of footsteps and broken branches that led to a goat trail winding up this side of the mountain.

"Looks like Miss Pakistan here is as good a tracker as me," Martin said.

"Keep dreaming, shorty," she replied, before looking up over her shoulder. "Fancy a night hike, chaps?"

71

Close Encounters

**WEST OF COMPOUND 57. SULAIMAN MOUNTAINS.
SOUTHERN AFGHANISTAN.**

Zahra had heard the commotion in the distance, echoing across the range, a fierce battle just east of her position, a mix of AK-47s and various American weapons. Crawling to the edge of a rocky overlook, she had seen the firefight raging around three miles away. And if the GPS was remotely accurate, it had taken place awfully close to her primary target, an old Soviet bunker where Akhtar, Pasha's brother, had his supposedly secret headquarters.

So much for that plan.

Fortunately, her alternate target had been in the opposite direction, and after a five-hour hike, including sneaking past a detachment of American marines trying to cordon the area, she was finally approaching it.

Less than a mile away—if she could trust her GPS.

But she now heard another noise, beyond the bend in the trail as it hugged the edge of the gorge before it widened into a rocky clearing.

The dozen men sitting by a wall of boulders were noisy—at least by her standards. They ate fruit and bread and smoked cigarettes while one of them stood guard. Their beards and loose clothes told her they were local, but that didn't mean they were necessarily friendly. And besides, they were not in the right location.

She inspected the group again, noticing the man standing guard in front of the group, dressed all in black and armed with what she recognized as a Russian SVD Dragunov sniper rifle with a large scope mounted on top.

Sniper, she thought, trying to make out their faces, to see if she could recognize Pasha among them, but it was too dark and she didn't want to risk getting any closer to take a better look.

Zahra checked her GPS once more before moving away, shifting like a shadow from tree to tree while working her way around the bend in the mountainside. Moonlight cast faint shadows across her path, perspiration forming on her forehead and over her lips even as temperatures dropped into the forties.

Wiping the sweat off with a sleeve, the Kurdish warrior paused to scan the woods with the scope on the suppressed UZI, all senses operating as one—the picture ahead, the clicking of insects, the aroma of pines, and the feel of the soft terrain through her boots. Any discrepancy in any of them would disrupt the natural rhythm and trigger an alarm in her operative mind, which would further elicit trained responses.

Clear, she thought, moving again, her degree of caution increasing as she realized that the trail at the edge of the mountain continued to circle the red dot on her wrist GPS, set to nighttime mode, which she had further dimmed and also covered with a sleeve.

She finally stood on a narrow outcrop surrounded by stone pines under a sky that would have seemed majestic with its blanket of bright stars and distant snowcapped peaks glistening in the moonlight. But it was all lost on Zahra as she tried to make sense of the GPS coordinates while recalling what Mani had said about not placing complete trust in maps in this part of the world.

The gadget marked her alternate rendezvous in the middle of the gorge separating her from the clearing where she had spotted those locals thirty minutes ago. If she were to believe the map completely, it meant that the secondary location would be at the bottom of the gorge.

She used the scope to look down into the abyss, which bottomed out in what looked like a riverbed and appeared completely deserted—which didn't make any sense as a rendezvous. The base of that canyon had to be at least a day's trek down switchbacks and goat trails.

She lifted her sights and trained them across the narrow void, where she could still make out the locals a quarter mile away, just as she had left them, hugging one side of the rocky bluff.

Was that my team?

To be certain, she gradually covered the entire perimeter of tree line skirting her clearing, almost a thousand feet of it, while remaining thirty feet from the edge, her motion fluid and inaudible, like a phantom. Her eyes probed deeper, in small arcs of ten to fifteen degrees. She let her sight adjust to each tunnel-like picture, searching for any abnormalities that could indicate a hidden warrior.

Finally deciding she was alone, she turned on her transceiver, tuning it to the predetermined frequency while looking at the locals through her scope.

She said in Pashto, "Courier in position at alternate."

But she just got static through her earpiece in return and noticed no abrupt movement from the men.

Double-checking the frequency, she tried again, with the same result.

You are early, she thought, checking her watch, realizing that dawn was still two hours away. Plus, one of the risks of using these radios in the mountains was that ridges played havoc with the gadget's range—not to mention that the wrong people could also intercept her transmission, even if it was encrypted.

She spent another ten minutes searching for the best vantage point to wait it out, finally opting for a wide branch a dozen feet off the ground on a pine protruding over the precipice. Although it was a bit unnerving, since she could stare straight down a couple thousand feet into the dry ravine, it provided her with a perfect view of the clearing from all angles. And the thick foliage did wonders to break up her slim form.

To maximize her stealth edge, she decided to switch to the suppressed Ruger. Its subsonic rounds and lack of a muzzle flash would make it impossible for anyone approaching the clearing to locate her—

"*We're here, Zahra. Signal when you arrive.*"

She blinked at the mention of her name, and also at the comment. *Seriously? Signal when I arrive?*

Frowning, she said, "*I'm* in position, Pasha. Where the hell are *you?*"

"*Akhtar sent me here to get you and the components safe passage to our*

new headquarters up the mountains. Our old headquarters is under at-
tack. We've been waiting for your arrival for a few hours."

"Well, you're not off to a good start. I'm *exactly* where I need to
be and there's no one here."

"What are your coordinates?"

Zahra frowned at the realization that this could be a trick.
Someone—perhaps American intelligence—could have intercepted
Pasha, forcing him at gunpoint to draw her into a trap.

"Actually," she said. "You tell me where *you* are."

After another static pause, Pasha provided his GPS coordinates,
which matched hers—down in the middle of the damn gorge.

"Wave your arms," she said, while looking through the scope.

A moment later the man in black with the SVD rifle behind his
back waved his right arm.

So that was he?

"Hold your position," she said. "I'm coming to you now."

Pasha ordered his men into defensive positions while he scanned the
clearing across the narrow canyon with his binoculars, but he could
not see any movement. Then he panned about the surrounding
ridges, and again, all seemed quiet.

Yet Zahra obviously had eyes on him, which he found discon-
certing.

Growing frustrated, he checked his surroundings again, this time
slowly, remembering his training, limiting his movements to ten-
degree arcs at a time. But after a few minutes, he still came up empty,
nothing but rocks, trees, canyons, and bluffs.

Yet Zahra was out there, stealthily moving toward him—and she
was a damn woman!

He frowned. The Muslim in him had had a hard time wrapping
his head around that ever since Akhtar had conveyed the instructions
to rendezvous with her, whom he remembered clearly from those
meetings between Prince Mani and bin Laden. But he had accepted
his brother's orders, just as he had agreed to collaborate with her
while working the security for those secret meetings, even if it con-
flicted with Sharia law.

Putting away the binoculars and switching to the Dragunov, he used the Leupold scope to scan the clearing across the gorge, the only place where she could have been. Everywhere else, like the ridges above them, was hours away by foot.

Too far.

But even with the night scope, he still came up empty-handed. For the life of him, he could not locate—

"Pasha, you have company," she said on the radio.

"What in Allah's name are you talking about?" he asked.

"I just spotted a force of men closing in on your position. They are trying to encircle you. Get out of there. Now!"

Before he could reply, the crack of a gunshot thundered across the outcrop and one of his men fell, clutching his chest. More reports followed, a mix of AK-47s and other small arms fire he did not recognize.

Ambush!

He heard the thumping sound of an unseen grenade launcher before three shells landed on the far side of the clearing in bright explosions, engulfing two of his men. Realizing they were surrounded, with the canyon to their backs, Pasha rushed to the opposite end from the blasts, locating a collection of boulders that offered a sniper's perch from where he could attempt to flank the incoming team.

As his men put up a defense, he scrambled up the rocks with the Dragunov in hand, cursing himself for having given away his coordinates over the radio.

72

Tackle

Clutching the Colt 1911 in both hands, Vaccaro followed Aaron and Nasser as the group surrounded the Taliban on that outcrop, cutting off their escape before opening fire with their mixed weaponry.

The Shinwari warriors had the advantage, with the dark forest to their back, while the enemy had the moonlit clearing gleaming behind theirs, making it relatively easier to discern them.

Five hours ago she had argued against coming here, especially after hearing the unmistakable sound of an M2 Browning, along with dozens of UMP45 submachine guns and M4A1 carbines, the preferred weapons of the United States Marines.

"The firefight is that way," she had said, pointing to the east.

"But you heard what we just heard," Aaron had replied, the Taliban radio in his hand, flanked by Nasseer and Hassan.

Vaccaro had stared at the Shinwari soldiers, hating to accept the brutal reality that they were right, that the real fight was to the west. They had to prevent the female courier—someone named Zahra—from delivering components to Pasha, the insurgent Aaron had been tracking since Islamabad. There was already too much action on that compound for any of them to make a difference.

So she had come along, running alongside Aaron, the mystery man assisting these determined warriors joined behind a common and noble cause.

They had approached the clearing carefully, waiting for Zahra, the courier, to arrive before engaging the Taliban contingent. But somehow she had spotted them and had warned the men in the clearing, forcing Aaron and Nasseer to launch the attack.

"Over there!" Aaron screamed, pointing at two figures trying to escape the ambush.

Vaccaro spotted them, loose clothing swirling as they tried to escape Nasseer's noose. She tracked the closest one, letting his silhouette come to her, squeezing the trigger as the rebel's center of mass aligned with the Colt's sights.

The flash splashed the forest with orange light and the report thundered in her eardrums as the .45 jacketed hollow-point round tore into the insurgent, who dropped out of sight.

Vaccaro went after the second target, who was scurrying to hide in the darker woods. Once more, she waited, biding her time, letting the rebel enter her sights. She fired twice, the first round splintering wood, the second catching him on the shoulder. The impact spun him around and he crashed face-first into a tree.

She considered following up but chose instead to stay with the group, rejoining Aaron and the others as they moved steadily against the trapped rebels.

And that's when she saw the shadow off to her far left, shifting from tree to tree. But unlike the two rebels she had just shot, this one raced in the opposite direction, *toward* the clearing. And also unlike the two rebels, every time she tried to bring it into her sights, the figure, much smaller and nimbler, would vanish, as if swallowed by the mountain, but not before she was able to discern the profile of a petite woman.

The courier?

"It's . . . the courier," she hissed, before shouting, "Aaron!" over the rattle of AK-47s and the detonating grenades. But he was too far away to hear her through the racket.

Dammit!

She ran up to him as he huddled shoulder to shoulder next to two of Nasseer's men, their weapons trained on four insurgents on the right side of the ridge. "Aaron! I think I just spotted the—"

Both men next to Aaron dropped to the ground as silent rounds smacked their temples, but he never noticed it, keeping his focus on the clearing, firing his UZI while standing next to a stone pine.

Vaccaro reacted, tackling Aaron from the side. It took effort on her part, considering his formidable bulk, but she had a running start, using her momentum to take him down, landing on top of him just as bark shattered where his head had been.

"What the hell?" he mumbled, hands on her shoulders as he lay on his back under her, his face inches away in the darkness as splintered wood rained on them.

Vaccaro felt his breath on her as she pointed at the two dead Shinwaris. "Not *what* but *who*," she said. "I just spotted Zahra. She came in from over there, and very fast!"

She rolled off him and rose to a deep crouch, trying to reacquire. Aaron joined her, UZI at the ready, as she aimed her Colt at the woods.

But the courier, like a ghost, was long gone.

73

Rescue

WEST OF COMPOUND 57. SULAIMAN MOUNTAINS.
SOUTHERN AFGHANISTAN.

Zahra fired the suppressed Ruger while moving, killing another man, punching a hole in the leftmost edge of their offensive line as they closed in on Pasha and his team, who had their backs to the gorge. But she was surprised so see that the assault was being carried out by another group of locals, not by any of the U.S. Marine platoons she had seen a couple of hours ago while making her way to the alternate rendezvous.

Perhaps a warring tribe?

In a crouch, she sneaked through the break she had created, using the thundering battle to hide her presence, hustling between trees, shrubs, and boulders, concerned primarily with her right flank, where the battle raged.

Muzzle flashes dominated the clearing now, their stroboscopic light peppering the attacking forces closing in for the final kill as the ensnared men started to panic. Apparently recognizing the futility of their situation, some of them abandoned their cover and made a run for it while firing wildly, until well-placed shots smacked their chests, their faces.

Where are you, Pasha?

Maneuvering along the far side of the ridge, she leaped across waist-high brush, taking aim at one of the attacking fighters rushing to this side of the clearing, weapon aimed at a spot just ahead and above her. And that's when she noticed the man in dark clothes hiding behind the rocks, trying to bring his large Dragunov sniper rifle around.

Wrong weapon, Pasha, she thought, lining up the incoming threat and smacking a .22 subsonic slug into the middle of the man's forehead. He crash-landed headfirst, tumbling in one direction while his AK-47 skittered in the opposite.

It happened very fast. In one instant Pasha witnessed the onslaught of mixed-caliber volleys decimating his team, and in the next he saw one of them swinging an AK-47 muzzle in his direction. He was about to hoist his sniper rifle around when the man fell from a round to the face.

Pasha stared at him, puzzled, wondering who had just saved—

"Pasha!"

He turned to see the woman huddled by the tree line, calling out his name, a suppressed pistol clutched in both hands. He recognized her features in the pulsating glow of the gunfight as the last of his men made a final stand.

Zahra.

He clenched his jaw at the thought of being saved by someone who defied the very essence of his beliefs.

"Now!" she pressed, as the last two surviving warriors, huddled behind a large rock by the edge of the canyon, returned fire.

Pasha jumped off the boulder and scrambled off the ridge, running into the forest, landing on his knees next to her while she kept watch over the final moments of the bloody fight, which ended when the last two warriors jumped into the abyss rather than let themselves get captured alive.

But the enemy managed to surround one who was alive, shot in the shoulder. They kicked his Kalashnikov away, holding him down.

Pasha lined up his Dragunov on the man's chest, but Zahra stopped him. "Are you insane?" she hissed. "That will give us away!"

"But he knows where we're going."

"Then let's hope he doesn't talk. But *shooting* him will guarantee we won't make it off this hill." Then she shot up the incline with surprising elasticity and stealth.

"Fine," he replied, scurrying after her silently, avoiding twigs and fallen branches—anything that could give them away—clambering away for a couple hundred feet undetected.

But they didn't get far.

Two men armed with Kalashnikovs came running toward them from their right like shadows in the night. It was the backup team, left behind to make sure no one escaped the carnage by the bluff.

As Zahra brought the suppressed Ruger around, the first man fell, some forty feet from them, before she could fire. His associate also tumbled, crashing headfirst, succumbing to silent rounds fired from an unseen vantage point.

"Who the hell was that?" asked Pasha.

"I don't know," she replied, peering into the darkness through the sights of her pistol but seeing nothing. Not a damn thing. "But what I *do* know is that we need to get the hell away from this place right now."

74

Pillars

WEST OF COMPOUND 57. SULAIMAN MOUNTAINS. SOUTHERN AFGHANISTAN.

"Nicely done," Sergei Popov mumbled from the branch next to the GRU Spetsnaz team leader, lying flat, halfway up the stone pine where they had observed the attack on the courier's team, waiting for the right opportunity to intervene. "And without a real sniper rifle."

Her shooting eye pressed against the night vision scope of her suppressed AK-9 assault rifle, Kira Tupolev watched the courier—the same woman who had accompanied Prince Mani to Moscow—pause and scan the woods with her weapon, obviously confused.

Tracking her had been relatively easy, thanks to the transponder signal overlaid on the GPS display on her tactical helmet, and Kira had been tempted to simply capture Zahra and force her to yield her destination. But Kira knew how easily plans change, and for all she knew the courier's original destination may have already changed, given the men following her and the attack on that old Soviet compound.

No, she thought. Initiative and ingenuity had gotten them this far. Now patience was the key pillar. And Kira had plenty of that, having waited seventeen years for the opportunity to redeem her family's name and avenge the brutality inflicted on her father by these monsters.

She would follow and wait, and if required, apply some initiative and ingenuity, as she had by intervening from a distance to keep the courier's mission—and therefore her own mission—alive. Nothing else mattered but locating the weapon and destroying it.

Nothing.

Sergei had suggested terminating the team that had ambushed the courier, but she had resisted the temptation to get directly involved. Right now she had the upper hand. Her Spetsnaz team was invisible, operating in complete anonymity, and she did not wish to relinquish that edge by acting overtly.

Initiative, ingenuity, and lots and lots of patience, she thought, as the courier and her companion overcame their surprise and took off into the darkness.

"Run away, little courier," Kira mumbled, following them with the scope. "Run away and show me the way to my bomb."

75

Dirty Business

**WEST OF COMPOUND 57. SULAIMAN MOUNTAINS.
SOUTHERN AFGHANISTAN.**

It ended as fast as it had begun, with the contingent of Taliban either dead or dying, and those who had not perished in Nasseer's effective assault had chosen to jump off the cliff rather than be captured alive.

All except for one: the insurgent Vaccaro had shot in the shoulder.

With the man gagged and secured, Nasseer was forcing a terrain map in front of him as Hassan forced a pair of single bow sheep shears to the genitals.

She stepped away from the brutality of the moment, as corpses littered the ridge, as the insurgent cried out.

Aaron stood by the other side of the ridge, where large boulders spanned the forest from the gorge. She joined him.

"Sorry you have to see that," Aaron said, tilting his head toward the screams. "Dirty business."

"I last saw the woman heading this way," she said, checking the Colt's magazine and counting two rounds left. She replaced it with a fresh one from her vest, cycled the slide to chamber a round, and thumbed the safety before securing it in its holster.

"Yes, and another one joined her . . . a man." He pointed at the deep tracks of desert sandals running from the boulders to the forest, before running his fingers over the disturbed leaves and dirt by the tree line. "And he knelt here, next to her, before heading in that direction."

Vaccaro leaned down to take a look.

"And thanks," he said, his rugged face, filmed with sweat, widening as he smiled, unveiling that gap in his front teeth.

"Thanks for what?"

"You can tackle me anytime." The grin broadened.

She shook her head and said, "Only if you tell me where the hell you're from. You're definitely not from around—"

"I'm Mossad . . . if you must know."

"And I'm Laura," she said. "If you must know."

"And I prefer 'Red,'" he replied with a wink. "It suits you."

She tugged at the ends of her hair with two fingers and frowned. "Not for long, I'm afraid."

"What do you mean?"

"It's slowly turning brown. Used to be much redder when I was young."

Aaron tilted his head. "Fiery enough for me."

Nasseer walked up to them, the map in one hand and his Kalashnikov machine gun in the other, the ammunition belt thrown over his shoulders. Hassan was behind him, wiping the blood from the shears.

"I know where they're going," the Shinwari chief said.

"How do you know he didn't lie?"

Nasseer dropped his gaze to the bloody instrument in his brother's hands and said, "There is a level of pain after which a man sticking to his story means he's telling the truth."

Vaccaro blinked at that.

"We reached that point a minute ago," the Shinwari added.

"In that case," Aaron said, getting up, "I'm betting it's *that* way."

Nasseer stared at the direction the Mossad operative pointed, then back at the map, and slowly nodded.

76

Not This Time

WEST OF COMPOUND 57. SULAIMAN MOUNTAINS. SOUTHERN AFGHANISTAN.

"Where is your *hijab*?" Pasha asked in the darkness, as he caught up to her halfway up the incline.

Zahra sighed, already regretting the decision to rescue him. But in spite of her hatred for what this man represented, she had a mission to complete.

That, however, didn't mean she had to put up with the asshole.

"Really, Pasha? I just saved your miserable life and that's all you have for me?"

"I am grateful, Zahra, but it is still the law," he said.

"Yeah, well . . . good luck with that."

Before he could reply, she whispered, "And clamp the chatter, would ya? They're right behind us." Then she once more bounded up a steep incline.

He caught up to her again, and they continued in silence for another thirty minutes, scaling on all fours, using roots and outcrops to hoist themselves, finally reaching a ledge roughly a thousand feet above the ambush.

"They know we're up here," she said, thoroughly soaked in

perspiration in spite of the cold temperatures, peering over the edge. She couldn't see anyone but she could hear distant rustling noises. "They're tracking us."

"I'm counting on it," he said.

She turned, glaring at him in the moonlight. He could be attractive if it weren't for his dumb-ass beliefs, which made him look as grotesque as her uncles. "What are you talking about? We may hold the higher ground, but we're outnumbered, with limited ammunition."

"Not for long," he replied, reaching for his radio

She placed a hand over his. "No radios. That's how they found your jihadist ass in the first place."

"Not this time, Zahra," he said, pulling away. "Not this time."

77

A Means to an End

WEST OF COMPOUND 57. SULAIMAN MOUNTAINS. SOUTHERN AFGHANISTAN.

Aaron and Vaccaro remained at the back of the line, walking side by side while Nasseer, who knew these mountains and apparently was also a master tracker, led the way. Hassan followed close behind, and then the others. The pace fell somewhere between relaxed and neck breaking—so, manageable, especially given the cold breeze, which she inhaled.

The line suddenly stopped, and a moment later Nasseer walked up to them. "Wait here," he said. "I'm going to scout the area ahead to make sure they are not leading us to a trap."

"I thought you said he didn't lie," Aaron said.

"Just because the bastard Hassan castrated told the truth, doesn't mean there could not be more of them along the way."

And he was gone.

The Shinwari warriors quickly sat down to relax, and so did Aaron and Vaccaro, finding a small rocky ledge that provided them with a spectacular view of the Sulaimans and the desert under a blanket of stars.

"So, is there a boyfriend, Red?" asked Aaron. He was drinking from a canteen, his features somewhat obscured in the moon shadow cast by the pines towering over them.

"Excuse me?"

"Girlfriend, then?"

"Oh, boy," she whispered, staring at this very nosy man. "Is that one of the lines the Mossad teaches you to pick up women?"

"Among others. So, boyfriend? Yes?" He handed the canteen over.

She took a swig while closing her eyes, swirling the water in her mouth before swallowing. The image of John Wright in his jogging shorts and Semper fi T-shirt loomed somewhere in her mind. Handing the canteen back, she said, "Sort of."

"Sort of? That's not an answer. You either have a boyfriend or you don't."

"Yes. Fine. A boyfriend. What about you, Aaron? Got a pretty wife and kids back home?"

"I did, actually," he said, drinking again before screwing the top back on. "Long ago."

"Divorced, then?" she probed, aware that intelligence types usually had bad marriages, with all the time away from home.

"Widow," he replied matter-of-factly while leaning back, resting his head against a smooth rock, hands behind his neck. As he did so, the next button of his shirt became undone, revealing more of his hairy chest. It was freezing and this man walked around with half his chest exposed like he was on some Caribbean beach.

"Ela was twenty-nine," he said, his green eyes staring into the distance. "David was three and Sarah five. Palestinian militia attacked our kibbutz on the West Bank, raping the women and killing the children while the men—myself included—were out working the fields. Cowards."

"I'm so sorry," she said, sitting cross-legged while facing him, placing a hand on his shoulder. He was very warm to the touch, like a furnace, and she liked that, giving him a soft squeeze. Although large, the man was also solid, and for a moment Vaccaro felt something stir inside her.

"So was I, Red. It happened a long time ago. But I know I will see them again . . . just not yet." He stared at the stars, his eyes glistening as he narrowed them. "Just not yet."

"Aaron, I—"

"Do not worry about it," he said, winking. "That is life on the West Bank. A day later our army razed a neighboring Arab village whose inhabitants probably had nothing to do with the attack on our kibbutz. But that's been our way of life since our nation was forged. They hit us and we hit them, and the blood cycle continues. I joined the army six months later and was eventually recruited by the Mossad, where I became a Kidon."

"Kidon?"

"Assassin."

"I see. And who is it that you are trying to assassinate up in this lovely corner of the world?"

"Osama bin Laden."

She cocked her head at him. "But . . . I thought you were tracking this nuclear bomb?"

"A means to an end."

"I'm not following."

"If al Qaeda, working with the local Taliban, has kidnapped a nuclear scientist, presumably to get this weapon operational, then it is a pretty good bet that bin Laden is involved . . . somehow."

"So follow the bomb to find your mark?"

"I knew there was a brain inside that very pretty head attached to that very pretty body."

"You *really* need to work on your lines."

"They seem to be working just fine," he said, grinning at her hand still massaging his shoulder.

She blinked, just realizing she had kept doing that, and pulled it away.

"Don't stop on my account, Red," he said, grinning, revealing that space between his front teeth.

Vaccaro slowly shook her head. For the first time in her life she was not sure how to handle a man. After a moment of awkward silence, she said, "So, you've killed a lot of people?"

"Some," he said. "Though probably not as many as you at the controls of that A-10."

She had to think about that for a moment. "And your motive for becoming an assassin for the Mossad? Revenge?"

He shrugged and rubbed his short dark beard. "I prefer 'righteousness,' or perhaps the survival of Israel . . . but I will take 'revenge.'"

She thought of Lieutenant James Vaccaro and said, "I actually understand."

He slowly turned to face her. "Do you?"

"Dad flew A-4s in Vietnam. He was KIA when I was six. I guess we are the product of our pasts."

He just stared at her with those penetrating eyes, and for a moment she felt he could see right through her as he said, "We are indeed, Red. We are indeed."

78

Circus

KANDAHAR AIRFIELD. SOUTHERN AFGHANISTAN.

Just fucking shoot me now.

Monica Cruz felt her head was about to explode as she watched the shitstorm created by the images displayed on the projection screen at one end of the conference table.

She sat next to Harwich on folding chairs against the back wall of the same room they had crashed the day before. However, this time their intelligence finding, plus the fact that Colonel Duggan was tied up briefing Defense Secretary Donald Rumsfeld in Washington, had gotten them seats at the table in his place.

Well, almost at the table, she thought, observing the two dozen men occupying the high-back leather chairs, discussing options, now that they had been given the undeniable evidence that the Taliban was in possession of an RN-40 tactical nuclear bomb.

And at the head of the group sat Major General Lévesque, hands behind his neck while listening to opinions on how to handle fanatics armed with a bomb two times more powerful than the one that leveled Hiroshima.

Off to the general's right stood Corporal Darcy and his partner, who had tried to stop Monica yesterday. Their bulky figures guarded the entrance while Darcy worked hard to avoid her gaze.

But Monica couldn't care less about those two clowns. She was growing steadily frustrated at the freckle-faced NATO commander for allowing the endless presentations on how to handle the situation, prepared by the heads of the British, the Canadian, the French, and even the damn Afghan forces. Most of the battle plans presented on the large projection screens on both side walls were of the vanilla variety, a combination of bombing raids and missile strikes in support of massive troop deployments to seal off the mountain while even more troops made an unheard-of wide-area sweep to track down the relevant threat.

"This is beyond FUBAR," Monica mumbled under her breath, while an Afghan colonel stood by the screen on the wall opposite her. The comment earned her a sideways glance from Harwich, who slowly shook his head, pressing a finger against his lips.

"Fine, boss, but it's still beyond FUBAR," she hissed, shifting her weight on the plastic seat and crossing her arms while letting out a heavy sigh—loud enough to turn several heads, including Lévesque's.

"Agent Cruz?" the NATO commander said, smoothing his thick orange mustache with an index finger while looking over the heads of the men sitting in front of her. "The FBI wishes to comment on our battle plans, eh?"

And just like that, the spotlight focused on her.

"Don't do it," Harwich whispered in her ear.

"I do, General," she replied, standing, while Harwich pressed the thumb and index finger of his right hand against his closed eyes.

"Then by all means," Lévesque said. "We're all ears."

"Very well. It is my opinion that all you're going to accomplish is wasting money *and* lives."

"And how's that, Agent Cruz?" he asked, as heads turned toward him before shifting back to Monica.

She pointed at the screen next to the Afghan colonel, who had remained standing, holding a laser pointer. The screen depicted a terrain map of a section of the mountain with an overlay of thick red and blue arrows representing various troop movements.

"One word, General: tunnels," she finally said. "The thinking in this room isn't tridimensional, but the enemy's is. The Taliban is just going to march right under your bombs and your thousands of soldiers."

Lévesque stood slowly and placed his palms on the table as the group's attention returned to him. He was a tall and stocky man, with broad shoulders and large hands that were also covered in those orange freckles. "I appreciate the candor, Agent Cruz, but rest assured that our plan, which represents the thinking of the finest multinational military minds, is designed to overwhelm the enemy and force it to yield the weapon."

"General, the only thing that is likely to be *overwhelmed* is the Role Three MMU, from all of the wounded your plan will produce by sending so many troops to so many IED-uncharted grids."

More silence, and Monica could see the man's jaw muscles pulsating for a moment, before he took a deep breath and asked, "So . . . what would you suggest, Agent Cruz?"

"Simple," she said. "Pull everyone out of that mountain . . . and nuke it."

Lévesque blinked. "Excuse me?"

"The whole mountain, General," she said, making two fists before extending her fingers. "Megaton range. Poof. Gone. Along with those tunnel rats."

"You're . . . *serious*, eh?"

She shrugged. "It's the only way to be sure. You either vaporize a bunch of rocks, goats, and goat fuckers, or you risk those very same goat fuckers vaporizing one of our own cities if they manage to smuggle that nuke out of the country."

Every head swung back to Lévesque, who simply nodded and sat back down while saying, "Thank you for your opinion, Agent Cruz. It has been most . . . enlightening. *And* noted. Rest assured I'll include it in my report." Then he motioned for the Afghan colonel to continue with his brief.

But before the man could say a word, Monica added, "General, you are aware that the Taliban has more tunnels in that mountain range than there are subway tracks on the island of Manhattan, right?"

"Agent Cruz, you've already made your point, and—"

"We had over nine hundred marines encircling Compound Fifty-Seven, General, and they *still* got away—through a fucking tunnel! Now you're telling me that the lessons learned from that snafu is to repeat it again on a grander scale?"

Lévesque stood again, now visibly angry. Dropping the pitch of his voice, he said, "You are out of your depth, Agent Cruz. You are here out of courtesy to Colonel Duggan and the CIA." He stretched a finger toward Harwich. "We are the experts when it comes to military strategy against local insurgents."

"Yeah, General, and how's that expertise been working out for you lately?"

"Please remove yourself from this room, Agent Cruz, or I will have you removed." He looked toward Darcy and his partner, who glanced at one another and frowned, shifting their pleading stares to Monica, hoping that she'd just leave on her own.

Monica stood and opened the door, but before stepping out she turned around to face her stunned audience and said, "Based on the number of recent deaths by friendly fire, including the CIA men your airstrike killed and the intelligence lead you blew by storming Compound Fifty-Seven, I'd say *you* are the one who needs to remove himself from this room, since you're obviously out of *your* depth."

"Enough!" Lévesque shouted, slapping the table with one of his massive hands, making quite the racket. Most people sitting at the table jerked back. "I want you to get the fuck off my base, eh? And by nightfall!"

"Gladly," Monica said. "I don't want to be a part of your circus, which I will report as a gross military mishandling of a great multiagency intelligence lead."

And she closed the door and walked away.

But she didn't get far. Harwich caught up to her before she could leave the building, reaching for her forearm.

Monica paused, staring at him and then at the intruding hand. "Not a good time to put your hands on me, boss."

Harwich blinked and let go of her, before saying, "You really had to do it?"

She shrugged. "Told you I would. The man's all brawn and no brains."

Harwich looked away, hands now on his waist. "That may be the case, but there are ways to go about this." Pointing to the conference room, he added, "And *that* wasn't one."

"Well, not my fight anymore. So if you'll excuse me, I think I need to go pack my things."

"Don't go anywhere. I'll find you after we're through in there."

"That's not what the Canuck said in there, *eh*?"

"Cruz," Harwich said, almost breaking a smile, "you're a piece of work, but just the same, I'm telling you to *stay put*. I'll take care of it."

"Yeah, boss," she said, walking away. "Good luck with that."

79

Coping Mechanism

SULAIMAN MOUNTAINS. SOUTHERN AFGHANISTAN.

Bill Gorman thought he was in shape, given his morning runs and visits to the embassy gym three times a week.

But after following Maryam up the side of this mountain, hiking endless narrow switchbacks and rocky inclines, it dawned on him that there was a crucial difference between being in shape and being in *mountaineering* shape.

The sweat dripping down his face, his inability to suck in enough air, and the cramps torturing his hamstrings and calves—not to mention the heartbeat throbbing in his temples—told him he certainly fell in the former category.

Christ Almighty, he thought, as Maryam dashed up a wooded hill like a damn goat, her figure in those tight fatigues always shifting, conforming to the bends in the terrain and surrounding shrubs under towering stone pines. At the beginning of the climb Gorman had not minded the view from behind. In the eternal words of the Commodores, the woman was a brick house. But half a day of nonstop climbing had long since washed away every impure thought as he tried like hell to keep up with her catlike agility.

But at least he wasn't alone in his misery. Chief Larson had also started to show signs of fatigue, though, in his defense, the giant man looked ten years his senior. And on top of that, he hauled that massive M2 Browning, plus the heavy .50-caliber belt stored in the custom backpack and feeding into the side of the weapon.

Danny Martin, apparently proficient at tracking insurgents, was right up there with Maryam, making the climb look easy while also making passes at the ISI officer—something Gorman suddenly started to mind.

Hagen and Ryan followed them closely, while Colonel Stark fell somewhere in the middle, in spite of being the oldest in the team.

As the group crested yet another hill, Maryam and Martin pointed to the west, where they had apparently picked up their trail. Stark decided to take a short water break, which Gorman fully appreciated, given the nonstop march since exiting that tunnel out of Compound 57.

He sat in between the colonel and the chief, reaching for his canteen and taking a few sips, swirling them in his mouth before swallowing. Maryam sat some twenty feet above them on a rocky ledge, while Martin hit on her under the amused stare of Ryan and in the face of the indifference of Hagen, who was already smoking—something that amazed Gorman, given the former SEAL's stamina.

"Quite the crew, Colonel," Gorman said, wiping the perspiration from his forehead. "I'm glad Glenn pointed me your way."

Stark poured some water over his head, rubbed his face, and nodded while pulling a small GPS tablet from a side pocket of his utility vest. "Been together awhile. Seen some shit."

"Yeah," said Larson in his baritone voice. "But there are still worse ways to make a living."

The man reminded Gorman of one of those oversize World Wrestling Federation fighters as he sat cross-legged with the Browning over his thighs while Stark rested his back against a boulder and studied the terrain map on his tablet.

Gorman heard Maryam laugh and shake her head at something Martin had said, while Ryan smiled and Hagen just smoked.

"You even have a comedian in the house," Gorman said.

"Yeah," Stark said with a heavy sigh, looking up from the black gadget. "That's how the man copes."

"Copes? With the job?" Gorman asked.

The colonel considered that for a moment, regarding Gorman with his ice-cold blue eyes before leaning closer. "Danny . . . He was married . . . had a young son. The kid was . . . how old, Chief?"

Larson held up four fingers.

"Yeah, four. Danny tells the wife to lock the gun safe while he's rushing out of the house to do a job."

"Bogota. Last year," added Larson. "Danny flew the helo."

"That's right. CIA job," Stark said. "Anyway, she forgets and the kid ends up shooting himself in the head. Brains all over . . . a fucking mess."

"Oh my God," said Gorman. "That's . . ."

"Yeah," Stark said. "And we can't be reached. Agency rules. So the wife ODs four days later. Sleeping pills. By the time Danny gets home, two weeks later . . . well . . ."

"Danny jokes a lot, Mr. Gorman," said Larson. "But he *never* smiles."

80

Compromising Position

SULAIMAN MOUNTAINS. SOUTHERN AFGHANISTAN.

The climb became tedious, following endless trails, traversing the face of a hill, followed by switchbacks and more trails.

Vaccaro walked in front of Aaron, who brought up the rear. The Shinwari led the way, with Nasseer and Hassan up in front, following the tracks left behind by the insurgents.

The line suddenly stopped again, and word got passed down that Nasseer was going to scout ahead once more.

Aaron sat down, drank from his canteen, and then offered it to Vaccaro, who slowly shook her head. "In a moment. First I need to . . . go," she said, pointing to the trees behind him.

Aaron was about to stand when Vaccaro waved him down. "If you don't mind," she said, "I think I can manage."

The Mossad operative grinned. "Of course you can, Red . . . but stay close."

"Roger that," she replied, stepping off the trail and walking a dozen steps over a layer of pine boughs, reaching a nearby tree, and going around it. Her back against its wide trunk, she glanced in both directions before lowering her pants and squatting.

But as she shifted her weight back and began to urinate, she heard a metallic click under her right heel.

"Oh, God," she mumbled, freezing, eyes closed as she waited for the inevitable, but whatever it was that she had stepped on did not explode.

Slowly, she reached down with her right hand, feeling through the layer of dry boughs and pine needles, fingertips coming in contact with a small round metallic object right under the heel of her boot.

This isn't happening.

She contemplated standing and pulling up her pants before calling for help, but she was worried about shifting her weight and setting it off. Besides, most IEDs and mines would have already detonated, which meant this one could be a dud, or perhaps a type of mine she didn't know about.

All the more reason not to move your ass.

"*Aaron!*" she hissed, trying not to scream. "*Hey! Aaron!*"

The Mossad man was over an instant later, stepping around the tree and staring right down at her pale legs and buttocks in the semi-darkness, the smell of urine hovering in the air between them.

"Red? I thought you said you could manage?"

"I think I stepped on a mine. Under my right boot."

He frowned, looked over toward the trail, whistled twice, and took

a knee next to her. "All right," he said. "I need you to remain perfectly still, okay?"

"I don't think that'll be a problem."

As the Shinwari clan gathered at the edge of the trail but remained
a safe distance away, Aaron lay flat on his belly, reached between the
tree and her right boot, and began to shift the layer of pine needles
out of the way.

"How screwed am I?" she asked, feeling the top of his head slowly
nudging against her bare right buttock, his hands by her boot as he
parted the boughs.

"Aaron?"

"Hold still, Red," he said, as she stared at the bark of the tree, unable to see what the hell he was doing, her heartbeat rocketing.

"It's Russian," he said a moment later. "And that's good."

"How can that possibly be . . . *good*?" she asked, feeling her voice
starting to break.

"An IED would have already gone off. No warning. Plus, these
Russian mines have a very small explosive charge compared to IEDs,
usually around fifty grams of a TNT–RDX mix meant to just
mangle a foot."

"How comforting."

"Better than blowing off both legs and your tight little . . . *chamor*."
He tapped her bare butt.

She wanted to laugh, but raw fear gripped her gut, and the reaction confused her. How could she feel so scared after thousands of
combat hours in her Warthog?

"Aaron . . . I'm scared . . ." she mumbled, before she could stop
herself, though she realized that she felt comfort in telling him so.

"I'm right here, Red."

He whistled again and Nasseer approached them.

"Russian PMN-4," he told the Shinwari chief, before switching
to Pashto.

Nasseer reached into a small rucksack, produced what looked like
one of those Leatherman multi-tools, and handed it to Aaron before
backing away slowly. She was able to catch a glimpse of the man's thin
face and did not like the look in his raccoon eyes.

"They're keeping their distance," she said. "Never a good sign."

Aaron ignored her while using the tip of a fingernail to pull a screwdriver out from the Leatherman.

She breathed deeply and asked, "Have you done this before?"

Aaron laughed. "Tell me about your boyfriend."

"What?" she asked, as he fiddled with the mine.

"Your boyfriend," he repeated, working the screwdriver against the side of the device. Holding on to her boot with his other hand, he added, "Tell me about him."

"Seriously? You literally have your head shoved up my ass and you want me to talk about John? You really need to work on your lines *and* your timing."

"So he has a name. For a while I thought you were just making him up to keep me away."

"Captain John Wright. U.S. Marines. Why do you ask?"

"Just curious about the competition." He stopped the screwdriver action and switched to a pair of pliers before trying to pull something out from the same side of the mine.

She closed eyes while suppressing a laugh. "You think he's your . . . *competition*?"

"You love him, yes?"

She narrowed her gaze while staring at the forest, considering the question. "Too soon for that," she finally said. "We just met . . . during a weekend in Qatar a few months ago."

"Sounds romantic."

"He's very sweet, Aaron."

"What does that make me?"

"The man who has his face an inch from a Russian mine to save my foot."

Aaron set down the multi-tool and whispered, "Dammit."

"What is it?"

"The striker . . . won't come out. It's stuck."

"I was wondering if it was a dud."

"Possibly. Once armed, these Russian mines only require a slight downward force on the pressure plate, which overcomes the upward tension of the creep-spring, sliding the metal gate holding back the spring-loaded striker. That all means it should have gone off the instant you stepped on it. But it didn't. The metal gate and striker are rusty after so many years, and I think your weight is the only thing now keeping the mechanism from releasing the striker."

"Meaning it could go off the moment I step off of it?"

"Or it could stay as it is. No way to tell while you're putting weight on it."

"Great. Is this when you walk away and join your friends while I step off the mine and hope for the best?"

Aaron whistled again and Nasseer returned. They exchanged some words in Pashto. The Shinwari boss left and then came back with three Kevlar vests.

"What's going on?" she asked, only able to get a partial picture of what was happening.

Nasseer returned to the trail while Aaron slid back, stood, and walked in front of her.

"Aaron? What do you think you're—"

"Do *not* move, Red."

Slowly, he pressed the sole of his left boot over the instep of her right boot, apparently to make sure she didn't shift, before reaching under her armpits and helping her stand, while also pulling up her pants to her waist.

"There," he said, as he fastened her belt. "Let's get you some dignity back."

"Appreciate that," she said.

"Stay like this now," he said, staring at her before slowly leaning down to reach for one of the vests, wrapping it around her lower right leg and his own left leg all the way to the ground. He then tightened the straps to press their knees firmly against each other.

"No, Aaron. You can't do this."

He cupped her face and grinned. "And leave you like this, now that I know you are a true redhead? That's a negative, *Red* One One."

She just stared at him.

"Now stay still," he added, as he leaned down again.

She placed both hands over the top of his head, running her fingers through his hair. His face pressed against her belly while he wrapped the second vest around her left leg and his right leg.

"You know, Red," he said as he stood, "I think in some cultures this is considered a marriage." He tapped the tip of her nose.

This time she managed a slight smile and showed him her left hand, wiggling her bare ring finger. "No diamond, no marriage, mister."

"Ah," he said. "We will get to that, yes? But first things first."

Aaron laid the third vest on the ground, leaning on the side of their legs, so that part of the vest would fall over the mine the moment they jumped off of it.

"Now," he said, standing and embracing her, "the acoustic energy will bounce against the tree, so we need to jump to the side to get away from the worst of it. Makes sense?"

"Aaron," she insisted. "You don't need to do this. I'm the one who—"

"Hush, Red," he said, kissing her forehead before wrapping his left arm against her back, his hand pressed against the back of her head, wedging it under his chin, forcing her face against his chest. His right arm went lower, below her waist, securing her firmly against him. "On three, okay?"

"Okay," she whispered, her lungs filling with his scent and that of her own urine as he nearly lifted her off the ground while keeping her right foot anchored over the mine.

Vaccaro let it all go, arms wrapped around him, allowing him to do as he pleased, surrendering to this most intimate of bear hugs.

He counted and they jumped together, as one, and Aaron further surprised her by shifting in midair with agility, placing his body between the Russian mine and her.

The PMN-4 detonated with deafening force, the shock wave nearly flipping them in midair as the forest lit up with a blinding white light.

She felt the heat, felt the shrapnel peppering the vest as he tightened his grip on her while shifting once more to land on his back, cushioning her fall with his own body.

They remained in an embrace for a few moments, the smell of cordite overpowering all others, his breath on her reminiscent of when she had tackled him hours earlier.

"You okay, Red?"

She flexed her ankles, rubbing her boots against his. "I think so. But the question is, are *you* okay?"

"Never been better," he said, a hand suddenly grabbing one of her cheeks, over her pants, squeezing gently.

"I bet you are, mister," she said, grinning.

"So what's the answer?"

"To what?"

"Do you love this John Wright?"

"Aaron?"

"Yes?"

"I think it's time."

"Time for what?"

"To let go of my ass."

81

Bloody Winch

SULAIMAN MOUNTAINS. SOUTHERN AFGHANISTAN.

They continued along a narrow footpath carved right into a vertical section of rock. Gorman didn't fear heights, but there was something about a thousand-foot drop just an inch from his feet that had a way of screwing with his mind. But at least the path was relatively flat, allowing him to recharge.

Martin was point, followed by Maryam, then Ryan and him. Stark followed a dozen feet back, then Hagen, and Larson at the rear.

The trail widened as it reached the other side of the tight mountain pass. Maryam and Martin paused to inspect a number of broken branches along a rocky track leading into a wooded valley at almost ten thousand feet, surrounded by rising terrain. They had reached a plateau buried deep in the range. Snowcapped ridges rose up beyond the canopy of stone pines, stabbing a layer of gray clouds blowing in from the west.

And that's when it happened.

Gorman watched Stark and his men suddenly dispersing, as if on cue, though not a word was spoken. One second they stood by him and the next they had vanished. Ryan was already scrambling halfway up a hill, Hagen and Martin rushed for the cover of a cluster of pine trees thirty feet away, and Stark and Larson disappeared behind a clump of boulders twenty feet in the other direction.

What the—

The first shot rang out from across the narrow meadow before he could complete the thought.

Gorman too had reacted, jumping in front of Maryam as the forest exploded in stroboscopic muzzle flashes—as sharp stabs pierced his shoulder and abdomen.

He landed next to her while a barrage of automatic fire mowed down the forest, zooming overhead, shattering bark, ricocheting off rocks, echoing off the surrounding mountains.

Trembling, Gorman put a hand over his vest, feeling the punctures right over the pain on his right shoulder and left abdomen. Bloody fingers confirmed it. The bastards had used a large enough caliber to punch through the Kevlar—

"Bill!"

He looked at Maryam as the world around them seem to catch fire—as explosions shook the ground and the thunder of Larson's Browning overwhelmed all other reports.

But it was Maryam's face that filled his world, and it was her hands that he felt on him, unfastening his vest before ripping his shirt with a knife, exposing the wounds.

"Stay with me, Bill!" She rolled him on his side for a moment before opening his individual first aid kit and slapping patches of gauze impregnated with zeolite powder on each wound.

He cringed and then screamed, tensing as the zeolite absorbed the water from the blood flowing out of the bullet holes, bringing platelets and other clotting factors together through an intense exothermic reaction that felt as if he was on fire.

"Suck on this!" she shouted, shoving a fentanyl lollipop from his

IFAK into his mouth. In an instant, the blood vessels in his mouth absorbed the powerful opioid, and Gorman felt his body relax as the berry-flavored drug killed the pain.

Grasping the tails of a field dressing, Maryam pressed it against the lower right side of his torso, over the zeolite patch, and wrapped it tightly before applying a second one to his shoulder.

Breathing rapidly, suddenly feeling cold, Gorman rolled on his side and vomited, arms trembling as the firefight raged around them.

His vision rapidly blurring, Gorman saw Maryam reach for her encrypted CIA radio, screaming over the noise of the gunfight a call for a "bloody winch."

82

Bloody Fool

SULAIMAN MOUNTAINS. SOUTHERN AFGHANISTAN.

Stark moved quickly across the enemy's right flank while Larson did his thing, tearing everything in sight, forcing the rebels to the ground through sheer brute force. He spotted the insurgents off to his left, huddled behind tree trunks and boulders while .50-caliber bullets singed the air around them.

"*In position, Colonel,*" reported Ryan from his perch.

"*Ditto,*" said Martin, which also meant that Hagen was poised to strike from the left flank.

"We're good, Chief," Stark said into his MBITR. An instant later the Browning went silent and, as expected, the rebels rose from their hideouts to return fire.

Ryan took out three in rapid succession from his spot on the hill as Stark closed the gap, firing headshots while running. His MP5A1's silent rounds, in sharp contrast with Larson's racket, dropped them before they realized what had happened.

"Clear," he said, before Martin reported from the other side of the narrow forest that the insurgents were neutralized.

Stark ran back to the spot where he had seen Gorman and Maryam diving for cover, and he was surprised to see Gorman on his back, with bandages on his shoulder and lower abdomen. Maryam hovered over him, working an IV into his left forearm. She had tears in her eyes.

"What happened?"

The CIA man seemed out of it as he sucked on a fentanyl lollipop.

Raising her wet gaze to Stark before placing a hand on Gorman's cheek, Maryam said, "Bloody fool. He had to be the hero . . . My bloody, bloody fool!"

"Chief!" Stark shouted. "Need immediate exfil for two!"

Maryam looked up. "For *two*?"

"Yes," he said. "You're going with him."

"But—"

"No argument," he said. "Things are about to get nastier, and I operate better with just my team."

"But I can handle myself," she said.

"And I noticed that," Stark replied. "But you're in intelligence. Go do what you do best and collaborate with Harwich at KAF. See if you can help us from over there . . . And look after him. He's one of the good guys."

Maryam dropped her gaze to Gorman. "He is," she finally said. "Even if he's a bloody fool."

83

Following Orders

KANDAHAR AIRFIELD. SOUTHERN AFGHANISTAN.

Monica leaped inside the Royal Canadian Air Force Black Hawk helicopter, dressed for violence, which included an MP5A1 as her primary weapon and a SIG P220 in .45 ACP for backup. She also carried her McMillan TAC-338 sniper rifle slung behind her back, her ever-present SOG knife strapped to her right thigh, plenty of extra magazines for all weapons, and a half dozen assorted grenades.

The call from the field had arrived just a minute ago. Someone in Stark's team had gotten shot and needed immediate evac.

That had been her cue. Grabbing her gear, she had hauled ass to the tarmac in time to join the rescue crew, while hoping like hell the wounded wasn't Ryan. The bastard hadn't called her since Scottsdale, but she still felt something for the asshole—certainly far more than for any other asshole she had ever dated.

"You can't be here, ma'am!" the operator behind the port M240 machine gun shouted over the noise of the rotor, his visor reflecting Monica's distorted features.

"I'm here by orders of General Lévesque!" she retorted. "Call him!"

The gunner shook his head and said, "Screw it! We're short a crew member! Know how to fire that, eh?" He pointed at the starboard M240.

"You bet!"

Monica secured a David Clark headset, already jacked into the intercom system, and settled behind the gas-operated weapon anchored to the floor of the cabin. The noise-cancellation system immediately dampened the rotor noise.

She tensed as the Black Hawk took to the skies like a damn elevator on steroids, something civilians never experienced when flying commercial or private helicopters, whose pilots were trained to be gentle with their passengers.

Kandahar Airfield rushed beneath them at a crazy speed, a blur of metal and canvas roofs, pavement, and shipping containers soon replaced by desert, and then hills, leading to the foot of the Sulaiman Mountains.

They flew west for ten miles along the southern face of the range while climbing, reaching nine thousand feet as the terrain transitioned from bare rocks to light vegetation and finally to woods so thick it made her think of places like West Virginia or North Carolina.

Monica enjoyed the cold mountain air while keeping watch through the sights of the M240, shooting finger resting on the gun's trigger guard, ready to engage anyone crazy or gutsy enough to fire at—

"Are you Agent Cruz?"

Monica turned around when she heard the gunner through the headset.

"Yeah. Why?" she asked.

"Because there is a Glenn Harwich on the radio asking for you, eh?"

That didn't take long, she thought, before saying, "Patch him through."

Static, followed by, *"Cruz?"*

"Hey, boss."

"What the hell are you doing?"

"What I'm supposed to be doing, boss."

"What are you talking about?"

"I'm following Lévesque's orders. I'm getting the fuck off his base."

84

Visions

SULAIMAN MOUNTAINS. SOUTHERN AFGHANISTAN.

Gorman felt as if he were falling, swallowed by a deep and endless abyss. But he no longer felt any pain—no longer felt the stabbing wounds or the burns from the coagulant patches as a strange sense of peace descended over him.

It might have been the fentanyl, or just his body shutting down, but whatever it was it enveloped him, taking him from the madness of his profession while projecting brief images, flashes of his life flickering in the twilight of this surreal world. The visions were gone as fast as they appeared, mixed with the reality of the moment. He saw Jeannie in one instance, her face radiant on their wedding day. But her eyes suddenly widened in fear as she jumped from the North Tower, as she fell into the same void that was swallowing him. He felt the intense fire, as dust and debris shrouded him, as screams and explosions overwhelmed him.

But her hands . . . they held him tight, shaking him, dragging him out of his drug-induced trance as her face hovered over him. But it wasn't Jeannie's. Her hazel eyes, replaced by large brown ones under thick brows crowning the face of an angel, glared down at him as her lips moved in haste.

Maryam was screaming at him. But Gorman could not hear her—not over the noise of the helicopter hovering over them.

Helicopter?

He saw it through the tunnel that was his narrowing field of view, high above her, and also noticed the object descending from the hovering craft, at the end of a winch.

Stretcher.

It spun slowly in the rotor downwash. A rescuer hung off a secondary cable next to the stretcher as it sank through a break in the canopy.

That's when Gorman noticed the oddest thing: the rescuer wore tactical gear, including a sound-suppressed MP5A1 strapped to the chest and a sniper rifle secured across the back.

And it was a woman.

85

Miss Cruz

SULAIMAN MOUNTAINS. SOUTHERN AFGHANISTAN.

Monica approached the ground, gloved hands gripping the side of the stretcher as debris swirled up in a funnel around the wounded man, whom she could now clearly see wasn't Ryan or anyone else from the contractor team.

The moment her boots sank into a layer of pine needles, Monica disconnected the heavy-duty latches of her harness and helped the woman kneeling next to the wounded man move him into the stretcher, with the assistance of Chief Larson.

"Hey, Miss Cruz!" he said with a grin, over the noise of the helicopter.

"Hey to you!" she replied. "Where's everybody?"

"Busy! Somewhere up that ridge!"

"I've been ordered to go back to KAF with him!" the woman said in a British accent. She looked a few years older than Monica, though it was hard to tell with her camouflage cream.

"Fine by me!" Monica replied, pointing at the harness swinging next to the stretcher.

"What about you?" the woman asked.

"I've been ordered to get the hell out of KAF!"

Larson did a double take on Monica, and she ignored him while securing the wounded man inside the stretcher. The moment the woman put on the harness, clicking it tight, Monica signaled the gunner, and the two went airborne.

"You cleared this with the colonel?" Larson asked, looking up as the pair cleared the upper branches and were pulled aboard.

Monica reached for the MP5A1, verifying a chambered round while glaring up at the giant man. "Cleared it with Lévesque."

"Good for you," he said, extending a hand toward the woods. "Your boyfriend is up on a hill somewhere."

"Not my boyfriend!"

"Of course not," he said with a laugh while walking away.

Monica shook her head and followed him as the Black Hawk vanished from view.

86

Edge

SULAIMAN MOUNTAINS. SOUTHERN AFGHANISTAN.

Colonel Stark kept watch on top of a ridge as the Black Hawk disappeared to the east, the rotor noise echoing in the range before fading altogether.

He sighed, regretting the decision to allow Gorman and Maryam to accompany his team on this job. Although they were both quite capable, considering their chosen profession, they lacked that extra edge developed by operators in the Special Forces Operational Detachment–Delta or the Navy SEALs. And in the case of Stark and his team, their experience went well beyond the years spent in those elite military units. Through collaboration with other nations' special forces, like the British SAS, the Russian GRU Spetsnaz, or the German KSK and GSG 9, they had picked up unique skills, gleaned from each style of special warfare operations.

At the end of the day, his team played at the Super Bowl level while intelligence officers never got past college football. And it wasn't really due to ability or lack of it. It was simply . . .

Practice. Practice. Practice.

As much as Stark regretted a talented guy like Gorman getting shot, and while he hoped the man made it and went on to continue his field ops, the colonel was glad that he and that woman were out of his hair.

Let operators do what operators do and let God sort out the rest.

In his mind, everyone had a seat on the bus. And as long as everyone knew their place, things just had a way of working out, especially when the shit hit the fan, as no plan ever survived the first shot.

Right now the seats on his bus were clearly assigned and occupied: Martin was somewhere west, picking up the trail of the hags trying to get the weapon deep into the mountains, while Ryan kept watch overhead. Hagen worked the other side of this ridge while Stark covered this end and Larson wrapped up the exfiltration of Gorman and Maryam.

And speaking of the chief . . . Stark spotted his silhouette approaching in the woods, the Browning held in front, left hand under the massive muzzle, right hand on the pistol grip, the .50-caliber belt fed into the side of the weapon, ready for business, and—

Someone accompanied Larson.

Did Maryam disobey my direct order and not go with Gorman?

But it wasn't the Pakistani operative. This woman was a bit shorter and built thinner than . . .

Stark squinted, recognizing FBI agent Monica Cruz, armed to the teeth, hauling not just an MP5A1 but also a TAC-338 sniper rifle.

For the love of . . .

He stomped over to meet them halfway.

"Boy, that man looks *really* pissed," mumbled Monica, as she walked side by side with Larson.

"Choose your words carefully, kiddo," the chief whispered, stepping aside to clear the way for his incoming boss.

Monica wasn't easily intimidated, but there was something about Colonel Hunter Stark that made every cell in her body want to jump at attention. And it wasn't his size. The man was shorter than the chief and not nearly as bulked. Maybe it was his stare of ice-cold blue eyes on a face hidden with camouflage cream. Or perhaps it was his posture, his overall commanding presence oozing with natural confidence and strength as he held his MP5A1 in front of him, always at the ready, as if expecting an attack at any moment.

And that impressive authoritative stance was now being aimed squarely at her as he said, in his equally imposing voice, "What the *hell* do you think you're doing, Cruz?"

"Couldn't take those NATO assholes for another second, Colonel," she replied.

"So?" Stark asked. "What's that got to do with you standing in the middle of my operation?"

Monica sighed and decided to try a different angle. "Figured you'd need an extra set of hands, since you just lost two."

"Well, Cruz, you figured wrong. Those two were here because they were footing the bill, but in the end it was obviously a mistake to expose them to the unforgiving nature of what we do. What could you possibly have to offer . . . besides Agency attitude?"

"FBI, actually."

"Same bullshit, different T-shirt."

"Come on, Colonel, check with Ryan. I can actually shoot *and* take care of myself," she said.

Stark briefly closed his eyes, inhaling through his nose and exhaling through barely closed lips as he replied, "Cruz, this isn't fucking training day. I don't have the time or the inclination to show you the ropes and—"

"I don't need you to show me the—"

"Chief, call KAF for another exfil." Stark started for the tree line.

"Wait," Monica said as Larson reached for his radio. "I can't go back."

Stark stopped midstride and turned back to her before slowly raising his brows.

"I . . . well, have been declared persona non grata at KAF."

"What'd you do, Cruz? Piss off your boss?"

"General Lévesque, actually. Pissed in the big Canuck's Cheerios."

"Oh," Stark said, before looking over at Larson, who just shrugged and grinned ever so slightly. "How'd you manage to do that?"

As she gave him the one-minute version, Monica noticed something changing in the colonel, though she couldn't quite put her finger on it. If she had to guess, she would have sworn that something resembling pride replaced some of the anger glinting in his azure stare.

"You actually told Lévesque he wasn't fit to command KAF?"

She dropped her gaze. "Something like that."

"In front of his entire staff?"

"Didn't mean to."

"Sure you did. What did he say?"

Monica pressed her fists against the side of her waist and, deepening her voice, replied, " 'I want you to get the fuck off my base, eh?' "

Stark stared at her, and for an instant she thought he smirked.

" 'And by nightfall,' " she added, before returning to her normal voice. "So I guess I exceeded the asshole's expectations by—"

"I understand that you and Ryan were at the same sniper school?"

Monica blinked. "Ye—yes. Two years ago in Scottsda—"

"You any good with that?" He pointed at the TAC-338's barrel, which was projecting behind her like an antenna.

"I can hold my own."

"How well?"

"One inch group at twenty-five hundred yards."

"You served in-country?"

"Four tours supporting the Seventy-Fifth Ranger Regiment. Two in Iraq and two here."

"Confirmed kills?"

"Thirty-seven."

"And then the Bureau?"

"With five years in between, with the LA SWAT. Master sniper."

"I see."

"Look, Colonel, if you really want me out of your hair, I'll go, but—"

Stark tapped his MBITR. "Delta One?"

"*Sir?*"

"Get your sorry ass down here. Now."

"*What's up?*"

"Your girlfriend," he said, turning around and starting again toward the tree line. "She's down here with the chief. Keep her on a leash."

"Dammit," Monica hissed at his departing figure. "I'm *not* his fucking girlfriend."

But Stark had already vanished into the woods.

87

The Throne of Solomon

SULAIMAN MOUNTAINS. SOUTHERN AFGHANISTAN.

Kneeling on a snowy ridge, Mullah Akhtar Baqer opiated while watching the rescue helicopter disappear around a bend in the mountain, some three thousand feet below them. A minute later, its rotor noise also disappeared.

The battle had lasted but a couple of minutes, during which he had hoped the team he left behind would put down anyone foolish enough to track him this high up the range. But as he had observed just one wounded being airlifted, followed by radio silence from his team, he had to assume the worst.

"What now?" demanded Dr. Khan, who was standing next to him, his dark woolen tunic being pelted with snowflakes. "They're still coming, and we're now leaving a perfect trail in the snow!"

Feeling the drug reenergizing him, Akhtar set down his pipe and picked up his binoculars, fingering the focusing wheel, estimating no more than a couple of miles of switchbacks between them and those men.

A couple of hours' hike, he thought.

Pointing at the storm clouds sweeping in from the west, he said, "Allah will cover our tracks by morning."

"Good of him," Dr. Khan replied, his head now covered in a woolen *keffiyeh*. "But I thought you said that if the explosives and the soldiers you left at the compound didn't stop them, those men down there would."

"Professor," said Akhtar, lowering the binoculars, "you worry about the well-being of the bomb. I'll handle everything else."

Dr. Khan pointed at the men transporting the weapon on the makeshift stretcher, their skin boots sinking in fresh snow to their ankles as they waited atop an icy ridge that would lead them to the north face of the range. "That's *precisely* my point," the scientist said, hugging himself while shivering. "I need a place to work and get the device ready to receive the new components. And *this* . . . this *frozen hell* isn't it."

"And you shall have it *and* the components," Akhtar replied, remembering the emergency signal he had received from Pasha the night before. His younger brother had connected with the courier, but they were being pursued, just as *he* was being hunted.

"*Meg ze jawaze safar na kawom.*" *We're not traveling alone.*

The simple phrase told him everything he needed to know—everything he needed to do to ensure safe passage of the components to their mountaintop hideout.

Akhtar shifted his attention to the north, to the high, jagged peaks of the southern extension of the Hindu Kush mountain system, where the Sulaimans continued for another hundred miles to form the eastern edge of the Iranian Plateau. He panned the binoculars to the highest peak in the vicinity, the Takht-i-Sulaiman.

The Throne of Solomon.

Just south of the summit named after the renowned king stood a secret and dangerous high pass—Qais Kotal—named after Qais Abdur Rashid, father of the Pashtun nation, who was buried on top of Takht-i-Sulaiman. Legend had it that Solomon himself had hiked the perilous footpath during his historic climb to look over the land of South Asia.

Akhtar had no idea if the king had actually crossed it, but the pass was very real, very difficult to negotiate—and very difficult for American UAVs or satellites to spot from above. Rising to over twelve thousand feet and very narrow and heavily wooded, it had been used by generations of jihadists to traverse the Sulaimans in their constant fight for independence from foreign invaders.

The mullah set down the binoculars, picked up the pipe, and took a final hit, closing his eyes as he inhaled deeply, feeling his body absorb the pure drug, letting it do its magical work while a cold Sulaiman wind washed over him.

Dr. Khan continued his incessant whining about being hungry, cold, and tired, disturbing this moment of peace. Thoughts of reaching for his pesh-kabz and just putting an end to the annoying little man crossed his mind, but the ancient wisdom of King Solomon kept the curved knife sheathed.

Although Akhtar didn't share the religious convictions of his younger brother and Akaa—or the thousands of jihadists who called him "mullah"—the title meant he was actually versed in Holy Scripture. Allah, for the guidance of mankind, had privileged four prophets by trusting each with a holy book. Moses received the Torah. King David the Zabur, or Book of Psalms. Prophet Isa—who Muslims believe was Jesus—was bestowed the Injeel, or true Gospel, not to be confused with the Christian Gospel written by Matthew, Luke, John, and Mark. And finally, Allah bequeathed to Muhammad the Holy Koran.

But it was King David, Solomon's father, who one day gathered his sons and put forward a number of profound questions, one of which had always resonated with Akhtar.

What is that action the result of which is good?

Solomon's answer: patience and forbearance, not haste, in the face of anger or peril.

Patience and forbearance.

Akhtar put his pipe and binoculars away in his rucksack, which he shouldered while turning to Dr. Khan. The palm of his right hand resting on the pesh-kabz, he said, "This way, professor."

As he followed the group across the southern face of the mountain, Akhtar could only hope that his younger brother, who was certainly facing his own share of peril, would choose patience and forbearance rather than haste.

88

The Color of Islam

SULAIMAN MOUNTAINS. SOUTHERN AFGHANISTAN.

Pasha recalled Akaa's tactics and chose to let the enemy get close.

Real close.

Zahra took a position just a couple of feet to his right, wedging her UZI's silencer between two exposed roots while lying on a bed of pine needles, settling her shooting eye behind the Leupold scope.

If he were to be completely honest with himself, Pasha would admit that she was as capable as—if not more capable than—any warrior he'd ever met, friend or foe. But his own feelings couldn't play a part in forming an opinion of a woman, even one as capable as

Zahra. The law was the law, and it was not up for debate. Yet, his own Akaa, the man he respected more than any other, had sent her to him, and it was this conflict that continued to tax him as they had hiked through the night and into the morning.

A contingent of men from the Noorzai tribe, who had been engaging Canadian troops north of their hometown of Girishk for the past year, had met them here an hour ago, courtesy of his brother.

Pasha now had twenty-three rugged warriors under his command, all veterans and armed with a mix of AK-47s and RPK light machine guns, plus loads of 7.62×39mm ammunition common to both platforms. Their leader was Jamil, which meant "handsome," though the man was anything but, missing most of his front teeth and part of his nose and right ear, lost to the shrapnel that had scarred his face and neck. Jamil's hair and beard, long and unkempt, were dyed green, the color of Islam, in the tradition of Noorzai chiefs. His dark eyes had fallen on Zahra the instant he had crested the ridge where they hid, and the man's reaction had been to pick up a rock to stone her—an action followed by his men. Only Pasha's reminder that Osama bin Laden had sent her on this holiest of missions had prevented a bloodbath, as Zahra had her UZI already leveled at the Noorzais.

So an agreement was reached: Pasha would keep Zahra out of sight from Jamil's men for the duration of their collaboration, and Jamil in turn would keep his men from tearing her apart for disrespecting Sharia law.

Two of Jamil's men, deployed thirty minutes ago down the hill to wait for visual contact with the incoming posse, now ran back up the same incline, purposely breaking branches and breathing heavily, even groaning with feigned effort. The two made quite the racket, to draw the enemy, before joining their comrades on the left side of the predetermined kill zone. A second group of Noorzais focused on the center while Pasha and Jamil kept Zahra away from the locals by covering the right flank.

Ten minutes later their effort paid off as the first figure loomed in the woods, under the shadows cast by towering pines under a midday sun. Under orders from Jamil to wait for Pasha to make the first move, the disciplined team remained hidden.

While he let them get closer he lined up in the crosshairs of his

Leupold scope a short, slender man dressed in dark khet partug under a wool tunic and a *karakul* hat, which indicated his status as leader. He held a heavy Russian PK machine gun and wore the ammo belt over his right shoulder.

89

Instincts

SULAIMAN MOUNTAINS. SOUTHERN AFGHANISTAN.

Aaron put a hand on her shoulder and Vaccaro paused, taking a knee in some of the waist-high bushes that were scattered through the sparse forest.

"What is it?" she whispered, the Colt 1911 in her right hand, safety off.

"Not sure," the Kidon replied, his knees sinking in the layer of pine needles as the Shinwari clan proceeded up the shallow knoll where a moment ago two figures had crested the plateau at the top of the grade. "Something isn't right . . . Too damn quiet."

Aaron had an UZI in his hands and one of Nasseer's M32 grenade launchers strapped behind his back. Before she could reply, he said, "Hold this for a second," and passed the UZI to her. Switching to the M32, he checked the 40mm shells loaded in the six-shooter gun barrel.

"Come," he finally said, standing. "Let's catch up with—"

The slow rattle of an AK-47 echoed down the hill, followed by other weapons, including machine guns.

90

Final Fight

SULAIMAN MOUNTAINS. SOUTHERN AFGHANISTAN.

Nasseer rolled away from the gunfire, his right shoulder burning, and finally crawled behind a boulder as the—

Another shot, this one from the right flank, made his thigh go numb.

They have us surrounded, he thought, as the two men who were right behind him on the plateau fell victim to the cross fire, multiple rounds going right through them as they stood immobile for an instant before collapsing.

Dropping the Russian machine gun, he reached behind his back, ignoring the blood soaking his chest and leg, fingers gripping the M32 grenade launcher. He had to try to give the rest of his men on the hill a chance.

He pressed the stock against his left shoulder as rounds stabbed the ground around him. Pointing the muzzle at the closest set of muzzle flashes to his right, he fired three times, just as Aaron had shown him. The 40mm shells thumped out of the tube and arced across the clearing.

The grenades detonated in sequence, bursts of light and thunder tossing men in the air while Hassan and two others joined in the fight, emptying their AK-47s into the surviving machine gun emplacements. But their volleys were short-lived as their chests exploded from single shots fired by a sniper from a vantage point up on a stone pine.

Nasseer's eyes narrowed in anger as Hassan dropped to his knees, still firing his Kalashnikov, before another round smacked him in the face.

Rolling away from his hideout, Nasseer aimed the launcher at the offending tree but was able to fire only one shell before a bullet found him, stabbing his chest.

Suddenly paralyzed, his vision tunneling, Nasseer stared at the cover of pine trees swirling in the breeze as the shell detonated in a bright explosion that rocked the ground.

And that was the last sound he heard before his world went dark.

91

Hasty Retreat

SULAIMAN MOUNTAINS. SOUTHERN AFGHANISTAN.

"AKs, RPKs, and grenades!" Aaron shouted, as the top of the hill ignited with muzzle flashes and shell blasts. Shinwari warriors careered down the hill, shooting their assault rifles back over their shoulders. But their hasty and uncoordinated retreat and attempt to return fire failed to overpower the multiple volleys of tracers screeching down the hillside from vantage points across the summit, stabbing trees, bouncing off rocks, and punching men in the back, chests exploding with crimson exit wounds.

Many figures now emerged above the Shinwaris, hunting down the surviving members of Nasseer's clan.

Vaccaro couldn't return fire for fear of hitting the retreating men, but Aaron popped his shells over their heads—all six of them—in rapid succession while sweeping the M32 from left to right.

The grenades arced up the terrain, creating havoc as the wave of enemy rebels atop the mountainside vanished behind multiple detonations.

"That's our cue, Red!" he shouted, tossing the empty M32, grabbing the UZI from her with one hand and her wrist with the other, tugging her down the incline.

"I'm not a little girl!" she shouted, pulling her hand away while running side by side with him. A few rounds flew past them, splintering bark and sparking off boulders.

They didn't look back, ignoring the buzzing of near misses, focusing on the rocky slope below them, using tree trunks, branches, boulders, and anything else they could grasp to manage their hasty descent.

Pasha fired his Dragunov at the departing figures, a man and a woman, his eyes blinking in sudden recognition of the figure seen through the powerful scope.

It's the pilot!

He forced himself to relax, exhaling while aligning the crosshairs with her runaway figure. But as he pulled the trigger, the man shifted left, blocking the way, the round pushing him forward. Unfortunately, he was big and didn't fall, though he pressed a hand to his side, obviously wounded.

By the time the Dragunov's recoil chambered another round, the pair had vanished around a bend in the trail. Off to his right, Jamil and his surviving men went in pursuit.

"Come," he told Zahra. "Let's finish this."

92

Sacrifice

SULAIMAN MOUNTAINS. SOUTHERN AFGHANISTAN.

The terrain leveled off and curved onto the same goat trail they had used on the way up, and Aaron let Vaccaro lead. She ran as fast as she could, cruising through alternating patches of brightness and darkness as pine trees projected ragged shadows across her path. Her lungs burned from the effort as she inhaled the thin and cold air—as the firefight stopped as abruptly as it had started.

Her heartbeat throbbed in her temples, in her ears, blocking all other sounds as she flexed her legs as fast as she could, trying like crazy not to trip.

The trail continued curving, narrowing as the grade steepened. Flanked by a rocky wall and the gorge, it followed the contour of the mountain to another rocky outcrop nestled among more pines.

She reached it, panting, pausing for a moment to catch her breath—only to realize that Aaron wasn't with her.

What the hell?

She looked up the trail, confused. He had been with her a moment ago.

Doubling back, she found him just beyond the bend in the footpath, sitting with his back against a rock and the UZI pointed up the trail.

"Aaron? What are you doing?"

"I'll hold them here," he said.

That's when she spotted the blood on his shirt.

"You're hurt!" she hissed, dropping to her knees, hands pulling up his shirt.

"We don't have . . . time for this," he said, swallowing, reaching for a map in his pocket and shoving it in her vest. He also clipped to her belt the radio she had taken from the Taliban.

"What do you think you're doing?"

"You need to go."

"No way. I'm not leaving you here with those bearded grim-fucking-reapers," she said, finally getting a look at the wound. It was an exit wound the size of a lemon, to the left of his belly button.

What kind of caliber was that? she thought, running her hand behind his back and locating the entry point, cringing when she found it just over his right kidney. The large round, probably hollow-point, had traversed his body, tearing him up. "It went through clean," she said, trying to sound reassuring, as she reached for her individual first aid kit inside her survival vest and slapped coagulant patches on both ends.

The Kidon reacted like the pro he was, not even blinking at a field treatment she knew burned like hell—on top of what had to be a very painful belly wound. Rather, he just kept the UZI aimed at the path, focused, steady, managing his breathing.

An assassin to the end.

Unfortunately, no amount of training or field experience could counter a sudden and very large loss of blood—plus the trauma to his lower abdomen. Aaron was already pale and sweating profusely.

He's going into shock.

"I just stopped the bleeding," she said. "Come. I'll help you up."

"We're wasting . . . time," he insisted. "Get out of here. Take that map . . . Call your people. It has the spot . . . where they're . . . taking the components."

She ignored him and, with considerable effort, helped him to his feet, forcing him to come with her down the trail until they reached the same clearing surrounded by pines.

"No use," he said, pointing at the path behind them.

Vaccaro saw the trail of blood. Even with the coagulant patches, he was still bleeding. A lot.

"I . . . can't . . ." he mumbled, collapsing by a large boulder at the edge of the precipice. "I'm sorry . . . Red. But you need to get that to . . ."

He cringed, bending over and cursing under his breath before sitting back up and resting the UZI on the rock, aiming it at the trail. "Get out of here. Now."

"Aaron, I can't leave you in—"

"I'm done . . ."

Vaccaro just knelt there next to him as he started to tremble.

"Dammit," he cursed. "Leave . . . or all of this . . . is for nothing."

She heard distant shouts, followed by the cries of men. It sounded like they were in severe agony.

"Taliban," he whispered, lips quivering, "Cutting survivors."

She felt a chill at the thought of those bastards getting their hands on Aaron, on her.

"That weapon," he continued, "can't become . . . functional . . . Bastards will take it to . . . Israel . . . or America."

Vaccaro felt paralyzed at this turn of events, angry at the choices laid out in front of—

Aaron grabbed her by the lapels and pulled her toward him. "Get . . . out . . . of . . . here."

Putting a hand to his cheek, she said, "I'll never forget you."

"Good," he said. "I guess my lines and my timing weren't so bad after all."

"No," she said, tearing up. "They were just . . . *wonderful*."

"And now for my best line yet. Go *now*, Red." He pointed at the drop behind him.

"Down that cliff?"

"Safest . . . way."

She eyed what looked like at least a seventy-degree precipice of bluffs, with trees growing out of the side of the mountain. It dropped about a thousand feet to a wooded plateau, reminding her of the one she had tumbled down the night before.

"Go . . . now," he said, his skin ghostly, eyes fixed on the trail.

The Kidon didn't have long, and he knew it. He professionally turned away from her as more cries echoed down the mountain, evoking images of Nasseer and Hassan castrating that man the night before. It was now payback time.

"Don't . . . worry," he mumbled, the UZI's stock pressed against him as he reached for a grenade. "Taking . . . the bastards with me . . . and then . . . meeting Ela and the kids . . . It's time."

The comment took her momentarily aback, and it also made her think of her father. She could hear him screaming at her to get going. There was nothing she could do for this man, but there was plenty he could do for her, for the mission—if she acted quickly.

"Good bye, Aaron Peretz," she said.

"Never stop fighting . . . Red One One. Never," he said, winking before turning around to face the direction of the threat. "And make your life matter."

Stunned by his words, Vaccaro stared at Aaron's very large and very bloody figure as he kept the muzzle of his UZI aimed toward to enemy.

Which will be here any moment.

Realizing there was nothing left to say—nor the time to do so—she began feetfirst, facing the wall, pressing the toes of her boots over small protrusions on the rocky wall while grabbing exposed roots and branches.

You can do this, Red.

Vaccaro looked down. She focused on small niches to use as footholds, letting the strongest muscles in her body do the heavy lifting while using her arms as fulcrums, reserving their strength for guidance and to keep her upper body against the wall.

She soon developed a rhythm, foothold after foothold, using rocks, roots, trunks—anything that could help slow the pull of gravity, managing her descent.

Branches snapped as she pushed through, scratching her, but she ignored them—just as she forced herself to ignore the shouts echoing in the clearing, now a couple hundred feet above her. Gunfire followed.

Aaron putting up a fight.

She picked up her speed as the reports intensified. She rushed past dozens of trees growing out at an angle straight off the side of the incline, using their roots, branches, and trunks to clamber down, losing sight of the clearing.

A blast reverberated across the mountainside, silencing the gunfire.

Vaccaro paused, aware of what it meant.

And just like that she was alone again.

She felt a lump in her throat at the thought of him, of what could have been.

Never stop fighting, Red One One. Never.

And make your life matter.

She persisted, determined to honor his sacrifice by protecting this vital intelligence he had given her—intelligence she vowed to deliver.

Or die trying.

Pressing her lips together, fueled by the ultimate sacrifice made by Aaron and his Shinwari friends, she persisted, ignoring her burning muscles, her throbbing hamstrings and calves, and the cuts on her hands and face as she crawled through the thicket.

The blast pushed Pasha back as the man huddling behind a boulder, surrounded, detonated a grenade. Four of his men lay on the ground next to the man's mangled body, one of them trembling.

He had to give that infidel warrior credit for surviving a shot from his Dragunov, plus putting up one hell of a fight. He had taken out several of Jamil's men with marksmanship-level shooting of his UZI, before running out of bullets and then killing four more with the grenade.

But there was no sign of the American female pilot.

Pasha reacted quickly, shouting orders, directing Jamil and more than a dozen of his men down the goat trail, watching Jamil's half-disfigured face under a mound of green hair disappear around a switchback while Pasha kept two soldiers with him.

Zahra walked past them and approached the edge of the gorge, peering down.

"What is it?" he asked, joining her.

"Look," she said, pointing at several broken branches a couple dozen feet below. "I think she might have gone this way."

"Stand back," he said, before grabbing an AK-47 from one of Jamil's men and emptying a clip into the vegetation lining the side of the hill. Zahra joined him, unloading a fusillade that mowed down the brush.

The gunfire erupted above, raining down, zooming past her, smacking trees and ricocheting off rocks, before her right cheek burst in pain. Blood suddenly covered the side of her face.

"Aghh!"

Vaccaro let go on instinct, falling back, crashing against a tree trunk, bouncing and falling again, plummeting through pine branches, bending some and breaking others as the skies, the trees, and the boulders traded places.

Her hands slapped wildly at anything to break her fall. She finally snagged a root with her right hand, hanging for a moment before planting her right foot over a rock.

She paused and took a deep breath.

Jesus.

She wiped the blood off her face as bullets continued to zoom past her. Relieved to still be able to see out of her right eye, Vaccaro managed to reach a branch with her left hand, letting go of the root and swinging under a wide trunk growing at an angle out of the side of the incline.

Her face throbbing, taking the pain with her jaw clenched, she wedged her body into the space between the pine tree and a narrow ledge. Rounds pummeled everything, some tearing into the trunk above her, others whooshing past her, clipping the vegetation below her.

And the firing stopped just as fast as it had begun.

"Do you think we got her?" Zahra asked.

"Can't see a damn thing," Pasha replied, staring into the wooded drop. "For all I know she may not even be down there but over on *that* trail." He pointed in the direction where Jamil had vanished. "Only one way to be sure," he added, and he ordered his two warriors down the cliff.

"What about this?" She pointed to the rucksack strapped to her back. "It's the priority."

Pasha frowned while watching the men climb a dozen feet down the hill. "That's why I need to comb every square inch of this hillside. She knows the way here."

Zahra shook her head and pointed at the GPS on her wrist. "Fine, but she doesn't know the way to Qais Kotal."

"Maybe," he said. "Maybe not. They captured one of my guys alive. Remember?"

Zahra frowned and said, "Then we need to divide and conquer. I'll go to Akhtar and get the bomb operational and out of here. You ensure that pilot doesn't talk."

"But Jamil's men . . ." Pasha said, actually feeling concerned. "I can't trust them alone with you. They wanted to stone you."

"That's why I need to go solo," she replied. "Besides, I work better alone, especially when the other choice is being in the company of assholes."

"Okay," he said.

"Then I need the coordinates." She offered him her GPS.

It only took him a moment to enter the coordinates and explain the route. "Go," he finally said, heading down the cliff. "I'll catch up to you."

As he watched Zahra rushed back up the trail, Pasha peered down the precipice again.

I am not through with you yet.

Vaccaro persisted, pushing herself through the pain, just as her father had done, refusing to give up, reaching the bottom of the rocky incline nearly out of breath, becoming weaker.

She knew they were coming, could hear them high above her, their shouts echoing in the void between them. And she had to assume others would be heading her way from the trail beyond the bend in the mountainside.

It's now or never, she thought, reaching for the radio and dialing the military air distress frequency of 243.0 MHz, hoping like hell someone would be listening at the other end—someone other than the Taliban.

93

Ooh-Rah!

KANDAHAR AIRFIELD. SOUTHERN AFGHANISTAN.

Captain John Wright was running—running like a damn Olympic sprinter—and so were a dozen of his men. They reached the tarmac just as the Chinook's twin Lycoming turboshafts spooled into action, turning the massive rotors.

The distress call from Red One One had arrived just minutes ago, picked up by the same Black Hawk helicopter that was returning with the wounded CIA man, and was relayed to KAF.

"Hold that bird, soldier!" Wright shouted, as his marines scrambled up the rear metal ramp.

Inside, four Royal Canadian Air Force crewmen, two of them medics, hovered over their equipment. Door gunners, one on each side, loaded their M240s with 7.64mm belts. Beyond them the pilot and copilot worked the instrument panel between them, throwing switches and turning dials.

One of the gunners stepped up to the cockpit to inform the pilots of the Yankee invasion. The copilot unbuckled his harness and headed toward Wright.

"Sir? What are you doing here?"

"You're going into a hot zone," Wright said. "You're gonna need some muscle on the ground."

"But we have no notice of marines—"

"Look," Wright said, as his men made it inside and helped themselves to the flip seats built into the sides of the massive helicopter. "She saved our bacon out there yesterday. No way we're abandoning her now. We owe her."

"I hope you know what you're doing, eh?" he said, before returning to the cockpit and updating the pilot, who looked over his right shoulder and shook his head at Wright before returning to his controls.

Wright took his seat next to Gaudet, who was checking his M4A1 carbine, as the twin Lycoming turboshafts unleashed their combined 9,500 horsepower, whirling the rotors into clear disks, lifting the craft off the blacktop. Wright noticed two Boeing AH-64 Apache helicopters tagging along as escorts.

"All set?" he asked.

Instead of replying, Gaudet turned to his men. "Marines! Are you ready to kick some ass?"

All eyes met the gunnery sergeant's, followed by a unanimous, "*Ooh-rah!*"

94

So Be It

SULAIMAN MOUNTAINS. SOUTHERN AFGHANISTAN.

Vaccaro ran down the side of the mountain toward the closest large clearing that could be used as an exfiltration point, ignoring her throbbing face, which burned like hell after she had patched it with QuikClot. But at least the blood had stopped, allowing her to see clearly out of her right eye.

But she had bigger problems: the Taliban.

She could hear them in the distance, beyond the bend in the trail as it curved around and up the mountain.

Bastards get an A for effort, she thought, pushing herself, reaching deep into her reserves to gain as much distance from them as possible, to prevent another failed rescue attempt—though this time she had warned KAF of hostiles in the area. Two Apache gunships accompanied the Chinook, call sign Hook Three Two.

She kept the channel open, using it as a beacon for the incoming rescue crew, which was still ten minutes away—the time she had to find an area large enough for the large helicopter to land.

With luck, she hoped to keep enough distance from the posse behind her that the Apaches could lay down a wall of destruction to enable a safe—

A round ricocheted off a boulder in a burst of pulverized rock, followed by another one hammering a stone pine to her left.

Cutting right, she decided to take her chances down another steep incline, this time sliding on her back, feetfirst, pressing the heels of her boots against the terrain, creating enough friction to manage her semicontrolled plunge.

Her back stung as she skidded down the abrupt grade, so she half stood, committing herself to almost running down the slope but taking the pressure off her back and passing it to her legs while she accelerated, widening the gap.

The increased speed, however, came with added risk of losing her footing and tumbling forward, especially as she started to get dizzy, as she briefly lost focus.

Mustering control and blinking to clear her sight in spite of her pounding right temple bringing tears to her eyes, she used her hands to snag low branches, fighting to keep her balance while kicking up dust and making a lot of noise. But at least no one was taking potshots at her.

For now.

She continued, clamping down the pain, remembering the long line of female warriors before her, drawing strength from their iron will, from their unwavering determination to persevere against all odds. She thought of the WASP, of Jackie Cochran and Nancy Love, of their leadership and sacrifice. She recalled their bravery, as well as that of all the women who'd ever served their country, even if that country had failed to recognize their selfless sacrifice for decades. Her thoughts then drifted to Aaron, to her rugged Mossad assassin—a real-life Kidon—who had managed to ignite something in her before sacrificing his life so she could live.

So Vaccaro pushed herself for the sake of her nation, for the sake of the oath she had vowed to keep. She persisted in honor of those who had come before her and out of respect for those who had given their lives for her—to protect the bloody map in her vest, marking the location of a weapon that was unthinkable in the hands of these fanatics.

After a few hundred feet the terrain leveled off into another plateau, this one wider—large enough for the Chinook—with a rocky outcrop at one end where she could hide and wait it out.

Feeling steadily weaker, the throbbing in her head nearly unbearable, Vaccaro brought the radio to her lips and, nearly out of breath, said, "Hook Three Two . . . Red One One has found . . . a clearing large enough. Home in on my . . . beacon . . . Beware . . . hostiles in the area.

"Red One One, Hook Three Two, roger. Five minutes out."

As she heard the reply, Vaccaro noticed a wide fracture in the near-vertical wall of rock next to the outcrop—hairline at the top but widening enough for a person to sneak through as it reached chest level.

A cave?

She approached it, the Colt 1911 in her right hand and the radio in her left, leaning down a bit to peek inside, letting her eyes adjust to the darkness, the smell of mildew and the cooler temperature washing over her. It felt like heaven, especially on her burning face, and she took a lungful of cold and humid air, fighting the dizziness rapidly overtaking her.

She looked behind her and then back inside the cave, the interior of which widened and curved into darkness. Biting her lower lip, Vaccaro considered the trade-offs. The cavern would keep her out of sight, plus she could spot people coming in, as they would be backlit while she remained in the dark recesses. But, on the other hand, she would be trapped, without an escape route.

Making her decision, she stepped inside, her exposed skin goose bumping from the drop in temperature as she said, "Hook

Three Two, be advised Red One One hiding in cave at north end of clearing. Anything that moves out there is hostile."

"Roger that, Red One One. Three minutes out. Pop smoke."

"Roger," she replied, reaching for her last MK-13 flare. She hesitated before pulling the rings at the ends of the five-inch-long cylinder, realizing doing so was a double-edged sword that would signal the incoming crew as well as her pursuers.

"So be it," she said, pulling on the rings and tossing the flare as far as she could before vanishing into the cave.

95

Lock and Load

SULAIMAN MOUNTAINS. SOUTHERN AFGHANISTAN.

Wearing a green David Clark headset, John Wright tightened the grip on his Heckler & Koch UMP45 submachine gun when he heard her voice.

Suddenly everything felt as if it was moving too slowly, including this damned helicopter. Never mind that it was the fastest troop transport model at KAF. It still didn't get him to her *now*, when she needed him.

Not in three fucking minutes.

Focus.

So he did, checking his weapon, making sure he had a full magazine of thirty .45 ACP jacketed hollow-point rounds plus one in the chamber—plenty of punch to counter the enemy's AK-47s. He ran a hand over his armored vest, fingers checking the four spare magazines and assorted grenades tucked into various compartments.

Drawing the SIG Sauer P220—also in .45 ACP—he performed a quick ammo check, including the spare magazines clipped to his utility belt. In total, Wright had almost 175 rounds—a bit overkill for such a short mission, but he wasn't in the mood to take any chance of this op going sideways, especially when he knew he could get in trouble for not checking with Duggan first. But sometimes it was better to ask forgiveness than permission, especially if it helped to ensure the safe return of Laura Vaccaro.

"Two minutes!" the pilot warned.

Wright looked over at Gaudet, who nodded, turned to his marines, and shouted, "Lock and load!"

Then, looking back at his superior officer, the gunnery sergeant said, "We'll find her, sir! We'll find her!"

96

Bad Omen

SULAIMAN MOUNTAINS. SOUTHERN AFGHANISTAN.

"Find her! Down there!" Pasha shouted, when he connected with Jamil's men at the next switchback. He had spotted the red smoke in the clearing below as the sound of helicopters echoed in the range.

Jamil's men shot down the hill with impressive nimbleness, like mountain cats on steroids, careering past trees and rocks, leaping from boulder to boulder with feline agility. Pasha tried to keep up, the Dragunov slung behind his back, his hands clutching a more manageable AK-47, though neither weapon could do much damage against the incoming Americans. The same was true of Jamil's team, which lacked RPGs.

Their best shot was to locate the pilot and either take her alive or silence her, then retreat before the rescue team arrived.

But to do so they needed to hurry.

By the time he reached the clearing, Jamil had already spread out his men—all fifteen of them—across the long and narrow overhang and had set them to searching the tree line and the edge, some vanishing in the red haze hovering like a bad omen.

"Where are you?" he mumbled under his breath, his eyes searching the clearing before settling on the rocky outcrops at the edge of the gorge, recalling how she had hidden in a similar area two nights ago.

97

Hold Your Breath

SULAIMAN MOUNTAINS. SOUTHERN AFGHANISTAN.

Vaccaro waited. The cave dampened the noise of the incoming helicopters, making it difficult to assess how far away they were.

She was tempted to head back out but decided to wait. The rescue crew knew she was hiding here, plus her eyes had adjusted to the darkness enough to have the upper hand on any—

A figure came into view, partially blocking the tall, narrow triangle of light that pierced the first dozen feet of the cave and formed a twilight zone bordering the darkness in which she hid. The silhouette was classic Taliban: baggy pants and tunic, plus the evident profile of an AK-47 with its long, curved, high-capacity magazine. He was sweeping the weapon back and forth, searching for a target in the darkness.

Holding her breath, Vaccaro lifted the Colt 1911 and fired two rounds into his center of mass. The flashes revealed a glimpse of a disfigured face, large hooked nose missing a nostril, brown teeth, and—interestingly enough—very green hair and beard. He looked like a cliché caricature of a bad guy—only he was real. Very real.

The insurgent arced back while squeezing the trigger of the AK-47, carving a track into the cave's ceiling and splashing the interior with stroboscopic yellow light. He finally collapsed, as dust and debris rained down on him.

Very real, indeed, she thought. *And now very dead.*

Darkness returned, but not before the reports had shown her a wide crevice to her left, a deep fissure in the rock wall that seemed wide enough to hide in.

Standing by the edge of the clearing, searching for the woman pilot behind rocks, Pasha saw the flashes and heard the shots. Two singles followed by the brief rattle of an AK-47 coming from inside what looked like a cave at the end of the clearing.

"This way!" he shouted to Jamil's men, as the helicopter loomed into view. But to his surprise, what emerged from below wasn't a Chinook. The twin rotors belonged to two Apache attack helicopters rising like a pair of demons, their stub wings loaded with death.

The Noorzai warriors turned their AK-47s toward the gunships and opened fire.

Pasha understood the senselessness of the attack, as their rounds ricocheted off the crafts' armored skin.

Painfully aware of what would come next, he broke into a run, toward the cave's entrance.

98

Grand Scale

"Thirty seconds!"

Wright watched the Apaches approaching the clearing, their rotors spiraling in the red smoke oozing from a single flare.

Gunfire erupted from multiple places along the tree line, primarily from the left and center sections.

The response was brutal and overwhelming as the gunships unleashed a mix of Hydra and APKWS 70mm air-to-ground rockets, lighting up the side of the hill before sweeping it with their M230 chain guns. It was destruction on a grand scale, unequivocal and swift, quenching any visible resistance by the time the Chinook's rear ramp lowered.

Wright scrambled out first, his UMP45 up and ready, scanning the long ledge through its sights.

99

Ladies First

SULAIMAN MOUNTAINS. SOUTHERN AFGHANISTAN.

Vaccaro spotted another figure near the entrance as gunfire intensified outside, followed by explosions that shook the entire mountain, and for a moment she feared that the cave would collapse.

She lined him up in the Colt's sights, but before she could fire, the figure tossed something inside, which skittered over the rocky floor.

She jerked away on instinct, pushing her body inside the adjacent crevice until the walls wedged her torso. In the same motion, she brought both hands to her ears, closed her eyes, and opened her mouth.

The blast inside the enclosure pounded her, compounding her head wound as she collapsed on her side, trembling, losing her grip on the Colt, which slid away, disappearing into a crack in the cave's floor.

Dammit!

On her knees, nauseated, breathing deeply, the headache so powerful she could barely see, Vaccaro gutted up, her eyes veiled with grit and an unbending resolve—a determination she had seen glistening in Aaron's dying eyes.

Reaching deep into her core for any shred of energy, swallowing the lump in her throat, her fingers curled around the handle of her SOG knife.

Pasha had tossed the grenade into the cave as the hill ignited behind him, tearing some men to pieces while setting others ablaze, running and screaming figures collapsing near the arriving Chinook while the Apaches steered out of the way and hovered overhead.

His back pressed against the wall next to the entrance, Pasha waited for the blast, which shot out of the jagged opening like a cannon shot. He rushed inside through the inky smoke swirling by the entrance, ignoring the smell of cordite and the soldiers scrambling out of the rear of the helicopter and spreading across the ledge. Surviving Noorzai warriors opened fire, engaging the marines, making a final stand.

Darkness engulfed him, but rather than pausing by the entrance, where he knew the light forking through the ingress would betray him, Pasha scampered inside and quickly shifted to one side while firing at waist level.

Through the flashes, he noticed Jamil's green-headed figure on the ground, mouth wide open in a final scream, dead eyes staring at the cave's rugged ceiling, fingers clutching his Kalashnikov in a death grip.

I know you are in here.

Reloading—and realizing that those marines would soon be coming up behind him—Pasha pushed deeper, stepping over Jamil, committing himself to finishing this, one way or another. The soldiers outside would have the place surrounded by now, as intense gunfire, a mix of AK-47s and American carbines, foretold the final battle.

But Pasha's battle was in this murky and damp chute, against this woman, this blatant violator of Sharia law who could also be carrying the secret of Qais Kotal, betraying Akhtar's ultimate hideout.

Not on my watch, he thought, moving slower now, his eyes peering into the obscurity, ears listening intently to every sound, filtering the racket outside, focusing on the—

A shadow separated from the wall to his right, surging toward him and stabbing his chest before he could bring his weapon around.

Stunned, Pasha stepped back as the figure vanished. His hands, trembling momentarily from the shock, dropped the Kalashnikov and he stared in disbelief at the rubber handle of the blade, protruding from his chest, just below his neck.

Instincts overcame surprise, forcing his mind to ignore the knife.

It wasn't going anywhere, and the fact that he could actually think meant it hadn't cut into anything vital—plus, pulling it out could cause him to bleed out. What he needed was a weapon in his hands, but reaching down for the AK-47 by his feet could expose him to another attack by the woman pilot.

So Pasha did the only thing he could: he drew the old Makarov, gripping it just as the shadow reappeared, firing once as a crippling pain in his groin made him drop to his knees.

Vaccaro had used whatever reserves she had left to surprise and stab the insurgent, but she lacked the strength to retrieve the SOG knife or to follow up on her strike as the man stepped back in obvious shock, dropping his AK-47.

As she felt her strength leaving her, draining from her core, the last thing she could think of doing before collapsing was to kick the bastard in the balls.

Resting most of her weight on her left leg, she brought her right boot up in between the rebel's legs as a gunshot cracked between them.

Her right shoulder went numb as she fell, landing on her back.

The insurgent dropped to his knees, staring at her, pistol in hand. She could see him clearly now: young, with angry brown eyes, a camouflage bandanna wrapped over his hair, her SOG knife still protruding from his chest.

Slowly, with apparent effort, he stood and aimed the semiautomatic at her face.

John Wright had rushed ahead of everyone else, making a beeline for the cave at the end of the ledge, the one Vaccaro had mentioned in her last transmission.

A man emerged off to his right, AK-47 in hand as he opened fire from a distance of fifty yards, shooting from the hip.

Good luck with that, Wright thought, the UMP45's stock pressed tight against his right shoulder, iron sights in front of his shooting eye perfectly aligned with the target's center of mass. He squeezed the trigger twice without breaking his stride, the .45 ACP slugs finding their mark.

Wright kept his momentum as the rebel dropped from sight, focusing on the wide crevice in the rock wall, on the place where she—

A single gunshot flashed from inside the cave.

No!

He pushed even harder, kicking his legs, reaching the entrance seconds later, running inside and screaming, "Laura! Laura!"

Vaccaro blinked when she heard her name.

John?

Was she imagining it? Did John Wright just call her name?

The shout prompted the insurgent to turn around and fire twice at the figure of a helmeted marine backlit by sunshine, the flashes splashing the walls with yellow and orange light.

Wright felt a sting in his right leg and a punch on his armored vest as the man shot his pistol twice. Doing so, however, marked the target for the veteran captain, who didn't blink while firing twice into the rebel's center of mass, before the bastard could fire a third time.

The insurgent just stood there, in apparent shock, before collapsing on his side.

Wright ran up to him and grabbed the pistol, a Makarov, flipping the safety and tucking it into his vest before kneeling by Vaccaro's side.

She lay on her back, a hand on her wounded shoulder, a QuikClot patch on the right side of her face, where he could see a cut across her forehead and right temple.

Slinging the UMP45, he reached down and picked her up, ignoring the pain in his leg, cradling her against his chest while whispering, "I've got you, baby. I've got—"

"John," she whispered.

"Don't talk," he said, carrying her out of the cave. "Save your strength."

The moment he cleared the entrance, he shouted, "Medic! Medic!"

The two Canadian operators rushed to his side, hauling a stretcher between them. Gaudet and his marines had already secured the clearing and had formed a perimeter while the medics helped Wright lower her into the stretcher.

"Sir!" one of the medics said, pointing to his leg. "You're bleeding!"

"Later, son!" Wright replied. "Ladies first!"

One of the Canadians cut through the right side of her shirt, exposing the wound on her shoulder, which fortunately seemed superficial. The other medic applied a patch of QuikClot before bandaging it enough for the return trip.

"John," Vaccaro said again, coming in and out of it.

"Don't talk," he said, kneeling by her side while one of the paramedics worked an IV into her right arm and the other looked at his leg. "It's going to be—"

"Listen!" she snapped, lifting her head and grabbing him by the lapels of his utility vest, getting his undivided attention. "The map . . . John." She let go of him and tapped the side of her vest before resting her head back on the stretcher and closing her eyes.

"Flesh wound, sir," the Canadian medic working his leg reported, squirting on an antibiotic cream, followed by a QuikClot patch.

"Thanks," he replied while frowning at the sudden heat on his wounded leg, before reaching into Vaccaro's pocket and pulling the map out. It was stained with blood. "What about this map?"

"Marks . . . the . . . location . . . of the bomb."

100

Legends

**QAIS KOTAL. SULAIMAN MOUNTAINS.
SOUTHERN AFGHANISTAN.**

The entrance to the underground facility was located almost two-thirds of the way across the pass, beyond an arch-shaped rock formation rising twenty feet over the snowy trail. It led to a narrow corridor that wound its way between soaring walls of icy granite before reaching the massive metal front doors.

The choke point, thought Akhtar, as he greeted two dozen warriors charged with defending this secret and sacred location, named after Qais Abdur Rashid, father of the Pashtun nation and thirty-seventh descendant of King Saul.

"We're here, Professor," he said, without turning around.

In true Afghan costume, Akhtar removed his gloves, using his left hand to shake hands while placing his right hand over his heart, gesturing respect.

According to legend, Qais discovered this place in the sixth century, shortly after meeting the Prophet Muhammad, who inspired him to seek a secluded place of worship "near the heavens." Over the centuries, kings had used it as a retreat, a place to escape the dangers and worries of the world. Military leaders saw it as a strategic hub connecting central and southern Afghanistan, while mullahs and sheikhs sought it as a place of prayer and meditation. But in recent times—at least for the past five years—it had been among the preferred hiding places of the current leader of the Pashtun nation: Osama bin Laden. And like prior chiefs throughout the history of this country, Akaa was being persecuted by the powers of the world. His predecessors had been hunted by the powers of the world—all of whom eventually regretted their decision to invade this landlocked nation.

And now the Americans.

Akhtar stepped through the long and winding corridor formed by walls of black granite—typical of the region—leading to the large, ornate, heavy doors, which, like everything else here over the centuries, had been brought up on the backs of mules. The doors protected the entrance to the central hall, a cavernous opening used as a hub linking man-made caves that served as a prayer room, sleeping quarters, a kitchen and dining hall, and a few private chambers and offices.

He stood there a moment, under the flickering yellow light of ancient oil lamps. Akhtar always thought it was ironic that one of those invaders—the feared Tamerlane—had rebuilt most of Afghanistan sometime during the fourteenth century, after his Mongolian predecessors had destroyed it. And that had included revamping this primeval cave, excavating additional chambers, and adding a tunnel to the northern face of the mountain, with a path down to a dry riverbed that led through the Koh-i-Baba mountains into the lush plains of Bamyan in central Afghanistan. After the Mongolian retreat in the fifteenth century, the Pashtuns took it over, using it as a secret artery to transport troops and weapons across the mountains, a tradition that had continued throughout the Soviet invasion and to this day.

"My father . . . he told me stories about this place," Dr. Khan said as he stood next to Akhtar, trying to take it all in. "But I thought it was just . . ."

"A legend?"

"Something like that, yes," he said

"Well, professor," Akhtar said, when he spotted Akaa emerging from one of the caves, followed by a tall man wearing Western clothes and lacking the obligatory Sharia law beard. "Prepare yourself to meet a real-life legend."

101

Mushroom

John Wright stood in the back of the room while Harwich and Duggan spread the map over the table. He was just too physically and emotionally drained to care about it while Vaccaro was being tended to at the Role 3 MMU.

He would rather have remained by her side, especially since she was unconscious, but Duggan had summoned him here. Plus, the doctor had told him that her wounds were minor but still needed attention to prevent infections. So he had made a pit stop to check on Gorman, who had survived his surgery but was still in critical condition. While he was there, he had a doctor check his leg, which earned him two staples and a shot of antibiotics, but otherwise he was good to go. Finally, he had headed to Duggan's office.

His reading glasses balanced on the tip of his nose, the marine colonel discussed the location of the coordinates relative to the current location of Stark, who had already been provided with the coordinates of the target.

"They're close, sir," Harwich said. "They have been tracking the men that escaped Compound Fifty-Seven, and the trail is leading them in the right direction."

"Looks like . . . what? Six clicks?" Duggan asked.

"Just about," Harwich said.

"Any chance we can get him some help?"

Harwich frowned, and Wright knew why, of course. The last time the marines had tried to "assist" Stark they had simply allowed the Taliban to escape with the weapon. "What do you have in mind?"

"Relax, Mr. Harwich," Duggan said. "I may be on a NATO base, but I'm *not* NATO."

"What about the general?"

"Mushroom treatment."

"So you're not telling him?"

Duggan angled his big head slightly and said, "I'll bring him into this at the right time. But first I wanted to see about getting a rifle platoon up there," he said. "And maybe SEALs, if they're available," he added. "I know some of the guys from SEAL Team Two."

Harwich rubbed his bearded chin. "The problem is accessibility. The southern face of that mountain is a bit high for helicopters, and the pass is too narrow for our planes. Plus, the ledges bordering the pass, carved straight out of the gorge, are too small a target for even the best HALO operator. Maybe we can drop them off here, near the entrance to the pass, but that will put them about a day and a half behind Stark. The other option is to bring them up the northern face of the mountain, where the terrain is more accessible by helicopter. But it would take a team at least four days to cross over to the south—assuming they can find a way to do so on the surface. Remember, we've never been up there."

"Shit," he said. "Neither option is—"

The door to his office burst open and Major General Lévesque marched in, followed by his typical entourage of foreign officers.

Rugged and tall, Lévesque reminded Wright of those tough Canadian loggers. Smoothing his orange mustache, Lévesque said, "Colonel I got word from—"

"Ever heard of knocking, General?" Duggan snapped.

Lévesque stopped and regarded the marine colonel, who was no lightweight; he resembled a pit bull, down to his strong jaw and chin. On top of that, Duggan just happened to be in charge of one of the largest forces assembled at KAF, and he was incredibly well connected and respected at the Pentagon and at the White House.

The general lowered his voice a decibel or two but did not back down. "Fine. Apologies for that, eh? Now, did one of your pilots deliver a map to your marines that may contain pertinent intelligence on the whereabouts of the bomb?"

"You mean *this*?" Duggan pointed at the map. "I'm assessing its value now to see if it merits your attention."

"I'd like very much to believe that," he replied.

"Believe what you wish, General, but know this: if I were to pass on to you *everything* that comes through my desk, you'd be neck deep in *shit*."

"Very well, Colonel," Lévesque said, glancing at his watch. "You've had *two hours* since the helicopter arrived from the field. What's your *assessment*?"

Wright checked his watch, wondering if Vaccaro was up.

He listened to the discussion for the first few minutes, while slowly backing away to blend with the entourage standing by the door, before slipping out and heading to the hospital.

102

Whatever It Takes

KANDAHAR AIRFIELD. SOUTHERN AFGHANISTAN.

The light stung her eyes.

Slowly, Vaccaro opened them, revealing a blurry world that slowly resolved into a white ceiling and overhead fluorescents, then a plastic bag hanging from a pole. She followed the clear tube connecting it to her right forearm.

"Hey, Captain."

She heard him but could not see him, turning her head slightly to the left as Wright pulled up a chair, a hand taking hers.

"Hey . . . Captain," she replied, as his face came into focus. She was feeling groggy, her eyes returning to the IV. "What . . . the hell . . . you people have me on?"

"Oh, you know, just your usual lifesaving cocktail after nearly getting killed by the Taliban."

"Ha-ha," she said, smiling without humor while bringing a hand to her face, feeling the narrow bandage over the right side of her forehead and temple.

"Took them a little while to clean that up," he said. "Nasty cut. But superficial. Just character building—plus, it's earned you at least a Purple Heart, not to mention the other awards coming your way for risking your life to save my marines."

Vaccaro inhaled deeply. "How . . . long?"

"Just a couple of hours," he replied. "And you got lucky on that shoulder wound. The bullet went through clean and was a small caliber—three eighty automatic. I took it from the bastard who shot you. Here, take a look."

He produced a small shiny black pistol. "Russian," he added. "Used to belong to a Colonel M. Tupolev, according to the inscription." He tapped the side of the muzzle.

Vaccaro signaled him to sit her up, and he reached for a small hand controller tethered to the bed through a white cord. He pressed a button and the back of the bed slowly rose, allowing her to get a view of her surroundings.

She breathed deeply, feeling reenergized after sleeping for a couple of hours, plus the cocktail they had pumped in her.

"Water," she said, while flexing her shoulder. It hurt some but nothing she could not manage.

Wright produced a water bottle with a straw already in it.

She sipped it, closing her eyes as the cool water refreshed her. "Where am I?"

"Role Three MMU, where you've been getting your beauty sleep."

She lay somewhere in the middle of a long and narrow room with beds lining both walls. Most patients were out of it—and most were missing a body part. The soldier across the aisle from her had no legs below the knees; likewise, the guy next to him. The bed to her right housed a kid probably still in his teens, who was missing his entire right arm and even part of his shoulder as well as both legs above the knees.

"That's Corporal Franklin," Wright said. "Nineteen. Ran right into a cluster of IEDs the same day you got shot down."

"Sorry, John."

"Actually, you were directly responsible for preventing any more of my men from getting hurt. As it turned out, because you stayed in the fight, I only lost one man, my gunnery sergeant. That makes you one helluva hero in my book, Laura."

She looked away, thinking of Aaron, of the Shinwari clan, of the crew of that ill-fated Chinook—the real heroes in her survival story.

Her eyes landed on a woman sitting by a bed to her left. Her skin color and features suggested she was local, though she was dressed in U.S. Army fatigues. She kept watch over a man lying unconscious, with bandages on his abdomen. An IV fed each of his arms.

"Bill Gorman," Wright said. "CIA guy. Shot in the gut. Heavy caliber. He's still in critical condition."

The wound also made her think of Aaron, who might have survived if there had been a way to . . .

Stop that, she thought, before asking. "Who's the woman?"

"One of Gorman's assets, according to Harwich."

"Harwich?"

"My civilian counterpart. I'm working intelligence for Colonel Duggan now. Guess you got your wish. Got me a desk job."

"Harwich is Agency, too?"

"Yeah. And they're a secretive bunch. You should have seen his face when I showed him this Makarov and he read the inscription. The man looked like he'd seen a ghost."

"Why?"

"He wouldn't say."

"Yeah," she said, remembering how guarded Aaron had been at first. "They can be mysterious."

He smiled. "Well, technically I've crossed to the dark side. We're collaborating in tracking the whereabouts of the missing Russian nuke. And you, my dear, provided us with a central piece of intelligence."

"The map?"

"Yep. Harwich and I briefed Colonel Duggan, and we passed the coordinates to Colonel Stark, who was already in the vicinity.

Vaccaro nodded, remembering him.

Wright made a face.

"What is it, John?"

"Well . . . Duggan was planning to bolster Stark's force with SEALs, and also a contingent of marines, but keeping it from NATO for the time being, given its recent track record."

"But?"

"The medics . . . they were Canadians, so it leaked to Lévesque that you gave me a map that marked the location of the bomb. When Lévesque confronted Duggan, the colonel had no choice."

"Dammit," she said, repeating Aaron's words. "To NATO everything looks like a nail. I bet they're preparing to launch a big airstrike."

He frowned and checked his watch. "When I left them a few hours ago, they were just starting to talk options. But the problem is one of accessibility to the target from the air. The coordinates are smack in the middle of this very winding and narrow pass—too narrow for our jets and a bit high for our helicopters, plus no place to land or drop troops. The closest ground asset is Stark and his team, and they're headed there now. Meanwhile, I'm sure that Lévesque and staff will review high asset imagery to figure out how to best hit it from above. But in addition to it being narrow, the mountain walls angle in over the target, preventing us from getting a clear view of what we're dealing with; thus the team on the ground. We're still looking into getting SEALs and marines up there, but the closest we can drop them in still puts them at least a day behind Stark."

She stared at her IV and unceremoniously pulled it out of her arm.

"Hey . . . what do you think you're—"

"I need a clear head, John."

"But the pain."

"The pain I can take," she replied, before checking her arm again. The shoulder was sore but functional. "What I *can't* take is another FUBAR directive from NATO. Now, get me some clothes, would you?"

"What do you think you're going to do?"

"Whatever it takes to keep that bomb from leaving that mountain, John," she replied, while thinking of Nasseer and Hassan—while thinking of Aaron. "Whatever it *fucking* takes."

103

Motion

QAIS KOTAL. SULAIMAN MOUNTAINS. SOUTHERN AFGHANISTAN.

Kira peered at the gray clouds partially blocking the last of the late afternoon sun filtering through the snowy woods, which hulked over the west side of the narrow mountain pass snaking south to north at almost twelve thousand feet.

Shivering, she took the opportunity to breathe deeply, forcing what little oxygen she could into her aching lungs. Even someone as fit as her and her team were having a difficult time keeping up with the nimble courier, who continued trekking the pass at a fast clip, seemingly impervious to the cold or the altitude.

Until a moment ago, when she had stopped for a quick water break and to check what looked like a GPS on her wrist.

But something else had captured Kira's attention. The movement had been subtle, a shape vanishing in the trees off to her far right, almost imperceptible, but not to her.

Someone was up on that hill—someone besides the courier. But for the life of her, she could not pinpoint the exact location of the motion.

Sergei Popov crawled up next to Kira as the sun finally sank beyond the western rim rock.

"What is it?" he whispered.

Kira didn't reply right away. Her eyes were fixed on the probable source of the disturbance, farther up on the same incline they were traversing while following the courier's advance on the snowy footpath.

The branches on stone pines near the top of the hill, about three hundred feet above them, had shifted ever so slightly in the wrong direction—opposite the prevailing wind—revealing a figure for just an instant.

But it's gone now, she thought, following the slow, lazy motion of the branches as the wind swept down from the jagged peaks of the Takht-i-Sulaiman.

The Throne of Solomon.

She compressed her lips, shifting her gaze between the offending tree and the telemetry painted on her helmet's display, wondering for a moment if the lack of oxygen was starting to muddle her senses.

"Someone might be out there," she finally said.

"Where?"

"To our right, up by those trees."

Sergei just nodded, knowing better than to risk a look.

"What do you want us to do?"

"Them? Nothing," she said, pointing at the other two Spetsnaz operators. "Tell them to keep after her. But you stay with me," she said, as the courier started up the trail again.

"What do you have in mind?"

"We'll see," she said, resuming her stride while her eyes searched for the right spot along the trail to make her move.

104

Bird in Hand

QAIS KOTAL. SULAIMAN MOUNTAINS.
SOUTHERN AFGHANISTAN.

"We're too close," Monica whispered, huddled next to Ryan on the lower branches of a pine.

"The colonel wants eyes on that courier at all times." Ryan replied.

"Still worried the intel is shit?" Monica asked.

They were observing the contingent of four operatives who were wearing some sort of advanced battle dress and were following a woman heading straight for the coordinates passed to Stark's team via Harwich. Unfortunately, maintaining visual contact with the courier required Monica and Ryan to get a bit closer to the operatives also on the courier's tail than their training prescribed. Judging from their advanced assault weapons—suppressed AK-9s—the team appeared to be Russian, and their sophisticated battle dress suggested GRU Spetsnaz.

He tilted his head and gave her that smile that reminded her of Scottsdale. "Something like that. You know . . . bird in hand?"

"Yeah," she said, "and our little bird is getting away."

Ryan tapped his MBITR to update Stark and the team a couple hundred feet behind them, as Monica slowly crawled down the tree. "Target's on the move again."

She followed Ryan, managing the contour of the bluff in the twilight of dusk, careful not to kick rocks or debris down the snowy hill to the team tracking the courier.

The cold and very dry air this high up chapped her lips. Monica wetted them with the tip of her tongue, uncomfortable with her current predicament. They were not only too close to their mark but also moving faster than she would have preferred.

She scanned the hillside beyond Ryan's slim silhouette, leaning in to the steep terrain while shifting between boulders and trees, keeping an eye on the group of four—

What the hell?

Monica squinted at the trail below while pausing by a mass of boulders that formed a short wall skirting her path. Settling behind it, she rested the TAC-338's muzzle between two rocks, using the powerful Leupold scope to scan the bottom of the hill, confirming her observation. There were now only two figures tracking the courier.

"What's going on?" Ryan asked. He had doubled back, holding his TAC-50 rifle, the .50-caliber big brother of her TAC-338. He fell in beside her.

"We're missing a couple of operatives down there."

"What?"

"Yeah. Look," she said.

He settled behind the scope of his own rifle to survey the base of the steep incline while mumbling, "Where the hell did they go?"

"Right behind you, yes?" came a heavily accented female voice behind them.

Ryan and Monica spun to face the wrong end of a suppressed AK-9 in the hands of an operator dressed in futuristic battle dress, standing on a ledge over them. She wore some sort of space-age helmet. Monica tried to bring her weapon around, but the woman released a single silenced round.

Metal sparked between Monica's hands as the round struck the TAC-338's stock, ricocheting into the forest, the vibrations forcing her to release it. The heavy rifle skittered down the icy hill, kicking a rock loose, which dislodged others, triggering a small avalanche.

The woman glanced over their heads and down the mountainside while frowning and saying into a hidden microphone, "Go in pursuit."

She was slim, and quite agile to have been able to circle them and then crawl up that outcrop—and without either of them hearing her. The woman's black, skintight battle dress, combined with her catlike hazel eyes and high cheekbones, made Monica think of Catwoman, the fictional DC Comics character.

"Now tell me," the woman said, as the rolling debris reached the bottom and silence returned to the pass, "what are American Special Forces doing this high up the Sulaiman Mountains?"

105

Zombies

QAIS KOTAL. SULAIMAN MOUNTAINS.
SOUTHERN AFGHANISTAN.

Zahra heard the commotion behind her. Spinning around, she spotted the rocks and a rifle tumbling down the side of the hill a couple hundred feet behind her—also catching a glimpse of a figure trying to hide behind a tree.

She had simply reacted, following her instincts, breaking into a run and taking off in a flurry of kicked snow while glancing at her GPS. If the gadget could be trusted, she was less than two miles from her objective.

Ignoring anything behind her, she raced down the narrow pass. The cold wind brought tears to her eyes as she focused on the slim trail before her, winding its way north, her boots ripping through a fresh layer of snow. At times, the opposite wall flanking the deep gorge angled less than forty feet from her, its trees nearly touching the upper branches of the snow-layered pines above.

Taking in lungfuls of cold air, she pushed herself, covering a mile in five minutes, exhaling through her mouth, her throat burning, as

well as her thighs. But it was her back that ached the most, in anticipation of a bullet.

A fallen log blocked the trail, and Zahra leaped over it, landing
in a crouch on the opposite side while whirling around, hands on her
UZI, the fire selector on single-shot mode as she aimed it at the trail.

The first figure came into view within seconds—tall, slim, and
helmeted, holding a suppressed rifle. She fired twice into his center
of mass, the bulky suppressor absorbing the reports.

The man fell back as another came into view, and she fired again,
also dropping him. But to her surprise, the first man sat up, reminding Zahra of one of those zombies in American horror movies that
could not be killed. Only this wasn't Hollywood. This was body armor capable of withstanding her 9mm Parabellum rounds.

Dammit, she thought, as she fired at him for sport, dropping him
again.

But not for long, she thought, scrambling away from the two operators recovering on the snowy trail, starting again north, up the
winding path.

She forced her stride for another half mile, exhaling puffs of warm
breath, the cold stinging her face, her eyeballs. But she persisted, the
sides of the trail blurring into a wall of brown and white.

Hoping she was now close enough for the winding path to not
block her radio communications, she spoke into the voice-activated
lapel mike connected to her Wouxun KG-UV6D transceiver.

"Mani . . . please tell me . . . you're there," she hissed, right before
a silenced round stabbed her left thigh.

106

Mexican Standoff

**QAIS KOTAL. SULAIMAN MOUNTAINS.
SOUTHERN AFGHANISTAN.**

"Last chance," Kira said. "What are you doing up here?"

The pair of snipers remained impassive, staring back while keeping their hands over their heads, as instructed. But that marked the extent of their cooperation. It was clear she was not going to get anything else from them. They were pros, like her, probably going after the same threat.

But Kira had her orders, and she had also had enough of these two characters. She needed to get back on the—

A muzzle nudged the back of her neck, right between the top of the battle dress and the helmet. Her skin tingling at the feel of ice-cold steel, Kira tensed, gloved fingers instinctively tightening her grip on the AK-9. In addition to the gun behind her, she spotted three men emerging from the forest to her right. One was a massive soldier, armed with a Browning machine gun. He was flanked by a muscular man with features darkened by camouflage cream and a shorter man with blond hair and mustache, also heavily camouflaged. Both carried MP5A1s.

"How about putting that fancy rifle down nice and easy," said a familiar gruff male voice behind her.

Kira blinked, but before she could reply, Sergei came out of his hideout behind a tree, AK-9 aimed at the incoming trio. "No one moves," he said with a heavy Slavic accent.

The three warriors froze a dozen feet from her, eyes gravitating from Sergei to the man behind Kira while she kept her weapon trained on the snipers.

"What we have here," the voice behind her said, "is a Mexican standoff."

Images of that raid on the Dubrovka theater and that bottle of Stolichnaya filled her mind as she continued staring at the two snipers.

"What is that?" Sergei asked.

"Chief, why don't you tell this Russian what is a Mexican standoff."

The large man with the Browning slowly turned to Sergei, though he kept his machine gun pointed at the ground. "You have guns on us . . . and we have guns on you. No side wins without taking heavy losses."

"Damn right," said the voice behind her. "A Mexican standoff."

Lowering the AK-9 while staring at the snipers, Kira said tentatively, "Janki mishka?"

Stark dropped his brows at the mention of his name.

That voice . . . That accent . . . Those Stolichnaya shots . . .

Slowly, he pulled the MP5A1 away as he mumbled, "Kira?"

The woman removed her tactical helmet, letting her auburn hair fall to just below her shoulder blades before she turned around, regarding him with those large hazel eyes over her pronounced Slavic cheekbones. A fine scar traversed her forehead and temple.

"What are you doing up here, Janki mishka?"

Quickly overcoming his surprise, he replied, "Same thing you're doing."

"Kira?" asked Sergei, who still had his rifle aimed at the trio to her right. "What is happening?"

"Lower that, Sergei," she said. "This is Colonel Hunter Stark. He helped me with the raid at the Dubrovka theater some years back."

"No wonder you look familiar," said Larson. "That's where Mickey got hooked on those damn Russian cigarettes."

Hagen nodded ever so slightly.

"I remember that red hair," said Danny, waving and winking at Kira, who just shook her head.

"I don't remember that raid," said Ryan.

"That's because you were still sucking on your mama's tit, Romeo," said Larson with a grin.

"Or maybe sucking on . . ." Martin pointed at Monica.

"Hey!" she snapped.

"That is all good," Sergei replied, tapping the side of his helmet. "But the courier is getting away."

"The man's got a point, Colonel," said Larson.

"So, Janki mishka," Kira said, strapping her helmet back on. "What do you say? Second run around?"

"What does 'janky whatever' mean?" asked Ryan.

Stark grinned, eyes on her. "It's second *time* around, Kira," he replied. "What are your orders?"

"Recover the weapon . . . or destroy it. But it cannot leave this—"

Gunfire reverberated across the pass.

"In that case, that's our cue," Stark said, pointing his MP5A1 at the path below them.

107

Speedy Delivery

**QAIS KOTAL. SULAIMAN MOUNTAINS.
SOUTHERN AFGHANISTAN.**

Her pulse roaring in her head, Zahra fired at the two dark shapes closing in on her, ignoring her throbbing leg. The UZI's recoil chambered round after round, but it was no use. The 9mm Parabellum slugs lacked the punch to pierce their battle dress. The black figures fell back but then would charge up again moments later, steadily closing the gap.

She cringed in pain, taking a moment to look at the wound. The round had gone through cleanly, missing the femur. But she was bleeding, in need of medical attention.

Dropping an empty twenty-round magazine and inserting a fresh one while limping through the deepening powder, Zahra winced in pain, the wind raging at her cheeks, blood staining virgin snow. She veered right, then left, following this winding, capricious white path as the sound of a near miss swooped past her left ear.

Feeling dizzy, light-headed, she made the next turn as another silent round walloped into a trunk hugging the trail. Snowplowing behind it, she brought the UZI around, firing another volley into the incoming shapes now less than a hundred meters away. One jerked sideways on impact, the snow enshrouding him. The second dove behind a tree. But a moment later both figures were back up, charging after her.

Whirling back on the trail, the cold gnawing through her clothes, the wound sapping her strength, Zahra sprang away, making the next turn. She ignored the blood-soaked leg, the peppered trail of crimson left on fine powder amid her footsteps, finally reaching the black granite walls that formed the narrow corridor leading to the hideout's entrance.

And that's when she saw him, standing taller than life, holding an AK-47 under a massive arch formed by granite boulders overhead.

"Get down!" Mani screamed.

Zahra lunged out of the way, sliding in the snow as Mani blasted a thirty-round magazine of 7.63×39mm cartridges at the two figures running behind her, forcing them to hurtle out of sight.

"Now!" he shouted.

Stifling a groan, Zahra staggered from the side of the trail blanketed in snow, rushing toward him. Ignoring her burning lungs, her aching leg, the heartbeat pounding her temples, she dashed across fifty meters of trail separating her from him, trailing blood, as others joined the fight—jihadists armed to the teeth. They ran toward her, letting her through before closing into a defensive wall, a mix of AK-47s and RPK machine guns.

"You've made it!" he said, embracing her.

But she was too damn weak to speak, trembling, scrunching her eyes in pain, chest heaving, feeling dizzy.

"Take me," she mumbled, falling in his arms. "Take me from this."

108

Pissing Contest

KANDAHAR AIRFIELD. SOUTHERN AFGHANISTAN.

"But . . . she's an ISI spy, eh?" Major General Lévesque said, in the rear of the trailer that Wright and Harwich had converted into a war room. They flanked Colonel Duggan by the wall of LED screens, fed by a half dozen UAVs hovering over Qais Kotal, while NATO analysts combed through the captured imagery.

Gorman sat in a wheelchair next to Maryam. At his insistence, she had rolled him from his hospital bed shortly after he regained consciousness, when he'd gotten word that NATO was planning to remove her from the base and fly her back to Islamabad.

The general, backed by four Canadian Army MPs, had come to escort Maryam to a plane that would take her back to Islamabad.

"She is . . . the *only* reason . . . we know there is a Russian nuke on the loose in the first place," Bill Gorman countered from his wheelchair, wincing in pain while placing a hand on his belly.

"Easy, love," Maryam whispered in his ear, leaning down while standing behind him.

"KAF is my domain, Mr. Gorman, and you need to abide by my—"

"This is a joint CIA–ISI–USMC operation . . . sanctioned by Langley and the commandant of the United States Marines, the secretary of defense, and ultimately the president of the United States of America . . . and it has *only* worked because we are playing . . . on the strengths of . . . our respective teams," Gorman said, suddenly feeling nauseated. "You want that bomb found and destroyed? Then I respectfully request that you . . . let us do our job." He closed his eyes when a pain stabbed his gut, and for a moment he almost pissed his green hospital gown.

"You need to head back to bed, Mr. Gorman," Lévesque said.

"Not until . . . we agree that . . . *Dammit*," he cringed, looking at his gown and noticing a bloodstain on his bandage.

"Bollocks!" Maryam said. "This isn't worth it, and we're just wasting time arguing when we should be working the problem. I'm taking you back to ICU, Bill, and then I'm getting on that bloody plane. I've had enough of this pissing match!"

"Contest," Gorman whispered. "Pissing . . . *contest*. And no . . . way you're leaving," he replied.

"General, the man's got a valid point," Harwich interjected. "She's a valuable asset to our mission. If it weren't for her, we wouldn't have known where to look. Remember that the Taliban captured a Pakistani scientist, which is what tipped the ISI in the first place. And it was *her* contact with the opium cartel that yielded Compound Fifty-Seven."

Lévesque exhaled heavily. "So the CIA is vouching for her?" Lévesque said, looking directly at Maryam, who held his gaze.

"*And* the United States Marine Corps," added Duggan.

Lévesque looked away, arms crossed. "Fine. But I want her confined to this war room . . . or the ICU, eh?" he said, apparently realizing she wasn't about to leave Gorman's side. "*And* she must be escorted by . . ." Lévesque turned to look at his MPs, finally pointing two fingers at Corporal Darcy, "by *him* at *all* times. Clear?"

The tall, blond Canadian Army MP shifted uncomfortably.

Duggan nodded. "Crystal."

"And if this backfires, it's on you, Colonel."

"Thank you for your understanding, General."

"All right," Lévesque said. "Back to work, eh? Find me that damn bomb. And get him back to the damn ICU before I'm blamed for the death of another damn CIA operations officer."

With that, the NATO chief and his entourage stomped off to his headquarters—minus one Corporal Darcy, who stood to the side, eyes on Maryam.

And that's when Gorman noticed that the man's throat was bruised.

109

Deception

They treated her wound in one of the rear chambers, under the yellowish light cast by an oil lamp, while a short and skinny Pakistani named Dr. Ali Khan inspected each component carefully.

Zahra sat on a bench, regarding the little man, while someone else—a medic of sorts who kept staring at her uncovered head—applied an anticoagulant disinfectant to her thigh before stitching it. She ignored him, just as she had ignored the red-eyed glare from the opium-smoking Akhtar and the rest of his men, who were silently judging her for violating their stupid laws and for arriving here alone, without Pasha or his men.

Zahra had already explained how they had gone after the American female pilot because they suspected she might have knowledge of this place. And since the enemy was at their doorstep, the sentiment in the room was that Pasha had been captured and broken, forced to yield this secret hideout.

"The round went through cleanly," the man said in Pashto, rather tersely. "It left the femur intact. I need to close the wound on both sides. But I lack anesthetic. Will that be a problem?" He waved a large curved needle in front of her for effect.

Zahra glanced at the small rucksack that Akhtar carried behind his back, from where he had produced the pipe and a bag of the dark green powder a minute ago. She considered opiating before this asshole stitched her up, but the last thing she needed was to get high.

"Stop talking about it and get it done," she told him.

The medic grinned and went to work.

Zahra ignored the sting as he began to suture the exit wound, her eyes on Dr. Khan. Behind him, Mani and Akhtar conferred with Osama bin Laden, who was dressed all in black, a Dragunov rifle similar to Pasha's slung behind his back. She was angry at all of them for making her trek this damn mountain, hauling those components, when she could have just remained with Mani in the Cessna and waited for Akhtar to arrive with the bomb and the professor. Unfortunately, Akhtar's message that the old Soviet compound had been compromised was not relayed before she jumped, which once more proved how the best plans could go to shit in a heartbeat.

Dr. Khan reviewed a bundle of colored wires and placed a tag on them before making an entry in a small notebook. Next he removed a small printed circuit board card and checked it by using probes connected to a laptop computer.

"Problem," he said after a moment.

Zahra sat up, moving her leg, which caused the medic to jerk the needle, making her wince.

"What kind of problem?" she asked, as the medic resumed his work and Mani glanced in her direction.

"This PCB . . . it's the primer circuitry that creates the voltage spike that sets off the conventional explosives."

"It's broken?" asked Zahra.

"No," he said. "It's been *tampered* with."

"Tampered?" asked Mani, now flanked by bin Laden and Akhtar.

"See here," Dr. Khan said, using a probe to point at one of the electronic components soldered to the PCB. "This capacitor has been added to dampen the voltage spike below the threshold required to detonate the explosive charge."

"Can it be fixed?" asked bin Laden, kneeling down to take a look.

"This is why I'm here, yes?" Dr. Khan said, reaching for a small pair of wire cutters and working the tip to snip off the offending component.

He again applied the probes to the PCB and nodded before regarding his small audience through his round glasses. "We're in business."

"That's it?" asked Mani.

"That's it," Dr. Khan replied.

"Who could have tampered with it?" bin Laden asked Mani.

"I don't know, but I will find out. I paid a fortune for those—"

"Please," Dr. Khan interrupted. "This is delicate work. Take the conversation outside."

Akhtar rolled his eyes as both bin Laden and Mani grinned and slowly backed to the front of the room.

Next, Dr. Khan opened the bubble wrap sleeve of the largest component, a battery pack roughly the size of a small shoebox, before reaching for a voltmeter and pressing the probe leads to its terminals.

"Another problem," he mumbled.

Zahra sat up again, and again shifted her leg as the medic worked the needle.

"What it is now?" she asked.

"The battery level in one of the cells . . . it's low."

Mani walked over, followed by Akhtar and bin Laden. "My people in Moscow checked it before we left. It was fully charged."

"Well," Dr. Khan replied, opening the compartment, "not anymore."

"It's a new pack," Mani insisted, "and it doesn't have a load draining it, so why would it be low?"

"Only one way to find out," the professor said, opening the pack and using a small screwdriver to disassemble it, removing six batteries, each shaped like long cylinder resembling a stick of dynamite. "There are three primary cells required to power the electronics, plus three more in standby as backup, in case there is a problem with one or more of the primary cells. Good redundancy," he explained, checking their respective voltage levels, nodding approvingly, until he reached the last one.

"It's one of the backup cells," he said. "It's low and . . ."

He made a face.

"What is it, Professor?" asked Akhtar.

Dr. Khan didn't reply. His hands toyed with the battery, and he ran his fingers along what looked like a very small seam toward the lower third of the cell. He twisted the top and bottom in opposite directions and the lower section began to unscrew.

"What the hell?" asked Mani.

"Not *hell*," Dr. Khan said, removing something from the battery and inspecting it. "A *transmitter*."

All of them looked at the device in his hands, and Zahra suddenly remembered the silent party on that ridge, shortly after she had rescued Pasha. Someone had fired on the enemy, allowing her to escape.

So they could follow me here.

And she suddenly recalled that woman at the meeting, the way one of the Russian captains had glanced in her direction.

"Your whore," Akhtar hissed, glaring at Zahra before getting in Mani's face. "She is the one who brought the enemy to our doorstep! Not Pasha! Where is my brother, whore? Where is he?"

"I don't know where your brother is!" Mani retorted, an index finger in Akhtar's face. "But what I do know is that my *wife* risked her life to bring your damn components! Which, by the way, cost me a fortune beyond your imagination!"

Zahra wasn't surprised often, but Mani had just shocked her with the way he had defended her.

Bin Laden got between them as both men reached for their weapons. "Enough!" he said. "The enemy is *outside!*"

The room quieted as Akhtar and Mani stopped, keeping up the staring contest for a few more seconds before slowly backing off.

"Now," bin Laden said, turning to the professor, "what are our options?"

"We turn the tables on them," Zahra said, pointing at the transmitter.

"What do you mean?" asked bin Laden, glancing in her direction.

"If you can't beat their technology . . . then deceive it."

110

Déjà Vu

QAIS KOTAL. SULAIMAN MOUNTAINS.
SOUTHERN AFGHANISTAN.

"It is the Dubrovka theater all over again, yes?" she whispered, while focusing the ATN DNVM-4 digital night vision monocular he had loaned her.

Stark sighed, realizing the futility of an overt assault.

Kira huddled beside him under a thermal blanket, looking down on the entrance to the winding passage formed by two nearly parallel walls of rock more than fifty feet high, crested by jagged peaks. From the looks of it, the corridor continued for at least three hundred feet before reaching the side of the mountain, where he presumed the entrance to their hideout was located.

Snowflakes trickled from unseen clouds, through a sparse canopy of pine boughs, as temperatures dropped into the twenties on what promised to be a very cold night.

They had deployed their combined teams in pairs. Sergei and Larson were perched high on a rocky outcrop overlooking the entrance, with a clear line of sight into the first line of defenders. Martin and Hagen covered the lower ground, close to the actual snowy path leading into the corridor. The last two members of Kira's team covered their rear, in case the Taliban decided to send a team from behind. Stark had ordered Ryan and Monica along the bend in the mountain that ran parallel to the towering wall forming one side of the corridor, to find a suitable spot to scale it in the hope of getting above the enemy.

"Just like the hot gates," he mumbled. The corridor reminded him not only of that damn theater but also of the legendary Spartans defending the mountain pass against the Persian army in the historic Battle of Thermopylae. Problem was that the Taliban represented the Greek force, now armed with machine guns, against his smaller force.

"The hot gates?"

"Ever studied the Greeks fighting the Persians at Thermopylae?"

"I saw the movie," she said. *"Three Hundred?"*

"Good enough," he replied, thinking of a way to level the playing field, just as they had done in Moscow.

Just as the Persians did, he thought, recalling the goat path that led behind the Greek lines and had been revealed to the Persian army. He hoped Ryan and Monica would find such a path, though they had the darkness and a winter storm playing against them.

Stark frowned, staring at Kira's profile in the dark as she worked the monocular. She had removed her helmet to use it, revealing not just that red hair but also the scar traversing her forehead and right temple. He recalled how she had pushed him out of the way in the final seconds of the assault, as a grenade fell on them from the stairs at the end of that corridor.

"What is it, Janki mishka?" she said, giving him a sideways glance before resuming her scan.

"I . . . wish you didn't call me that."

"You didn't seem to mind that night, *da?*" She tapped him sideways with her hip.

Stark felt color coming to his cheeks. No one besides her had been able to warm his very cold heart since Kate had walked out of his life. "In any case, I never thanked you," he said, a finger shifting her hair out of the way and tracing the fine scar.

Kira grinned but kept her eye on the monocular. "You would have done the same for me, Janki mishka, yes?"

"In a New York minute."

"I do not know what that means."

He smiled. "Means da . . . yes."

"Good." She snuggled against him, though he wasn't sure whether it was more for warmth or for affection.

Stark ran his fingers over her right shoulder, feeling the smooth surface of her battle dress.

"Enjoying yourself, yes?"

"Kevlar?" he asked.

"Woven with titanium fibers and polyethylene plates over vital areas . . . among other . . . *classified* features."

"Impressive," he replied.

Kira had already told him how they had tracked the components halfway around the continent, and about their powered HALO jump and the loss of a third of her team before they reached their designated landing site. Unfortunately, her GPS tracker had lost line of sight with the overhead satellites the moment the courier vanished inside that cave, which likely had a back door to another part of the mountain.

"Do you still have that tattoo?" he asked, since the battle dress covered her neck.

She turned to him and smiled before reaching just below her chin for a hidden zipper and tugging it down just enough to expose her neck and left clavicle, both covered in that amazing body art.

"You remember, yes?"

"Time of my life," he replied, as he pictured it hovering over him.

She winked before zipping her suit back up and returning to her scanning.

He cleared his throat, then asked, "Those components you sold them . . . they're the real thing?"

"Da . . . unfortunately. We tampered with the primer circuit board, so it won't detonate the conventional explosives. But they can still turn it into a dirty bomb."

Stark had told her how they had gotten here, thanks to the combined intelligence of the CIA, the ISI, and that red-haired air force pilot who reminded him of this Russian woman he'd never expected to see again. For a moment Stark wondered how Vaccaro was doing. Last he'd heard via Harwich, she had been in surgery at the—

"Do you think there is another way out of that cave?" Kira asked, setting down the monocular, her eyes on him.

"It's how they operate, which is why I requested those high assets," he added, referring to the UAVs currently combing every inch of this mountain with their sophisticated arrays of electro-optical/ infrared sensors. And to be on the safe side, they were armed with

Hellfires, with orders to fire on anything that moved or that resembled a cave entrance.

And while all that sounded great, Stark cringed at the fact that the same NATO command that had nearly incinerated him and his team just a few days ago had its finger on the trigger of those drones circling overhead. He had been careful to detail the precise location of their combined teams, but the seasoned colonel still didn't trust—

"*Sierra Echo One, Delta One,*" Ryan said over the operation frequency.

Stark exchanged a glance with Kira, feeling her warm breath on him as the blanket came over their heads, leaving just enough of an opening to use the monocular that rested between them.

"Go ahead, Delta One," Stark replied.

"*Delta One starting our climb.*"

"Copy that, Delta One. Report back when you crest that wall."

"*Roger.*"

"Now we wait," he said, turning to face Kira, just as his Casio vibrated on his wrist.

"What is it?" she asked.

He frowned and reset the alarm before reaching for the Ziploc bag.

"What is that?" she asked again.

Tilting his head while removing the pills, then replacing the bag, he said, "They keep me from going crazy." He popped them in his mouth and swallowed them with a sip from his canteen.

"I see," she said, understanding. "But I heard they affect your . . . *khuy.*"

"Khuy?"

"Penis. And that would be . . . a shame." She winked.

"Ah," he said, his face blushing again. "I wouldn't know. It's been . . . awhile since . . . well . . ."

In the darkness and silence that followed, Kira surprised him by pressing a hand against his groin and smiling.

"Well, no problem so far," she reported, giving him a slow romantic kiss on the cheek and squeezing twice before releasing him. "Just a little something to remember me, Janki mishka."

Then she turned back to the night vision monocular and resumed her scanning of her side of the woods.

Stark needed a minute, filling his lungs with cold air to regain his composure. Finally exhaling heavily while settling behind the night vision scope on his MP5A1, he resumed his scan.

He quietly savored the moment, even while realizing that they were both professionals operating in the world's most hostile nation, carrying out what could very well be the most important mission of their lives.

That small kiss and her playful touch was all that Kira could offer at the moment—maybe ever—as neither knew what the future would bring.

And it would have to be enough.

111

Painting

QAIS KOTAL. SULAIMAN MOUNTAINS.
SOUTHERN AFGHANISTAN.

"He wants us to report back when we crest *that*?" asked Monica, staring up at almost a hundred feet of near-vertical rock, through the layers of snowflakes dancing overhead.

"That's what the man said."

"Well, that's being hopefully optimistic."

Ryan shrugged while inspecting the rock. "What can I say? He trusts our abilities."

"How? He barely knows me."

"*My* skills then."

She smiled without humor before glancing back up the black granite. "It's been a while since I've done this, and it looks ominous."

"That's what she said."

Monica punched him on the shoulder.

"It's like riding a bike. Just follow my lead and my route and you'll be fine. It'll come back to you," he said, wedging the toe of his right boot into a small protrusion at knee level, hoisting himself up, then reaching for a small ledge with his right hand and sticking the fingers of his left hand into a vertical crevice that ran almost the entire length of the wall. In fact, the long crack had been the selling point for Ryan to select this spot.

"Remember to relax your grip," he added. "If you overgrip you'll wear out your forearms, and then you're done. Use your legs to support most of the weight."

He demonstrated how to hang, using the friction of his right sole against the rock while using fingertips for balance, keeping his upper body angled toward the rock. His left leg hung for a moment, before he lifted it up to reach another small imperfection in the wall.

Monica squinted, trying to see the foothold. It was barely visible, just a slight flaw, but enough for his left sole to grip it, allowing Ryan to climb another two feet. Again he rested his weight on his legs while keeping his arms stretched.

"It's called hanging smart," he said. "Avoid bending your arms, 'cause that overworks your biceps, triceps, and shoulders."

He shot back up again, making it look too damn easy.

Here we go, she thought, following his movements, leveraging the friction between the rock and her rubber soles, climbing a couple of feet but flexing her arms in the process. Slowly, she bent her legs to stretch her arms, noticing the instant relief on her muscles.

I'll be damned.

Running the fingers of his left hand up the vertical crevice, Ryan continued his slow ascent, foothold after foothold, though most weren't more than slightly angled sections of rock. She mimicked him, keeping her upper body away from the rock while resting her weight on her legs, forcing the soles into the rock.

They moved in nearly vertical fashion, with an occasional shift here and there for better footing. She tried hard to minimize bending her arms but kept catching herself trying to lift with them instead of her legs, which Ryan explained from above was a classic rookie mistake. Slowly, she got into a rhythm, left hand running up the crevice, legs bent to force her weight into the rock, and arms stretched, building her confidence.

Roughly two-thirds of the way, Ryan reached a narrow ledge, no more than a foot deep by three feet wide, but enough to sit on. He helped Monica up onto it.

Despite constant reminders to keep her arms straight, they still throbbed. She shook them while breathing lungfuls of cold air, exhaling wisps of warm air.

"You're doing great," he said, smiling as snowflakes fell on them, peppering their armored vests.

"Yeah, sure, but what goes up must come down," she said, looking down at the wall.

"No sweat," he said, reaching into his backpack and producing a climbing rope. "Standard equipment when on a mission with the colonel."

"You mean to tell me you could have climbed up here and then tossed a rope down for me?"

He grinned. "Where's the fun in that?"

She punched him on the shoulder.

"Ever done it on a ledge, Miss Cruz?" he said, embracing her.

"In the words of the great Prophet Tyler . . . 'Dream on,'" she said, but she didn't push him away. The man was very warm, and she was freezing.

"I really meant to call," he said.

"Whatever."

"Let me show you how much I care about you," Ryan said, reaching into the rucksack and producing a couple of heavy-duty carabiners, clipping one to his utility vest and another one to hers.

"What's this?"

"You'll see," he said. "Now, stay where you are . . . and control yourself. No monkey business."

"What are you talking about?"

Getting up and turning around, Ryan placed his legs on either side of her for balance while reaching up and inserting an anchor into the vertical crevice, running it down until it caught. Doing so, however, pressed his groin into her face.

"Really, Ryan?" she said, shifting her head to the side.

"Boys will be boys," he said, helping her to her feet before running the climbing rope through the anchor and threading it through each carabiner before working some strange knots she had never seen.

"Now we're officially hitched," he said with a wink.

She ignored him, inspecting the setup, noticing how they were still free to climb, but any sudden motion, such as in a fall, would tightened the rope, arresting it. "Not bad," she said.

"Not bad, my ass," he said, scrambling up again like Spider-Man.

She waited until he was a good five or six feet above her before following, the safety rope dangling between her legs. The wall angled inward as it neared the top, making it easier to scale. She focused on the basics, legs bent and arms stretched, left fingers in the crevice and at least one boot pressed against the rock, right hand gripping something above her, usually another crack or some protuberance.

Again she developed a tempo, controlled, relaxed, managing her breathing, remaining over her center of balance while in motion, and allowing enough rest in between. Her movements became precise, deliberate, visually locating a hand- or foothold before committing to it. As she started to feel good about herself, she managed an upward glance to see how Ryan was making out, but she was staring at nothing, just rock, snowflakes, and dark skies. He was gone, already on top somewhere.

Bastard, she thought, clambering away, getting through the moves quickly to save upper body strength, using arms to shift weight and legs for support, fluidly covering the final dozen feet.

Ryan lay on his belly along the ridge and waved her over, pointing at the corridor below. It resembled a snake poised to strike, with armed men at every curve, leading to an entrance protected by a heavy metal gate. Metallic oil lamps flickered among them, casting a yellow glow on the granite walls.

"Delta One has visual on six DFPs . . . staggered," Ryan whispered into his MBITR, referring to the Taliban defensive fighting positions at each turn. "Heavy gate into compound, but clear line of sight to the sky."

"*Delta One, Echo One. Paint it,*" Stark said.

"Roger that," Ryan replied while staring at Monica, who slowly nodded, signaling understanding.

Slowly, Ryan reached inside the rucksack and retrieved a gadget shaped like a carton of cigarettes with a lens at one end. Monica recognized it as a Northrop-Grumman ground laser target designator. A small tripod unfolded from the bottom, and she helped him set it up on the ridge while Ryan looked through the side scope to aim the crosshairs at the middle of the door.

Flipping a switch on the side and entering an activation code powered up the athermal diode-pumped laser system, which lacked an active cooling system and was therefore silent.

"Delta One painting," Ryan replied.

"*Call it in, Chief,*" Stark said.

"And *that* would be our cue," Ryan said to Monica.

They slid off the top of the ridge and hung side by side from the rope, just low enough to get out of the blast zone.

112

Eye in the Sky

KANDAHAR AIRFIELD. SOUTHERN AFGHANISTAN.

The General Atomics MQ-1 Predator flew at a cruising speed of ninety knots, just south of Takht-i-Sulaiman, its flight surfaces slaved to the remotely piloted aircraft operators manning the Royal Canadian Air Force ground control station inside a trailer just outside NATO headquarters.

Glenn Harwich, John Wright, and Maryam stood next to Colonel Duggan, behind the RPA pilot, who slowly tilted the control column, entering a holding pattern just a thousand feet over the northern portion of Qais Kotal. Remotely piloted aircraft was the trade name for what was known to the general public as a UAV, or to use its more mundane name, a drone.

"Pretty tight for the MTS, sir," observed the sensor operator sitting next to the pilot, tasked with management of the AN/AAS-52 multi-spectral targeting system, which included a thermographic camera for low light or night ops. His eyes focused on the flat screen painted with flight telemetry and images of the ground.

"Can you take the shot, son?" asked Duggan.

"Now I can," he said, the instant a window popped on his screen marking the spot painted by the ground laser target designator.

"What type of warhead is on that missile?"

"Thermobaric, sir."

"Good. Send it," Duggan ordered.

"Roger that, sir," the operator replied, entering the activation code.

A moment later, the solid-fuel rocket of the AGM-114N Hellfire ignited beneath the right wingtip of the Predator, its semiactive laser homing guidance system locking on to the target painted by the GLTD.

Accelerating to Mach 1.3 in seconds, the 104-pound missile arced toward the ground in a blaze, shooting through the forty-foot break in the mountain pass and slamming the target. The eighteen-pound metal augmented charge generated a high-temperature explosion and an ensuing blast wave that whited out the flat screen.

Harwich could only hope that Stark and his team had sought proper cover.

113

Thermobaric Reaction

The 100 percent fuel warhead sucked up all of the available oxygen within its blast radius and melted through the heavy metal gate with nuclear force, turning it into white-hot shrapnel that shelled the interior of the cave along with superheated air. Outside, the ensuing shock wave twisted its way through the corridor at nearly the speed of sound, taking the shape of a glowing serpent while incinerating men and equipment, before shooting its scorching venom into the pass.

Monica hugged Ryan tight as the blast erupted over the walls, orange flames licking the sky, the sonic boom shaking the bedrock like an earthquake.

She felt the heat above them, scorching, suffocating, like the breath of the devil.

But it ended as fast as it had started; smoke replacing flames, the ringing in her ears superseding the sound of the blast.

"Hey," he whispered.

"Hey," she replied.

"Ever done it on a rope, Miss Cruz?"

"Really? Something's seriously wrong with—"

"Delta One SitRep."

"Delta One still here," reported Ryan, winking at her.

"Cover us, Delta One. We're going in."

"Roger that," replied Ryan, climbing while whispering, "Maybe another time, Miss Cruz."

They crawled back onto the ledge, momentarily enjoying the heat absorbed by the granite as it hissed in the cold air. This time they stood on the ridge, but they soon realized that there was really nothing for them to cover—nothing but charred hardware and bodies tossed about in the winding path. And if that was what the blast did outside, where it could actually expand, Monica couldn't imagine the type of havoc it wreaked in the enclosed space of a cave. The acoustic energy alone would have crushed its occupants with the force of a thousand flashbangers.

Never mind the flames and shrapnel, she thought, inspecting the smoldering carnage while Ryan provided Stark with an update.

114

The Hot Gates

QAIS KOTAL. SULAIMAN MOUNTAINS. SOUTHERN AFGHANISTAN.

Hagen and Martin led the stack, wearing their night vision goggles while rushing into the corridor. Stark watched their greenish figures running ahead of Kira and him while Larson and Sergei brought up the rear. Ryan and Monica kept overwatch while the last two Russians in Kira's team remained covering the pass.

The smell of burned flesh overpowered all other smells. Luckily both teams were all too familiar with it. It hung in the hazy air as they jumped over carbonized figures at every turn, amid twisted and charred hardware. The heat absorbed by the walls during the seconds following the blast now radiated from shimmering surfaces. Invisible waves of warmer air bent the surrounding colder air, distorting the picture in front of them like a mirage in the desert.

"Definitely the hot gates now," Kira said, earning a sideways glance from Stark as they negotiated the corridor, cruising through the scorched violence of a Hellfire missile.

They were inside in another minute, scanning the large, hazy interior with overlapping arcs of fire, searching for anything that moved, but the place was largely empty, just burned furniture and a handful of seared bodies thrown about by the explosion.

The entrance room connected to three corridors. Stark looked at Hagen and Martin before stretching two fingers toward the hallway to their right, ordering Larson and Sergei to the left passageway while he and Kira took the center one.

Even with the blast, there was still a reasonable chance that some-one might have survived it, perhaps locked inside some interior vault-like enclosure. So caution called for tossing concussion grenades at every turn. The echoing blasts pounded their eardrums as the combined teams cleared each chamber.

It didn't take long for Stark and Kira to realize that something was seriously wrong. Aside from the three bodies in the main hall, each space they checked was devoid of people. Kitchen, bedrooms, everything. And the other two teams reported similar results.

"What is happening, Hunter? Where is the bomb? Where is everybody?" Kira asked, walking inside the last chamber, a lab of sorts, with tables and walls packed with tools. Blood stained the floor next to a small pile of bandages and other medical supplies.

Stark stared at everything in disbelief as Kira's slim figure, cloaked in black, suppressed AK-9 in hand, inspected the closets and under each table. She poked at everything, opening cabinet doors and desk drawers, rummaging through the hardware on each lab table, but in the end there was nothing even remotely close to resembling a nu-clear bomb. Just general electronics equipment of the Radio Shack variety and assorted tools.

Nothing, he thought. *We have nothing.*

"Did they trick us?" Kira asked as they walked back into the hall-way.

"I don't see how," he replied. "You said that your tracking device pointed to this hideout."

"It did. But it has gone silent."

Stark looked down the long and hazy hallway, trying to get inside the heads of an enemy that was as crafty as it was deadly. He could not conceive of any scenario in which the Taliban would have not left itself a back door to escape, and that meant that his team just had not been able to find it.

It has to be here. Somewhere.

"What do we do now, Janki mishka?"

"The only thing we can do. We check it again. Top to bottom." She looked up. "What top?"

Before he could reply, Larson came on the ops frequency.

"Colonel . . . the place is cleared, and no one—and I mean no one—is fucking home."

115

Back Door

KANDAHAR AIRFIELD. SOUTHERN AFGHANISTAN.

"Wait for it," Maryam Gadai said, pointing at the right side of the flat screen depicting the infrared imagery captured by a Reaper drone circling above the northern face of the mountain just as the Hellfire struck. The left side of the split screen showed the actual missile strike on the southern wall. The operator sitting behind the controls had synchronized the two feeds.

Wright and Harwich flanked her as the operator slowed the video to frame-by-frame speed, showing the missile's progressive advance to the target before the left screen whited out. Corporal Darcy stood to the side, maintaining a respectful distance from the trio.

"There," she said, stretching a finger toward the right side of the screen, where a brief speck of heat—depicted as yellow on the otherwise dark purple image—glowed through the woods layering the side of the mountain, about a second after the blast.

"What's that?" Harwich asked.

"That would be the cave's arse, Glenn . . . the bloody back door."

Harwich frowned. "But where? Stark combed the place and there is no rear exit."

"This heat signature contradicts that," she said. "But it is not at the same level."

"What do you mean?" asked Wright.

She tapped the operator on the shoulder and he worked the keyboard to pull up a view of the mountain superimposed with blue contour lines marking relative height north to south. A red dot marked the location of the Hellfire target, and a green dot marked the spot of light on the northern face.

"According to the terrain map, the rear is almost two hundred feet lower than the front. So I'm guessing a hidden staircase or angled passageway? Something similar to the one behind Compound Fifty-Seven? Except this one is going down while the one in Compound Fifty-Seven went up."

Harwich and Wright exchanged a glance.

"How in the world did you figure this out?" Harwich asked.

Maryam shrugged. "What else am I supposed to do, Glenn? I'm confined to this bloody room when I'm not calling on Bill, who's out for a while from some bloody IV cocktail." Pointing at Darcy, she added, "And my cheeky babysitter is such a bore. Chap is mute."

"Throat . . . sore, eh?" Darcy mumbled in a very raspy voice, pointing at his bruised neck.

"See," Maryam said, as Harwich and Wright headed for the door to go update Duggan. "A bloody bore."

116

You're It

They found Colonel Duggan in the long line near the entrance to the DFAC adjacent to his headquarters, chatting amiably with a few marines who were also waiting their turn, and who seemed fresh out of basic.

Perhaps from the group that arrived the other night, Wright thought, deciding this was another reason he liked the colonel. Most senior officers didn't mingle with the men, much less wait in line with them, typically dispatching an aide to fetch them food. Duggan was a rare breed in any uniform.

Stopping a prudent distance from the crowd, Wright signaled him.

Duggan turned his heavyset face to them, reading glasses hanging from his neck. He sighed and walked over.

"Just lost my spot, guys," he said, pointing his Roman nose at the end of the line wrapped around the building. "And Lévesque made me skip lunch, so please make it worth my while."

They took turns briefing him, taking a couple of minutes to explain, while also giving Maryam credit for the finding.

"Glad we kept her," he said, crossing his arms, dropping his gaze for a moment, before directing it at Wright. "All right, this is what we're going to do. I need you to pull together the best damn rifle platoon in the company. No rookies. At least two rotations. I don't care if you need to steal them from other teams. You get the pick of the litter. Then I'm taking Mr. CIA here with me to brief Lévesque and get some helos to drop those marines right up the Taliban's ass on the north face of that mountain and take the damn bomb back."

"Am I leading them, sir?"

Duggan looked at Wright as if he had two heads. "What kind of dumb-ass question is that, soldier?"

"Well, sir, you said I was now in intelligence with Mr. Harwich, so I figured—"

"Like you figured to hop on that Chinook to rescue the pretty captain?"

Wright had wondered when that was going to come up. "Sir, I—"

"Does your head still hurt from the other day?"

"No, sir. All good up here."

"And the leg?"

"Leg's fine, sir."

"Then that makes you an active asset of United States Marines, son." Leaning closer, Duggan added, "And if you ask me, the best *damn* captain in the Corps. So, *yes*, you're it."

117

Smoke

QAIS KOTAL. SULAIMAN MOUNTAINS. SOUTHERN AFGHANISTAN.

Stark just had to come out for air. He was standing by the entrance to the cave, eyes closed, feeling the cold draft blowing in from the pass, whistling in his ears as it tunneled through the entryway.

They had spent the past two hours checking the stuffy and mildewed place inch by inch, searching every crevice, every wall, and every chamber. Hagen had even used his lighter to get some of the oil lamps going to preserve the batteries in their night goggles.

And still they had failed to locate anything remotely resembling the back door that the Taliban had used to escape—and which Harwich claimed had to exist, based on UAV imagery of the missile strike.

Stark watched as Kira stepped away with Larson and Martin to find a clearing large enough to get line of sight for her satellite phone so she could update Moscow. He had already briefed Harwich, who was hopefully working his way up the chain of command to update President Bush. Kira had told him that Bush had contacted President Putin a week ago to find a way to work together. Unfortunately, Putin, true to form, had blown him off.

Idiot, Stark thought, hoping that the partnership he had struck with Kira would force Putin's hand. But even if it did, there was little Putin could do to assist, given that President Bush already had KAF focused on this effort.

Stark forced world leaders out of his mind as he watched Kira walk away, while Martin hit on her and Larson laughed.

The rest of her team was somewhere up on the hill, covering them. Hagen was out of sight, probably smoking somewhere, and he had no idea where Ryan and Monica were—and maybe he didn't want to know, given the way those two kept looking at each other.

Though he couldn't really throw stones at them, given his own glass house situation with Kira, who glanced over her right shoulder and gave him a slow female wink.

Martin, who had already figured out the "Janki mishka" nickname, said to her, loudly enough for Stark to hear, "Hey, Kira can I be your Yankee cub?"

"What is cub?" Kira replied.

"It's like a little horny bear," Larson explained.

Stark shook his head at Kira's laughter echoing in the corridor, while he focused on his current dilemma: the vanishing insurgents.

"What am I missing?" he mumbled, staring at the soaring walls of granite. Kira's team had seen the courier run this way, and there was no other option, once someone entered the winding passageway, but to go inside the cave. And to rub salt into the wound, Kira's receiver no longer picked up the signal from the transmitter embedded in the replacement components, which could mean that the Taliban had discovered it, or perhaps that they were out of range.

So no sign of the hags and no way to track them.

Every second they spent here with their thumbs up their asses was a second the enemy used to get away—an enemy now armed with the components and know-how to get that nuke operational.

"Why is it always so fucking hard?" he said out loud, frustration making him tighten his grip on the MP5A1.

"That's what she just said, Colonel," Ryan blurted, walking outside with Monica, who gave him the bird.

Hagen stepped out next, using his lips to pull a Sobranie Classic from his pack. He cupped it while working the lighter, next to Ryan and Monica. Monica's TAC-338 was slung behind her back, her arms crossed in apparent frustration.

"So, does he actually speak?" Monica asked Ryan, tilting her head at the former Navy SEAL as he took a long drag and exhaled through his nostrils.

Stark sighed and looked away.

"Once," Ryan said. "In Venezuela."

"Colombia," Stark corrected.

"Same thing. Anyway, we're deep in the jungle, late at night. Third day on some Agency job," Ryan continued, while Hagen shook his head and kept smoking. "So Mickey here has watch while the rest of us are getting some shut-eye. But somewhere in the middle of the night he needs to go. You know?"

Monica dropped her brows at him. "Take a piss?"

"No. Number two. So he takes a bag, some TP, and walks out a hundred yards to get some privacy. Next thing you know, we're woken up by what sounds like a woman screaming at the top of her lungs. But it's Mickey here. Apparently a tiger came out of the bush and caught him, pants down, dick swinging, and—"

"It was a jaguar," Stark corrected again. "No tigers in Colombia."

"Hey," Ryan said, "the man here started screaming '*Tigre! Tigre!*' That's 'tiger' in Spanish."

"That's what the locals call jaguars," Stark said. He looked over at Monica and whispered, "*Jaguar.*"

Hagen slowly nodded.

"So," Ryan continued, "this Venezuelan tiger is staring at Mickey, who's still squatting over his shit bag, screaming at the top of his lungs—so much that the tiger does a one-eighty and runs the hell away. That day we figured out why the man's so quiet. Mickey here's like Mike Tyson—scary, intimidating, and damn strong, but with a voice that doesn't match the package. Go figure."

Stark sighed while Hagen just took a long drag and exhaled through his nostrils.

"True story, huh, Mickey?" Ryan said.

Hagen remained impassive, the Russian cigarette wedged between the middle and index fingers of his left hand while his right remained glued to the pistol grip of the MP5A1, shooting finger resting on the trigger guard.

Just then, Martin returned alone from around the bend in the corridor and stretched a thumb over his shoulder. "Your girlfriend's back there calling her people, sir."

Stark looked at Hagen. "I guess we both gotta take some shit today."

Martin paused. "Who's been giving Mickey shit?"

"This guy," said Monica, pointing at Ryan. "Told us the Venezuelan tiger story."

Martin said, "Bet he didn't tell you his Romeo story."

Hagen actually smiled, while Stark rolled his eyes.

"Don't you have some place to be, Danny?" Ryan asked.

"No, he actually doesn't," said Monica, also smiling. "I want to hear this."

Danny unwrapped a lollipop, pointed it at Ryan, and said, "We're down in Mexico, south of Juárez, going after this drug boss. Agency job . . . like a year ago."

"Eight months," Stark said.

"That's right. So we took him out—Ryan here did it. Headshot from like a thousand yards."

"Seventeen hundred," Ryan corrected.

"Whatever," Martin continued. "Bastard's dead. Mission accomplished. So we're driving back to the border in two pieces-of-shit Kia SUVs. I mean we're really hauling ass, 'cause any moment now the whole Mexican cartel is going to figure out what happened and is gonna come looking for us. I'm in front with this character here," Martin said, pointing at Ryan again. "And the colonel and the rest of the gang are behind us in the second SUV. Remember that, Mickey?"

Hagen nodded, taking a drag, while Stark said, "Last time we let Ryan drive."

"Damn right," Martin said. "Pretty Boy here is driving, but he's also checking texts from some señorita he met in Juárez on the way down—you know, the ones that love you long time by the hour?"

"C'mon, man!" Ryan protested, while Monica crossed her arms and shook her head at him. "She was the daughter of—"

"Hey, if it looks like a duck and quacks like a duck . . . well . . ." Martin said.

"That's disgusting, Ryan."

"I'm telling you, she wasn't a—"

"Anyway," Martin said, "Ryan is sexting and don't see this massive bull that's coming charging from some field to our right."

"A bull?" Monica asked.

"Yeah. Big fucking *toro*. But Pretty Boy here has his eyes off the road. So it smashes into our tin can, and I mean *hard*, man. The bastard rips the roof right off with its horns before going airborne and landing somewhere on the other side of the road."

"Oh my God," Monica said.

"And while we're all wondering where the roof went, this Mexican guy comes running out of the same field screaming, 'Romeo! Romeo! *Gringos hijos de puta!* You kill Romeo!'"

"That was the name of the bull?" Monica asked.

"Yeah. Why? You thought we call him Romeo because of his pretty mug?" Martin said. He tried to grab Ryan by the chin, but Ryan moved away.

Monica shrugged.

"So get this," Martin continues. "The little Mexican bastard wants us to pay for his big-ass toro laying dead on the road, never mind that *it* hit *us*. But it's Mexico, right, and it's also the middle of cartel country, so all logic goes out the window. By now, several of his amigos have caught up to him and are blocking the road while pulling out their machetes, so the colonel, Mickey, and the chief get out with their guns. But we don't really want to use them, 'cause nothing draws more attention from the cartel than shooting guns. Plus, the whole idea is to get away quietly, right?"

"So what happened?" Monica asked.

"Bull returned from the dead," Ryan said. "That's what happened."

"Yep," Martin said. "Romeo suddenly wakes up, stands, shakes his big-ass head, and stares at us for a moment, apparently confused, before taking off toward the field across the road. So there go all of the Mexicans, running after it and screaming. 'Romeo! Come back! Romeo!' Right, Mickey?"

Hagen took another long drag, nodded, and exhaled skyward.

"Look," Ryan pleaded with Monica, "the girl really wasn't a—"

"Hey," Monica said to Hagen, ignoring him. "Do that again."

Hagen just stared at her.

"Exhaling smoke. Do it again."

The former Navy SEAL complied, directing a puff of smoke at the narrow sky above the parallel rock walls while Stark, Martin, and Ryan looked on.

Instead of rising, the haze streamed right into the cave, as if in a wind tunnel.

Well, I'll be—

"Your knife," Monica said, pointing at Hagen's massive twelve-inch serrated weapon that could qualify as a double-edge machete. The fixed blue steel blade had a gut hook on the back of the tip, designed to inflict more damage on the way out than on the way in, by latching on to entrails. "May I?"

Hagen looked at Stark, who nodded.

Unsheathing it, he handed it to Monica by the rubber finger-groove handle. She took it, feeling the weight and balance, before looking back at Hagen and smiling.

"Nice. Who makes this?"

"Custom," said Ryan. "Some dude in Germany made it just for him. What was his name?"

"Boker," said Stark. "In Solingen. And it's too big for you, Cruz. What do you have in mind?"

Ignoring him, she looked about her, locating a piece of half-burned green canvas that had belonged to one of the men guarding the corridor. She used the Boker to slice several two-inch-wide strips, each about two feet long.

Stark looked on with interest as she wrapped one of the strips around the knife's gut hook before locating an oil lamp, opening it, and dipping the tip into it.

She threw the other strips over her shoulder before walking back up to Hagen. "How about a light, cowboy?"

Hagen grinned, producing his lighter and igniting the soaked canvas.

The makeshift torch worked perfectly, producing a bright yellow flame that immediately bent in the direction of the breeze sweeping into the cave.

"All right, boys," she said, heading back in with the fire pointing the way. "What do you say we go find us a nuclear bomb?"

118

Night of Nights

KANDAHAR AIRFIELD. SOUTHERN AFGHANISTAN.

Eight Sikorsky UH-60 Black Hawks leaped off the ground, powered by twin General Electric T700 turboshafts, soaring over the tarmac in the early evening breeze, dark shapes vanishing in the western sky.

Captain John Wright removed one of several twenty-five-round magazines secured to his vest and inserted it underneath his Heckler & Koch UMP45 submachine gun before pulling the bolt mechanism to chamber the first round.

"We're in for one hell of a night, sir!" Sergeant Gaudet shouted over the rotor noise, while taking his seat next to Wright in the lead bird. They formed the tip of NATO's spear, an elite rifle platoon deployed to encircle the location identified by Maryam as the likely escape point of the insurgents from their mountain hideout. The gunnery sergeant held a standard M4 carbine, already loaded with a thirty-round box magazine, as did some of his men. The rest were armed with either M249 light machine guns or the heavier M240L machine gun. A dozen more rifle platoons from the marines, as well as several units from the Rangers and the Canadian Army, were being deployed to lower altitudes by the larger Chinooks, in an all-out effort to seal off the area.

"Yeah," Wright replied, looking back at the airfield as countless helicopters took to the skies. It was quite a sight to see. "A hell of a night indeed, Gunny."

Everyone in Lévesque's staff was now painfully aware of the strong possibility that the insurgents could vanish inside other caves in those mountains. So time was of the essence, and that's where Wright and his handpicked team came in.

Typically it took only four Black Hawks to haul a rifle platoon of forty-three men and their gear into battle, each carrying a maximum of eleven soldiers. But the helos were only half-loaded this evening in anticipation of the high-altitude insertion, marked on the contour map at thirteen thousand feet, which would place them two miles from that speckle of heat in the UAV infrared video.

Meaning the enemy could be waiting for them.

And there were other problems besides a night insertion with hostiles in the area, including dropping into largely uncharted terrain. The face of that mountain just north of Qais Kotal was so damn inaccessible and located so far west of KAF that it had not merited NATO's attention until now. And while there were plenty of UAVs circling the place, their cameras could only do so much, especially at night and in a mountainous terrain so heavily wooded that Vaccaro had told him it reminded her of Colorado Springs.

Wright stared out the side window and into a sea of stars and a silver moon, but in his mind he saw the feisty air force captain as he had left her at the edge of the tarmac. She had not been happy about him heading back into the line of fire, but she certainly understood, especially given the stakes.

Whatever it fucking takes.

Wright grinned when he thought about her pulling off her IVs and crawling out of bed with her pale ass exposed in that hospital gown, red hair swinging, cursing like a sailor when a nurse had tried to stop her.

But there was something different about her—something he couldn't quite put his finger on. He had gone through her debrief in detail, piecing together a most amazing survival story, including her encounter with that Shinwari tribe that knew Harwich. It was the stuff of legends. But there was something missing in her account—or someone. And whatever that was, it had altered the way she looked at him.

He sighed, staring into the cold darkness while feeling a chill gripping his gut, suddenly uncertain about their future. But then again, fighting in Afghanistan meant he couldn't be certain about the next hour—even the next minute. No one could.

But if the Good Lord did indeed allow John Wright to survive this night of nights, plus the remaining 107 nights before the end of his rotation, he wondered if maybe, just maybe, he still had a chance with Laura Vaccaro.

119

Every Last One of Them

KANDAHAR AIRFIELD. SOUTHERN AFGHANISTAN.

Sipping her third energy drink in an hour, Vaccaro remained at the edge of the ramp, gazing west, until the last set of red and green navigation lights faded in the ocean of darkness separating KAF from the Sulaimans.

Waiting for the mild painkillers to kick in and take the edge off her throbbing shoulder and forehead, Vaccaro stared at the spot where they had disappeared. She hugged herself, but in her mind she didn't see John Wright as he had left her, all geared up for violence.

She saw Aaron Peretz, her Kidon, as she had left him on that cliff, and she silently cursed the fact that she could not get him out of her mind.

There was something about that man—something that Wright, with all his charms, attentions, and even bravery, had not managed to stir.

Vaccaro was angry, not just at her conflicting feelings but also at the fact that she had been grounded until the fight surgeon cleared her. That decision had left her standing at the edge of the flight line while a dozen A-10s took off in support of the troops.

I should be with them.

But orders were orders, and that meant she wasn't going anywhere, and neither was her new bird, one of the new A-10Cs incorporating upgraded electronics for work at night and in bad weather. The advanced close air support aircraft was even fully fueled, ready to go at a moment's notice, as were all active planes on this ramp.

She sighed. The queasiness from the anesthesia had already worn off, and once those Tylenol-Codeine tablets kicked in, she would be good enough to grab her helmet, climb in, and get back in the war.

But orders were . . .

Never stop fighting, Red One One. Never.

And make your life matter.

There was that Mossad man again, staring at her with his dying eyes.

"But how?" she mumbled.

If you feel the urge to do something, then go see Harwich in the war room.

Wright replaced Aaron's face as she recalled the marine captain's parting words, just minutes ago, before he followed his men into the waiting Black Hawks.

So she did, stomping away toward a nondescript shipping container located near the rear of the USMC headquarters.

But when she tried the door, it was locked.

She stared at the digital lock, frowned, and knocked three times.

The door opened, but instead of Harwich, the Pakistani woman she had seen by Gorman's side at the ICU stuck her head out.

"Hiya!" she said, before dropping her thick brows at the bandage on Vaccaro's forehead and over her right temple. "Bollocks . . . Please tell me the cheeky bastards who did that are dead."

Vaccaro nodded. "Every last one of them."

120

Torch

**QAIS KOTAL. SULAIMAN MOUNTAINS.
SOUTHERN AFGHANISTAN.**

Stark had read about this and had even seen it in the movies, but he never thought it would work so precisely. The tip of the flame pointed the way at every intersection, steering the group toward one of the rear chambers, which he and Larson had already scrubbed. Twice.

He looked about the room, the torch splashing rock walls with a yellowish glare. This had been the place with the large tables loaded with trays housing various tools, presumably to work on the nuclear device—though at a glance they could have belonged in your typical mechanic's shop. He scanned a variety of screwdrivers, wrenches, wire cutters, pliers, and socket sets. There was also a hydraulic lift and tons of odds and ends, including hardware he had seen before at Radio Shack—and at IED factories—like timers, detonators, and wires, but no explosives in sight. Some of the tools hung from make-shift wooden peg-boards on two walls, next to an acetylene torch and some power tools connected via an inverter to a set of large truck batteries. As with every chamber in this cave, the wood here was a bit singed from the intense heat following the missile strike, but because this was the last room in the beehive-like interior, it had sustained minimum damage.

Stark saw no sign of any door or exit hatch, nothing to support the UAV images reported by Harwich—until Monica followed the flame to the back corner, where two peg-boards met.

It was there, in the half-inch vertical gap between the peg-boards, that the tip of the torch flickered nearly horizontally, as if fighting the end of a vacuum cleaner. Stark frowned, not certain how he had missed it when inspecting this room an hour ago.

Placing his fingers along the crevice, he felt the air rushing between his fingers. Pressing his palm against one peg-board, he pushed firmly, but it felt solid, anchored to the rock. However, the second peg-board, and its supporting wall, gave a little under pressure, widening the gap to almost an inch. He also noticed that the whole lab table, also secured to the wall, moved as well.

"Ryan, Danny, Mickey, get in here," he said, pressing his weight into the table while his guys also leaned their bulks against it, and the whole thing, peg-board, table, and even hanging tools, swung inward.

It was another hidden door, like the one in Compound 57. Almost five feet wide and as tall as the ten-foot ceiling, it was spring-loaded, designed to swing back into a closed position.

"Clever bastards," he mumbled as they pushed it fully open.

Monica stepped forward, the torch held high, while Stark and Hagen covered her with the MP5A1s in case of hidden rebels. The yellowish light revealed a set of hazy stairs cut straight into the rock, going down into darkness. Everything smelled of smoke and cordite.

"So the shock wave must have pushed the door open for the duration of the blast before the spring-loaded mechanism swung it back," Stark said.

"But long enough for the hot gases to reach the bottom of the stairs and get captured by the passing UAV's thermal imaging camera," Monica added, completing his comment.

Stark just stared at her, nodding slightly, before turning to

Hagen and saying, "Mickey, Danny, go tell the chief to get word to KAF that we've found it, and get everybody over here. We'll meet you down wherever the hell this leads. Cruz, Ryan, with me."

Then he rushed down the stairs.

121

Into the Fire

SULAIMAN MOUNTAINS. SOUTHERN AFGHANISTAN.

They flew in from the east, very low and very fast, following the rising terrain, leaving the main force behind somewhere down the mountain. Turboshafts worked overtime to compress the thinning air into turbine chambers, mixing it with jet fuel to propel eight Black Hawks above ten thousand feet.

Wright did a final check of his gear. The dim red glow of the cabin's light—designed to illuminate the interior without impairing night vision—washed the camouflaged faces of his men. Hands on their weapons, eyes glinting with the shared determination of launching into something worth doing, the warriors maintained the impassive demeanor of tried-and-true veterans.

Calm. Focused. Ready.

He turned back to the picture beyond the window, a nearly solid layer of pines sprinkled with fresh powder rushing just below the helicopter's belly.

Vaccaro had been right. The place did indeed look like Colorado Springs in early winter, after the first blizzard—except for the bearded insurgents hidden beneath that tranquil sea of snowy boughs.

"*Two minutes!*" came the warning from the copilot over the intercom system.

Feeling the adrenaline rush in anticipation of battle, Wright flexed his hands, protected by a pair of leather gloves with hard-shell knuckles, just the tips of his fingers exposed, to retain dexterity.

He clutched the Heckler & Koch submachine gun, feeling confident in his ability to place all twenty-five .45 ACP rounds in the detachable magazine with crazy precision from any stance—even running—and in any lighting conditions.

"Goggles," he told Gaudet.

"Marines! Goggles down!" the Louisiana native shouted.

The men complied, lowering their helmet-mounted AN/PVS-14 monocular night vision devices over their nondominant eyes. The single-eye design provided superior depth perception and night adaptation, leaving their shooting eyes free for a matching AN/PVS-14 attached to every weapon.

"Sixty seconds!"

The side gunners trained their M240Ds on the incoming clearing, a rocky outcrop just wide enough for one bird at a time. The machine guns were mounted on pivot arms and fitted with front and rear sights and a trigger group that accommodated the spade grip devices, and were fed by extra-large magazine boxes filled with disintegrating M13 linked belts of 7.62×51mm cartridges.

Wright looked at one of his men, who was armed with an M240L, the lighter version of those side-mounted guns, incorporating titanium into the design to achieve an 18 percent weight reduction.

Filling his lungs with the cold air streaming through the side openings as the gunners scanned the LZ, Wright waited for the pilot to flare the Black Hawk a foot over the rocky ledge, then he jumped out the side door and ran to the trees. He took less than fifteen seconds to cover the fifty feet of clearing, by which time the first Black Hawk was already out of the way and the second was rushing into its place, dropping its load.

Ten seconds per helo. Eight helos.

Eighty seconds, Wright thought, his UMP45 aimed at a forest painted in a palette of green, as he searched for anything that moved.

That was plenty of time for insurgents in the area to reach the LZ and unleash hell on the incoming Black Hawks at their most vulnerable moment. So the marines spread efficiently around the edge of the clearing, progressively covering each bird until the entire platoon had safely infiltrated the woods and the helicopters vanished down the mountain.

Automatically breaking up into their three rifle squads, led by a three-stripe sergeant, the marines fell in line while Wright had Gaudet call it in.

Speaking into his MBITR, the gunnery sergeant said, "Bravo Niner Six, Six Six Zulu on the ground."

The reply came a few seconds later, as the transmission had to go through a pair of UAVs circling the top of the mountain and acting as relay stations. *"Roger that Six Six Zulu. Proceed to target. Be advised we still don't have eyes on hostiles."*

"Of course," Wright whispered to himself, though loud enough for Gaudet to turn his head. "Where would be the fun in that?"

"Sir?"

"Nothing, Gunny. Let's just go finish this," he replied, staring at the picture before him, a fresh layer of snow mixed with pine needles angling up at around twenty degrees under a virgin forest of stone pines.

It could actually be a Christmas postcard—peaceful, serene, even beautiful—if it weren't for the fact that somewhere beyond the range of his night optics hid a whole lot of crazies armed with a nuclear weapon.

122

Back in Business

The mountain wind brought tears to Stark's eyes, and as he inhaled, the chill seemed to squeeze his chest. But the air wasn't just cold. It smelled of burned wood.

MP5A1 at the ready, he stepped out of the cave at the bottom of the stairs and onto a bed of singed pine needles, noticing the nearly circular pattern around the exit.

Monica extinguished the torch before exiting what had been a long and winding series of descents, sections of steps between long inclines cut in the rock. Ryan followed as the three of them stared out into dark wilderness.

Stark peered through the night vision scope mounted on the MP5A1. Monica and Ryan already had their night vision monoculars out and were scanning the scenery.

To his right, the mountainside slanted into green darkness at a shallower angle than the hill to their left. The dim silver moonlight filtering through the canopy showed that the hill led to the same gorge they had seen on the southern face, which had been lined with river rocks after a thousand-foot drop. But it wasn't until he stood here that Stark got an appreciation for the strategic value of this place high up in the mountains, secretly bridging the country's northern plains with the southern section of the Sulaimans skirting Kandahar and Lashkar Gah. It was the ideal route to run guns and soldiers between the northern and southern war theaters.

And who knows how many other passages like this one exist in these mountains.

Stark believed in his core that such secret compounds, mountain passes, and the tunnels that connected them all were the primary reason why the Taliban could never stay defeated. NATO could pound the hell out of it for months—just as the Soviets had in the 1980s—driving them out of a region or a town, but a month later the rebels were back in force.

Monica tossed the smoldering rags from the end of Hagen's knife before wiping it against her pants, walking to the edge of the burned forest floor.

Kneeling, she loosened pine needles with the tip of the knife.

"What are you thinking, Cruz?" Stark asked, while Ryan took a knee next to her.

She lowered the monocular and pointed the Boker knife at the trail of crushed pine needles in the direction of the abyss. "Some went this way."

Peering through his scope, Stark made out what looked like a goat trail disappearing into the chasm, likely leading to switchbacks down to the riverbed.

"And some went that way." Ryan stretched a gloved finger at the hillside to his right.

Stark stood between them, scanning the woods with the sight on the Heckler & Koch submachine gun.

No one in sight.

"Bastards are long gone," Monica said, reading his mind. "But which group has the bomb?"

"Sierra Echo One, Six Six Zulu. SitRep."

Stark heard the marine contingent through the earpiece connected to his MBITR, as did Ryan and Monica, who stood up.

"Six Six Zulu, Echo One at northern egress."

"Six Six Zulu is two miles northeast of your position. Negative enemy contact."

"Roger," Stark replied.

The rest of his team, as well as the Russians, joined him ten minutes later, and everyone gathered around Kira as she activated her receiver, which came to life with a series of beeps.

She paused, removing her helmet and turning the GPS screen over so everyone could see it. The location of the hidden transmitter was overlaid on a color GPS map.

"It is picking up the signal again," she said, zooming in on the map.

"Makes sense," Stark said. "The cave must have blocked it."

"Da," Kira said. "And it is moving . . . *that* way, one and a half miles from us." She pointed in the direction of the gentle grade, away from the gorge.

"That's the same direction Wright and his platoon are coming from. Chief, relay those coordinates to Six Six Zulu right away. The insurgents are just a half mile from them. Keep updating them every minute until they make contact."

While Larson got on the horn with Wright and his marines, Stark divided the team into pairs to head downhill. Leaning over to Kira he asked, "What did your boss have to say?"

She shook her head. "He was busy, so I left a message with Anton."

"Anton?"

"His boy."

"Son?"

"No, Janki mishka. His aide, but a boy just the same. No hair on his *yaytsas*."

"His what?"

"His balls."

Before Stark could reply, Kira headed out.

123

Picks and Shovels

SULAIMAN MOUNTAINS. SOUTHERN AFGHANISTAN.

They advanced methodically, the forest painted in shades of green as he surveyed it through the scope of his UMP45 submachine gun, safety off, fire selector on single-shot mode. Gaudet covered his right side, closely followed by one of his three rifle squads, Six Six Zulu Alpha. Squads Beta and Charlie flanked Alpha by a predetermined distance of fifty feet in each direction. All squads had split up into their respective fire teams of four marines each at fifteen-foot intervals. Together, Six Six Zulu formed a mobile and unified offensive fighting force of mixed-caliber weapons more than two hundred feet wide, advancing uphill.

Wright had already entered into his wrist-mounted GPS the coordinates provided by Chief Larson, marking the location of the enemy, indicating it was less than a half mile away and closing.

The woods became sparser now, allowing moonlight in, which shimmered over the layer of freshly fallen snow.

Pausing, which made the entire line pause, Wright glanced at the surrounding peaks, now visible through breaks in the trees, before looking over at Gaudet in the greenish twilight of their optically enhanced world.

"Get the men into static DFPs. We're going to wait for them right here. And hold fire for my signal."

Gaudet conveyed the order to the squad sergeants, who relayed it to the rifle team leaders, and within a minute the entire platoon had dug in behind boulders and trees.

He received a new set of coordinates from Chief Larson that told him the Tangos were less than fifteen hundred feet away and moving steadily in his direction.

Wright settled behind a cluster of ice-slick rocks half buried by pine needles and fallen boughs amid patches of snow. Settling his shooting eye behind the AN/PVS-14 monocular atop the UMP45, he focused on his fire arc of roughly ten degrees to either side of his direct line of sight. Anything beyond that was the responsibility of either Gaudet to his right or the corporal to his left.

Any moment now, he thought.

Cold and dry air, both chilling and invigorating, filled his lungs as he relaxed his breathing. The thing about the incoming enemy was that Wright had no idea of its size. All Chief Larson could provide was the location of the GPS transmitter, and KAF had no eyes on them because of the tree coverage, so it could be just one insurgent or a whole bunch of the bastards.

His index finger caressed the trigger as seconds ticked by, while he scanned the edge of his optics' range, a greenish terrain dotted with sparse trunks backdropped by darkness.

The murky background suddenly shifted as a shadow slowly detached itself from a tree: a man in loose clothes and a turban, wielding an AK-47, moving in a deep crouch, slowly but deliberately. Then another. And another.

He risked a scan beyond his assigned arc of fire and noticed others emerging through the darkness, counting at least a dozen, probably more.

As he returned to his assigned arc, Wright noticed that a couple of the men were holding not AK-47s but picks and shovels.

He frowned, just as Gaudet leaned over and mumbled what Wright was already thinking.

"Sir, who the hell brings picks and shovels to a gunfight?"

But a moment later, he understood why.

124

Flanks

Stark and Kira paused the moment gunfire echoed down the mountain, a blend of UMPs, M4 carbines, and M249 and M240 machine guns, mixed with AK-47s.

"It's begun," he whispered, following the trail of what looked to be at least twenty or thirty men, perhaps more, moving in five columns spread about a dozen feet apart.

Once more divided into pairs, Stark and Kira tracked the rightmost trail while Monica and Ryan handled the next one, then Hagen and Martin, Larson and Sergei, and finally the last two Spetsnaz soldiers at the other end.

"Our trail is breaking right, Janki mishka," she whispered back in the dark, her slim black figure glued to his left flank, the suppressed AK-9 up by her shooting eye, polymer stock pressed against her right shoulder.

Stark nodded. Their mark's trail was indeed veering farther and father to the right, away from the other four columns of rebels.

"But the signal is coming from over there," Kira said, pointing in the direction of the other tracks, which were headed into the firefight downhill.

"I know," he replied, spotting the crushed pine needles and broken branches marking the rightmost group's path. "But these assholes might just be breaking right to try and flank our guys down there."

Kira hesitated, obviously ordered to follow the signal from the embedded transmitter. "Okay, Janki mishka," she finally said. "I guess there are too many chefs in that kitchen."

Deciding to let that one go, Stark spoke into his MBITR. "Chief, looks like we're breaking right to follow our guys, who might be trying to flank the marines. Stay with the main force. The signal is coming from one of your columns. Hit them hard from the rear."

"*Roger that.*"

Stark and Kira pressed on, rushing across a narrow clearing to a series of switchbacks that veered up the side of the mountain but headed east, circling the fighting.

And that's when Stark heard the shots coming from just beyond the next bend in the trail, which led to a ledge overlooking the battle in progress.

Wright knew something was seriously wrong less than thirty seconds into the battle, as he fired at the incoming insurgents. Some fell, but the rest took immediate cover and returned fire.

It wasn't the shots they fired back at his marines that bothered him. The counterattack was expected, just as he expected his men to overwhelm the enemy with their superior weaponry and tactics.

It was the enemy, however, that was surprising him.

The first marine, a corporal with Bravo Squad on Wright's left flank, fell on his side. Then another man collapsed—also from Bravo Squad.

And again, falling on his side.

Damn!

The soldiers were not snapping back as if shot from the front. They were being fire upon from . . .

"Gunny! We're being flanked!"

"Where?" Gaudet said, firing another three rounds into a man hidden behind a boulder, the M4 carbine reports deafening.

Shots zoomed overhead, most from the enemy ahead, but one walloped into the tree just to his right.

"Up there!" Wright shouted, looking toward the wooded terrain rising to their left, spotting the distant muzzle flashes. "Somewhere the hell up there!" As more shots blasted overhead from that vantage point and others punched the ground just behind him, he shouted, "Call it in! Get a damn Hawg over there!"

125

The Stars

SULAIMAN MOUNTAINS. SOUTHERN AFGHANISTAN.

Akhtar watched bin Laden work the Dragunov sniper rifle with unparalleled skill. In the first ten seconds he had eliminated two enemy soldiers from a distance of at least five hundred meters—and at night.

The six men they had brought with them were also firing in the direction of the enemy's muzzle flashes, clearly visible across the dark meadow below them. But at that distance their AK-47s lacked the accuracy of the Russian sniper rifle. So they offset exceeding their weapons' effective range of three hundred meters by unleashing volleys of 7.62×39mm rounds in full automatic fire, emptying magazine after magazine into the cluster of marines spread along the length of the mountainside.

Akhtar also fired his Kalashnikov at the maximum cyclic rate of six hundred rounds per minute, emptying thirty-round magazines in seconds, reloading, and firing again.

He glanced over at Akaa, perched over a branch at the far end of the ledge, which gave him a nearly perfect line of sight into the—

One of his men dropped his rifle, hands clutching his bleeding chest as he tumbled over. Then another.

What in Allah's name is happening!

He turned in the direction of the threat, catching a glimpse of two figures firing suppressed weapons.

The world seemed to slow to a crawl for Akhtar as he stared in disbelief at the incoming enemy, at their bulky silencers, while his AK-47 remained pointed in the wrong direction. He knew it would be impossible to bring it around in time.

But he still had to try.

Just before two rounds stabbed his chest.

Akhtar fell to his knees, dropping the assault rifle, his vision tunneling as his body went numb.

He finally collapsed on his back, staring at the stars. He was having difficulty breathing.

And that's when he realized he was choking on his own blood. But he noticed that the pain was gone, all the pain—the cramps, the spasms, the incessant craving for another shot of opium.

Akhtar found himself suddenly at peace—at peace with the stars.

126

Elvis

SULAIMAN MOUNTAINS. SOUTHERN AFGHANISTAN.

Stark and Kira had divided the enemy, capitalizing on the element of surprise.

She took on the closest rebels while he focused on the farthest ones, whose flank was exposed as they focused their attention on Six Six Zulu's DFPs.

The MP5A1 with the night vision scope made his job easier, allowing him to align a target while running, firing two shots into each center of mass before switching targets.

Kira did the same, mowing down the enemy efficiently.

It didn't take long to neutralize all seven of them on that ledge, all wielding AK-47s.

Stark paused, scanning the kill zone next to Kira before speaking into his MBITR. "Six Six Zulu, Sierra Echo One. The threat to your flank is neutralized."

"Roger that, Echo One. We'll call off the airstrike on that mountainside."

"Yeah, Six Zulu. That would be appreciated."

He turned to Kira, who was staring at one of the insurgents who was still alive, though not for long. Blood spurted from his mouth as he exhaled. The right side of his face was badly scarred from old burns, as was his neck and exposed upper chest.

"Friend of yours?" he asked.

She didn't reply. She knelt in front of him, looking a bit spellbound, mouth wide open. Her gloved right hand reached for a large gold ring dangling from the end of a leather strap on the man's neck.

Stark blinked and narrowed his eyes at the ring, which looked awfully like the one in the image that Harwich had—

"This," she told the insurgent, grabbing the ring and tearing it off his neck, "belonged to my *father.*" She waved the ring in his face before aiming the AK-9 at his forehead. "You understand, you piece of shit? This is my father's! My *father's!*"

The wounded rebel stared at her, before mumbling, "Shuravi. Shuravi."

"That's right. I'm that *Shuravi's* daughter, and I hope you rot in hell, you son of a—"

A single shot rang out from the far side of the ledge.

Stark dropped to the ground on instinct, rolling away just as a tall man hauling a sniper rifle crawled down from a stone pine. He recognized the weapon's wooden skeleton stock. It was a Russian SVD Dragunov.

From a distance of just forty feet, Stark stared at the insurgent, bringing his MP5A1 around, but then he momentarily froze, not believing his eyes.

He recognized the beard, the prominent nose, the full lips and high brows, the tall and thin frame—all matching the physical description etched in the mind of every American soldier deployed to Afghanistan.

That's . . . impossible!

Stark blinked, thinking his eyes were playing tricks on him. But it was definitely the elusive terrorist mastermind, the architect of 9/11—the world's most wanted fugitive.

And as he watched him take off into the forest, the Dragunov in his hands, Stark lined him up, firing three shots aimed at the middle of his back.

Osama bin Laden shifted with unexpected agility, almost reading his mind. The 9mm rounds sparked off a boulder, missing him altogether.

Dammit!

Stark started to go after him, then he spotted Kira's figure sprawled on the ground a few feet from the dying rebel. He glared at the vanishing figure of bin Laden, then back at Kira. The bastard had shot her with the powerful sniper rifle.

He shifted his gaze between the blood pooling under her and the terrorist's silhouette as he disappeared in the woods. If he went after bin Laden, Kira could bleed out in under a minute.

Making his decision, and hoping he didn't live to regret it, he jumped over the dying rebel with blood foaming in his mouth and reached her side, turning her over.

"I forgot . . . to duck," she whispered, eyelids fluttering, lips quivering. The round, a powerful 7.62×54mm, had enough energy to breach her battle dress just above her left breast.

"Hang in there, baby," he whispered, unzipping the armored fabric from her neck down to the side of her midriff, exposing her right breast and the intricate compass rose tattoo surrounding it—now smeared in blood.

The slug had punched her just above the polyethylene plate, which was shaped like a brassiere, following the contour of her breast while protecting her heart. Still, the Kevlar and titanium woven fibers had stripped enough energy from the 181-grain bullet to keep it from shattering her shoulder and even severing the arm. But in the process of absorbing the impact, the battle dress had spread the energy across her upper torso, shocking multiple webs of nerves. To Kira, it felt as if someone had kicked her in the ribs.

Upon closer inspection, he saw that the slug had managed to lodge itself under her clavicle bone, so the first order of business was stanching the hemorrhage before she went into shock.

Reaching for QuikClot gauze from his survival pack, Stark pressed it against the wound.

Kira cringed and muttered something in Russian, her chest heaving, hands clutching his arms, wide-eyed stare on him, lips quivering as she took the pain.

"Easy there," he said, unwrapping a fentanyl lollipop. "Suck on this."

Kira complied, rolling it in her mouth. The chemical had an immediate effect, relaxing her. She breathed deeply, releasing his arms, allowing Stark to work the wound.

He packed more QuikClot gauze into the bullet hole, letting the hemostatic agent in the fabric stem the blood flow, before using the remainder of the roll to wrap the shoulder.

He checked her vitals, and they seemed strong enough. But she seemed out of it, a mix of the shock and the strong opiate.

Satisfied, he partially zipped the battle dress back up and over the dressing to secure it in place before speaking into the MBITR.

"Six Six Zulu, Sierra Echo One. I need a winch for one wounded."

"*Roger Echo One. Three helos are already on the way.*"

Stark glanced at his GPS before looking in the direction where bin Laden had escaped, and said, "On second thought, Sierra Echo One is requesting an airstrike east of the following coordinates." He provided them and added, "Drop everything you've got. Elvis is up there."

"*Say again, Echo One.*"

"Elvis. Confirmed sighting," he said. "Bastard shot Kira. Torch the hillside."

"*Roger that.*"

Slinging his MP5A1 behind his back, he picked Kira up, cradling her like a baby.

She leaned her head into his chest, and as Stark doubled back to get away from the incoming strike and to find his team, he noticed the leather strap clutched in her right hand.

And the gold class ring dangling from it.

127

Angels

Akhtar stared at the starry heaven as his mind grew dizzy, cloudy. He had seen the woman dressed in black take the gold ring and scream words he did not understand . . . except for one: *father.*

She had waved the ring while shouting the word over and over. *Father! Father!*

Or did he imagine that? Was his mind simply losing focus as he bled out alone on that hillside?

But a moment later, after the infidels left him to die of his wounds on this sacred mountain, as his vision blurred and it became impossible to breathe, Mullah Akhtar Baqer thought he heard a choir of angels humming in the night, welcoming him to paradise.

However, it was just the distant sound of jet engines on full afterburners echoing across the Sulaimans.

128

FLIR

"What the hell is that?" Vaccaro asked, staring at a sequence of UAV thermal images from the bottom of the gorge adjacent to the northern face of the mountain and about two thousand feet below the rear exit of the cave.

"*That* is what I wanted to show you," Maryam said, working the keyboard in the CIA war room. The operator assigned by Duggan had been called away to NATO headquarters to assist the small army of specialists tracking all of the information streaming from the dozen UAVs circling the many battles in progress. In addition to the firefight at the top of the mountain, where Wright's platoon was still engaged in a fight of their own, the main force deployed down the mountain was encountering heavy opposition. In all, there were close to a thousand soldiers, plus air support, duking it out with as many insurgents across almost fifty square miles of mountain—at least based on the reports reaching Lévesque's staff, which included Duggan and Harwich.

Vaccaro flexed her shoulder while leaning over Maryam, noticing that it hurt a tad less than it had thirty minutes ago—and so did her forehead—meaning the Tylenol-Codeine was working its magic. The pain was still there, but it was now manageable. And best of all, she had done it without resorting to stronger meds that, although far better at tackling the pain, would have impaired her ability to think.

"What do you think that is?" Maryam added, pointing at a sequence of images captured before that particular UAV was rerouted to the main battle down the mountain.

Unlike night vision devices, which amplified the available light to produce greenish images, thermal cameras, referred to as forward looking infrared, created pictures from heat, not visible light. But an FLIR lens detected more than just heat. It captured and showed minute *differences* in heat—as little as $0.01°$ Fahrenheit—displaying it in the shades of gray painted on the screen.

"I think that's people, eh?" offered Corporal Darcy in his raspy voice.

"Possibly," Vaccaro said. "But what are they doing down there?"

"Hard to tell," Maryam said, advancing the images depicting what could be—maybe with a little imagination—the figures of rebels, colored light gray, moving across the bottom of the ravine.

"Well, given the proximity to the exit of that cave, it merits a closer look," said Vaccaro.

"Aye," Maryam said. "The problem is that we captured these by accident while circling over the cave's exit, so the camera's lenses were not optimized for the bottom of the abyss two thousand feet down."

"Looks like they stopped walking right there, eh?" offered Darcy.

"Tell me why you're here again, Corporal?" Vaccaro asked, glancing over at the tall Canadian.

"My cheeky friend is here to make sure I don't steal any bloody secrets of state, right mate?" Maryam said, without turning around, trying to zoom in on the last image.

Darcy nodded. "Something like that."

"How did you even find these shots in the first place?" asked Vaccaro.

Maryam shrugged and looked at Darcy.

"She hates my guts, Captain," Darcy explained. "So she'd rather spend hours scrubbing these images than—"

"Bloody hell!" Maryam said, zooming in enough to delineate something resembling a structure shaped like a cross, though the image was just too grainy. "What is that?"

"Could be anything," Darcy said. "A cabin of sorts."

"A cabin shaped like that? And in the middle of a dry riverbed? Really, mate?" Maryam said. "That's why I don't fancy you."

"But what else could it—"

"We shouldn't be guessing," Vaccaro said. "Not when there's so much at stake. What we *need* is another high asset pass over that spot with the FLIR cameras optimized for that depth. Then we'll know for sure."

"Good luck with that, Captain," Darcy observed. "In case you haven't noticed, there is a major battle in progress twenty miles away that requires *all* of our assets."

"See what I mean?" Maryam said, looking over her right shoulder at Vaccaro. "A bloody bore."

"How old are these images?" Vaccaro asked, massaging her shoulder.

"Three hours."

"Damn," Vaccaro said. "Let's go find Harwich and Duggan."

"You are free to do as you wish, Captain, eh? But Miss Gadai is confined to this room or the ICU."

"He really *is* an asshole," Vaccaro said to Maryam, who just shrugged again.

"Just following orders from General—"

"Are you seeing what we're seeing, Corporal?" asked Vaccaro. "There is a nuke on the loose and these here are images that show a group of people—probably Tangos—less than a mile from that fucking cave. What part of *that* doesn't just scream 'Oh, shit' to you, eh?"

"Captain, I—"

"I'll be right back," Vaccaro said, and stomped out of the room.

More debris blasted past them, cooking the woods, the heat nearly unbearable.

But Stark understood NATO's logic. The first jet took care of the surface while the second went after the tunnels.

"Please . . . Hunter," she said. "You must—"

"Never," he repeated, as molten shrapnel landed all around them

He shielded her with his own body as the thundering shock wave passed over them, ripping branches and dislodging rocks, turning everything into lethal missiles.

In the middle of this madness, he found her catlike eyes gazing up at him, and she mumbled, "*Spasiba.*"

"Anytime," he replied, as he heard two more jets in the distance, their engines also on afterburners.

Holding her tight, he scrambled toward the next switchback.

130

Enclaves

SULAIMAN MOUNTAINS. SOUTHERN AFGHANISTAN.

"I want fire on those boulders now!" Wright shouted at Gaudet, pointing toward the insurgents huddled behind each of three rock formations closest to him, some one hundred feet away, sporadically firing their AK-47s. The rest of the force was too far left or right to matter and was already engaged with the other squads.

The hillside to their left was in flames as multiple sorties shelled the woods, igniting the sky in more explosions than he could count.

That wasn't his fight, though for a moment he could almost

imagine his grandfather in the snowy Ardennes as German artillery shelled the woods.

Focus!

Gaudet grabbed three sets of marines armed with either M249s or the larger M240s, and within another thirty seconds multiple volleys of mixed-caliber slugs enshrouded the enclaves in crushed rock and dust.

"Stay here!" Wright shouted.

"Sir?"

"Just keep those guns on them! I'll be right back!"

"You want me to pop some smoke, sir?"

"Hell no! Don't feel like catching one in the ass!"

Smoke was a two-sided sword. It could hide you from the enemy but also from your own guys, who could also confuse you with the enemy.

"Eyes on me, Gunny!"

He left the protection of his tree without waiting for a reply, running around the leftmost enclave while the rebels behind it remained pinned down.

There was a risk with this approach, as slugs ricocheting off the rocks could get him, which is why he came alone. But he had no choice. He had to make a move. The Taliban had engaged them for far too long, almost as if they had an ulterior motive, stretching the moment instead of vanishing as they always did when facing a superior force.

And what about the picks and shovels? What the hell are they burying?

He scrambled in a zigzag pattern, remaining low, closing the gap in seconds, the UMP45's polymer stock pressed against his shoulder, right hand clutching the pistol grip, shooting finger on the trigger and left hand on the vertical foregrip beneath the muzzle.

He spotted the first group, three rebels clustered almost on top of each other as the incessant volleys pounded the rock formation. Their greenish shapes clearly visible in his night vision monocular, Wright fired two-round bursts into their heads. The insurgents were totally unaware of what had killed them.

"First enclave cleared." He spoke into his MBITR while rushing to the next enemy enclave, noticing the sudden cease-fire on this spot, meaning that Sergeant Gaudet was actually tracking him, managing the attack.

He took off toward the second enclave, just slightly uphill and fifty feet over, rushing like a shadow, firing while moving. One of the men in the group raised his head, eyes blinking in recognition. He screamed, alerting his companions.

Wright put one in the middle of the man's forehead and a second in his throat before mowing down the rest—all four of them—by quickly thumbing the fire selector lever to full automatic fire and emptying his magazine into the cluster of men.

"Second enclave down," he reported, dropping the spent twenty-five-round magazine and inserting a fresh one as the covering fire stopped on the third enclave.

But before he could pull on the bolt to load the first round, an invisible force punched him straight in the chest, tossing him back. He crashed against the side of a boulder, hitting the back of his head hard, the helmet cushioning the blow. He lost his grip on the UMP45.

Momentarily dazed, realizing that his vest had managed to absorb the impact, though not without shocking his upper chest, knocking the wind out of him, Wright tried to reach for his sidearm. He knew he had only a handful of seconds before whoever had fired that round came in for the kill.

He tried to breathe, to fill his shocked lungs with frigid air, while his hand slapped the holster of his SIG P220, but he could not bring his fingers to grab the pistol grip.

Focus, kid. You can do this.

Wright looked about him in the snowy woods.

Pops? he thought.

Now, kid. Get it done.

Gasping for air, he freed the P220 from its holster, bringing it up as two rebels appeared out of the darkness, AK-47s on him, eyes glinting in the night, their bearded faces contorted in anger.

The rebels approached him, leveling their assault rifles at his face just as Wright fired once at the closest figure, whose head snapped back in a bloody mess that sprayed his companion.

Realizing he didn't have time to switch targets, Wright tried anyway. But the Kalashnikov's reports never came. Instead, the second rebel dropped to the side, head exploding from suppressed rounds fired from somewhere up the hill.

Wright just lay there in pain, confused, his chest aching, while he tried to get his diaphragm and the muscles between his ribs working again.

In the middle of his agony, he saw her, like a greenish apparition materializing from the darkness beyond his night optics, gloved hands holding a TAC-338 sniper rifle with a bulky sound suppressor attached to the muzzle.

Behind her, the shape of a second sniper loomed through the woods. It was a man holding an even larger rifle, also suppressed.

At the same instant, as he managed his first lungful of air since getting shot, Wright noticed figures rushing down the hill, firing suppressed rounds into the backs of the insurgents.

The woman reached his side—Hispanic, long hair tied in a ponytail that swung behind her. Special Agent Monica Cruz.

"You okay, Captain?" she asked, leaning down and offering a hand.

Wright took it, breathing again, feeling his own strength returning. He was surprised at her strength, since she was so small, as she easily helped him to his feet.

"Need a minute . . . and thanks," Wright replied, blinking while holstering the SIG and locating his UMP45.

"No problem," she replied, as her sniper companion joined them, followed by three helmeted men dressed in black gear and armed with different weapons. The largest of the group, Chief Larson, wielded his massive M2 Browning. A much smaller man, Martin, stood next to him, armed with an MP5A1 and sucking on a lollipop. A third man appeared, Hagen, the former SEAL, also armed with an MP5A1 but smoking a cigarette. Three more figures materialized behind them, all clad in some strange black battle gear, clutching what he recognized as suppressed AK-9s. They wore equally weird helmets, which resembled those worn by cyclists.

Colonel Stark appeared behind the Russian trio, cradling a woman who was wearing that same black uniform

"Who are they?" Wright asked.

"Russians. Spetsnaz. They're with us," Stark replied.

131

No Entry

KANDAHAR AIRFIELD. SOUTHERN AFGHANISTAN.

"Sorry, Captain," one of the three Canadian MPs said, blocking her way. "The general is busy with his staff. Big war going on, eh?"

"That's precisely why I must see him," Vaccaro insisted, glaring at the three soldiers planted in front of NATO's war room in the rear of Lévesque's headquarters.

Her rank and the name she had built for herself around KAF had been enough to get her past the door and all the way down here. But these guys were not budging.

"Could you at least ask for Glenn Harwich, please? It's about the missing bomb."

"No can do, ma'am. The general was very specific. No one goes in there."

"But—"

"No one means *no one*—even you, Captain Vaccaro. But I'll let him know you need to speak with him as soon as he gets a break, eh?"

"Don't fucking bother," she replied, stomping away.

If she could not convince NATO to get eyes on that gorge, then she would do it herself.

132

Decoy

SULAIMAN MOUNTAINS. SOUTHERN AFGHANISTAN.

Stark had carried her for nearly a half mile, and his arms were burning, as were his legs and back. Kira had insisted that he leave her behind. Then, as her strength returned, she had wanted to walk. But he kept her tight against his chest, wanting every ounce of her energy to go toward keeping her alive.

Wright spoke into his MBITR. "Gunny, where are those helos? We have wounded!"

"En route, sir!" Gaudet shouted from thirty feet away, as he and the rest of the marines emerged from their DFPs and approached them. "ETA three minutes!"

"The bomb," mumbled Kira, lifting her head while pointing to the GPS screen in her hands.

Stark laid her gently on a cushion of pine needles and took a look at the screen, then started to his right, toward the source of the transmission. Wright and the others followed, tracking down the origin of the signal, near a group of dead insurgents.

The colonel moved them aside with the help of Monica and Ryan, but he soon realized there was nothing there that remotely resembled a nuclear device.

Are you kidding me? Stark thought. The signal intensified the moment Monica rolled one of the rebels onto his back, revealing a canvas bag.

"Are you kidding me?" she shouted, opening the bag and producing a cylindrical object roughly the size of a stick of dynamite. "What the hell is this?"

"That," said Kira, limping over to them assisted by Sergei, "is part of a battery pack, plus our embedded transmitter."

"So where the hell is the damn bomb?" said Stark, standing up.

"The picks and shovels," Wright offered. "I'm betting the bastards—"

"Buried it?" Monica blurted.

"What else they could be doing with them?"

"Gunny!" Wright shouted. "I want this entire hillside combed for anything that resembles freshly dug ground! Get everyone not involved in the exfil of the wounded to—"

"*Sierra Echo One, Red One One*," Stark heard through his earpiece.

He blinked at the call sign, and also at the fact that it wasn't Vaccaro but a woman with a strong and quite familiar British accent.

"Maryam?"

"*Aye.*"

"What the hell are you doing calling here?"

"*I'm conveying a message from Red One One. Get eyes on the gorge west of the cave's exit. Repeat, get eyes on the gorge west of the cave's exit.*"

"What are we looking for?"

"*The bomb, Echo One. The bloody bomb.*"

"Where is Red One One?"

"*Don't know. She asked me to pass this message before she went off to do, and I quote, 'whatever it fucking takes.'*"

133

Gunslinger

KANDAHAR AIRFIELD. SOUTHERN AFGHANISTAN.

U.S. Air Force Second Lieutenant Jessie James worked ground control at the KAF control tower in the predawn hours. She had been handling traffic between the tarmac and the runway since the attack began, the previous evening, and she was damn tired.

Her relief, however, wasn't due for another two hours, at the 0600 shift change, when Jessie could look forward to a breakfast pit stop at the closest DFAC before crawling into bed for some well-deserved shut-eye. But what Jessie looked forward to the most was the end of her rotation, in another eleven days. Then it was back home to her fiancé in Oklahoma City for a long-planned wedding and the start of her new life as a married woman and air traffic controller at Tinker Air Force Base.

New life and *new last name*, she thought, staring at the A-10C starting up at the far end of the flight line. She looked forward to shedding her last name, which, combined with her first, had been the source of countless jokes and pretty much the bane of her existence for most of her twenty-three years of life.

But her dad, rest in peace, had loved the Wild West, and she had been an only child, so . . .

Jessie dropped her gaze at the lone Warthog as it started taxiing onto Taxiway Echo One without requesting permission, heading straight for the beginning of Runway 23. She turned to First Lieutenant Vargas, who was in charge of the tower frequency that controlled the traffic on the runway and in the vicinity of the airport.

"Who's that?" she asked.

Vargas pulled up a pair of binoculars to try to read the tail number. "That's Mike India Niner Six Seven . . . Not on the list for to-night. Let me check who it belongs to." He put down the binoculars and worked his terminal.

Jessie tapped her radio. "Mike India Niner Six Seven, Ground Control, please state intentions."

"Ground, Red One One. You guys okay with me taking my new ride out for a spin? I heard there's a war out there."

Jessie blinked, recognizing Captain Vaccaro's call sign and voice. She had followed Vaccaro's inspirational story closely, from the unprecedented landing of that crippled Warthog to her getting shot down to protect the lives of those marines, her survival in the middle of Taliban country, and finally her daring rescue. It was truly the stuff of legends, and Jessie, like most women—and quite a few men—on the airfield, had become fans of the gutsy air force officer.

"That's her bird all right," confirmed Vargas, looking up from his screen. "But this says she's grounded until the flight surgeon clears her."

And that made sense. Last Jessie had heard, the captain was in the hospital.

Frowning, Jessie finally said, "Red One One, Ground. Hold short of Runway Two Three at Echo One."

"Roger. Red One One holding short, Two Three at Echo One."

Looking at Vargas again, Jessie said, "She must have clearance, right?"

Vargas shrugged. "I guess . . . but she's not on the list. Maybe there was a mistake at NATO headquarters, given the large number of flights we dispatched earlier. Most of them are due back by dawn."

"You think she might be . . . ?"

"Winging it?" Vargas said.

"Something like that, yes."

"She could be . . . you know . . . shooting from the hip," Vargas said, shaping his right hand like a revolver and pretending to draw, gunslinger style. "Takes one to know one, right?"

Jessie shook her head. It was an old joke, one of many she looked forward to leaving in the past after her—

"Ground, Red One One still standing by. Just burning good fuel here, folks. Don't want to keep those troops on the ground waiting for their air cover."

"Technically, it's your call, Jessie," Vargas said. "I handle runways and airspace. Any aircraft you hand over to me, I have to assume it's already been cleared by you."

"Yeah, thanks for that," Jessie replied, shaking her head, eyes back on the A-10C waiting just short of the runway threshold.

Vaccaro knew the folks in the tower were checking the clearance list and noticing she wasn't on it. And she also knew that they could get in trouble if they let her go. On the other hand, she was already in a world of shit for even getting this far.

Never stop fighting, Red One One. Never.

And make your life matter.

She had already tuned in the tower frequency on her second communications radio and knew there was no one on final approach for Runway 23, meaning she could just go.

"This one's on me, guys," Vaccaro said, nudging the throttles and taxiing beyond the threshold before aligning the nose down the runway and pushing full power.

The Warthog kicked her back as it accelerated. Her eyes shifting between the end of the runway and the airspeed indicator, she pulled back gently on the control column at 180 knots and held that airspeed during her climb out.

The airfield fell behind her as she stared at an ocean of stars beyond her bulletproof canopy. Reaching fifteen thousand feet, she turned to her self-assigned vector of 230 degrees, placing her bird in a direct course with the north side of that damn mountain.

She settled the Warthog at a cruise speed of three hundred knots, which placed her precisely eighteen minutes from her objective.

Vaccaro blinked to clear her sight. Just sitting up was a pure effort of will. The meds she had decided to take were her limit, considering her weight and that she needed to be very present and in the moment, so some pain would have to be tolerated.

As she scanned her instruments, the KAF departure controller came on the radio.

"Red One One, Bravo Niner Six. RTB. Repeat RTB."

Vaccaro grinned under her oxygen mask, before flipping a switch to cut them off. Instead, she dialed the ops frequency of the marines up on that mountain.

"Six Six Zulu, Six Six Zulu, Red One One. How do you read?"

A pause, followed by, "*Please tell me . . . that you're not . . . airborne.*"

It was John Wright, and he sounded out of breath. "Six Six Zulu, do you have eyes on that gorge?"

"*Negative . . . Two clicks away . . . Running.*"

"Then, John, darling," she replied. "Run *faster.*"

134

Running on Empty

SULAIMAN MOUNTAINS. SOUTHERN AFGHANISTAN.

Stark watched Hagen, Martin, Ryan, and even Monica disappear up that hill as he and Larsen tried to keep up. But it was no use. There was something about the vigor and stamina of youth that no amount of exercise and diet could replace. He was hurting, and that was after shedding everything except for his night vision monocular, his MP5A1, and six spare magazines.

Chief Larson and Captain Wright ran alongside him, also hauling the bare essentials. Sergeant Gaudet and the rest of the platoon—plus the Russians—had remained behind to search for a potentially buried bomb and to tend to Kira and the rest of the wounded until the helos arrived.

"Go, Janki mishka," she had told him. "Go find my bomb."

And to add a degree of surreal to the situation, Captain Vaccaro had decided to join in the fray after appropriating an $18 million U.S. government military aircraft. Apparently, she had been denied entry to see Lévesque, currently holed up in one of his conference rooms with his staff, which included Harwich and Duggan. So the air force captain, convinced that the Taliban attack across the mountain was just a decoy, had taken matters into her own hands.

And based on what they had just discovered in that dead insurgent's canvas bag, Stark had to agree with her—thus the running back to where they had exited the cave, which, ironically, had been less than a thousand feet from the edge of the precipice.

"That pilot," Stark said to Wright, as they clambered up icy rocks leading to a snowy switchback. "Quite the pistol."

"You have . . . no idea," he replied, checking his watch. "But shit's about to hit the fan . . . at KAF headquarters."

They reached the switchback, turned, and faced another snowy hill.

But at the moment Stark would much rather be here—exhausted, cold, hungry, and nearly out of breath—than at KAF, where the good Major General Lévesque was about to receive some most unsettling news via Six Six Zulu.

135

Around the World

JAFABAR. SULAIMAN MOUNTAINS.
SOUTHERN AFGHANISTAN.

Osama bin Laden exited the tunnel that led to the outskirts of the village of Jafabar, back on the southern face of the mountain. To the north, he could hear the massive battle of his own creation, near the distant foot of the mountains leading to the Panjshir Valley. Over nine hundred of his battle-hardened warriors drew the attention of NATO forces, keeping the enemy looking in the wrong direction.

But not for long, he thought, realizing that by now the group that had killed Akhtar—and nearly killed *him*—would have realized the ruse.

Escaping the strafing had been easy in their tunnel systems, which nearly traversed the mountain. They were used primarily to allow contingents of men to recover from their holy jihad, to shift forces from one theater to another, and of course, to survive the onslaught of bombs on the surface.

The enemy had sophisticated and highly terrifying weapons.

His men had deep caves and tunnels, which had been good enough to defeat all previous invaders.

And now the mighty United States.

This remote headquarters in the Taliban-controlled town in the middle of Taliban-controlled territory was away from NATO's prying eyes in the sky.

Greetings gave way to orders. Messages were dispatched via encrypted radio and relayed as far south as Lashkar Gah to trigger desired activities on the planned escape route, along the bottom of the gorge and over the desert leading to the Indian Ocean.

His strategy during this war had never been to defeat American technology but rather to deceive it—to deceive it by capitalizing on the enemy's arrogant dependence on it.

Making them predictable, he thought, as he accepted a cup of hot tea from the young daughter of one of his men, her head covered in a traditional *hijab*, her face nearly shielded by a *niqab*. The dark veil allowed a view of just an inch of light-olive skin and a pair of mesmerizing brown eyes, which were averted from his stare.

"Thank you, child," he said, sipping his tea while standing next to a crate that his men had dragged to the edge of a clearing overlooking Quai Kotal, which eventually led to the desert.

Distant explosions speckled the northern range like lightning flashes, brief moments of twilight seen through jagged ridges, followed by rumbling thunder as his forces continued distracting the enemy, setting the stage for his ultimate act of destruction.

Which will be felt around the world.

136

Religious Beliefs

SULAIMAN MOUNTAINS. SOUTHERN AFGHANISTAN.

Zahra remained in the rear of the cabin with her leg up while Mani did a preflight check and Dr. Khan finished his work on the device, replacing the damaged components and installing the battery pack.

They worked in near darkness, save for the flashlight she kept pointed at the bomb while the scientist accomplished his work—quite a bit faster than she had anticipated, given the complexity of the task.

And that's a good thing, she decided, given their time constraint.

They had exited the cave just in time to avoid the inevitable and quite predictable NATO strike, before splitting forces per her plan, using the hidden transmitter to turn the tables and trick the enemy, drawing them in the opposite direction from the bomb.

It had taken Prince Mani, Zahra, Dr. Khan, and a contingent of ten men almost two hours to make it down the countless switchbacks to the dry riverbed. Bin Laden and Akhtar had kept all attention away from them, making their short but arduous journey rather uneventful, considering NATO forces had been on their heels. Still, the hike had been quite difficult for Zahra, with her wounded leg. She had worked through the pain, refusing to accept Mani's help for most of the way to avoid appearing weak in the eyes of men who would just as soon stone her for refusing to wear a hijab.

Screw them, she thought, *and the religion they use as an excuse to subdue and maim women.*

Fortunately, those men now waited outside, protecting the plane in case the enemy decided to look this way. And that had allowed Zahra her first rest since she had jumped off this very plane, four days ago.

She stared at the diminutive bald-headed man with round glasses and a long, skinny nose that he kept shoved into the guts of the weapon. She had to give the little guy credit for being both feisty and efficient, standing up to Akhtar and the rest of his—

The device came alive with a series of beeps.

She leaned forward. "Is that thing on?"

Dr. Khan looked up from his work, regarding her over the rim of his glasses. "That would be the point of me being here, yes?"

Mani walked in from the cockpit wearing a set of night vision goggles and pointing at his watch. He looked a bit like an alien with those goggles, but they were necessary. Darkness was their friend.

"We need to get going. Dawn is just over an hour away."

"Good. Because my work here is done," Dr. Khan replied, before spending a few minutes showing them how to activate the device. "I have rigged this timer to the trigger mechanism," he added, pointing to a small digital timer attached to the battery pack. "You can set it in thirty-minute increments, up to six hours, so you have time to get away."

"That would be useful," Mani said.

"I thought so," Dr. Khan replied. "You two don't come across as . . ."

"Jihadists?"

"Then be sure to be at least seven kilometers from the blast," he replied, showing them how to operate the device, before turning it off to preserve the battery and securing it in the compartment behind the seats for its upcoming flight.

And with that, the scientist excused himself and stepped outside, where he joined the contingent of men who would head back up the gorge.

Mani pulled up the stepladder and closed the door before heading to the cockpit. He was followed by Zahra, who also donned a pair of night vision goggles. Turning them on, she stared at the short greenish runway of river rocks leading straight into a section of the pass too narrow for the Cessna's wings.

As Mani strapped into his seat and put on a Bose headset, he looked over at her and smiled, apparently reading her face. "I got in, Zahra, and the wings are still attached, yes?"

"Looks that way."

"And they will remain attached on the way out. Trust me," he said.

Having already completed the prestart checklist, Mani turned the starter. The turboprop kicked in right away, whirling the propeller into a clear disk. He completed the engine start procedure but kept the navigation lights and beacon off.

Zahra stared at engine gauges coming to life, getting the strange feeling that she just might be in for the ride of her life.

137

The Plane

SULAIMAN MOUNTAINS. SOUTHERN AFGHANISTAN.

"Are you hearing what I'm hearing?" Wright asked, huddled between Larson and Stark at the edge of an outcrop, with a clear line of sight into the void.

The colonel looked down from their vantage point. He could certainly hear the unmistakable sound of a turboprop revving up, echoing inside deep canyon walls. Unfortunately, his night vision optics could not see a damn thing beyond the first few hundred feet of the gorge.

"Ryan? Anything?" he asked his Delta sniper, who had taken a position farther north, along with Monica and the other nimbler operators, who had beaten them to the edge by almost ten minutes.

"*Negative, sir. Too dark. Just the sound. But how could it be coming from down there? It's looks too narrow for any plane.*"

Stark frowned, remembering the tight pass on the way up. The walls were not only less than fifty feet apart but also misshapen, with protuberances and trees growing at angles from niches and shelves. Plus, the path twisted like a damn snake, making those turns impossible in a plane.

But the sound intensified, meaning it was headed this—

"Six Six Zulu, Red One One. Do you have eyes on that ravine?"

Stark sighed in frustration. His MP5A1 was pointed into the abyss, but without a target.

"Too dark, Red One One," Stark replied. "But we can hear a plane revving up down there. What's your ETA?

"Three minutes."

138

Hand Grenade

KANDAHAR AIRFIELD. SOUTHERN AFGHANISTAN.

With so many battles in play across so many square miles of mountain, it actually didn't surprise Harwich that it took almost ninety minutes for the message from Six Six Zulu to make it up the NATO chain of command. But when it did, it felt like a hand grenade tossed right in the middle of Lévesque's long conference table.

Denial took hold first, as the realization that they had been played sank in. It was followed by anger, starting with the general's fist crashing on the table.

Standing, the NATO chief looked around the room. He looked as tired as Harwich felt, with dark circles around bloodshot eyes and a two-day orange stubble taking over his freckles.

"Can someone please tell me how it can be that, with the hundreds of millions of dollars in equipment and trained personnel at our disposal, our breakthroughs are coming via a *Pakistani spy?*"

He asked this of no one in particular while pointing at the infrared images on the screen behind him. But he did glance over at Maryam, who stood between Harwich and Corporal Darcy, and added, "No offense intended, Miss Gadai, eh?"

"Aye. None taken," she replied.

"So, how soon before we get a flight of jets over there?" he asked.

"They're taking off right now, sir," said one of his aides, a Lieutenant Garrison, also Canadian, looking at his tablet computer. "ETA twenty minutes."

Colonel Duggan, sitting to Lévesque's right, shook his head and said, "General, this thing will be over in *twenty seconds.* Captain Wright has just reported engine noises in the area that he believes belong to a turboprop plane, probably the bastards flying the bomb out of there."

"What about planes already in the air . . . over the battle zone?" Lévesque asked.

"RTB to refuel sir," Garrison said. "They've been out all night providing air cover for our troops and are flying on fumes."

Visibly frustrated, Lévesque just sank in his chair.

"General?" Harwich said.

Lévesque lifted his gaze at the CIA man. "Yes, Mr. Harwich?"

"There's a Warthog two minutes out, sir."

He leaned forward. "Who?"

"Captain Laura Vaccaro."

"The one we rescued yesterday?"

"Yes, sir."

"I thought she was in sick bay, eh?"

Harwich looked at Garrison, sighed, and said, "Long story."

"How did she get there so fast?"

"She had a head start."

"But . . . we just got the report."

Harwich looked again at Garrison, who said, "Ah . . . she went rogue, sir."

"Rogue? What do you mean, *rogue?*"

"She came over to alert you," Maryam decided to interject. "After

I showed her those images. But your blokes outside wouldn't let her through."

Garrison shifted uncomfortably. "Miss Gadai is right, sir, and I just learned that as well. The captain did come by—over an hour ago—but the MPs turned her away."

"Why?"

"Because they were following orders."

"Whose orders?"

"Ah . . . yours, sir."

"Fuck me," Lévesque mumbled, before turning to Harwich. "So . . . a Warthog, eh?"

"Yes, General."

"Well? Let's get her on the horn!"

139

Short Field

QUAI KOTAL. SULAIMAN MOUNTAINS.
SOUTHERN AFGHANISTAN.

Part of the trick to a successful short-field takeoff was to let the plane rev up while stepping on the brakes. Zahra had seen Mani do it many times before, but always while operating on dirt or grassy field. Never on river rocks, which resulted in slight forward movement as the tundra tires slid over the stones under the power of the Pratt & Whitney PT6A-140 turboprop.

"Looks like the goggles give us about five hundred feet of visibility," he said, applying twenty degrees of flaps for added lift during the takeoff run, before releasing the brakes. "Here we go."

The Caravan lurched forward, gathering speed.

The plane trembled for about fifteen seconds, until Mani applied just enough rear pressure on the yoke to transfer some of the weight from the tires to the wings. Another twenty seconds and he tugged harder, and the Cessna leaped into the surrounding darkness.

Mani left the flaps in place while cutting back power, since they would not be climbing much this night. They entered a slow flight, which the airspeed indicator marked at ninety knots, or half the Cessna's cruising speed, but it was required to negotiate the tight turns ahead.

Before that, however, they needed to clear a very narrow section of the canyon, which he had apparently managed on the way in.

Even with the night vision goggles it was difficult to see that far ahead, but they could not risk turning on the halogen landing lights. This had to be stealth all the way, lest they wish to paint an X on their backs.

Mani banked the wings almost thirty degrees while applying opposite rudder, presenting a narrower wingspan while adding power to offset the loss in lift.

"Easy now," he whispered, as dark green walls rushed by. They were cruising at just a hundred feet over the bottom of the canyon, working the delicate balance between power and drag to hold airspeed and altitude. This required constant minute adjustments of all control surfaces and power settings while he slowly nursed the airplane through the narrow pass—even more so as the ravine turned, compounding the problem.

"So *this* is what I missed," she mumbled, gripping the sides of her seat as he increased the angle of bank to forty-five degrees, adding more power and rear pressure on the yoke, which he achieved by working the elevator trim.

"Almost done," he whispered, covering another five hundred feet before the canyon widened to almost a hundred feet, allowing him to level out the wings. But as he did so, muzzle flashes erupted high above them.

140

Firing Blindly

"Don't let up! It's got to be down there!" Stark shouted, emptying an entire magazine into the darkness below as the engine noise peaked.

Wright followed suit with his UMP45, blindly unleashing volleys of .45 ACP slugs into the void while Larson opened up the Browning, vomiting rounds at a ridiculous rate.

Their combined muzzle flashes splashed the walls with stroboscopic light, but they still could not see that far into the gorge, even with the goggles, which forced them to fire indiscriminately into the greenish darkness from where the sound had originated.

"Red One One, Six Six Zulu. SitRep."

"I'm here, boys, and I see your muzzle flashes. Hitting anything?"

"Who the hell knows?" shouted Wright, swapping magazines. "Goggles are useless that deep in the ravine!"

"Roger that. Got word from KAF that reinforcements are on the way. Circling overhead now to get a better view."

Stark raised his gaze. Although he could hear the jet engines, he could not see the Warthog. Vaccaro had kept her exterior lights off to be on the safe side.

Dropping a spent magazine on the frozen ground and inserting a fresh one, he pulled the cocking lever with his non-firing hand fully to the rear and then released it, chambering a round, before unleashing another thirty rounds into the void. He could only hope that a handful of the dozens of rounds being released each second by their combined force would actually hit something other than the frigid landscape.

141

Fighter Jock

She screamed, but not at the barrage of rounds raining on them, or even at the few that managed to punch a hole or two in the fuselage.

Zahra shouted obscenities in both Pashto and English when Mani banked the plane almost sixty degrees while applying opposing rudder, forcing it to the side of the canyon where the gunfire originated—so damn close she could almost touch the black granite wall.

The maneuver not only presented a much narrower target to the enemy but also made it harder for rounds to find him, given the angle at which they were being fired. One of the peculiar features of Quai Kotal was its granite walls, which angled inward instead of outward as was the case with most canyons. This made the bottom of the gorge wider than the top, which worked to their advantage as the Caravan hugged the eastern wall.

She watched in relief as the mixed-caliber volleys from above tore into the center of the ravine, kicking up clouds of dust but missing them by over a dozen feet as Mani continued flying at sixty degrees of bank.

And in another minute, as the canyon turned, they left the threat behind.

Leveling the wings once more, he pushed more power, increasing airspeed to 120 knots, while Zahra scanned the instrument panel, looking for any indication of a problem.

"Doesn't look like they hit anything vital," she observed, before inspecting the underside of the wings near the fuselage, where the fuel tanks were located. "No fuel leaks, either."

"Good. We barely have enough to reach our refueling stop south of the border."

She glanced at the GPS, which showed them as a dot in the middle of the twisting canyon traversing the Sulaimans. They had another thirty miles of this before they would cross the desert in the opposite direction they had come just four nights ago and then fly straight to Karachi to change planes again. Then it was straight to Paris, France, aboard the Citation X.

Just another Saudi couple headed for a weekend of excess.

Zahra stared at the shades of green beyond the Plexiglas windshield as the realization of what they were about to do suddenly became very, *very* real.

The City of Lights was scheduled to die in forty-eight hours.

By *fire*.

142

Lonesome Dove

**QUAI KOTAL. SULAIMAN MOUNTAINS.
SOUTHERN AFGHANISTAN.**

It took almost ten minutes before Vaccaro spotted them, and only for a moment, while flying a couple hundred feet over the twisting pass.

The forward-looking infrared camera under the belly of the Warthog interfaced with her helmet, painting in her clear visor thermal images of the darkness below. Something very hot was moving very fast near the bottom of the canyon.

The problem was finding it again, and keeping it in her sights long enough to lock on one of her two AIM-9X Sidewinder heat-seeking missiles. But the ravine was too narrow and winding for a clear shot.

"Red One One, Bravo Niner Six. SitRep."

Vaccaro frowned under her mask. Wright had convinced her to turn her other comm radio back on, tuned to KAF's frequency, and now the same controller who had requested her to RTB wanted a situation report.

"A little busy, guys," she replied.

"Red One One, this is Major General Thomas Lévesque of the Canadian Armed Forces and commander of NATO forces in southern Afghanistan."

Well, she thought, turning the Warthog back over the narrow pass, looking for the runaway plane, *that's certainly a proper fucking introduction.*

"Still busy, sir. Had eyes on the plane for a moment and—There you are!"

She spotted the heat signature again and immediately activated a Sidewinder, trying to get a lock. That was one of the advantages of the AIM-9X version of the venerable missile. When she used it in conjunction with her Joint Helmet Mounted Cueing System, she could point the AIM-9X's seeker and lock it by simply looking at the target, making her job easier, especially in her condition. Her shoulder continued to throb, especially when working the throttles, but it was her forehead that really bothered her, as the lining of her helmet pressed against her stitches.

Gut up, she thought, as the range finder reported the target almost two thousand feet below her and four thousand downrange.

But before she could release the Sidewinder, her missile warning system blared inside the cabin. Someone had achieved missile lock on her.

"What the—"

The side of the mountain lit up, and she reacted by throwing the Warthog into a tight right turn while pushing the throttles forward.

"Missiles!" she shouted. "Someone's firing missiles at me!"

———

Bin Laden led the group of men on the clearing overlooking the pass, aiming the launcher at the incoming jet, which was barely visible in the night sky.

He positioned the target in the center of the sight assembly range ring, trying to get the missile's heat-seeking head to lock on to the hot exhaust plumes of the large engines in the rear of what he recognized as an A-10.

The cold night and the lack of any other heat source gave the seeker the upper hand. It responded with the acquisition tone, a steady, high-pitched sound signaling missile lock.

Bin Laden pressed the Uncaging switch before squeezing the trigger, momentarily blinded by the blaze as the missile shot out of the launcher, leaving behind a yellow contrail as it streaked across the sky.

A moment later, two of his men also released their missiles.

The g-forces tore at her as Vaccaro cut hard right in full afterburners, losing sight of the narrow pass or the plane getting away, her senses focused on the three pulsating lights rapidly closing in.

She worked the SUU-42A/A countermeasures system, dispensing a combination of flares and infrared decoys, before dropping the nose and turning in the opposite direction, trying to increase the distance between her and the—

Two missiles went for the hot lures dropping behind the Warthog, detonating their high-explosive annular blast fragmentation warheads less than five hundred feet away.

The A-10C shook from the combined shock waves, followed by the sound of dozens of sizzling fragments, like red-hot hail, thrashing her armored skin.

She jerked her head back when a flaming fragment pounded the armor-glass, breaking up into dozens of smaller pieces. Like a burst of smoldering ash, the pieces vanished in her slipstream, leaving behind a dark, grazed spot the size of her fist on the canopy.

Two down. One to go, she thought, working through the pain in her shoulder and forehead while giving her instrument panel a quick glance, verifying no damage, before releasing more flares.

The countermeasures ejected from their underside pod stained the sky in bright crimson as she leveled out less than fifty feet over the forested mountain, cutting back power while turning hard left at almost three hundred knots to position the Warthog at a ninety-degree angle relative to the incoming missile.

G-forces slammed her into the seat, and the titanium frame screeched from the stress—as did her wounds. The A-10C's wings trembled as she pushed her plane, and her body, to their limits.

"Red One One, Bravo Niner Six. SitRep."

Seriously?

She couldn't reply even if she wanted to, not while the g-meter read 7.8 and her head felt as if it would burst at any moment. But she still managed to complete the turn, leveling the wings and pushing full throttle again, accelerating to 330 knots while searching left, then right, trying to locate the incoming—

The blast lit up the sky just above and to her right, where she had released the last load of flares, and the shock wave pushed the Warthog down into the trees.

Shit!

For a second, the belly of the plane sank into the upper branches as glowing shrapnel rained on her like molten lava, bouncing off the armored canopy while the airframe trembled, the control column almost slipping from her grip.

Airspeed plummeted from the sudden friction as branches tore into her undercarriage munitions.

She pulled back on the column while the afterburners torched the forest in her wake. The control panel lit up, signaling failures in multiple weapons systems, from Hydra rockets to her Sidewinders and MK77 incendiary bombs. Her port engine was also overheating.

But she had more immediate problems. Clutching the control column with both hands now, she pulled as hard as she had ever pulled, ignoring her shoulder while slowly inching the A-10C from the forest's deadly grip.

Her eyes glanced at the airspeed.

230 knots.

If it reached 120 knots, the Warthog would stall and sink in the sea of stone pines while she still had over half her fuel, triggering an inferno.

Never stop fighting, Red One One. Never.

She needed an edge, something to cut the friction.

And it came to her an instant later, as airspeed dropped to 210 knots.

She pulled the trigger on the Avenger 30mm gun, which came alive with a thundering blaze of depleted uranium hell, carving a wide track in the canopy directly in front of her—and producing a twenty-knot decrease in forward airspeed.

But she persisted, praying that the reduced friction created by the rotary canon mowing down the forest ahead of her would offset the increased counterforce of the 30×173mm rounds, each nearly a pound in weight, fired at the rate of 4,200 rounds per minute. The tops of pines in her path vanished in a blur of mulch and green debris, ripping away the mountain's hold, allowing her to spring skyward.

Airspeed shot back up, but not all the way to cruise speed. Her port engine continued to overheat and she had to throttle it back, using opposing rudder and aileron to counter the asymmetrical thrust.

She was free, accelerating once more in the night sky while searching for the runaway craft, but her FLIR camera was malfunctioning, unable to produce any heat images, likely damaged along with most of her underside systems.

Dammit.

Switching on the night vision optics in her helmet turned the darkness into shades of green. But like the team on the ground, who had been unable to see the plane at the bottom of the gorge, she was now blind, incapable of discerning anything deeper than a few hundred feet.

Unless . . .

As she considered the thought, KAF came back on.

"Red One One, Bravo Niner Six. SitRep."

Vaccaro shook her head, not at the controller but at the maneuver she might have to do in order to have a chance at catching the fugitive plane.

"I'm running out of options, boys," she replied. "Dodged three missiles and nearly bought the farm. All weapons systems down except for the Avenger. Where is the cavalry?"

"*On its way, Red One One. Ten minutes out. Hang in there. Try to keep eyes on the target.*"

"Roger that. Will—"

Another flash down by the edge of the pass.

Realizing she could not continue to play the enemy's game, Vaccaro used the only card she had left. Pumping the last of her flares, which she was thankful to see were getting dispensed in a red-hot stream arcing away from her flight path, she pushed both engines into full afterburners while dropping the nose and banking the plane, sinking into the chasm while topping 340 knots, just a dash below her maximum speed.

She was going way too fast and also stressing her port engine. But survival depended on proper spacing from the flares.

The blast came once again, from somewhere above and behind her, powerful, reverberating, splashing the canyon with yellow light. Shrapnel tore into her bird, the airframe once again trembling as the armored skin absorbed the detonation. More alarms blared inside her cockpit, more systems malfunctioning.

But her primary enemy now was her speed.

She needed to slow down fast or risk crashing inside the pass.

Deploying the air brakes while cutting back the throttles pushed her into her restraining harness, her shoulder stinging from the pressure.

Damn.

Mustering control, she swung the stick to the left and pressed hard on the left rudder pedal, shoveling the Warthog into a wickedly tight turn to clear the next twist in the winding canyon, her head pounding from the g-forces.

Airspeed dropped to 210 knots. 190 knots. 170 knots.

She adjusted the throttles to hold 160 knots, flying with flaps at ten degrees while diving almost to the bottom of the ravine, leveling off a couple hundred feet from the dry riverbed.

Her eyes scanned ahead now while she managed her speed, turn after turn, as walls of black granite and snowy trees blended into a green-washed corridor.

She had to constantly adjust, constantly compensate for the port engine, which she now kept at idle, letting it cool while she relied on the starboard turbofan to keep her in business.

And that's when she spotted the rogue plane, disappearing around the next turn, a few hundred feet ahead and just below her, its green silhouette clear against the canyon wall.

It's a Caravan!

"Bravo Niner Six, Red One One. Be advised target is a Cessna Caravan. Repeat. A Cessna Caravan."

No response.

What the hell?

She repeated the message and again got no response, which made her think that her comm radios were among the growing list of malfunctioning systems.

Adjusting power to avoid overshooting the Cessna, she slowed down to 150 knots. Doing so placed her dangerously close to her stall speed of 120 knots, but now she had a clear shot with the Avenger.

However, the Caravan turned again, momentarily disappearing from sight. She followed, only to realize that the turn led into a narrower pass. The Cessna had already gone into a slip, wings banked forty degrees with opposing rudder.

Since she had roughly the same wingspan as the Caravan, Vaccaro copied the maneuver, narrowing her profile, squeezing through the constraining walls until they opened up again after the next turn.

She leveled her wings at almost the same time as the Cessna, whose pilot seemed unaware of her presence. At a distance of just three hundred feet, she squeezed the trigger.

And nothing.

Not a damn thing.

Dammit, she thought, glancing at her systems, noticing the red warning light on the Avenger cannon, and also noticing her fuel gauge at 30 percent.

She didn't have enough fuel to get back to—

Gunfire erupted from the bottom of the gorge, the muzzle flashes pulsating in rhythm with the hammer-like blows to the Warthog's underside—the Taliban covering the Caravan's escape route.

Bastards are everywhere, she thought, while trying to diagnose the Avenger malfunction—and also while managing the constant turns, controlling airspeed, and offsetting the asymmetric thrust due to her overheating port engine.

She muscled her way through the volleys pounding her bird, trusting the Warthog's armored skin, and glanced at the GPS screen. It highlighted the canyon, which was splitting into dozens of fingers as it approached the desert in another fifteen miles, meaning the Cessna could take any one of them, disappearing in the sand dunes. And given the level of resistance she had witnessed inside this canyon, she didn't want to think about what awaited her in the open.

She had to act, and act now.

143

At Gunpoint

**QUAI KOTAL. SULAIMAN MOUNTAINS.
SOUTHERN AFGHANISTAN.**

"Bastards are shooting at her!" Wright shouted. He was hanging on to an overhead pipe on the forward cabin of the Black Hawk helicopter that had plucked them off the edge of the precipice a minute ago, before it hauled ass down the pass, using the FLIR camera to locate the two planes.

The Warthog cruised right over enemy positions deployed along the bottom of the ravine while rapidly approaching the runaway Cessna.

"Why isn't she using the cannon? She's close enough!" Stark shouted over the rotor noise. He was standing next to Wright, between the pilot and the copilot, staring at the large center display slaved to the infrared camera.

To Stark's dismay, this was the same helicopter that had rescued Kira—who had forced the pilot at gunpoint to head this way after hearing of the runaway plane.

"What the hell do you think you're doing?" he had screamed, when he boarded the Black Hawk and saw her standing by the pilot, holding a shiny Tokarev to his helmeted head while Sergei and the other Spetsnaz operative covered her with their AK-9s.

"It is my bomb, yes?" she had replied, her shoulder now properly bandaged, a fire burning in her hazel eyes.

"This might work in Russia, Kira! But you can't go around hijacking American military helos!"

"He would not do it otherwise," she had replied.

"Bitch is nuts!" the pilot, a Lieutenant Gonzales, had screamed, giving her the bird.

"See?" she had added, waving the gun. "The only way."

Stark had talked her into putting the gun away and then had convinced Gonzales to go in pursuit.

"Just keep those crazy fucking Russians away from me!" Gonzales had shouted, waiting for Stark to dispatch them to the rear before he would accelerate in the direction of the A-10C.

They had tried to respond to Vaccaro's message, which had identified the rogue plane as a Cessna Caravan, but apparently the air force captain could not hear them.

Stark stared at the infrared image, which showed the Warthog closing in on the seemingly unsuspecting Cessna—until the Warthog rammed its nose into the smaller plane's empennage.

"She didn't just do that!" Wright screamed. "Get me down there!" he shouted to Gonzales.

"Too tight, sir!"

"I don't care! Get me down there!"

"Can't do, sir!"

"Son," he insisted, "the battle is *down* there! Not *up* here."

"I get it, sir, but—"

Stark pulled out his SIG P220 and pointed it at the pilot.

"You too, *cabron*? Seriously?" Gonzales shouted, while Kira looked up from the main cabin and started laughing.

Stark ignored her, his attention on the young pilot. "*Very* serious, son. That plane's flying away with a nuke. I'll be damned if I'm going to let it out of my sight."

"Shoot me if you must, sir, but I am not risking everybody's lives! The opening is too narrow for the rotor!"

Stark frowned and looked past the very amused Kira, arms crossed, telling her guys something he could not hear. He spotted Larsen and Martin in the rear of the cabin, looking bored, sitting across from Ryan, Monica, and Hagen, who somehow had managed to fall asleep in the middle of all this.

"Danny! Get your ass over here!" Then, turning back to Gonzales, he added, "You are relieved, son!"

"Seriously, sir?" Gonzales asked, as Martin reached the cockpit.

"Very! This guy's the best stick in the armed forces. Plus this is on me!"

Gonzales motioned his copilot to head to the back while he swapped seats to yield the left stick to Martin.

"You better know what the hell you're doing," Gonzales shouted at Stark, as Martin strapped himself into the right seat.

Martin just grinned while settling behind the controls, left hand on the collective lever, right on the cyclic, touching the tips of his boots to the rudder pedals.

144

Knock Knock

**QUAI KOTAL. SULAIMAN MOUNTAINS.
SOUTHERN AFGHANISTAN.**

The A-10C's nose crashed into the Cessna's rudder with enough force to rip through the relatively softer aluminum skin, tearing off the top third. Debris flew into her armored canopy like shrapnel, grazing it before washing away in her slipstream.

"Knock knock, assholes," Vaccaro said inside her oxygen mask, keeping an eye on her airspeed, which had dropped to 140 knots.

The planes separated on impact, and the Cessna wavered while accelerating.

"What the hell was that?" Zahra screamed, slamming into her seat belt. "Did we hit a wall?"

"Not a wall," he replied, advancing the throttle, reaching 180 knots while pulling up his flaps.

"Then what?"

"Company," Mani replied, testing his control surfaces. The rudder was a little sticky, but functional, and so were the elevators as he dropped almost to the bottom of the ravine and slipped the plane into the next turn. "We have company."

"What are you talking—"

"Back there," he said. "Someone just rammed us."

"Where do you think you're going?" Vaccaro mumbled, advancing both throttles to catch up to the Cessna, reaching 180 knots, pushing not just the overheating port turbofan but also the airframe as she swung the stick to the right to negotiate a sharp turn.

The g-forces piled up on her as she banked the A-10C nearly onto its side, the pressure crushing her wounded shoulder, making it difficult to breathe. The pain was overwhelming.

Jesus!

But she kept control of the center stick, emerging into another straightaway. Leveling the wings while once more closing in on the Cessna, she noticed that her target kept changing altitude, bobbing up and down in the pass as the walls rushed past at a sickening speed.

She kept her cool, working through the pain, eyes straight ahead, making adjustments, working the elevator, rudder, and ailerons along with power settings to track her target like a missile, closing in very fast. She shoved the throttles into full afterburners just before ramming the Cessna again. The crash was overarching. Her harness dug into her flight suit, squeezing the wind out of her, and she felt the force ripping into the staples on her shoulder.

The Warthog trembled, her control column quavering as more alarms blared in her cockpit. The A-10C's nose crashed into the Cessna's tail section, tearing through it and into the main fuselage, white aluminum skin covering her canopy.

She stared in surprise into the rear interior of the broken Caravan—a mess of twisted metal, seats, and luggage.

And the bomb!

Clearly strapped into the rear cargo compartment.

Vaccaro could almost touch it, until she pulled back on the control column, trying to dislodge the nose of the Warthog from the Cessna's tail as both planes dropped to the bottom in a deadly embrace.

The shock from the impact dislodged Mani's seat from its anchors on the floor, sending him crashing into the control panel, while Zahra fell against her harness and the Cessna dove toward the riverbed.

Zahra leaned back, dazed, but conscious enough to see the sea of stones rushing up at them.

"Mani!"

But the Saudi was gone, his dead eyes staring at the floor, a wide gash on his forehead where he had struck the panel full force.

Mustering savage control, Zahra reacted just as he had trained her in case of emergencies, pulling on the yoke, but the Cessna was unresponsive. Lowering flaps, she shoved the throttle to the forward stop. The turboprop screamed, pushing a gust of air over the increased airfoils in the wings, but instead of breaking the fall, the wings mysteriously began to rock.

"What the hell is happening?" she screamed, as the bottom of the ravine filled her windscreen.

Vaccaro kept the rear pressure on the control stick, trying to break the Cessna's lock by banking the wings, but the Warthog's nose was jammed deep in the other plane's guts, embedded in the aluminum fuselage. Even so, she managed to pull up their combined masses several degrees, shallowing the angle just enough to avoid a head-on crash.

The planes collided against the riverbed, hard, the Cessna's propeller stabbing the creek, chopping into the layer of river stones before the tips bent backwards. Its nose landing gear collapsed on impact, tearing away, while rocks milled the main fuselage.

But that did the trick.

The Cessna broke off from the Warthog's nose and slid forward and to the side, spinning on its belly while the wings were ripped from the fuselage, rivets popping like a machine gun. The fuel inside them ignited while the cabin hurtled away from the flaring inferno, flipping sideways and into a line of boulders lining the eastern wall.

The Warthog gouged the ravine behind the Cessna, parting river stones as she slid right through the Cessna's burning wings. For an instant, as flames licked the canopy, Vaccaro considered ejecting, but the realization that the rocket booster under her seat could send her crashing into the canyon walls kept her hands on the control stick and throttles.

Thousands of stones hammered the armored canopy as she slid past the fire and continued beyond where the Cessna had wrapped itself around a large rock. And that's when she remembered the

turbofans, still thrusting the heavy jet as it carved a track in the ravine. But the plane's armored skin, combined with its hardened steel
and titanium frame, kept it from breaking up like the Cessna.

Still, the stress taxed the structure, rattling its very armored fabric to the brink of its design limit, and the turbofans sucked in rock
and debris, which tore at the fins whirling at thousands of revolu-
tions per minute.

The engines exploded just as she slapped the controls to shut them
down, igniting the canyon behind her, orange and yellow-gold flames
licking walls of black granite. The dual blasts tore off the Warthog's
tail, and the ensuing shock wave hurled the main fuselage like a damn
Frisbee. She was spiraling in a cloud of sparks, the ravine's walls swapping places.

Until she struck something hard, unyielding.

145

Judgment Day

QUAI KOTAL. SULAIMAN MOUNTAINS.
SOUTHERN AFGHANISTAN.

Zahra crawled out of the fuselage, cringing in pain and dragging her
broken leg across the riverbed, where she found a stick good enough
to use as a crutch. She limped away from the Cessna and past the
remains of the Warthog.

Don't stop.

Get out of here.

She pushed herself to keep going, continuing around the next bend in the ravine, leaving the fires behind, moving as fast as she could, trying to gain as much distance as possible from a place that would be crawling with NATO forces shortly.

Unfortunately, NATO was no longer her primary enemy.

Many figures emerged from behind boulders along both canyon walls.

Tall and thin, their loose clothes, bearded faces, and a mix of Kalashnikovs and RPG launchers were visible in the orange twilight glow of the flames reflecting on slick canyon walls.

But it was their condemning stares that made her gut twist with raw fear, as they surrounded her and pointed at her exposed head, her tight clothes.

"I'm Zahra Hassani," she said, forcing her mind to ignore the pain from her broken leg. "I'm with . . . the sheikh."

The men remained impassive, until one of them picked up a rock from among the millions lining the bottom of this ravine.

The others followed his lead.

"No!" she said. "You don't understand! I'm with—"

The first blow came from behind, overwhelming. Colors exploded in her mind as she trembled while falling on her side and urinating on herself.

But she still managed to put her left hand up while reaching with her right for her suppressed Ruger and shouting, "No! Stop! Please! I'm—"

The second rock struck her shooting hand, and she watched in horror as her fingers bent at unnatural angles and the pistol skittered away.

She tried a final plea, just as rocks rained on her from all sides, pummeling her as she cried out and tried to shield her face with her arms. But soon her arms were as useless as her broken leg, shattered under the brutal punishment.

And they didn't stop.

Wouldn't stop.

Couldn't stop.

The law was the law.

And as she lay there, scourged, paralyzed by inconceivable pain, no longer able to even whimper, a man approached her, holding a large rock with both hands.

The last thing Zahra would ever see was the insurgent raising the rock high above his head, eyes as dark as the sky while he recited a verse from the Koran.

146

Elevator to Hell

QUAI KOTAL. SULAIMAN MOUNTAINS.
SOUTHERN AFGHANISTAN.

"Danny! Lower! Now!" Stark shouted.

Martin idled the power to the turbines, shifting the cyclic to the left while applying opposing rudder and lowering the collective.

The Black Hawk banked nearly sideways as it plunged nose-first into an impossibly narrow opening, the fifty-three-foot-diameter rotor barely clearing the vegetation growing off the precipice.

"*Hijo de puta!*" shouted Gonzales from the copilot seat, hanging on to his restraining belts.

Stark grabbed an overhead handle, bracing himself while cringing at the downward acceleration, his stomach rising to his throat as the helicopter free-fell into the canyon.

"That little man has issues!" shouted Larson, still strapped to one of the fold-down seats, as the whole craft dropped into the chasm, almost on its side. "Right, Mickey?"

The maneuver made Hagen open his eyes, blinking as he realized they were plummeting sideways.

Stark kept his big frame locked in the doorway between the cockpit and the cabin, staring into the darkness through one of the open side doors, where the side gunner hung on to his anchored M240D machine gun for dear life.

The combined team strapped into their side seats in the rear clutched their weapons while Martin let gravity do its thing, squeezing them through an opening for what seemed to Stark like an eternity, until the canyon opened up.

Adding power and collective while centering the cyclic and rudders leveled out the helicopter, transitioning into a controlled descent.

"Nice move, cabron!" Gonzales shouted.

Martin grinned again, dropping to just a hundred feet above the uneven bottom.

"Hold it here!" Stark ordered, reaching for one of the coiled 40mm ropes on the side of the Black Hawk and tossing it overboard before grabbing a pair of heat-resistant gloves.

"Steady, Danny!" he shouted, looking out toward the bend in the canyon behind them, where he had seen muzzle flashes firing at the Warthog a moment ago. Those rebels were down there somewhere, probably racing this way.

MP5A1 strapped behind his back, he jumped, the rope wedged between his thighs and clutched with both gloves. Using the combination to break his fall, he dropped the hundred feet to the rocky bed in ten seconds.

He moved out of the way and aimed his weapon toward the bend to cover Wright, who followed him a few seconds later, then Larson, Hagen, Ryan, Monica, and Sergei. Kira remained in the helo with two of her guys to provide covering fire along with the side gunners.

Stark led the way, taking off in the direction of the fires near the crashed planes, leaping over rocks and fallen logs and skirting burning pools of spilled gas from the Cessna's severed wings. The flames lit up the ravine, boiling clouds of orange flames and smoke. Martin hovered behind them, finally reaching a spot wide and level enough for the helo.

"Try to set it down here!" Stark said into the MBITR, concerned about the relatively easier target the hovering Black Hawk made to any insurgents emerging from the turn in the canyon. But once it was on the ground, they could form a defensive perimeter to guard it until it was time to leave.

A moment later Martin settled the Black Hawk gently over the riverbed, the rotor wash kicking up a cloud of debris.

Kira climbed out and limped toward them, followed by her other two Spetsnaz soldiers.

"What the hell?" Stark shouted. "You're in no shape to—"

"Janki mishka!" she screamed over the rotor noise, glaring at him with those catlike eyes crowning her pronounced cheekbones. "I have my orders!"

"Fine!" he shouted, stretching two fingers like a snake's tongue at her and Wright. "But you and your team are with me! You too, Captain! Chief, Mickey! That way!" he said, pointing in the opposite direction, where he expected the Taliban to emerge at any moment. "Shoot at anything that moves, and tell those gunners, too." Then, turning to the snipers, he said, "You two, up on those boulders! Cover both ends of the pass."

Without waiting for a response, Stark and Wright took off while Kira, flanked by her team, tried to keep up, soon reaching the Cessna fuselage.

Stark went in from the massive hole in the rear, MP5A1 leading the way, and located the device a moment later.

"Kira! Your baby!" Stark screamed, taking a moment to stare at the damn cylindrical object that had everybody on edge. It was still strapped to the aluminum floor. Scrambling to the cockpit, he found a pilot dead. His seat had come loose during the crash, crushing him into the control panel. The copilot seat was empty.

Running back to the cabin, he found the Russian operative kneeling by the device. "You've got this?"

"Da! Go!" she screamed, giving him a thumbs-up before shouting in Russian at her men, who started releasing the straps.

"Let's go, Captain."

Stark and Wright rushed down the creek, past the Warthog's engines, which were still ablaze, illuminating the gorge—just as the pass came alive with muzzle flashes from beyond the A-10C's fuselage. At the same time, gunfire broke out behind them, from that rear turn in the ravine. AK-47s were immediately countered by M4 carbines, UMPs, the Black Hawk's M240Ds, plus Larson's Browning.

Stark frowned.

The enemy was closing in from *both* ends of the pass.

He aimed the MP5A1 at the distant figures closing on the Warthog's nose, their rounds hammering the armored skin and canopy, sparking off into the night.

He pulled the trigger just as Wright did, laying suppressing fire downrange from the downed jet, left to right, while screaming into his MBITR, "Ryan! Got eyes on the Tangos beyond the Hawg?"

The response came in the form of .50-caliber rounds zooming overhead, tempering the attack. Two rebels snapped back on impact.

Stark and Wright didn't let up, augmenting the counterattack by unloading their magazines, forcing the rebels back, catching their running silhouettes in their slack clothing disappearing behind boulders. But sometime during their hasty retreat, someone managed to fire an RPG.

"Get down!" Stark screamed, diving for cover alongside Wright. But the warhead arced not toward them but toward the A-10C's cockpit, scoring a direct hit.

The nose exploded in a radial pattern of metal and orange flames licking the night. The armored canopy shattered and the cockpit was set ablaze.

"Laura! *No!*" Wright shouted, getting back up and running toward the smoldering wreckage while Stark covered him, firing his MP5A1 at distant figures, forcing them down. Ryan assisted from his vantage point, .50-caliber rounds singeing the air a few feet above them.

They reached the A-10C a moment later, but the fire was too intense, the heat blistering, even from a dozen feet away.

Wright tried to get closer, but Stark grabbed him from behind.

"Let me go!" the marine captain shouted.

"She's gone, soldier!" Stark replied, his arms wrapped around Wright. "She's gone!"

"Laura!" Wright screamed again, as rounds pounded the rocks to their right, and both men immediately dove for cover. Two rebels emerged from behind the blaze, AK-47s pointed at them.

But as Stark and Wright brought their weapons around, multiple reports thundered from behind a line of boulders lining the western wall, the rounds smashing into the heads of both rebels.

Stark and Wright looked up at the source of the shots.

And right there, standing larger than life, Captain Laura Vaccaro appeared from behind a mound of rocks, right hand clutching a dark pistol.

Her long red hair swirling in the breeze, she shouted from behind a large boulder she was using for cover. "Hello, boys! What took you so damn long?"

Before Stark could reply, a small-caliber round ricocheted off his helmet. Just as he realized someone was taking potshots at them with a suppressed weapon using subsonic ammo, Vaccaro made a face, grabbed her shoulder, and shouted, "Someone just nailed me with a peashooter! And on the same damn spot!"

"Ryan!" Stark shouted, emptying another magazine in the general direction of the hidden insurgent as Wright got Vaccaro and they took off toward the Black Hawk.

Stark spotted the figure dashing across the ravine in a deep crouch, less than twenty feet away. As he lined it up in his sights, a .50-caliber round whooshed overhead, striking the figure's center of mass.

Nice shot, he thought, using the night vision scope to confirm the kill.

Several muzzle flashes ignited from behind the dead rebel, pounding the boulders around him.

"Ryan!" he screamed again.

"I'm on it, Colonel!"

A volley of .50-caliber shells seared the air above him, along with Monica's .338 rounds, while Stark swapped magazines and fired as he moved backwards, reaching the Cessna fuselage. He was pleased to see that Kira's team was already hauling the device out of there with some makeshift stretcher.

"Everybody to the helo!" he shouted, running backwards behind Vaccaro and the Russians while Wright doubled back to join him, laying down more suppressing fire, swapping magazines again.

Last one, Stark thought, pulling the bolt to chamber the first 9mm round.

Martin was already in a hover just a foot off the ground, the Black Hawk's dual turbines roaring over the noise of the firefight.

Kira and her team heaved the weapon on board before jumping in, followed by Vaccaro and Wright, while the side gunner worked the M240D. The combined vibrations of their rattling guns, plus the turbines and rotor, shook the fuselage to its core. On the other side, Ryan, Monica, and Hagen also climbed aboard, while Larson and the second side gunner covered them, unleashing insane barrages of mixed-caliber hell.

Sitting on the edge of the cabin, next to the gunner, Stark continued firing. The noise was deafening, the smell of gunpowder and exhaust fumes as overarching as the quivering of his body as he operated the MP5A1 in full automatic fire. Wright stood behind him, emptying two more magazines, hot casings raining over the cabin's floor.

"Danny! Get us out of here!" Stark shouted, dropping his empty MP5A1 and grabbing Martin's Heckler & Koch, firing every round before rushing to the cockpit after verifying that everyone was on board.

Martin responded by jamming the collective and twisting the throttle. The Black Hawk leaped skyward in gut-wrenching fashion while the side gunners, plus Larson and Wright, continued firing into the muzzle flashes at both ends of the ravine.

Rounds pinged the armored underside of the helicopter as Martin shoved the cyclic forward and rose five hundred feet—as far as he could go, given the narrowing canyon walls above him.

"You mind, Gonzales?" asked Martin.

Sitting in the copilot seat, Gonzales released a load of 70mm Hydras into what remained of the downed Warthog, leaving nothing for the Taliban to parade, and in the process scorching the bottom of the ravine, tempering rebel action.

"Thanks!" Martin shouted

"No problem, amigo!" Gonzales replied, before opening the dual GAU-19 Gatling guns on any remaining resistance as Martin accelerated through the smoke and flames.

The Black Hawk soared above the riverbed, rushing down the twisting canyon, leaving the flaming wreckage behind.

Stark once more anchored himself in the opening between the cockpit and the cabin. Everyone else found a seat and strapped in as Martin banked and twisted the Black Hawk, picking up forward speed.

They finally reached a section of the pass wide enough to climb another few hundred feet between the walls, almost to the top of the pass.

"Hang on!" Martin shouted, gathering enough momentum to bank the Black Hawk while pressing opposing rudder, reversing the maneuver he had used to dive into the narrow gully.

Stark clutched the sides of the doorway as the helicopter once more turned nearly on its side, presenting a narrower rotor profile to the soaring walls, clearing the pass, and rising into a clear sky that was stained in shades of orange by a sun barely looming on the eastern horizon.

They flew in from the west, fast, skimming the snowy treetops while dropping down the mountain toward Kandahar. But they were no longer alone. A pair of F-16s and three A-10s now escorted them.

Stark watched their reassuring silhouettes while sitting next to Kira.

"How are you feeling?" he asked, pointing at the bandage under her battle dress.

"I will survive, Janki mishka," she replied, before patting the side of the long weapon fastened to the metallic floor between her and her team. "And so will a lot of people."

Stark sighed as his gaze shifted from her Slavic features in the twilight of the cabin to her team surrounding the RN-40. Then he looked to Monica and Ryan, also sitting side by side, eyes closed, her head resting on his shoulder. Wright and Vaccaro sat across from them. Vaccaro's bleeding shoulder was being tended by a medic. Her head rested against Wright, eyes staring out the side opening.

And then there were Chief Larson and Mickey Hagen, standing guard by the side gunners, weapons pointed at an Afghan dawn.

Ready.

Always ready.

147

The Favor

President Bush sat at the head of the conference table in the Situation Room, flanked by Secretary Rice, Secretary Rumsfeld, and CIA Director Tenet. Counselor Bartlett worked the video conferencing equipment.

The president was dressed in a pair of jeans, a Texas Rangers T-shirt, and cowboy boots, sipping from a very strong cup of coffee. It was just past three in the morning on a Sunday, but the emergency call from someone named Anton, one of Putin's aides, certainly merited getting everyone out of bed.

Secretary Rice wore a white jogging suit and sneakers. Rumsfeld and Tenet were in jeans, as was Bartlett.

The mood was quiet, given the hour, but relaxed. The bomb was secured, and all that remained was a discussion that President Bush truly looked forward to but refused to initiate.

Slowly, after a series of beeps and messages on the computer display in front of Bartlett, the image of President Vladimir Putin wearing a business suit, no tie, materialized on the large flat screen at the end of the room.

He was alone, sitting stoically at the head of a table, hands on its smooth wooden surface.

"Kovboy, thanks for taking my call," he said in his deep voice.

"Howdy, Pootie-Poot," Bush replied. "To what do I owe the pleasure of getting my staff and I out of bed at this hour?"

"You have something . . . something that belongs to me."

Bush leaned back before looking at his guys, settling on Rice.

"Condi? You know what he's talking about?"

"No, Mr. President."

"Rummy? Have you been serving rum punches lately?"

"No, sir. Not this week anyway."

"Brother George?" he asked Director Tenet. "Has the Agency been behaving?"

"Always, sir."

"Oh, Danny Boy?" he asked Counselor Bartlett. "Have the pipes been calling down the rose garden?"

"No, Mr. President. All quiet here too."

Turning back to the camera, Bush said, "You see, old friend, we have no idea what the hell you're talking about. So I'm afraid you'll have to spell it out."

Looking to either side, Putin leaned closer to the camera and mumbled, "*Nam pizdets.*"

Bush frowned while showing his palms. "Sorry Pootie-Poot, but no parley Russkie."

"Da. Da," he said, before adding, "I . . . I . . . ah . . ."

"Yes? Come on, you old KGB bastard. I know you can do it," the president said.

"I . . . screwed up."

"And how'd you manage that?"

"The bomb we lost . . . I should have been . . . up-front with you."

"There you go!" Bush said, slapping the conference table. "That wasn't so hard, was it?"

Putin just stared back.

"Now, I take it you want your bomb back?"

"Da."

"You mean the RN-40 tactical nuclear warhead you lost in Afghanistan on the night of September 13, 1988?"

After hesitating, Putin said, "Da."

"The one that the Taliban discovered last week and we had to move heaven and earth to locate and recover?"

"Da."

"The one we have fully documented, with photos and serial numbers, so there is no doubt whatsoever of its origin and how NATO forces recovered it from the Taliban?"

Dropping his gaze to the table, Putin simply nodded.

"Of course you can have it back, Pootie-Poot."

Putin abruptly looked up. "I . . . can?"

"Absolutely. I mean, we already have plenty of our *own* bombs, right Rummy?"

"Plenty, Mr. President," Secretary Rumsfeld replied. "Enough to level the world many times over."

"See. Many *times* over," Bush repeated. "But look, this little incident will remain between us friends, okay, Pootie-Poot? No sense in advertising it to the world, and *especially* to your . . . political enemies."

Putin nodded. "That would be *greatly* appreciated."

"But that's the thing," Bush said. "I don't want your *fucking appreciation*."

Putin blinked. "N-no?"

Bush slowly shook his head.

"Then?"

"Just a small favor."

After another pause, Putin said, "Anything, Kovboy. You do this for me and you can have . . . *anything*."

"That's the spirit, old boy," the president said, before looking at his staff. "See, fellows? I told you the man's a team player."

"What . . . what would you like?" Putin asked.

President George W. Bush simply smiled and said, "I will let you know, Pootie-Poot. I will *certainly* let you know."

148

The Gift

MOSCOW. RUSSIA.

Snowflakes pelted her long parka as Kira left Sergei by the black Mercedes and went up the icy concrete steps at dusk, pushing one of the double glass doors with a gloved hand.

Her left shoulder ached from the effort, though it pretty much bothered her anytime the weather changed, especially on these bitterly cold Russian nights. In fact, in the past few weeks, since returning from Kandahar with the bomb, it had become her very own personal meteorological predictor.

Kira stepped inside the lobby and Andrei, sitting at the guard post, looked up over the edge of his newspaper. Checking his watch, he said, "You're just in time. He's due for his meds in thirty minutes, and then he's out for a while."

Kira despised the sight of the little man as much as she hated this building. It was certainly no place for a hero such as her father—no way for Colonel Mikhail Tupolev to live out his days.

She walked straight to the set of doors leading to the patients' rooms and faced the same utterly depressing corridor under the same dull glare of humming fluorescents recessed in the ceiling, evenly spaced down its entire length. The smell of disinfectant was pungent, almost making her eyes water.

But this time it all felt different, or so she hoped, heading for the fifth door on the left, the heels of her black stiletto boots clacking flatly on polished floors.

Slowly inching the door open, Kira found her father in his brown recliner, facing the layer of white covering the gardens and the early evening traffic on E30.

Colonel Mikhail Tupolev just sat there, frozen in time, eyelids sewn shut, right hand a mere stump. But it was his left hand, resting on the recliner's arm, which drew her focus—the one that always looked as if it held a gun while he flexed his index finger, squeezing his imaginary trigger.

She took his hand in hers. "Hello, Daddy," she whispered.

As was always the case, Mikhail offered no reaction, resembling one of those Greek statues in the garden.

Her eyes inexorably gravitated to Nemesis, still wielding that sword in the midst of winter—a winter that had lasted seventeen long years for the once formidable Soviet pilot, recipient of the coveted Hero of the Soviet Union award.

Reaching into her coat pocket, Kira produced his Gagarin class ring. Without a word, she slid it on the ring finger of her father's surviving hand.

And waited.

It took a moment.

Slowly, Mikhail Tupolev did something he had not done for some time: he visibly responded. He stopped the finger flexing and ran the tip of his thumb over the ring's features. His lips parted, and for a moment she thought he said something, perhaps a whisper of gratitude, or maybe of surprise.

"I found it, Daddy," she said, resting a hand on his thigh and squeezing gently. "I found the bomb *and* your ring . . . and I killed them all."

A single tear ran down the side of the colonel's left cheek, and at that moment, as Kira shifted her eyes to the frozen garden, she felt his hand reaching for hers, gently interlocking fingers.

She looked over and he was still facing the window, his sunken and wrinkled features impassive, shut eyelids fixed on that miserable Russian winter sky dumping a wall of flurries on the evening traffic.

But I'll take it.

Just as dawn broke slowly, with a faint trace of orange and yellow-gold dancing against the distant horizon at the end of the darkest night, perhaps Kira had just witnessed the first sign of his rising sun, his first steps toward the light.

If only for a little while, she thought. Soon the nurse would come with another dose of those radical PTSD meds, snuffing out any semblance of brightness from his soul, dragging him back to that shadowy world of complete indifference.

Glaring at this most depressing of rooms in this most depressing of institutions, Kira decided this was certainly no place for such a hero, forced to live out his days in the stupor of the very drugs that protected him from reliving the nightmares.

Imprisoned in his own mind by those bewhiskered assholes, and again by his own country.

Kira sighed and returned her gaze to Nemesis, before looking skyward. She needed to be strong for the both of them, and she needed to do so right now, before the nurse returned.

Producing the Makarov that John Wright had given to her before boarding that Antonov flight to bring the bomb home, Kira let go of Mikhail's hand and pressed the semiautomatic against his palm.

"Daddy . . . I also found this. It belongs to you."

The colonel straightened as he gripped the pistol with instant familiarity, leaning forward, feeling its cold steel, its balance, and his index finger no longer twitching but resting on the trigger casing.

Again, he mumbled something, but she could not make it out.

"There is one in the chamber, Daddy," she said, hating herself for doing this. But she wanted to give him the option, to allow him a moment of control over his destiny. Plus, she could no longer bear seeing him like this. Perhaps he could no longer bear living like this.

But now he had a choice.

Hugging him tightly, she added, "Now, if you so wish, you can finish what you started on that mountain . . . and take your rightful place among the fallen heroes of our *Rodina*, our Motherland."

The moon hung high over the Sulaimans as Colonel Mikhail Tupolev raced through the darkness, his heartbeat rocketing, his lungs burning as he filled them with cold, frigid air. The rotor sound of the rescue helicopter reverberated across the hillside, searchlights stabbing the forest as he tried to reach the clearing.

He hated this country, hated everything about it—especially those bearded insurgents, their loose clothing flapping in the breeze as they encircled him, as they tightened the noose.

Pesh-kabz knives glinted in the moonlight as unseen hands forced him onto his back, as two demons crawled over him, chanting in tongues.

But this time it was different.

This time he had his gun, his old and trusty Makarov, his fingers curled around the pistol grip, index finger on the trigger.

The curved blades would not cut him again.

Not tonight.

Not ever.

But he still had to fight them to free his hand, pulling as hard as he'd ever pulled, jerking his wrist from their grip, and finally pressing the muzzle against his temple.

Now, he thought. *Peace . . . at last.*

Kira was halfway across the lobby when the single gunshot echoed from behind the double doors leading to the hallway.

She briefly closed her eyes as Andrei jumped up from his seat, tossing the newspaper and reaching for the radio strapped to his belt, barking orders, which Kira ignored as she pursed her lips and continued to the exit.

A sense of peace enveloped her while pushing the double glass doors, leaving behind the chaos of Andrei running amid orderlies, medics, and other guards, filling her lungs with cold and humid air under a gloomy November sky.

But she found the brisk Russian winter scene refreshing, revitalizing. And as she headed down the icy steps toward the waiting sedan, she noticed a colorful Eurasian bullfinch perched on Nemesis's right shoulder.

She paused and observed the chubby little bird, its bright red chest and grayish wings and cap contrasting sharply with the surrounding whiteout.

It turned its short and thick black bill toward Kira, regarding her briefly while chirping a song that resembled fluted whistles, often described by Muscovites as mournful.

Ruffling its feathers to shake off a thin layer of flurries, the bullfinch winged skyward, vanishing in the winter snow.

Kira watched it, through her tears.

EPILOGUE

TWO MONTHS LATER . . .
COLORADO SPRINGS, COLORADO.

Laura Vaccaro swooped through mounds of fresh powder, veering sharply down the extreme slope, cutting left then right to stay on the challenging course following the northern face of the mountain.

The air, cold and invigorating, filled her lungs, and adrenaline shot into her bloodstream as she buckled down, tucking her helmeted head, poles under her armpits when reaching a steep straightaway, gathering speed.

The wind whistled in her ears as her world turned white beyond her goggles, as her heart pounded her temples, as a liberating feeling of complete exhilaration overtook her senses.

She shot past another skier, the number pinned to the back of his jacket flapping in the wind, losing him in the silvery flurry kicked up by her skis.

Grinning beneath her mask as she reached the next turn, Vaccaro dug the edge of her downhill ski just enough to cut left. Her ankles, knees, and waist bent, the edge gripped the snow, shifting her momentum, negotiating the turn before she pushed her poles to gain on the last racer.

More speed. More speed.

She again curled down into the traditional downhill position, helmet and poles tucked in tight, her stomach churning as the terrain steepened, as a wall of pines caked in snow to her right and the gorge on her left blurred into a world of blinding chaos.

One more turn, then the final straightaway.

Last chance to overtake the final competitor.

She remained in a deep crouch, visualizing the upcoming turn, biding her time as the guy currently in first place began to slow down in anticipation of the last sharp right in the course.

Wrong move, pal.

Holding her downward energy just long enough to overtake him in a flurry of whirling powder, Vaccaro caught him, out of the corner of her right eye, swinging his helmeted head toward her as she rushed by.

Adios!

Keeping her feet eight inches apart and her thighs an inch from touching, she reached the turn, shins angled forward, applying a very light pressure on the tongue of each boot by bending her knees ever so slightly.

Bringing both skis equally on edge, she carved the track deep, kicking up a wall of snow while sticking the turn and shifting her momentum to the right, maintaining a steep angle between her feet and her shins, moving her hips toward the center of the turning arc.

And once more she pushed the poles vigorously, entering the final slope, not bothering to look back, cleaning up her downhill pose for the last stretch.

The crowd flanking the last section of the course, as well as those gathered at the bottom, exploded in cheers, their roar overpowering the wind shrilling in her ears.

Speed. More speed.

She continued accelerating, refusing to yield one ounce of advantage, shooting across the finish line at full speed before jerking sideways, digging in both skis firmly, bathing excited spectators in white powder. Looking up the slope while lifting her goggles, Vaccaro caught the first racer of the all-male competition cross the finish line a full two seconds behind her. He was officially the winner, but camera crews and reporters rushed to her, the rogue skier who had been denied entry—even with her hero status as recent recipient of two Purple Hearts, a Silver Star, and the Medal of Honor. The latter she had received directly from President George W. Bush at the White House, the previous month.

But rules were rules.

So she had done what she did best: gone rogue and broken them, proving once again that she could do the job of any man—and then some.

The Fox Sports reporter reached her first, a woman in her late twenties. She had tears in her eyes.

"You did it, Captain Vaccaro!" she said, thrusting a mike in front of her. "You beat them all!"

"Oh, I'm just having a little fun . . . It's a glorious morning for skiing in our wonderful state of Colorado," she replied, catching her breath while the crowd continued to cheer, ignoring the winner and the rest of the racers crossing the line.

"What are your plans now that you have officially retired from the air force, Captain? There are rumors floating out there that you plan to enter a bid in the next U.S. Senate race."

Before she could reply, the ESPN crew as well as CBS Sports, ABC Sports, and a couple of local stations also managed to get their microphones in front of her puffs of condensation as she tried to control her breathing, her chest still heaving.

Vaccaro stared at the crowd as all eyes focused on her, and she knew the entire country would also be watching, given her hero status and the controversial nature of this race.

This was her moment—a moment no one had given to her. She had earned it through hard work, through sacrifice, through countless hours stuffed inside a Warthog cockpit, protecting the backs of soldiers. She had unleashed hell on America's enemies during her multiple tours, beating the odds, refusing to capitulate, and never— ever—backing down from a fight worth fighting.

Never stop fighting, Red One One. Never.

She inhaled deeply, recalling the rugged face of her Kidon, his cheesy lines, and his ultimate sacrifice—the very unexpected way Aaron Peretz had forever changed her on that remote cliff in that godforsaken land.

And every time she thought of Afghanistan, she inexorably thought of John Wright, still on his rotation and still respecting their decision to keep it friendly until they were both stateside. No sense in making plans for the future until they were both completely out of harm's way.

But that may be awhile, she thought, as the crowd quieted down and she stared into the whirling automatic lenses of a half dozen cameras.

Wright had received an official notification from Duggan that the Marine Corps was stop-lossing him, extending his tour due to a shortage of experienced officers. It certainly wasn't fair to either of them, but the nation needed him to continue fighting the war on terror—and the very same nation now waited for her response.

Smiling at the cameras, she shrugged and replied, "What are my plans, you ask? Well, today I'm skiing."

The crowd burst into laughter, as did the reporters.

The ESPN woman reacted first, asking, "And tomorrow, Captain? What about tomorrow?"

"Tomorrow . . ." Vaccaro said, pursing her lips while looking at the snowy mountains.

Never stop fighting, Red One One. Never.

And make your life matter.

Returning her gaze to the cameras, she said, "Tomorrow I'll do whatever it takes to serve the great people of the State of Colorado . . . whatever it *fucking* takes."

KANDAHAR AIRFIELD. SOUTHERN AFGHANISTAN.

His gold oak leaves arrived on the same day as his stop-loss papers, and although Duggan would never admit it, John Wright was certain that the battlefield promotion to major was the colonel's way of softening the blow.

Plus, that also meant no more field excursions. For the remainder of his extended tour, Wright would serve his country from within the relatively safer confines of the airfield.

But his contributions were nonetheless significant, spending his days reviewing intelligence reports with Harwich and Monica, co-ordinating with the U.S. Air Force, the U.S. Army, the Canadians, and even the Afghan Army on troop deployments, and providing the daily briefings to Duggan. His ability to work successfully in such a multinational setting—a skill he never knew he possessed—had also earned him the privilege of representing the Corps at Major General Lévesque's staff meetings.

Privilege, my ass, he thought, wondering if perhaps that had been the real reason why Duggan had promoted him. It was no secret that the colonel wasn't a NATO fan, while Wright seemed to thrive in such a highly political environment, earning everyone's respect—even Lévesque's—while gaining more and more responsibility.

But sometimes, late at night, after the meetings and the dinners, after visiting the wounded, awarding Purple Hearts, and writing letters home, Wright would sit alone at the edge of the tarmac under a blanket of stars and watch the planes and helicopters come and go.

And think of her.

At first their communications had been frequent, almost daily. But as weeks turned into months, and as the world of politics exerted its life-sucking force on the senatorial candidate, the phone calls stopped and the emails became irregular, shorter, less personal.

She was busy on the other side of the planet, moving forward, making new friends, new connections, getting catapulted onto the national scene, while he was forced to remain behind, fighting this noblest of fights.

Wright had another nine months to go, and by then, if one could believe the polls, Senator Vaccaro could very well be on her way to Washington to represent the good people of Colorado.

But there was already talk of a Pentagon assignment for him after KAF. Duggan had mentioned it twice. So perhaps there was still a chance for them, at least geographically.

But, either way, John Wright would never, *ever* forget the precious time they'd spent together, including that perfect weekend in Qatar.

Three A-10s taxied toward the runway, red and green navigation lights glowing, their tail beacons blinking. They took off a moment later in formation, afterburners igniting the air as they accelerated toward the distant Sulaimans.

John Wright watched them as they disappeared in the darkness.

LAS VEGAS, NEVADA.

Stark had not wanted to come—and still could not believe he was actually here.

But Ryan, Martin, and the chief had convinced him, while Hagen had just looked on, smoking his damn Russian cigarettes as his buddies made their case.

C'mon, Colonel. What better place to spend our downtime—and our bonuses—in between contracts than Sin City?

Stark could actually think of a few places, including a remote beach in Costa Rica, a jungle retreat on Hawaii's Big Island, or even a ski resort in Colorado, where he had gotten word that Vaccaro was ahead in the polls for the race to the United States Senate.

Good for her, he thought, checking his Casio while jogging past the impressive fountains in front of the Bellagio, feeling the cold steel of his 9mm Glock 19 inside a leather holster in the small of his back, pressed against his spine and covered with a black T-shirt.

He paused briefly to watch the water and light show amid a crowd composed primarily of vacationing families, honeymooners, bachelor parties, and college kids.

And lone wolves like me, he thought, continuing down the Strip toward the Mirage, the opulent establishment that had been home for two long days, with five to go. The only good thing, besides having his very own suite, was the food. For the past forty-eight hours he had feasted, slept, and worked out while his team did whatever it was that young guns with cash to burn did to blow off steam.

Stark didn't ask and he really didn't want to know. And he *certainly* didn't want to be anywhere near them until it was time to head back to the jet. His guys were raunchy enough while in-country; he didn't want to think what they were doing in a place like Vegas.

He shook his head and picked up his pace after crossing Flamingo Road, running past the massive complex that was Caesars Palace.

The air was cold and dry. For a moment Stark blocked out all sounds while pretending to be on some remote road in Arizona, Hawaii, Montana, or New Mexico—anywhere but here.

But the team had wanted to come, and he could not tell them

no—especially given the brutality of the missions they had completed. Following their arrival at Kandahar Airfield, a top secret videoconference had been held between Putin and Bush to decide the fate of the recovered nuke, the United States finally opting to let the Russians keep it.

Brief good-byes had followed as Kira and her team boarded a transport to complete the journey started by her father seventeen years before.

Harwich and Monica had returned to their intelligence duties, along with John Wright, who got stop-lossed while Vaccaro was honorably discharged, because of her multiple injuries, and went home to Colorado. Gorman and Maryam headed back to Pakistan, while Stark and team spent another two weeks at KAF supporting Duggan before boarding their C-21 jet to fulfill new Agency contracts in Baghdad, Colombia, and Nigeria, spending almost a month at each exotic destination.

And now Vegas in April.

He slowed a half mile from the Mirage, located across the Strip from the Venetian, to start his cooldown period, finally fast walking as he reached the parking lot. He went straight for one of the many sets of glass doors leading to the very flashy lobby. But then again, what wasn't gaudy in this town?

Visitors queued in front of a ridiculously long front desk, backdropped by an equally long and quite impressive saltwater aquarium, to facilitate check-in on a grand scale under an array of soothing lights and music. In the distance, beyond a walkway through one of the world's most elaborate indoor rainforests, the massive casino floor exploded with activity. Slot machines dominated the scene, their incessant bells and whistles mixing with hundreds of conversations in a dozen languages.

But Stark focused on the one thing that mattered most to him: the elevators to his penthouse suite, which would be followed by a hot bath and then room service, capped by another great night of uninterrupted sleep.

A minute later, tired and hungry, he slid the magnetic key on the pad by the door and stepped into his only semblance of a vacation, a very quiet and very beautiful top-floor suite overlooking the Strip, though he wasn't sure if it was worth the eight hundred bucks a night being charged to his American Express platinum card.

Still, Stark had to admit the place was something else, with its beautiful furniture, rugs, decorations, a wall of panoramic windows, and—

He sensed a presence behind him, near the bar leading to the bedroom.

Following professional habits, he spun while dropping to a deep crouch and reaching for the Glock.

But he never drew it.

Rather, Stark stood slowly, dumbfounded, shooting hand still behind his back, fingers curled on the pistol's grip.

Dressed in black, Kira Tupolev sat at the edge of the bar, smiling as she held up two bottles of Stolichnaya.